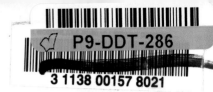
DATE DUE

JA 28 '03 '06			
JA 28 '06 SE 27 '06			
SE 26 '07			
DE 15 MY 14			

DEMCO 38-297

THE
VOW

THE

VOW

A NOVEL

DENENE MILLNER,

ANGELA BURT-MURRAY,

AND

MITZI MILLER

Amistad

An Imprint of HarperCollinsPublishers

HarperCollins books may be purchased for educational, business, or sales promotional use. For information, please write: Special Markets Department, HarperCollins Publishers, 10 East 53rd Street, New York, NY 10022.

FIRST EDITION

Designed by Betty Lew

Printed on acid-free paper

Library of Congress Cataloging-in-Publication Data
Millner, Denene.
The vow : 3 women, 2 carats, 1 year / Denene Millner, Angela Burt-Murray & Mitzi Miller.—1st ed.
    p. cm.
ISBN-10: 0-06-076227-6
ISBN-13: 978-0-06-076227-8
1. African American woman—Fiction. 2. Female friendship—Fiction. 3. Mate selection—Fiction. I. Burt-Murray, Angela. II. Miller, Mitzi. III. Title.

PS3613.I565V69 2005
813'.54—dc22   2005042124

05 06 07 08 09 ❖/RRD 10 9 8 7 6 5 4 3 2 1

ACKNOWLEDGMENTS

Denene Millner

I have taken this journey nine times and each is counted as an abundant blessing. None of this would have been possible without Him. This is for my husband, Nick Chiles, a constant inspiration, provider, and protector—I'm so glad to have taken my Vow with you, my one and only love; my two little princesses Mari and Lila, for giving me the most important, fascinating, wondrous title in the world, *Mommy*; my dad, James Millner, for being the wise, ever-calm presence who has always encouraged me to be smart and love with abandon; my mom, Bettye Millner, who, even in our Father's house, walks beside me; and the rest of my wonderful family: Troy, Mazi, Angelou, James, Miles, Cole, Walter, and Helen, Jameelah, Maia, Zenzele, and Imani. For my longtime agent, Victoria Sanders: no one does it better than you.

For the Amistad staff: thanks for the incredible journey and vision. And to my co-authors: Mitzi, thank you for inspiring me to tap into my nuevo black socialite within and most of all for being the funniest, kookiest, loveliest friend a girl could ever have. There's a tea party in ATL with your name on it. Angela, thank you for being an amazing god-mommy to my baby; your calculated brilliance has been the steam in our ABW caboose.

Angela Burt-Murray

To my thoughtful and poetic husband, Leonard Murray, thanks for always making it do what it do, baby! And for our two beautiful children, Solomon and Ellison, I quote the great western philosopher Mary J. Blige: *I took one look at you and it was plain to see that you were my destiny . . .*

At the heart of this glitzy novel is the enduring friendship of three women. And as such I'd like to give a special shout-out to all my girl-friends. Because without these women and their wisdom there would be no Vow . . . Thank you for the unconditional love, mommy getaways to the Ritz, late-night therapy in the Vineyard, dirty jokes, the champagne-induced secret-sharing sessions, emergency room recaps, playdates, shopping sprees at Short Hills, babysitting the Burt-Murray boys, and motivation. To my fabulous and fly BC girlfriends: Ché Baby, Denise, Miki, Kim, Desiree, and Tanya. BCFL! Special hugs to my girlz from back in the day, Nichelle, Erin, Karra, LaShawn, Ginia, April, Adriene, Romeldia, Pamela, Rolanda, Carla, Rocquelle, and in memory of Ursula. To my 1271 girlfriends Amy, Nina, and Sharan, thanks for always having my back, and chocolate cupcakes! To the South Orange crew, Jenny, Rebecca, Betsy, Denene, and Tatia, thanks for sharing motherhood and all the milestones. And special thanks to the coolest sister-in-law in the world, Tracey, and supportive mother-in-law, Brenda, and my superstar niece, Jovon. You're simply the best!

High five and hallelujah to my crazy, sexy, cool co-authors Denene and Mitzi, and our rock star agent, Victoria Sanders! And to the dedi-cated divas of Amistad, especially our editor, Dawn Davis, thank you for believing in this project and pulling out all the stops.

And to my beautiful mother, Diana Burt, and her special circle of best girlfriends, Lynda, Hazel, and in memory of Kathy, thank you for giving me a living example of what true friendship looks like. Through the window of your forty-five-year friendship you all have made me the daughter, friend, wife, mother, and woman I am today and for that I am eternally grateful.

Mitzi Miller

First and foremost, I would like to dedicate this book to God, Yemaya, and all the orishas that guide and protect me along my path.

To Elsa Miller, I am who I am because of you. I couldn't have asked for a better mother. To my sister Melissa, if I can do it, so can you—probably ten times better; my father, Guillermo Miller, for all those nights when Mommy was working and you let me have Burger King for dinner; my Tia, for making me laugh with your sarcastic sense of humor; and Uncle Ricky, for refusing to let a health condition get the best of you. I see it runs in the blood. I'd like to thank my entire family for their tireless support.

To Mali, Nikki, Carmen, Shayla, Dara, and Toya, thank you for creating safe spaces where I can always breathe freely. To Fatima, Melissa, Daina, Kenya, Ericka, KD, Takara, Lisa, Karina, and Maya, your collective determination to settle for nothing but the best keeps me focused. To Joyce E. Davis, my mentor and friend, for her infinite wisdom and kindness. To all of my wonderful, beautiful, progressive girlfriends who understand my drama and provide invaluable perspective, thank you for continually enhancing my quality of life.

To Victoria Sanders, my kick-ass literary agent, for believing in our vision from the very first phone call. To Dawn and the entire Amistad staff, for their hard work and enthusiasm.

To Denene and Angela, my dynamic and super-talented co-authors, for proving that the dream—a good black man, two healthy kids, and a big ol' house in the 'burbs—is more than reasonable. I know my "happily ever after" is right around the corner . . . but till then, I'll keep on giving you crazy escapades to live vicariously through.

I would especially like to acknowledge Drama, who held me down the entire summer in our sweltering apartment. Yes, we can play with the ball now.

THE
VOW

Mr. and Mrs. Calvin Jacobs

and

Dr. and Mrs. William Bradford Johnson II

request the honor of your presence as their children

Elise Erin Jacobs

and

William Bradford Johnson III

unite in Holy Matrimony

Saturday the Thirty-first of December

Two Thousand and Five

At half past six o'clock

Peachtree Methodist Church

325 Peachtree Street

Atlanta, Georgia

1

TRISTA

I have a wicked hangover. And as the Saturday-morning sunshine streams between the curtains into the hotel room and warms my face, I'm certain that a jackhammer has taken up residence behind my right pupil. Damn, I forgot to take my contacts out last night; they're stuck to my eyeballs. For a moment, I think about staying in bed all day and sleeping off my pounding headache, but as my splintered gaze slowly begins to focus, it falls on the strapless violet gown hanging on the back of the closet door. I groan and remember that duty calls. Today, my best friend, my homegirl, my soror, my ace boon coon Elise is getting married, and I'm the maid of honor. And no matter that we've been friends since we learned how to double Dutch, I don't think sistergirl would forgive me for even *thinking* about missing her big day.

Gently clasping my throbbing head in my hands, I sit up in the bed and wrap the sheet tightly around my naked body. Is the room actually spinning? I'm such a lightweight. I should have stuck to my self-imposed two-drink-max rule last night. As I feel my hair, I realize most of it has fought its way free of the sleek French knot Elise requested the bridesmaids get at the hair salon yesterday. It's a matted mess. We were supposed to wrap it tightly and have it lightly touched up today, if necessary. Elise is going to kill me.

What time is it? Pushing aside two champagne flutes, a half-empty bottle of Veuve Clicquot, my cell phone, and BlackBerry resting on the mahogany nightstand, I squint at the digital clock. Luckily it's only

10:17. I've got a while before I have to pull myself together and meet my girls Amaya, Viv, and the rest of the bridal party downstairs in the lobby to go take pictures before this evening's wedding ceremony.

My office is under strict orders not to bother me this weekend, but judging from the red voicemail light flashing rapidly on my cell, the vibrating pager, and the bright-orange message light on the hotel phone, some are still desperate to reach me. Ordinarily I would return all voicemails and emails first thing in the morning, but I drank so much champagne last night my head feels like it's being squeezed between the bellies of two sumo wrestlers.

Well, this is the first real vacation I've taken in the seven years since I joined The Agency (derisively referred to in the entertainment industry as T&A—Tits and Abs—for the high number of busty starlets and leading men with six-packs in our stable), so the demanding partners and my narcissistic clients seeking reassurance that they are beautiful, talented, and destined for Oscar glory (always in that order) will have to function without me for a few more days. Hopefully none of them have been arrested for intent to distribute, left their wife for the fifteen-year-old Scandinavian au pair, or gone AWOL from a movie shoot to check into rehab.

Gingerly turning my head toward the window, I think I hear rain. Damn, Elise has to be freaking out right now. Her ripped-from-the-pages-of–*Martha Stewart Living* dream wedding day is ruined. The bridal party was scheduled to take pictures outside at the botanical gardens prior to this evening's candlelight service. Didn't someone once tell me that rain on a wedding day was good luck? Whoever said it doesn't matter, because I'm not about to say that to Elise Erin Jacobs. And I know my girl Amaya, the diva of drama, and even Viv, who's the most rational of all of us, ain't trying to say that mess either. Let the man who will vow today to cherish her till death do us part get cursed out in front of four hundred of their closest friends and family members.

Elise is an only child, so this wedding is a big deal for her family. Her daddy hit the California Quick Pick Lotto Jackpot for $87 million back when Elise was in junior high school. Two weeks later, Big Poppa Cal bought three one-way airline tickets to Atlanta, where his brother lived, and told his family to pack only the family photos; that was all they would be taking from Mercy's Way Housing Projects in Compton.

Elise and I had lived next door to each other since we could remember; we were best friends. Whenever my mom was out on one of her drunken binges down at the dog track, my father was out looking for her, and my older sister was running the streets, I would spend the night with the Jacobs, no questions asked. Her mom—I call her Ms. Evelyn—would tuck me into Elise's narrow cot. If I was lucky, I would fall asleep before I heard my father dragging my mother, yelling and cursing, down the hallway, back into the apartment.

After Elise moved to Atlanta we vowed to keep in touch. We wrote each other long letters with glittery red pens on "Hello, Kitty" stationery. And every Sunday, I would wait by the pay phone in the hallway of our building for Elise's four-o'clock call. For an hour, I would catch her up on who was gang bangin' now, my sister's latest antics, and my nonexistent high school social life, and she would tell me about living in Atlanta. I loved hearing about their big new house, their heated swimming pool, Jacuzzi, tennis court, her new poodle Mercy. When she told me about some of the girls in her new school who called her "project girl," I teasingly told her, "Look, Wheezie Jefferson, you better let those bama-ass girls know you don't take no mess or punch them dead in the eye!" She'd laugh and say she'd try to do better. I thought she had the best life. When she came back to Southern California to go to UC with me, it was just like old times. We even pledged together.

And while Big Poppa Cal's lottery fortune hadn't exactly endeared the family to the local black elite over the years, Elise was marrying into one of the city's premier families. Will was Atlanta's crown prince, the son of the mayor, so the guest list was a veritable *Who's Who* of the Atlanta elite. *Jet* and *Ebony* had flown in their best photographers to record the white-tie nuptials. Knowing Elise and her mom, they were probably organizing a conference call with Jesus himself right now to negotiate a break in the clouds.

But I couldn't even be mad at my girl: she was turning out her New Year's Eve wedding first class. Guests who were traveling from out of town were met at the airport by gleaming black chauffeured limousines. A professionally shot "welcome video" featuring Elise and Will entertained us during the short ride to the Ritz Carlton Hotel. When we arrived, the desk clerk informed us that our room charges were taken care of, compliments of the Jacobs family.

Once upstairs, we were treated to even more surprises. A huge basket awaited us in our rooms. I dug into the assortment of makeup, perfume, cologne, a robe, satin slippers, CDs, scented candles, and fragrant bath salts. On the coffee table was a bottle of champagne, and a silver platter with strawberries decorated in dark and white chocolate to look like they were wearing tuxedos. A Tiffany gift box held a pair of crystal flutes engraved with the words *Elise and Will 2005*. An envelope held a list of additional amenities at our disposal—among them, a fleet of cars on standby to take us anywhere we needed to go, as well as in-room massage, manicure, and pedicure.

As I looked around the elegant suite and popped one of the decadent strawberries into my mouth, I mumbled to myself, "Shoot! Martha Stewart ain't got nothing on a black woman with a plan and a platinum Amex."

The extravaganza was on New Year's Eve, and, considering the welcome I'd received so far, I wouldn't be surprised if they had corralled Dick Clark into forgoing dropping the big ball in Times Square in favor of doing it at their reception.

I knew it was going to be a wedding to remember.

But for now all I want to do is forget about last night.

As a fresh wave of nausea washes over me, I collapse against the mountain of pillows. I need to get to the bathroom. Why can't I will my body to just get out of this bed, crawl across the floor, and get acquainted with the Ritz's porcelain goddess? But I immediately dismiss that idea when the sound of the shower running penetrates my foggy brain. I bolt upright in the bed. It's not raining outside. That's the shower I hear running. He's in the bathroom.

I sink back down in the bed and put one of the pillows over my face. I'm not ready to face him yet, and it has nothing to do with the hangover. I can't believe I slept with him last night. Again.

OF COURSE I NEVER intended to sleep with Damon. In fact, I had planned to do the total opposite: to be fabulous but frosty. Divine but distant. Play it cool. Yeah, I had it all planned. So what happened?

What happened was my backbone snapped like an old rubber band as soon as I saw him last night at the rehearsal dinner. I had just returned to my seat after taking some pictures of Elise and Will when he walked into the private dining room. While I knew that, as Will's frat brother, Damon had been invited, Elise had mentioned to me that he might not make it because he was in the midst of a big business deal. Secretly I had been disappointed. I had wanted to show him that I had made it. Without him. But there he was. Standing at just over six feet, with satiny-brown chocolate skin and a neatly trimmed mustache, dark eyes framed by lashes any woman would kill for, Damon Reynolds was still f-i-n-e. And judging by the expensive-looking suit, the last ten years had served brotherman well.

According to The Negro Network (TNN), the informal email gossip grapevine that allowed any young, black, and even mildly successful person to find out relationship status, job title, income range, and assorted other personal and juicy information on anyone within about six exchanges with friends, he was a vice president of a white-shoe investment bank in New York. Glad to hear his dream came true.

Well, he wasn't the only one that had made their dreams come true. After graduating from college and law school, I landed a coveted job in the mailroom of The Agency, where I had busted my ass seventy hours a week and was about to become a partner in the hottest talent agency in the world. Everything I thought I wanted was falling into place. I had a growing roster of superstar clients, maintained a Rolodex that many of my backstabbing coworkers would sell a kidney—or any other major organ or appendage—for, and owned a luxurious beach-front condo. Not bad for the scholarship student from the projects who arrived at the University of California with a suitcase full of donated clothes and fifty dollars in her pocket. I wasn't exactly the poor little girl from South Central that Damon last saw at graduation. I had made it on my own. Just like I said I would.

Elise liked to tease me that "on paper" I had everything. She said the only thing I was missing was a man. I tried to explain to her that being an SSBFDLA (a successful, single, black, female dating in L.A.) and finding a good man to date—forget falling in love with—was like navigating a full-contact sport. And besides, most brothers act like if they gave you the time of day you should come running, like Bob Barker just called your name for the Showcase Showdown. Why is it that the sisters who have men are always trying to tell those of us who don't that it's so easy to find someone?

But lately I had started to think about what Elise was saying. Watching a lot of my friends and coworkers getting married and starting to have children had me thinking that maybe there was more to life than work. I knew that I was on the right track to making partner at The Agency, and that would bring me the financial security I had been striving for, but maybe I want more . . . like someone to share my life with. I don't want to end up alone.

Unfortunately, the most serious relationship I've had was two years ago with Faison, a guy I met in a chatroom on blackplanet.com who I subsequently found out was addicted to internet porn. Most of the guys I meet are wannabe actors who just want to get into my panties in the hopes that they'll put it on me so good I'll take them on as a client or introduce them to one of my contacts. I only made that mistake one time . . . okay, maybe twice. It's rough out here.

My girl Amaya, who practically requires an IRS audit and a *Sports Illustrated* cover before she'll go out with a guy, hasn't exactly found her soulmate, either. Viv, on the other hand, is a hopeless romantic, in love and still in a "relationship" with the father of her child. Relationship. If you want to call it that.

And my work schedule is so demanding that the last thing I want to do if I actually have some spare time is play let's-get-to-know-each-other with someone my married friends think I'd like. Ever since Amaya, Viv, and I all turned thirty a couple of years ago, it seems like all our married friends have been on a mission to hook us up with guys they "think we'll find interesting." And every last hook-up is a disaster. With a capital D. Which is why I was at my girl's wedding solo.

At the rehearsal dinner, as Damon made his way around the room, greeting other friends from college, our eyes locked. Stay cool, girl. I tried to appear in control of the situation, I raised my champagne glass to him in greeting and then swallowed the contents to steady my nerves. His almond-shaped brown eyes took me in as his full lips curved into a sexy half-smile. He mouthed the word "Hello."

"Damn, girl, is that fine-ass Damon?" asked Viv as she jumped up from her seat, nearly knocking over her chair in the process. She craned her neck to get a better look.

"Yeah," I said, trying to act nonchalant, but Viv, the tenacious reporter, had always been part bloodhound. And after twelve years of friendship, she knew me better than anyone—especially when it came to my college romance with Damon.

"Yeah?" she said, putting her hand on her hip and snorting at my obvious discomfort. "Girl, don't even try to act like you still not sweatin' that brother."

Across the room I caught Amaya's eye; she'd turned away from one of the groomsmen, who seemed to be having a conversation with her breasts, to see if I'd noticed Damon's arrival. I hoped she wouldn't try to turn this into a big deal.

But I knew Viv was right. Who was I kidding? Damon hadn't been back in my life—or, rather, in my immediate proximity—for more than forty-five seconds and I was already perspiring all the way down to my thong. As my body temperature continued to climb, I prayed the sweat wouldn't cause any perceptible stains on my new Helmut Lang pantsuit. I slipped off the jacket and hung it along the back of my chair. My matching silk halter-top suddenly made me feel exposed. As I adjusted the narrow strips of fabric that barely covered my smallish B-cups, I suddenly regretted buying the flimsy top. While Viv and Amaya had both raved about it when I tried it on yesterday, saying it really complimented my caramel skin, I knew Amaya really wanted me to buy the top so she could borrow it when we got back to L.A. That heiffa ain't slick. When I looked up from adjusting my clothing, Damon was standing by my side.

"Trista," Damon said, enveloping me in a warm embrace. Even after all these years I still loved the way that man said my name. He always drew it out as if he were savoring the sound of the syllables on his tongue. As we pulled away from each other, one of his large fingers trailed down my bare back; I suppressed a shiver.

"Damon, how are you?" I asked coolly.

Viv assessed after a split second that this was a DEFCON 3 situation and slid between us to save her girl from making a fool of herself. "Hey, Dame," she said, as she hugged him, "it's good to see you. Toast the happy couple with us."

I accepted Viv's interference and grabbed the champagne, refilled my glass, and took a large swallow. When I turned back to Viv and Damon, they were staring at me.

"How about a glass for Damon, Tris?" said Viv as she nudged me sharply while continuing to smile at Damon.

"My bad," I mumbled as I filled the champagne flute in his outstretched hand.

Thankfully, before I could embarrass myself further, Will came up and pulled Damon away for a picture of the frat brothers. As I watched him leave, Amaya sidled up to me, smiling like she knew I was up to no good. I put up my hand to indicate I wasn't trying to hear anything she had to say and took my seat.

"Damn, girl," she said as she sat down beside me. "You hittin' that this weekend?"

"Hitting that?" I asked, and looked at her like she'd sprouted an extra head during dinner. "Please don't talk to me like I'm one of those wannabe rappers you like to date."

"Call it whatever you want, girlfriend, but you might need to break him off a little sumthin sumthin tonight," said Viv, who giggled loudly as she reached around me and high-fived Amaya. We were seated with the Jacobs family minister, who would be officiating tomorrow's ceremony, and his wife, a dead ringer for Coretta Scott King. She looked at us pointedly and whispered something to her husband.

"Look, ladies," I whispered tightly as I flashed Coretta a fake smile. "Can we try to act like we've matured in the ten years since I've last seen him?"

"Ain't nobody trying to say we haven't matured," said Amaya. "All we're saying is that Damon's looking good and this weekend is a prime opportunity for your celibate behind to ring in the New Year properly. And your girls ain't trying to let you miss out, acting like you all grown up and shit."

"Preach," said Viv, as she raised her glass in agreement.

"First of all, I am not 'celibate' . . ."

"When's the last time you had sex?" they both demanded as they cut me off.

"Let me rephrase," said Amaya. "When was the last time you had *good* sex?"

"Awww, damn, girl," said Viv as she snapped her fingers. "She's got you there."

"For your nosey information, I'm seeing someone." As soon as I said it I wished I could grab the words back. Why'd I go and say that?

"Who?" they both demanded.

"None of your business," I answered defensively, picking at my crème brûlée. I could see them out of the corner of my eye going down a short list of potential partners.

"Wait a minute, are you talking about that tired lawyer you introduced us to a couple of weeks ago at G. Garvins?" said Viv as she snapped her fingers at the memory of the three of us having a celebratory dinner for Viv's birthday.

"You guys did seem awful cozy," said Amaya, who nodded in agreement.

"If you all must be all up in mine, yes, it was Garrett James."

"Eww," they both screeched. Coretta shot us another sharp look. Instead of worrying about our convo, Mrs. Johnson needed to focus on her husband, the Good Reverend Doctor, who flirted with Amaya every time the old bat left the table.

"Garrett James, for your information, is a really great guy, and a very accomplished attorney," I said.

"Whatever," Viv said, dismissively waving a forkful of her dessert at me. "All I know is that when he realized Amaya and I weren't lawyers or potential clients he didn't have two words to say to us. And it's my guess that Garrett Lame couldn't put in work if instructions from the Kama Sutra were written into one of his legal briefs."

"I know that's right," said Amaya. "I mean, he's fine and all, but he did seem kinda siddity-acting."

"Shows what you two know," I said. "We've been having a great time together."

"So why haven't you told us about you spending time with him?" quizzed Amaya. "Because he's w-w-wack," she summarized by making scratching motions on an imaginary turntable.

"He's not wack," I shot back. After being in a dating black hole for nearly two years, honestly, I was just happy to have someone who called a second time when he said he would, and this looked like it might, maybe, sorta, possibly, if the moon, planets, and stars aligned in the right way, turn into something decent. Garrett and I hadn't actually done the do yet, but we'd had some heavy petting here and there, so the sex looked promising. And Lord knows I could use some.

"Please, girl," said Viv. "It's been so long since you've had some good 'n plenty that if he was laying the pipe right, he'd be sitting at this table with us right now."

"Whatever, ladies," I said. I returned to my dessert and tried to discreetly scan the room under lowered lashes to see where Damon was.

Shoot, who were *they* to talk? Neither one of them was doing any better than me in the relationship department. Viv, at thirty-two, was also another one who seemed to have it all "on paper." She was a senior reporter who covered the breakups and makeups behind the scenes and between the sheets of the celeb set for the *Los Angeles Daily News*. But on the personal tip, my girl Viv was a complete mess. Still hung up on her son's father, Sean, she was only having ex-sex with him and could never seem to make a clean break. He, on the other hand, didn't seem to have a problem seeing other people. But Viv continued to love his dirty drawers. And after each disastrous time they hooked up, Amaya and I would receive the teary recap. Viv had already excused herself numerous times during dinner to "call and check on Corey." Girlfriend thought we hadn't noticed but we both knew full well that Viv was really calling to see if anyone else was over there with Sean.

I've told her a million times she needs to let that one go.

And Amaya, well, she was probably the only one of us who *didn't* have it all "on paper." Sexy in a sort of young Pam Grier kind of way, she'd won a contest to be the spokesmodel in a hair-relaxer commercial while we were in undergrad. Bitten by the acting bug, she'd been doing the Hollywood hustle ever since. She supports herself with roles in music videos and small movie parts, but mostly sustains her lifestyle of the rich and scandalous thanks to the generous support of industry players, tattoo-laced athletes or rappers, plus the residuals from that old commercial, which airs during *Soul Train* reruns.

So, needless to say, I certainly wasn't about to take advice from the two of them regarding what to do about Damon.

"I'm going out for a cigarette," I said and excused myself before

either of them could get in another word. Ducking out of the room, I
asked one of the waiters where I could light up. He must have thought I
wanted to smoke some herb because he pointed to a dimly lit terrace
just off of the ballroom.

I opened the French doors and stepped out into the chilly air. I'd
run out of there so quickly I had forgotten my jacket, and the little top
provided zero protection. Shivering, I lit my cigarette quickly so I
could smoke and get back inside, where it was warm. I was so busy
hopping around, trying to heat up, that I didn't hear the door open behind me.

"Nice night," said Damon as he stepped out onto the terrace and
shut the door.

"Uh-huh." I immediately wished I'd gone to the bar. Did he follow
me out here? He is looking too good for the two of us to be out here
alone. Viv and Amaya were right—I hadn't had that itch scratched nicely
in a while. And he brought back so many memories.

A sister can only be so strong.

"Cold?" he asked as he slipped off his suit jacket and draped it
around my shoulders before I could answer. The warm fabric smelled of
his cologne. This man might make me hurt him.

"Thanks," I mumbled and pulled his jacket tightly around my
shoulders, continuing to puff on my cigarette. Even though he closed
the doors behind him, we still heard the band playing softly inside the
dining room.

"So how's L.A. treating you?" asked Damon. Hmmm . . . so he's
been keeping up with me . . . I told him that I was happily on track to
make partner.

"You've accomplished everything you always said you would do,
Tris." Without you, I wanted to say but held my tongue.

"Yeah, you're right. What about you?" I forced myself to ask. I didn't
want it to seem as if I was keeping up with him.

"New York is cool. Just doing my thing at the bank. You know, just
trying to make it." It was so like him to downplay his success, but I knew

he was doing more than "just trying to make it." At dinner someone had passed around a copy of *Black Enterprise*, which mentioned Damon in their roundup of the top black execs on Wall Street.

"How are your folks?" I asked as I looked up at him out the corner of my eye.

"Good. Howard and Diana sold their dental practice a few years ago and are now hell bent on seeing every corner of the globe," he answered. "I never know where they are until I get a postcard in the mail from someplace like Johannesburg or Anchorage, Alaska."

"That's great."

"What about your pops, your sister?"

"They're great," I said with a forced smile. If Damon noticed my discomfort, he didn't let on. "Daddy retired. My sister's still the same."

"That's good. So what about you?" he asked, turning to look at me, then copping a drag on my cigarette. "You're looking good. Real good, Tris. You must be beating brothers off with a stick out there in L.A."

"Oh, you know . . . " I said, unwilling to elaborate.

"Seeing anybody special?" he asked and looked into my eyes as if he could read the answer in them before I spoke.

"I wouldn't say special, but you know . . . "

"So, when did you start smoking?" he asked, changing the subject. "You used to give me so much grief about smoking in college."

"In law school it was either cigarettes or crack, and I didn't think being a crack head would help me make law review."

"Wow, you even choose your vices based on career impact. You always were focused."

"You'd know that better than anyone else," I shot back pointedly.

"You're not still mad about that, are you?" he asked as he passed the cigarette back to me.

"Of course not. I'm just saying that you should know better than anyone else about how focused I can be."

"Would it help to say I'm sorry for what happened?"

"Nearly a decade has passed since we had that fight. Surely you don't think I'm still mad?" I hoped he would believe me and let it go.

I met Damon our freshman year, when he was handing out copies of a black student newspaper on the quad. I had tried to walk by without taking a copy of the paper he had just started.

"Look, sister, there ain't but a few of us black folks on this campus. We got to stick together," he had called after me. I turned back around and looked at him. He smiled and wrote his phone number on the copy of the paper he gave me. I was hooked. We shared the same biting sense of humor, a love of blaxploitation movies, Langston Hughes's poetry, and greasy Chinese takeout. We coordinated our class schedules so we could see each other as much as possible. And then there was the sex. Damon had been my first and he studied my body like it was a required course he had to pass. We were adventurous, we'd do it anywhere. The library stacks, back in the stockroom at his job, on his little desk at the newspaper office, the bathroom at a party. We didn't care. Practically overnight I became one of those sorry sisters who drops all her girls for a man. Luckily, Viv and Amaya, who said they were just happy to see me getting some, also liked Damon, so they didn't give me too much grief. Not that it would have mattered, because Damon had me wide open.

The only thing we fought about was when he claimed I didn't have enough time for him. I tried to explain to him that I had to work hard. This degree was my ticket out of the 'hood. I swore I wasn't going back to South Central. And I was going to help my family get out, too. I wasn't like Damon; I didn't have an upper-middle-class family of medical professionals that I could fall back and depend on to write check after check for tuition. I had student loans to rival the national deficit. I had to make it on my own. There was no other choice. I was frustrated that he couldn't see that. Our disagreements became more frequent toward the end of our senior year, because nothing was going to stop me from graduating at the top of our class and getting into law school.

On the eve of graduation, Damon begged me to spend our last

night at school with him, but I'd been finalizing my valedictory address and told him I couldn't. We'd had a huge fight that ended with me storming out of Damon's apartment after he accused me of always putting everything else before our relationship. The next day I delivered my address and headed to a summer law program at the University of Chicago. He'd landed a job with Merrill Lynch and moved to New York. We tried to keep in touch, and he was always asking me to come to New York to see him, but I was too busy with my classes. Our strained conversations, with him accusing me of never having time for us, became less frequent and eventually just stopped. And we hadn't seen each other since.

I'd wanted to pick up the phone so many times. Just to call and hear his voice. Make sure that he was okay, but my pride wouldn't let me. I threw myself into my law studies, graduated at the top of my class, and buried all those feelings for Damon. Or so I thought.

"You know, I've thought about you a lot over the years," he said.

"Yeah?" I didn't want to admit that I had thought about him, too, but had been too proud to reach out. We were both silent for a few moments, each of us lost in our own memories. Suddenly he took my hand in his and brought it to his lips. Even though it was freezing outside on the balcony, I felt myself warm up, my pulse quicken. He kissed me on the lips. His lips were full and soft like I remembered. I opened my mouth just enough for him to slip his tongue inside. I dropped my cigarette and wrapped my arms around his shoulders, leaning into his body. His hands slipped underneath his blazer to caress my bare back.

"What are we doing?" I asked as I pulled away from him.

"You've always asked too many questions," he said as he smiled and pulled me back into his arms, then began to nuzzle my neck just below my ear. Damn, he *knows* that's my spot. He moved up to my cheek and then back to my lips before I could protest. My mouth seemed to have a mind of its own as I inhaled his intoxicating scent. Maybe Viv and Amaya were right: this should be my night to get some. I nipped at his lips. What's wrong with having one last night together?

"Feels like you're trying to start something out here," he said, his tone suddenly husky. Just the sound of his voice made me wet. It's been a long time since I'd felt this excited. I tried to run down a mental list of the pros and cons of starting something with Damon tonight. But as his hands moved around my back to reach inside the thin strips of silk covering my breasts, my mind was made up.

"Want to go upstairs?" I asked, smiling at him daringly.

Damon pulled my hips into his and let me feel how much he wanted to. I'd forgotten how blessed he was and couldn't wait to get reacquainted. He turned to open the door to the balcony. By the sound of the horns, the band was in the middle of an R&B flashback with a funky rendition of "Flashlight." We escaped upstairs to my suite while all the guests dipped to the Electric Slide—the perfect song to distract attention from the fact that we'd disappeared. By the time we made it to my room the sexual tension crackling between us was almost visible. As Damon made his way over to me, I stood by the bed and poured some champagne into the two monogrammed flutes. I put an Isley Brothers CD from the gift basket into the player resting on the nightstand. Elise should have called her little gift the Booty Call Basket.

"Here's to reunions," I said as I raised my glass and took a sip.

"To reunions," he said in agreement, and he also sipped. The champagne gave me courage. As I took his glass from him, a bit of the golden liquid dribbled down his chin and dropped onto his chest.

"Hey, you got me wet," he said jokingly.

"Don't worry about it, I'll clean it up." I clasped the back of his head and brought it down close to my face and flicked my tongue along his lips. Teasing him, I nipped at his full bottom lip with my teeth, sucking gently before moving along his chin, down his neck, and into the sprinkle of dark hairs along the opening of his shirt. As I unbuttoned his shirt I planted wet kisses along each peek of naked flesh, then helped him slip out of the shirt. My tongue traced the muscles along his shoulders, sometimes softly, sometimes hungrily. Before he could reach for me I pushed him down on the bed and stood between his legs.

"Relax, baby," I said, looking at him and letting him know that I was in control tonight; he should just do as he was told.

Letting his jacket slip off of my shoulders, I took a few sips of champagne before I started to undress myself. I unsnapped the clasp on my top and let the halter drop into a silky puddle at his feet. I turned around and worked my hips slowly to the Isley Brothers' beat, then let my pants drop to the floor. The moan that rose from the bed told me he appreciated the view, and the show. Turning around, I stood in front of him in my black La Perla thong and strappy Manolo Blahnik stilettos, and reached back to grab my champagne glass. The hungry look in his eyes told me my Pilates classes had been well worth the money, and the effort. I climbed onto the bed and straddled him. With a sly smile on my face, I took one more swallow before I tilted the glass and poured some champagne onto his chest.

"You going to clean that up, too?"

"But of course," I said mischievously, then leaned down and began to lick the top of his chest and work around to his nipples. I remembered that they had always been sensitive, so I bit at them softly, pinched and pulled. Damon groaned and tried to grab at my hips. I playfully moved out of reach, sliding down his body, dragging my hard, standing-at-attention nipples along the way. They tingled at the warm sensation of his body and the cool liquid of the champagne. Using my tongue I followed the delicious rivulets. When the trail ended at his pants, I looked up at him and watched him stare at me as I unbuckled his belt and slowly pulled down his zipper. I told him to stand up and take off his pants. Then I pushed him back down on the bed, turned around, and sat on his lap; he felt more than ready. Clasping his hands, I brought them up around my body and sucked gently on two of his fingers, and then used them to trace my nipple. As he tried to squeeze my breast with one hand I pushed it down on my thigh. Then I took his other hand and sucked sensuously on one finger to give him a preview of what was to come. I could feel his heart beating against my back and I arched and let him caress my breasts as I rubbed my bottom slowly back and forth against his hardness. My head rolled back and I moaned. I was trying to maintain control of my seduction, but then the hand that had been resting on my thigh slid down between my thighs.

"Open your legs," he whispered in my ear as he kissed my neck and pinched at my nipple with the other hand. I tried to resist him, to keep my legs closed, but the tables were turning on me. "Open your legs, Trista." I arched my back and slowly spread my legs. He laughed softly and slid his finger down into the velvety wetness and began to stroke me.

"Mmm . . . nice," he said in my ear as I rubbed harder back into his lap and then pushed against his large fingers. I wanted to feel him inside me, but he knew what I wanted and began to tease me. Two fingers danced around the edges of my lips, slipping in, slipping out, in, out.

"Oh God. Damon . . . Damon." Suddenly he grabbed my arms and pulled me up on top of him and kissed me hard. Our tongues flicked around each other as he rolled over on top of me. He sucked hard on my neck and massaged my breasts, softly pinched my nipples. He moved hungrily back and forth between the two mounds as if he couldn't decide which one he wanted. I arched my back to give him better access and wrapped my legs tightly around his. I was lost, and loved every minute of it.

When he gently pushed my legs apart, pushed aside the thin strip of lace with his tongue and then buried his face between my legs, I inhaled sharply. I couldn't even think, it felt so good. His tongue played with me, sucking and gently biting. I closed my eyes and threw my arms over my head saying his name over and over. And then when I thought I was going to explode, he thrust into me. Always smooth—I hadn't even noticed that he'd already put on a condom.

I put my arms around him and pushed him over, straddling him again. I put him inside of me, sliding up and down faster and faster, clasped my thighs tightly, and massaged my breasts. I rocked back and forth, up and down. I took him deep inside of me, rolling my hips, squeezing and releasing him until I felt the beginning waves of my orgasm.

"Oh, I'm about to come," I moaned deeply as I slid up almost to his tip and then came down. I felt my body convulse. He arched his back up off of the bed, grabbed the back of my head and pulled my hair as his body contracted with mine.

We both collapsed against each other in a tangle of sweaty limbs. I rested my head on his chest and fell asleep to the sound of his heartbeat.

OH MY GOD, what was I thinking? I was supposed to be putting it on him last night, so how did I end up getting turned out? Drinking and sex do not mix. Especially with the college ex you never quite resolved things with. Suddenly the bathroom opens. Steam fills the doorway. I see Damon slathering shaving cream on his face. Droplets of water from the shower cling to his broad chest, and a crisp white mono- grammed hotel towel hangs loosely around his hips. Good God, I could eat him alive.

Determined to look better than I feel, I assess my post-booty attrac- tiveness factor. Grabbing loose strands of hair with one hand, I feel around in the tangled sheets for a stray bobby pin to twist my hair back up. My mouth could use a HAZMAT suit right now, but seeing as there's no way for me to get to my toothbrush without breathing on Damon, I find my purse and pop a few Altoids in my mouth. My stomach contracts sharply but I clench my teeth and will the mints to stay down. Then I grab my tube of lip gloss from my bag and run it over my dry lips and then try to dig last night's makeup out of the corners of my eyes. *So not sexy.*

"Well, someone's finally awake," says Damon as he emerges from the bathroom and sits down on the edge of the bed next to me. Each word is like a nail being driven into the base of my skull. I pull the sheet over my head.

"Are you hung over, baby girl?" he asks, using his pet name for me in college. He laughs and tries to pry the sheet out of my hands.

"Hung over doesn't even begin to describe how I feel," I mumble hoarsely from under the sheet. My tongue feels puffy and rough like it's made of sandpaper.

"Must have been all the champagne you drank while you seduced me last night."

I lower the sheet just enough to flip him the finger. I would kick him out of my bed, but the effort to lift one of my legs would surely send me into cardiac arrest.

"Not that a brotha's complaining," he says, lifting the edge of the sheet and sliding next to me. He reaches around to cup my breasts, softly rolls my nipples between his fingers, and begins to kiss the back of my neck. He's lost the towel. He glances at the nightstand and sees the lights flashing insistently on my cell and BlackBerry.

"Looks like you're pretty busy these days. Must be hard for a man to compete with all of that."

"Well, lucky for me I still don't believe in all work and no play," I shot back. I can't believe he's bringing up our same old issue.

"Damn, what happened to the sweet girl I used to be in love with?" he asks with a chuckle as his hands begin to make their way down my body. "Now she's all hard with this edge."

Just when I'm starting to think that a little morning activity might be the perfect hangover remedy, my stomach contracts and I give a dry heave. Bolting upright with one hand over my mouth, I wrap the sheet around my naked body with the other hand and scamper across the bed to the bathroom. Lunging for the toilet, I kick the door shut behind me.

As Damon's deep laugh vibrates in my ears, I lie on the cold marble floor, cradling the toilet bowl, waiting for the waves of nausea to pass. How could I have lost control like that in front of him? I loved Damon a long time ago, and in a moment of weakness I let him get to me again. But what's past is past. I won't allow myself to go back.

Silently I curse the day I introduced myself to Elise on the playground; curse Elise and Will for getting engaged; for asking me to be in this stupid wedding; for that damn basket; for inviting Damon back into my life. And then I remember that I only have myself to thank for this mess.

2

AMAYA

"Amaya, if you don't stop moving your head, I swear to God I'll never do your hair again," says my hairdresser, Lily, for the umpteenth time this morning.

"If you don't stop pulling my hair, Lily, there won't be anything left on my head for you to work on," I shoot back as I screw the top on the bottle of clear nail polish and blow softly on my glossy French manicure. After all these years, I still hate getting my hair done. A blessing and a curse: I was born with the type of hair that makes men erect at the very thought of running their fingers through it, and women look for any opportunity to snatch it right out of my scalp. Long, thick, and midnight black—I'd never straightened my hair a day in my life until I was chosen to be the Dead Straight Hair Relaxer spokeswoman back in 1995. Even though a simple blowout was more than enough to keep my hair straight, the company insisted that I chemically straighten my locks. And, much like my life, it hasn't been the same since.

Between the mandatory six-week touch-ups and turning down the random weirdos with hair fetishes, I often wonder if winning that raggedy competition ten years ago was worth it. But then I remember my face plastered across every box of Dead Straight, and that the commercial campaign put me in front of—and underneath—some of the most powerful men in the entertainment business. Dead Straight is my launch pad to a career in the movies. Besides, the cute little check I'm still receiving from the nice folks at Dead Straight sure comes in handy when the first of the month rolls around.

Pain in the ass or not, having my do tightened up for today's big event is a must. I'm a staunch believer in looking on point at all times. As my acting coach, Ms. Lamar, always insists—fake it till you make it. Not to mention, there are going to be a whole lot of movers and shakers in the house tonight, and I'm certainly not going to blow this opportunity to make a connection by looking less than perfect.

More important than my career, though, Elise is my girl. From the moment I spotted her at the Alpha Delta Zeta informational tea sophomore year, I knew we'd become friends. While most of the girls were running around stressed out, trying to meet and leave lasting impressions with the room full of sorors, Elise looked completely relaxed. Her nonchalant attitude made it clear that none of the pomp and circumstance, much less catering to anyone's ego, mattered to her. Seated behind her, I nearly pissed in my knockoff Liz Claiborne pantsuit as I spied her nodding off during one of the boring Sunday-afternoon speeches given on the history of the organization. When one of the sisters tried to embarrass her by asking her to recite all the names of the seventy-five-year-old organization's founding members, I discreetly whispered the names in her ear as she rose from her chair. We've been tight ever since.

Ironically, Elise was one of the sorority's top choices for our pledge class. In addition to being a straight-A engineering student with a magnetic personality, Elise's parents are stinking rich. She easily made it onto ADZ's spring 1994 line.

I, on the other hand, wasn't quite as fortunate as Elise. The product of a severely dysfunctional single-parent home, and only an okay student, I was well into my sophomore year with no declared major to speak of and a bad attitude. However, it was common knowledge on the yard that the ADZ girls—and their parties—were the shit, and I wanted to be down. So just as I did in every difficult situation in my life when money and influence were in short supply, I'd compensate with deter-

mination. While the other interested girls studied the chapter's illus-
trious history and memorized the Greek alphabet, I studied the current
members of the campus chapter. After much intensive "research," I
located a copy of a sex tape starring the super-righteous Big Sister
Laqweeda that a member of the Alpha Kappa Omega fraternity had
secretly recorded after a particularly notorious keg party during her
promiscuous freshman year. I used this tape to "convince" her of what
an asset I would be to the sorority.

I always thank my lucky stars for those two inches that placed me in
back of Trista and made Elise my back on our pledge line. From the very
first time we were lined up to this very day, she's taken care of me. With
her quick thinking, there were plenty of times Elise saved me from a
long night of hazing during our eight weeks underground together.
Most memorable was the night our spiteful Big Sister DeTonya
attempted to cut my ponytail when she caught me nodding off during
one of our all-too-frequent night-long study sessions. Just in the nick
of time, Elise swatted the scissors from her hands. It cost her a good
paddling, but in many ways she literally saved my life.

It was to Elise that I first confided my desire to become an actress.
So when I finally worked up the nerve to enter the Dead Straight
Spokesperson competition, Viv, who, ironically, fell in line right
behind Elise, convinced her to drive us around town in the middle of
the night, so that we could tear down all the posted contest announcements—you know, to reduce the competition. And when I won, Elise was
the first person backstage with an armful of roses and a huge hug.

"I'm finished, Amaya," Lily says as she steps back and admires her
handiwork.

"Finally! Jesus Christ, Lily, were you reinventing my hair?"

"Sweetie, why don't you turn around and take a look before you start
running your mouth," Lily replies as she spins my chair around to face
the mirrored vanity table.

"Aww shit! Now this is why I love you," I exclaim as I admire the
thick cascade of glossy curls that Lily has brushed over to one side (the

right, of course, as this is my better side) to frame my face. Elise wanted us bridesmaids to wear our hair in a classic French knot but I'm sure by now, girlfriend knows I always do my own thing.

"Yeah, yeah, whatever, Amaya," Lily says. "Just pay me so that I can carry my behind home and get back in the bed. You done worked my nerves so bad I can't even go into the shop today!" she playfully complains as she packs up her curling irons, combs, and brushes into a black leather carrying case and drops it into her black nylon Prada tote.

"Now, Lily, you know you haven't been in the shop on a Saturday since you left L.A. and moved to Atlanta six years ago! Talking about you want to get back in the bed—you need to blame that man of yours for wearing you out, not me," I joke as I grab my wallet and remove two crisp hundred-dollar bills. "Anyway, you know you love me."

"Ugh, don't remind me," Lily grumbles as she tucks the money into her jeans, blows me a kiss, and heads out of the bathroom.

As the hotel door closes behind her, I pick up my Louis Vuitton cosmetics case and place it on the vanity. I turn back to my reflection and carefully study my face in the mirror. Not bad, not bad at all, I think to myself. All those damn yoga classes and expensive oxygen exfoliation treatments are really paying off. At thirty-one and a little bit (twenty-three on my head shots), my smooth chocolate skin is line-free and tight. I know I probably won't need surgery for years, but I am already saving for it. Some people have 401k's; I have a plastic-surgery account for a few nips, tucks, and lifts when the time comes. That's money I'll definitely need, since Viv won't even let me ask her ex-man, an A-list plastic surgeon and former classmate, for a little Botox hookup. But as I step back from the mirror open my robe and survey my still-perky 34C breasts, 24-inch waist, and 32-inch hips, even I'm impressed.

"Damn, I look good."

Taking a seat back at the vanity, I begin removing my sable makeup brushes, NARS eye shadow compacts, and foundation from "Louis" and place them on the marble counter. I've been on enough music-video shoots and movie sets to know how to do my makeup like a pro, so in addition to using my own hair stylist, I declined Elise's offer for a professional to come by this morning. I glance briefly at my pager and debate whether or not I should try Keith again before doing my makeup. I'd already paged him three times since arriving in Atlanta two days ago—and all of them went unanswered. There's nothing more aggravating than being ignored. I know for a fact that he received the pages because there are always two things you can count on with Keith Cooper: first, as the head of Beat Down Records, he always has his BlackBerry with him, and second, he'll always read the message. Its annoying vibration has interrupted many a sweaty sex session. I smile at the memory of our last encounter.

Last month Keith had to go to New York City on a promotional trip with his new rap artist, Killer Dun. At the last minute, he sent me a first-class round-trip ticket to join him for the weekend. With visions of long days of shopping on Fifth Avenue and even longer nights at the Plaza dancing in my head, I gladly threw on a pink Juicy suit, my favorite pair of Jimmy Choo sandals, and hopped a plane out of LAX. When the car he'd sent for me reached the hotel, there were keys to the room and an envelope with his platinum American Express waiting for me at the front desk. As much as I had hoped he'd be in the suite for me, I didn't trip because I knew the deal; Keith wouldn't be returning to the hotel until much later that night. Until then, the Big Apple was mine.

So I simply turned around without even going up to the suite, hopped back into the waiting car and headed over to Fifth Avenue. From Bendel to Gucci, Tiffany to Prada, I spent the rest of the afternoon working that credit card like Bella at Bliss does my deep-tissue massage. I purchased enough beauty products, clothing, lingerie, and jewelry to keep me stocked for the next two weeks, let alone the two days I'd be in the city. When I finally returned to the hotel, I had to tip two bellboys to carry all of my purchases to our suite.

The look on Keith's face when he opened the door and found me standing there waiting for him in only a new red lace Cosabella g-string and a pair of red lace-up stilettos holding a glass of scotch for him was priceless.

"Goddamn, girl, you are fine as hell," he said as he shut off the BlackBerry he had been talking into and grabbed me by the waist in one swift movement.

"Oh yeah," I answered huskily. "Well, if you think I look that good, can you imagine how I taste?"

"Mmm-hmmm, fuck the imagination," he whispered hoarsely as he dropped to his knees and nuzzled his face in my freshly manicured pubic hairs. "I'm about to eat you alive." Using only his tongue, he deftly pushed aside my underwear and proceeded to massage and suck until my clitoris swelled up to the size of a large pea.

"Jesus," I moaned as I stood over him and grabbed the back of his head to steady myself.

"Naw, girl, not Jesus— Keith."

"Fuck you, Keith," I tried to whisper but the words were caught in my throat as my body convulsed in what was sure to be the first of many orgasms that night.

"Funny, I was just about to," he said as he stood up and flipped me over the back of the couch. At the very sound of his zipper coming down and the condom wrapper ripping, my legs started to quiver again. Because if there's one thing in the world that Keith Cooper can do, it's fuck the shit out of me. When he's inside of me, I forget about the two long years I've wasted loving his married ass. I forget about all the broken promises to leave his wife and the times I've been stood up. I forget about the nights that I spent at home alone, crying my eyes out.

Just as I had felt the tip of Keith's penis on my inner thigh and braced myself for his entry, his BlackBerry went off. "Baby, don't answer it," I begged. "Please don't answer that."

"Amaya, you know I'm working. I got to answer at all times," he said as he hopped away with his pants around his ankles in search of the device he'd dropped at the door.

Instead of cursing Keith out, the idea that he is so important and busy that he can't be out of communication for more than two hours before his office sends out an electronic search party turned me on even more. So I stepped out of my thong and walked over to the bedroom, where he was sitting on the bed arguing with someone, and knelt down between his legs. As I circled his tip with my tongue and gently massaged him, he began replying to every question with a satisfied *mmmm-hmmm*. When I finally pulled him deep into my throat, he started stuttering so badly he was again forced to hang up the phone. I'd won. Love is a funny thing.

AN URGENT KNOCK at the door interrupts my reverie.

"Amaya, are you in there?" screams Viv through the hotel door. Lord, if she weren't one of my very best friends in the world, I'd curse this heifer out for yelling my name like she's on some playground.

"Amaya Tomasa Anderson!"

"Vivian Olivia Evans, I am coming!" I answer as I close my robe and make my way to the door.

"Chile, if you aren't the slowest-moving individual I have ever met in my life . . . " she exclaims as she sweeps into my room, dressed in the violet bridesmaid gown.

"That's because I don't move, my dear," I explain, "I sashay."

"Well, whatever the hell you do, get to it because we're supposed to be down in the lobby in twenty minutes."

"I'm about to do my makeup and put on my dress right now," I sigh. "Hope I look as good as you, hot mama." The violet satin gown, while not my first choice for color, had a sexy fitted bodice that flattered all of our figures.

"Hmph," she says brushing off my compliment like she always does. "Well, at least your hair is done. If there's one thing I can always count on it's Amaya having her hair done. But weren't you 'sposed to do it up like the rest of us?" she asks, smoothing the back of her own French knot.

"Now, you know I've never been one to follow a crowd," I answer as I return to the bathroom to finish applying my makeup. "Um, can you please tell me again why it is you felt the need to bring your big ass down here and harass me?"

"Whatever," she says dismissively. "You know you need me to keep your slow behind on track. Besides, I want to catch up on that last audition."

With every intention of becoming the next Halle Berry, I've been working on my big break for what seemed like forever. But life in Los Angeles is hard. Thankfully, my mama ain't raise neither a fool nor an ugly girl. There are countless men with money willing to pay to be in the company of a beautiful woman.

My first unofficial hustle was Clarence Tillman—my agent (despite my repeated requests to Trista, who said she couldn't represent me because I wasn't big enough for The Agency yet). Turns out he has semi-decent connections, and a thing for black women, so if I flirted with him a little and occasionally gave in to a little NC-17 foreplay; he tended to forget to take his percentage out of my meager checks. (Luckily, his triple bypass surgery last year had limited me to mostly hand jobs and letting him fondle my breasts.) The bottom line is that you need a killer agent to make it in this Hollywood game. Granted, there are times when I feel terrible about the way I'm living my life. But at the end of the day, that'll be for a therapist to sort out; right now I have to be willing to do whatever it takes to succeed. Clarence has pulled together a couple of print campaigns, local commercials here and there, as well as a few parts in some independent (read: straight-to-video) flicks to cover the costs of being beautiful and barely B-list in Hollywood. But unfortunately, between the cost of living in the 90210 area code, monthly appointments with the top dermatologist in the city, private acting lessons, and weekly sessions with my personal trainer, I've been living on a prayer and a generous gentleman friend for a hot minute.

Sometimes when I think about how successful Trista and Vivian have become through their hard work and determination, I wish that almost every measly "break" in my career didn't come from a traded

sexual favor or putting up with some kind of bullshit. There are definitely times when I call one of my girls and almost break down and confess my trifling lifestyle—but inevitably one of my "boyfriends" will
either show up with a diamond-studded trinket or get my name added
to a closed audition list and I get over it.

"Well, I was going to wait until we were all together to tell you the
news," I start to explain as I carefully apply my mascara. "But since
you're here harassing me I guess I might as well tell you . . ."

"Girl, if you don't spill the beans already!" Viv snaps.

"Easy," I chide. Patience was never Viv's strong point. "I just got a
call from Clarence, and your girl is up for the lead in the new Soular Son
film." And even though she is a senior reporter for the *L.A. Daily News*,
hopefully she won't say that "being up" for this part was just my way of
saying that I—along with most of the black actresses in Cali—have been
granted an audition, which will hopefully lead to a screen test, which
will Lord willing lead to my first major movie role.

"Shut up! Shut the hell up!" Viv screams while she hugs me.

"Yep, I swear."

"Okay, just who did you have to sleep with for that shit?" she jokes.

"Well, you know, they don't call me the good-head girl for nothing,"
I smirk.

"Girl, stop saying stuff like that before someone believes you one
day," she quickly replies. "I am so proud of you. I know it's been a long
time coming."

"Thanks, and feel free to drop that little item in your paper next
week so a sister can get some buzz going," I tell her as I study my finished
face in the mirror. I'd outlined my large brown eyes with a dusting of
shimmery gold eye shadow and finished them off with several coats of
mascara to make my lashes look a mile long, then sealed the deal with my
signature glossy plum lipstick. I am definitely ready for my close-up.

I silently wonder how proud Viv would be if she knew what I'd had
to do to land that opportunity.

"Looking good," Viv says, ignoring my last comment as she does anytime I ask her to violate her "journalistic ethics" and help me out with some press. I return to dusting body shimmer along the tops of my breasts and then walk past her back into the bedroom to dress.

Taking my gown out of the closet with one hand, I loosen the belt on my robe with the other and let it slip to the floor.

"Aren't you going to put on some underwear?" says Viv, looking at me with her mouth open as I slip quickly into the dress.

"Ruins the effect," I say, pulling the side zipper up quickly and then stepping into the Swarovski-studded silver sandals Elise's mom picked out for all of the bridesmaids. Snatching up the matching clutch from the dresser, I walk back into the bathroom to grab my LV cosmetics case and my pager.

"C'mon, girl," I say on my way to the door. "You know Trista is going to be downstairs fifteen minutes ahead of time, and I don't want to hear her mouth today."

"Um, I beg to differ," she says mischievously, following me out the door.

I search her eyes for details, but she isn't giving it up. I have to work for it. "Excuse me?"

Viv lets me sweat for a minute, then spills it: "Well, when I stopped by Trista's room last night to give her the jacket she left at the rehearsal dinner, all I heard was the Isley Brothers and a whole lot of moaning through the door."

"What!?"

"Yes, ma'am, whoever was inside that room was getting busy," Viv giggles as she pushes the button for the elevator.

"Do you think it was Damon?" I ask.

"Hell yeah it was Damon. And you know what? I'm not mad at her. He's looking good as hell, we all know their history, and if anyone needs to get some love, it's Trista."

"Whew, I know that's right," I reply as we step into the elevator. "Talkin' 'bout 'Garret isn't wack!' Trista knows she's dead wrong for even letting that arrogant asshole hit that."

"Stop! Stop! You're gonna make me cry and my mascara will start to run!"

Just as we step off the elevator into the bustling lobby my Sidekick sounds.

"Gimme a sec," I ask Viv. Before I even flip it open I know who it is. The message is from Keith: "Sorry I can't be there with you. There's a little something for you at the front desk. X&Os"

My eyes sting as I fight back the tears. I hadn't told the girls he was supposed to be coming because I didn't want to see the pity in their eyes if he didn't show up. They're the only ones that I would trust with the fact that I've been dating a married man for all these years, and even they can't help but feel sorry for me at times like this. I am so sick of his apologies and "get over it" gifts. I am sick of holding my breath—tired of being second best. I drop the pager back in my bag and start walking down the hallway.

"Who was that? Anything important?"

"Nope. Just a little friend of mine that heard I was in town and wants to hook up."

"So what did you say?"

"I told him thanks but no thanks, I'm rolling with my girls this weekend."

"Must be nice to have little friends all over the country," Viv muses.

"I guess. He mentioned that he left me something at the front desk so I guess we'll see how nice it really is," I answer, making my way through the lobby.

As Viv suspected, Trista is nowhere to be found when we arrive in the lobby. But what is waiting for me at the front desk is a small blue box. I untie the white satin ribbon and flip it open; inside is a blinding pair of diamond-and-platinum studs. As usual, no note included.

"Well, it looks really nice from where I'm sitting," says Viv.

"I guess," I sigh to myself as I remove the pair of amethyst earrings from my ears—the same ones Keith gave me when he stood me up on my birthday three months ago.

"Well if you don't want him, pass him and his gifts right along!"

I look at Viv and laugh, "Like you have eyes for anyone but Dr. Feel Good. I'm not going to even ask how many times you've called him this weekend. Plus, trust me when I say, you don't want no parts of this one."

Thankfully, just as she's about to hit me with Twenty Questions, Trista slides up behind us and drops into a chair next to a potted plant. She's trying to hide her bloodshot eyes behind a pair of dark sunglasses with the price tag still on the frames. As I quickly finish putting the latest "Keith consolation gift" in my ears, I catch Vivian giving Trista the evil eye.

"I'm not even going to ask who you're trying to fool with those ridiculous glasses, but what the hell happened to your hair?" she demands.

"Girl, I think my shower cap was torn and I didn't even know," she answers sheepishly as she tries to pat the matted mess. "I think it had a small tear and the steam must have gotten to it."

"Shower cap my ass, that's some straight up rolling-around-in-the-bed hair right there," I say. "And I guess you missed your appointment with the makeup artist."

"She must have come while I was in the shower. What am I going to do?" Trista says, groaning and dropping her head in her hands.

"All I know is, we better fix it before Elise sees you and falls out," clucks Viv.

"Is it that bad?" Trista asks, gingerly touching her head again.

"The real question is, was it that damn good!" I answer her as the three of us head into the women's lounge. Viv cracks up. "Don't worry," I say confidently as I tap my makeup case. " 'Louis' and I are going to fix your face, and Viv can work on that head."

By the grace of God, Viv and I work a miracle in a mere fifteen minutes. I loan her the pair of earrings that I've just removed to complete the look. Even hard-to-please Trista is impressed.

"Ladies, thank you so much for all your help," Trista says gratefully as she admires her mini-makeover in the mirror.

"Yeah, yeah, yeah, don't think we did this for your trifling behind. This is all about Elise. I just didn't want to mess up my lipstick trying to give her mouth-to-mouth when she passed out at the sight of your head," I laugh.

"I was kind of a mess, wasn't I?"

"We'll talk about all that at the reception," I say. "Elise is probably already in the lobby, so look excited. Or in Trista's case, should I say, just try to look alive?"

"Kiss my ass, Amaya."

"Seems to me someone already beat me to that, my dear."

IN TRUE BETTER-black-bourgeois fashion, the start of the wedding is delayed forty-five minutes. As we wait in the chapel lounge for the easily flustered wedding planner to give us the cue to line up, I distractedly watch Vivian and Momma Evelyn fuss over Elise. She looks beautiful. Standing in front of the mirror in a hand-beaded silk Vera Wang gown, she bends down so her mother can place the delicate veil on her head. So that's what the glow of true love looks like, I think to myself.

"Elise, you look beautiful. I am so happy for you," Viv says.

"I'm so nervous. Are you sure my hair looks all right?" questions Elise.

"I promise," I assure her. "You even look better than me for once."

"Mommy, I think I'm going to throw up," Elise whimpers to her mother.

"Chile, if you don't want your father to die of a heart attack, you better not vomit on that eighteen-thousand-dollar dress," she responds evenly.

As Trista and I burst into laughter, Vivian throws us the glance she reserves especially for little Corey when he cuts up in class.

"What? You know that was funny as hell," I say.

"Whatever, Heckle and Jeckle," Elise snaps. "I'm dying here and two of my best friends are laughing their butts off."

"Don't make me curse you out on your wedding day, Elise," I answer her as soon as I catch my breath. "You know you look amazing. Stop acting up."

"Not to mention, you're about to marry the man of your dreams," Trista adds.

Just then, the wedding planner bursts into the room: time to line up.

When the church doors open, I'm overwhelmed by the number of people who've turned out for Elise's wedding. I use my long walk down the aisle as an opportunity to profile all of the prospective hookups of the evening. Many of the guests try to place my face: sure, they've seen me on TV but can't quite place me. A lot of the women wrap their arms around their dates a little tighter as I glide past their pews. Doesn't matter, though, because their men are still checking me out. Can't be helped. And while plenty of good-looking faces fill the pews, none belongs to the one I really want to see.

By the time I reach the front of the church and assume my spot next to Vivian, my cheeks hurt from smiling so hard, while tears of disappointment again sting the corners of my eyes. When Elise finally appears in the doorway, looking breathtaking, I use that opportunity to finally let the tears fall. As I observe the look of absolute adoration on Will's face, I selfishly wonder if anyone has ever looked at me that way. Or will anyone ever. As much as my ego desperately wants to pretend, my heart won't let me deny the sad truth. The look on Will's face represents a love that will last forever, while the looks I receive last until sunrise. As the Good Reverend clears his throat and asks us to bow our heads in prayer, I am struck by the reality of just how alone I truly am.

3

VIVIAN

Maybe I shouldn't have yelled at him. I mean, he *is* home on a Saturday night taking care of his child, while I'm out partying it up with my girls. But then, expecting anything less from him would make me one of those low-expectation-having mofos, wouldn't it? He's doing what a man's supposed to do: he's taking care of his kid. But he should be doing it without the help of some drunk trick whose obvious mission tonight is to ply Sean with drinks so she can break him off while my son is somewhere being ignored or rushed off to bed with as little attention paid to him as possible. That ain't right. And I know Sean—my Sean—knows better.

Sean is my son's daddy, the boy I've loved since the moment I stepped onto the yard at the University of California. The first time I saw him, he was spinning his cane and stomping his size-twelve Timberland boots as he and his frat brothers hollered their organization's Greek letters at the newbies crowded in the atrium for freshman orientation. I was mesmerized. He was a little light for my taste, and slightly more buff than I would have liked him to be, but his perfectly manicured, blond-tinged locks were piled high up on his head (I'm a sucker for dreds), and when he shook himself with abandon in a fit of frat pride, they fell past his shoulders and into his beautiful face—a move so sexy it more than made up for his melanin deficit. Tall, beautiful, and the center of attention—that's what Sean Jordan was, and that's what I liked. Well, that's what I fantasized about. I had never actually hooked up with anyone like him because, um, let's just say I wasn't exactly Ginger the head cheerleader growing up, if you know what I mean. I'm not saying I didn't have the goods to get the boys to look. It's just that in the scheme of things, Vivian Olivia Evans' natural hair, extra hippy hips, quirky sense of humor, slightly-to-the-left political sensibility, and extremely big mouth couldn't exactly compete with the overproduced bombshells who showed up on campus with their expensive clothes, perfect bodies, and family credit cards. They'd come to get their M.R.S. degree alongside some of the most eligible black bachelors our people had to offer. I'd gotten used to playing the back in high school, being the girl who was "the friend"—the one everybody came to for advice when they wanted to get hooked up with someone else. But I was fresh at UC, and prepared to give myself a new start in a place where no one knew me, and that meant being bold enough to walk up to the hot boy and make his acquaintance.

Let's just put it this way: we made each other's acquaintance, all right—straight up until our little boy, Corey Jordan, took up residence in my womb and made two pink lines appear on my home pregnancy test. Sean never denied the child was his; he would never play me like that. But the birth of our son was the death of our relationship. Sure he wanted to have a baby, just not in his first year of med school at age twenty-two, and, to be real about it, not with me, a broke college senior who was desperately clinging to an on again/off again relationship that should have ended long before his seed hooked up with my egg. But I'm completely incapable of being totally honest with myself when it comes to Sean. He was my first. And my first love. My only love. The first man to ever tell me he loved me back. And he is the father of my child, the person with whom I created a life—the most precious gift God could ever give to a human being. And I choose to recognize that as a good thing. Because the fact of the matter is that even with all our problems, Sean and I are more right together than apart.

Which is what I'd been calling his house all night to tell him. I was feeling a little nostalgic—any wedding can get a girl's heart pumping, but there was enough warmth and romance at Elise's ceremony to make every woman within a three-state radius want to get on bended knee and convince her man that love's the place to be. But Sean wasn't answering. And, even tipsy on champagne and fruity mixed drinks, I knew that my child's father, who was supposed to be baby-sitting his baby boy in his posh mini-manse in Pacific Palisades, should have been looking at his caller ID and picking up his receiver when he saw my cell number pop up. I'm the child's mama. And what the hell was he doing that he was too busy to pick up the phone, anyway?

"Hello?" he finally answered, the annoyance in his voice more than apparent.

"Hey, babe—it's me," I said, glad to finally hear his voice. I didn't give him a chance to say anything; I just wanted him to listen to me. "You know, I've been thinking that maybe we should rethink our relationship—you know, make it work beyond pediatrician appointments and parent-teacher conferences and the occasional tryst. You and I were made for each other—I wish you would see that," I said, the alcohol making me ramble on. "I've been calling you all night to tell you that."

There was silence, followed by a sigh. "Viv? Aren't you at a wedding? Don't you have some bridesmaid duties or something to attend to?" Sean said.

Did he not hear a word of what I just said? I didn't think I could make it any more plain. Maybe I should have just said "I love you" or something. Because he was ruining our moment. "I would be attending to my wedding duties if my child's father answered the phone," I huffed, giving back to him a little bit of the tone he was giving me. "What—were you ignoring me? What are you doing, anyway? Where's Corey?"

"Viv, why you acting like I never took care of my son before?" he sniffed right back. "You don't have to check up on us—he's fine. I don't know why you can't just . . ."

Just as he was about to launch into his "you need to trust a brother" soliloquy, I heard her. "You want me to pour you another glass of wine, baby?" she said sweetly. Huh? Wine? With my man? Didn't that bitch know who the hell I was?

"Who the hell is that?" I shout into the phone, loud enough to surprise even myself in a crowded hallway. A few people toss glares in my direction. Talking on your cell phone is an inalienable right in L.A., but I'm not so drunk yet that I can't recognize that in this crowd you come off as classless cursing loudly into it. I was already a bit uncomfortable mixing with Atlanta's elite—I'm not one for fancy affairs—so wobbling around in these shoes and trying to look sexy but not too sexy in this dress, and choosing just the right words to say to a room full of strangers with more money, elegance, and attitude than the Kennedys isn't exactly coming natural for me. I'm not up for embarrassing myself any more than I already have.

My eyes dart around the hallway for an exit, somewhere quiet and empty. I quickly find two heavy French doors that open out to a balcony, and step out onto it, quietly closing the doors behind me. I can't really hear what he's saying until I get outside, but I pick up somewhere around "and it's not any of your business who the hell I'm with. Please tell me you have a reason for calling me."

"Tell me you don't have my son hugged up with one of your bitches," I seethe.

"Um, I wouldn't be calling anybody bitch if I were you," Sean shot back.

"You did not just call me a bitch, did you? I know you didn't just call me a bitch."

"You're right—I didn't call you a bitch. But you *are* drunk," he says quietly.

"You don't know what I am," I snap back. "I've had a little bit to drink, but I'm not so loaded that I don't realize the danger my child could be in if his father is too busy drinking and sleeping with some stranger to watch after him properly."

"Corey is fine," Sean snaps. "He's sleeping. In case you hadn't noticed, it's well after his bedtime. And as for who's in my house, that's none of your business. Good night, Viv." With that, Sean hangs up on me.

I hear silence, and pull the cell phone from my ear like it's scorching hot. I stare at the "call ended" message and, after a few seconds of catching my breath and realizing fully what Sean has done, I yell in a loud staccato, "Oh —no—he—did—*not!*" So consumed was I with dialing, dialing, and redialing Sean's number—I must have been at it for at least fifteen minutes—that I hardly noticed Amaya step through the heavy French doors.

"Please tell me you're not calling that Negro again," Amaya says, her voice so quiet I barely hear her. "I figured you'd be bouncing to the Star Spangled Banner up in this piece, seeing as you ain't been out on the town since Ice Cube left N.W.A."

Startled, I almost drop my cell phone as I rush to hit the end button and shove it into my clutch. "Amaya, what you want?" I ask her, annoyed.

"Stop sweatin' your baby daddy and get back into that reception and party with us—that's what I want," she says as she pulls a mirror out of her purse and starts checking her makeup. "All these bougie folks are jackin' my buzz up in here, and it would be nice if I could count on my homegirl to liven this ol' stale party up."

"Amaya? Why you all up in my business? See, if you weren't so wound up about what I was doing with my baby daddy, you might have one of your own. Now!" I respond, dotting my sentence with a chuckle. Damn. I didn't mean for it to come out like that. But she is speaking out of turn. And anyway, I'm mad.

"Okay, superstar—you got that one. I'm gonna let it slide, just because I know that's the Clicquot talking and not you," she says. "But that's going to be the last time you bring up my single status without getting your feelings hurt. Anyway, we weren't talking about my love life; we were talking about you enjoying yourself. Sean is a good dad; if there's something wrong, he'll call you. And I know Elise is probably looking for your behind right now as we speak. So come on, let's go get this party started right!"

That's my girl, Amaya—always looking out for my party interests. It was because of her that I'd gone from flirting with the idea of pledging, to standing front and center before a bunch of evil sorors who took great pleasure in torturing our pledge class for just over eight weeks. Though it was her good-time sensibilities that made me want to hang out with her, it was our shared backgrounds—and her willingness to let down her guard when she was around me—that made me count her as an irreplaceable friend.

"Viv, come here, I need to tell you something," she'd said to me conspiratorially one evening as we and our line sisters made our way back to our dorms from one particularly grueling pledge evening when we were ordered by one of the more demanding big sisters to hook up an elaborate four-course feast for her, five other sorors, and their boys du jour. The soror, the illegitimate but well-laced black daughter of a successful white TV producer who'd had a big career creating the most stereotypical black sitcoms ever to hit the airwaves in the seventies, was as rich and spoiled as they came at UCal—and she made a point of keeping those of us who didn't have a celluloid pedigree in our place. She was particularly cruel to Amaya and me, probably because she knew that neither of us came from Hollywood or cash. It's not that we were walking around broadcasting that we were straight outta Girlz in the Hood, but in L.A. it's crystal clear who has roots and who's an interloper. "And don't even think about coming up in this piece with some broke-down pasta dish, or some of that backwoods ghetto food," she'd warned as she stared into Amaya's eyes. "I want a chi-chi feast—no expense spared. I better feel like I'm sitting at the best table at Spago. That's the most exclusive five-star restaurant in L.A. for you country bumpkins who haven't been anywhere," she added, her spittle hitting my cheek as her words seared into my face.

Amaya later confided that she couldn't afford the forty dollars each of us line sisters needed to chip in to hook up that expensive dinner. I was the only one she could tell because I was the only one who knew she was broke as hell. During our long, grueling weeks on line, we'd gotten so close and identified with each other's poor backgrounds so readily that we started sharing meal cards and pooling money for groceries to make sure that neither of us would go hungry while we kept being forced to spend our pennies on the rich bitches who were continuously kicking our ass with their financial demands. Elise and Trista were our girls— we'd grown to love and admire them while we bonded on line—but neither of us was ready to reveal our monetary issues, so we weren't about to tell them that forty bucks was going to break our bank accounts. "What are we going to do?" I asked, terrified that we would be exposed for the broke 'hood girls we were.

I'm still not clear how she did it, but Amaya showed up to our pledge meeting later that night with $150 to split between the two of us. I felt guilty taking the money, and she wouldn't tell me where she got it—just that I should hold on to the cash, lest she "waste it on something unnec-essary instead of what it's for, even though that's pretty stupid." I stuffed the cash into my shoe; I don't know how she knew to get extra, but we ended up chipping in just under seventy dollars each for that damn meal that we couldn't even eat.

If it was Amaya that I could confide in, it was Elise that I could count on to make me feel good about myself—I swear, there's no one more peppy and glass-is-half-full optimistic than that girl. So sure was she that everything would be better in the morning, that I half-expected her to grow a red afro and start singing that stupid *Annie* song every time she walked into the room. Though Trista and I liked each other just fine, she was a little too much of a straight arrow—conservative, quiet, and a bit too pent up—for me to really start to care for her like a true friend, until we went over, got a little older, and realized that though our political sensibilities were completely opposite one another's, we had the same goal: to rule our world. In fact, it was Trista who, as we were about to graduate, helped me draw up the paperwork I needed to get into a com-petitive internship program—a paying gig—with the Associated Press in

New York, which, after L.A., was the best place a young wannabe entertainment reporter could be to not only get attention from the publicists
who grant celebrity access, but also to make some extra cash writing
freelance stories for some of the hottest magazines on the newsstands.
In fact, Trista came in from L.A. and drove me and a truckload of my stuff
from D.C. to New York—a four-hour pep talk came with her services—
then introduced me to the editors-in-chief of some of the hottest hip-
hop mags around, as well as a few New York—based celebrity publicists,
all of which put me on solid footing to getting into the highly competitive
industry. My mom had agreed to take care of Corey for the six months I
was in New York—I'd missed him something terrible even before we
pulled the U-Haul out of the driveway, but I knew I'd be able to send for
him once I got settled. So I, a single mom, had the rare opportunity to get
my career started without all the hurdles that come with caring for a
child. "I'm so proud of you, Viv, she said, hugging me tight. Today is the
beginning of the rest of your life, and you're going to win—I know it."

I guess I am playing to win. In the two short years since I walked
through the AP's doors, I've written over a dozen high-profile cover
stories for *Vibe*, *Essence*, *Rolling Stone*, and *Jane*, and, after a short stint
as an entertainment reporter for the *Baltimore Sun*, I finessed a gig covering movies, television, and music at the *Los Angeles Daily News*—a
dream job that not only let me write the kinds of stories I wanted, but
put me in the same town as Sean, whom I desperately wanted to be close
to, for Corey's sake. A boy, after all, needs his daddy.

My son's mama needed someone, too. But wasn't nobody picking
my ass up. Sure, there've been boys here and there that I've messed
around with—a fellow reporter who covered my beat for the *San Francisco Chronicle*, a music publicist I met when I wrote a story about a rapper he represented, and even a youth pastor at a local church who
ministered to B-list celebrities out in Compton. But being a single
mom in a cutthroat business—entertainment reporters are expected to
network at all hours of the day and night to get close to the players, and,
lately, to damn near rummage through people's garbage to keep up with

the glossy tabloid scoops—I'd hardly had the energy to sustain a healthy relationship. There wasn't anything wrong with those men; it was me. And, well, the fact that I was still having ex-sex with Sean.

I know, I know—I don't say this out loud too often. Who I have in my bed is, of course, my business, but I do realize that continuing to let Sean sleep with me in the nighttime but deny me during the rest of the day isn't healthy for either of us. But the sex feels so damn good. And he's so incredibly smart and strong and capable of treating me like the love of his life when he puts his mind to it. And Corey has his daddy around, even if it is under dubious circumstances. Besides, I can't help but think that after Sean finishes sowing his wild oats, he'll get tired of the women who only want him because he's a sought-after plastic surgeon. I don't care that he's a boob doctor. I don't care that he's easy on the eyes. I don't care that he's got cash and a pedigree. I just want him. And seeing as I'm not all that happy with our current "arrangement," I need to talk to the boy and let him know that it's time to stop playing games and be together already.

I was about to explain all of this to Amaya when Elise's crack-head wedding planner busts out onto the balcony and orders us back into the reception room. "Ladies, come," she says, clapping her hands. "It's time for toasts. Inside."

Startled by her demand, I jump up and start to follow her through the double doors. Amaya doesn't move; she rolls her eyes and reaches for her compact. I shoot her a look and signal with my head for her to hurry it up. "Oh, I'm coming, I'm coming—damn!" she says, rolling her eyes at the wedding planner's back. But Amaya doesn't move any faster. I'm laughing at her and shaking my head when I step back into the hallway leading to the reception area and see Trista running toward me, frantic. The crazy wedding planner foolishly tries to step in front of her, but Trista runs through her like a linebacker, and the woman has to scramble to keep her footing. Amaya busts out laughing; my eyes follow Trista to the ladies' room. "Come on," I say, grabbing Amaya's hand. "Something's wrong with Trista."

She is leaning over the sink, staring at herself in the mirror when Amaya and I bust into the bathroom. "Whose ass do I have to kick?" Amaya demands.

"Amaya—please, not so loud," Trista stage-whispers, her eyes darting around to see if anyone heard her.

Amaya sucks her teeth, and lowers her voice. "I don't care who hears me right now. What the hell is wrong with you?"

Trista looks at Amaya and rolls her eyes. "Nothing, Amaya. Nothing's wrong."

I look at Amaya with a "let me give it a try" nod, and then back at Trista. "Sweetie, what's going on?" I say gently. "Maybe we can help you fix it."

"Oh, there's no fixing this, unless you know how to take back the last two days I spent making an idiot out of myself," Trista says, her voice trembling. She is quiet for a moment, then turns around to face me and Amaya. "He has a girlfriend, and she's here."

"Who, Damon?" Amaya says, her mouth dropping open.

"She's here?" I say, simultaneously.

"Yes, and yes," Trista says quietly. "Out on the dance floor with her man, slow dragging to my damn song. I saw her when she came in—all six foot five of her—looking like she stepped out of the pages of *Vogue*, and I watched her sashay her lanky behind over to Damon and kiss him on the lips. And you know he had the nerve to not even look embarrassed, like we hadn't just made love less than twenty-four hours ago? I can't believe I let him talk his way into my bed. I *know* better."

"Oh sweetie, it's not your fault—the boy is fine, and he's your ex, and sometimes, you need a little ex-sex to get you by," Amaya says matter-of-factly. "Ask Viv."

"Amaya, please—this isn't BET's *Comicview*. Enough with the jokes," I say, shooting her a look before turning to Trista. "Sweetie, come on—let's get it together. I know you're hurting right now, but short of us going out there and beating her down, there isn't really much you can do about it right now. And Elise is waiting for you to come out there and make a spectacular toast on the happiest day of her life. Don't let Damon and his trick steal your joy or Elise's. Pull it together, Trista."

I look at Amaya, and she looks back at me, both of us unsure whether Trista will fall for my pep talk after being so badly embarrassed. After a few moments, she checks her lipstick in the mirror and turns around. "You're right," she says, standing up tall and smoothing out her dress. "I'm not going to worry about it. Let's go celebrate the bride and groom." That said, she marches out the door, with us close on her heels.

IT TOOK ONLY a few seconds for the wedding planner to get everyone to start tapping their expensive crystal champagne glasses with their forks—a signal for Elise to kiss her groom. And then, as if she were a conductor cueing the brass section, the wedding planner points at Trista with her index finger, and signals her to start toasting the happy couple. I look to my left and then my right: Trista is staring down at her drink, her focus clearly somewhere other than on the index cards on which she'd jotted her speech yesterday afternoon between phone calls to her office and a really bad movie we'd ordered on pay-per-view. Amaya is staring into space—Lord only knows what's going through her mind. Clearly we need to rally.

The room becomes quiet; all eyes are on Trista. She's good at getting plenty of attention for her clients, but she's never been one to hop on stage and strut her own stuff, so this is a particularly exquisite torture for her, as the audience is full of proper black folks who don't suffer fools easily. When she hesitates just a second too long, I know I need to step in. I stand up, take the microphone from her clenched fingers, and make a joke about how as the only writer in the bridal party it's fitting that I should make the toast. "Elise and Will," I start slowly, wracking my cloudy brain for words of love, faithfulness, and devotion that will pass as coherent and memorable. "There couldn't have been a more perfect day for a more perfect couple. But Elise has always had it like that—she's the lucky charm. Her parents had a hint that this was true when they brought their pretty little brown bundle of joy home, and they found out for sure when they marked Elise's lucky numbers on that lottery ticket—her birth date, her favorite number, her age, and the first and last numbers on her Social Security card. Trista's known the luck of Elise since they were toddlers, when they became best friends. Amaya and I were blessed with her presence when we pledged our sorority—she was always the calming, sweet one in the midst of the storm, ready to open her arms in a wide embrace, always saying just the right words to put everyone at ease. Through her we've all been blessed with good fortune, and now it's Will's turn to see just how lucky life is when Elise is a part of it." I turned to Will and looked him in his eyes. "Good fortune is sitting right there next to you, Will. Yours will be a life crafted by the angels—God will see to it, for yours is a union that is truly blessed. Here's to a true love—may it feel new, even through the years when the glitter fades, the children have moved away, and the wrinkles of time have turned both of you old and gray. To the beautiful bride, and her extremely lucky groom," I said, raising my glass to them. "May we all be so lucky to find what you two have today." The room rang out with *Hear! Hear!* and then fell silent as everyone took a sip. When I sat down, Trista reached for my hand and squeezed it; her eyes said "Thank you," even if her lips didn't.

DESPITE THE CHEER in the room, it is clear that Trista, Amaya, and I are hurting. If no one else notices, the bartender sure does. Trista and Amaya are at one with the champagne; I'm knocking back berry martinis. We hardly hear the music, couldn't care less about the merriment that increasingly fills the room as the party rushes toward midnight—and the New Year. "You think anybody would notice if we left?" Amaya asks, fingering her watch and looking over her shoulder. "I'm ready to go. For real."

"We can't leave yet. It's almost midnight, and you know Elise is going to want us close by," Trista says, practically slurring her words, "Besides, why leave now? If I go back to my room, I won't be able to see her and him with my own eyes—and remind myself never to be so damned stupid again," Trista says as she tosses her head in Damon's direction.

"Um, I think I get the dumb-ass award tonight," I say, raising my glass to my girls. "I called my man to tell him I love him, and instead accused him of being a heartless, neglectful father. I'm such a loser."

"Loser?" Amaya says, cocking an eyebrow. "Um, he had a woman at the house. That's grounds for getting upset."

"A woman?" Trista says, incredulously. "Hold up—that Negro had a woman all up in his house when he was supposed to be taking care of your son? You bet you had the right to call him out."

"I know, but Sean would never purposely hurt Corey, and it's not like our relationship extends beyond the parameters of eleven P.M. and six A.M., so there's no reason why he would think he couldn't have yet another fake-boobed freak at his house while I'm away. It just hurts to have it confirmed while I'm calling to tell him how much I love him."

"Look, we have about ten more minutes until the clock strikes twelve. We can give Elise a hug and kiss, wish her and Will well, and then go back to our rooms and drown our sorrows without anyone noticing," Trista says.

"Sounds like a plan," Amaya chimes. "I still have a bottle of champagne chilling in the mini-bar upstairs."

We are quiet, each lost in thought about the disastrous pall that hangs over what should have been a phenomenal evening for us. So absorbed in our own thoughts that we don't even notice Elise tossing her bouquet of calla lilies into a crowd of squealing women. Girlfriend was always a bad shot—the damn bouquet flies over all of their perfectly coiffed heads and lands on the bar, right in front of me, Amaya, and Trista. The crowd of disappointed singles turns around, looks over in our direction. Some were mumbling about a do-over under their breaths, but reluctantly begin to applaud.

Elise has a grin on her face a mile wide. Hanging on Will's arm, she shouts, "Ya'll are next, girls!" We all smile and then turn back to our drinks, leaving the bouquet sitting right there on the bar. I don't know about them, but I'm especially disappointed, not just because Sean is acting up, but because we're headed into a New Year feeling helpless and, even worse, hopeless. I grew up in an extremely religious and superstitious household: my mom taught me from practically my first independent breath that whatever you're doing as you head into the New Year is what you'll be doing for the next 365 days. And I took that to heart—always found something constructive, positive, and loving to do when the clock struck twelve. When I was little, my mother would gather us up, get us dressed, and march us on down to St. John's Episcopal AME to pray the New Year in. I continued the tradition until I went to high school, where being hugged up in some boy's arms was my mission, so sure was I that doing so would guarantee me a New Year filled with affection. By college I'd pretty much surmised that just because you were slipping some tongue to a boy as the New Year rolled in didn't mean you were going to get any more loving the rest of the year. In fact, for me, it was a crapshoot. So I got constructive: I decided to take fate out of the equation and make resolutions that could only come true if I put my heart and mind into it. They'd worked up until now: I vowed when Corey was born to be a good mother—and I am. I vowed to become a senior reporter at a top newspaper—and I have. Last year, I promised myself that I'd be taken a lot more seriously by my superiors and get promoted to either an editor's post or at least into a gig that would allow me to show off my true talents—either as an investigative entertainment reporter or a pop-culture critic. That resolution is still winding its course. My editor apparently has other plans for my career—but I've talked my boss into letting me do a few critical essays on blacks in Hollywood (or the lack thereof), and that's satisfied my gotta-move-on appetite for now. Yes, when I put my mind to it, I can do anything.

"Hey," I say, looking at my watch. It's 11:53—we have seven minutes. "I'd like to make a pre–New Year's toast," I continue, raising my glass.

"I'll drink to whatever—what you got?" Amaya says.

"Here's to a New Year where we take control of our romantic lives and find the men of our dreams," I say.

"Oh yeah? You been holding out on us, Vivian Olivia Evans? You got some men stashed somewhere? Some good ones who know how to act right? And respect a lady? And make money? That a girl can trust? Who give foot rubs on demand?" Trista slurs.

"Huh? You won't find any of those on planet Earth," Amaya says. "She must have a rocket ship waiting to take us to Pluto."

"Come on, guys—I'm serious. I want us to take a vow tonight that sometime this year we'll each find our soulmate, fall madly in love, and be happy, dammit."

"Oh, why stop at being happy?" Trista says. "Why don't we go all out and pledge to be married by this time next year?"

"Yeah—a triple wedding. What I always wanted," Amaya says dryly.

"Come on, you guys, I'm serious. My New Year's Eve pledges have always come true, and this will be no exception," I say confidently, though inside I know this resolution is going to be the toughest I've ever made. I don't want them to know that, though, so I look Trista and Amaya right in the eye. "Let's raise our glasses and promise one another that we will find us men who appreciate, love, and respect us, and who'll slip rings on our fingers before the year is over."

"Oh, come on, Viv," Trista says. "Surely you're not serious."

"Why not, Trista? If I were telling you to vow to make partner before the year is up, you'd be all over it. And you, Amaya," I say, turning to her. "If I told you that you had to find the perfect role by the end of the year, you'd be costarring opposite Clooney."

"True that," Amaya laughs.

"So then why is it so hard to believe that if you put your minds to it, you can find a man who loves you unconditionally and who's willing to pledge his undying love for you by year's end?"

They don't say anything, but I can tell they're thinking about it. I look nervously at my watch again. "Come on, guys—it's two minutes to midnight. Raise your glasses and let's do this."

Trista and Amaya look at each other nervously and let out giggles. I stare into both of their eyes and raise my glass, too. "Okay, girls: on this night, as the clock strikes twelve, we vow to find men who will love, honor, and treasure us enough to grace our fingers with rings, and walk with us down the aisle into a lifetime of happiness."

"To two carats or more," Amaya toasts enthusiastically.

"To success in romance," Trista says, raising her glass.

"To the Vow," I say.

"The Vow," we say together. Our glasses clink together as the room explodes in applause and cheers, with confetti and balloons falling from the ceiling and the band breaking into a funky rendition of "Auld Lang Syne." It's as if the room is cosigning our deal—as if they know our fate. I have a good feeling about it. Come this time next year, we aren't going to be crying in our champagne glasses—unless they're tears of joy.

4

TRISTA

I love driving through Beverly Hills at this hour. At 6:30 A.M. there's a crisp chill in the air—and barely any smog. It's almost too cold to have the top down on the car but I do it anyway and keep the heat at seventy-two degrees on my bare legs. As I roll past the designer boutiques on Rodeo, the mannequins in the window wait expectantly for the swarms of Japanese tourists and jaded Beverly Hills housewives to slap down platinum credit cards for their expensive wares. I turn up the volume on my Jill Scott CD. Listening to that sista's golden voice is like my morning therapy. Much-needed therapy for where I'm headed.

As I ease my 325i convertible up to the curb outside L'Ermitage, I glance at the clock and see that I'm early. Carlos, one of the valets, is spraying down the sidewalk in front of the swank boutique hotel, and when he sees my car he cuts off the water, drops the hose, and jogs around to the driver's side to help me out.

I grab my alligator portfolio and copy of *Variety* from the backseat. I glance at the main headline: INSIDERS SAY OSCAR NOMS TO FAVOR STARLET KIMBERLY SPRINGFIELD. As I digest this info, I catch my reflection in the hotel's glass doors. I smooth down the front of my black-leather Michael Kors skirt and adjust the matching silk blouse, brace myself for breakfast, and walk toward the hotel's lush outdoor dining area. I can see that Cassidy is seated in front of the waterfall, her famous face obscured by a copy of *Variety*. Shit.

Cassidy St. James is my most famous client—not that I would ever admit that to any of the other stars I rep. At forty-three, Cassidy is eccentric, to say the least. She lives at the hotel and can be seen wandering around the property with her spiky dirty blond hair askew, wearing a monogrammed terrycloth robe, oversize black Chanel sunglasses, and slippers. She got her start as a child star and went on to make a string of big hits back in the day. Movies usually have two parts for women: young bimbo girlfriend or younger bimbo wife. And once Cassidy veered north of thirty, Hollywood stopped calling. The firm dumped her on me when her last agent died. Last year I convinced her to consider an independent studio project. No one wanted her for the part, but I fought for her. She called twice a day from the set to bitch about her lack of a private trailer and the young director's lack of respect for her "craft." I tried to placate her by telling her this was her comeback vehicle. Most calls ended with her hanging up on me.

Now it looked like everything just might pay off. Last year Canaan Pictures released *Emma*, the story of a divorcée diagnosed with breast cancer who decides to undergo homeopathic treatment while holding together her dysfunctional family. The reviews were magnificent and the word of mouth spread like a California wildfire. An Oscar nod would put her squarely back on directors' radars.

"Good morning, Cass," I say, slipping into the chair across from her.

"Morning, Trista," she says frostily as she glances over the top of her paper at me and flicks her wrist, noting the time on her delicate gold Cartier watch. I give the waiter my order, certain that Cassidy has already ordered, intent on drawing attention to my lateness.

I know we were set for 6:45 A.M. But I drove here all the way from Santa Monica; all she had to do was roll out of bed and shuffle her bony butt downstairs.

"How was your trip?" she asks, not really caring about the answer.

"Wonderful," I say brightly, nodding my head vigorously to erase the image of Damon's face, which just popped into my head. "You've seen the paper," I continue, scanning the story to see what's got her so ticked.

"Yes, and according to Brad Townsend at *Variety*, Kimberly Spring-field is going to win Best Actress."

I'm going to need some food before I can piece back together her delicate ego.

"Brad Townsend doesn't know what he's talking about. He's just a writer. Everyone knows you're going to win for Best Actress," I say confidently.

"I better. You told me to do that piece-of-shit movie!" she shoots back testily.

"*Emma* was hardly a piece-of-shit movie, Cassidy." Shit movies were the projects she was doing before I took her on as a client, is what I want to tell her. "Everyone's saying it's your finest hour—brilliant performance, an instant classic," I say, feeding her blurbs that ran on the movie posters. "TA is firmly behind this project, and we're putting together an aggressive campaign to reach all the Academy members and media outlets to assure a steady stream of favorable buzz as they prepare to vote. You will win."

And if *she* wins, *I* win, because then they have to make me a partner.

As I EASE THE car back into the thickening traffic my cell phone rings. I adjust my earpiece and answer.

"Good morning, gorgeous," says a familiar deep voice.

"Garrett, good morning," I answer, smiling at the sound of the endearment.

"I missed you, why didn't you call me when you got back in town?" Garrett's heavy breathing tells me he's in the midst of his morning workout at home.

"Oh, you know, things have been crazy, getting back in the flow at work," I say. I'd received a message from him but didn't want to return his call immediately. I needed time to think about what happened in Atlanta. Having sex with Damon was a big mistake. I'll never lose control like that again. What Damon and I had is officially black history. And I need to get over that with a quickness.

"So when am I going to get to see you?" Garrett asks.

Ordinarily I'd tell him I'd have my assistant, Adriene, give him a call with the first available opening in my schedule, but today I'm going to focus on our Vow. I invite him to the Jerry Bruckheimer premiere I need to attend tonight. I'll blow off the after-party (something I never do) and we'll grab a late dinner.

We finalize our plans as I guide the car down the ramp into TA's underground parking garage. I scan the partner initials on the wall, longing for the day when I'll have my own designated parking spot.

Stepping into the cavernous art deco lobby, I'm once again struck with the same feeling I get every time I walk in this place. I can't believe I'm an agent.

I've been a film junkie since I was a kid. I knew I wanted to work in Hollywood, but I also knew I couldn't take rejection well enough to be an actress. After graduating from law school, I headed back to L.A. and got a job in TA's mailroom. My sister Tanisha joked that she could have hooked me up down at the Compton post office where she was working at the time and I didn't need two fancy degrees to do it. But she, like most of my family, didn't understand. I wasn't going to bust my hump at the mailroom for years and get nowhere. I was getting out of South Central. Everyone started in the mailroom to learn about the business—from the bottom up. Sure, it was a lot of bullshit—delivering the mail, dropping off scripts all over town, copying thousands of pages, running questionable errands (read: drug mule)—but if you hustled, you could make it to agent assistant and then the holy grail: your own desk.

My shot came when Brian Turrow, one of the firm's star agents with a nasty, but functional, cocaine habit and an even nastier disposition, became overwhelmed by a pile of scripts. When I rolled my mail cart past his office for his morning delivery of the trades, he yelled out to the hallway.

"Hey, you! Can you read?" I walked into his office. "My assistant has gone into fucking labor. I told that cunt to schedule a C-section after

Cannes!" He tossed a bunch of scripts in my direction and told me to give him notes on them by tomorrow morning. Grateful for the opportunity, I stayed up all night compiling detailed notes about character development, plot lines, and which of his megawatt clients should star in the vehicles. By the time I was finished the next morning, I'd put together a ten-page report on each script for Brian's review. Anticipating he wouldn't be in for a while, I straightened up his office and wiped down his glass desk which was "dusty" only in the middle. I placed my write-ups on his desk and sat back down in his assistant's cubicle. Around nine the phone began to ring, so I started taking messages.

When Brian came in he walked into his office and slammed the door behind him. After about thirty minutes, he asked me to come in.

"What the fuck is this?" he asked as he raked his fingers through his hair, which I wanted to tell him only accentuated the new plugs.

"Uh . . . the notes on the scripts you asked for . . ."

"What the fuck makes you think I've got time to sift through ten pages of bullshit from somebody from the fucking mailroom?"

I was dead. My first chance to show my stuff and get out of the mailroom into an assistant's job and I was through. I thought he'd be sending me to HR to turn in my ID. Instead he told me to break down my thoughts on one page by noon. I wasn't about to blow it. I put together a short memo on each script while juggling the phones. When Brian headed out to lunch, I tucked the revised notes in his briefcase.

The next day I wasn't sure if I should return to the mailroom but I took my seat back in the cubicle. When Brian came in he asked me to get Ben Stiller on the phone and didn't mention my notes. In fact, he never mentioned them and never formally hired me. I just kept showing up, and after two weeks my paycheck reflected a marginal increase, so I assumed I was hired and dug in.

Brian was a player and I was learning from one of the best. For four years I worked around the clock for him, and when he was tapped to run a studio, I got promoted to agent with Brian's recommendation. And when they divided up his roster, I was given a couple of names to get me started. The rest I hustled and built up on my own. And now with Cassidy positioned to win an Academy Award, I'm a shoo-in to make partner.

I FLIP THE LIGHTS on in my office and am greeted by the sight of a foot-high pile of scripts by the side of my desk with typed notes from my assistant, Adriene Madison. Good, at least she's gone through everything so I can skim her notes and pick out the best ones to possibly pursue before the Monday status meeting with department heads.

As I sit down I reach for the silver picture frame on my desk and remove the old picture of me, Amaya, Elise, and Viv flashing our sorority sign back in the day and replace it with one of all of us from the wedding reception to remind me of our Vow.

Adriene pokes her head in the door to say good morning. Girlfriend's got the Beyoncé long blond weave look going on today. This woman must blow half her paycheck on hair extensions. Sometimes the colors and style choices make me cringe. But who can blame her? Southern California is the weave capital of the world with the highest per capita horsehair usage in the country. I have to give it to her, though; whether she's sporting a jet-black, chin-length bob or a fiery red pixie cut, girlfriend's hair is laid.

And she's also the best assistant. Her instincts are on point, and, most important, girlfriend has my back. That's something worth its weight in gold in this piranha-eat-piranha office that isn't exactly a case study in compliance for the Equal Employment Opportunity Commission. She helps me stay sharp with my main competition for partner, Steven Banks, who is always looking to exploit any weakness. The nephew of one of TA's most powerful partners, Hunter Banks, Steven is a major prick. He'd started in the mailroom with me and raised a big stink when Brian put me to work on his desk. A few weeks later, one of the other assistants was let go for "stealing office supplies" and Steven was put on his desk. Soon he was promoted to agent and given a roster of strong talent, including the new "It" girl, Kimberly Springfield, Cassidy's Oscar competition.

"Hey, Adriene," I say as I scan my emails.

"Hi yourself," she says as she walks into my office and plops down in the chair in front of my desk.

"Thanks for pulling together notes on the scripts that came in while I was away."

"No prob."

"Please put Garrett's name on the VIP list for the Bruckheimer premiere and make a dinner reservation for us tonight at Koi."

"You the boss."

THE DAY GOES BY quickly. Adriene pokes her head in to tell me it's time to go. I touch up my makeup and then rake a comb through my shoulder-length flip. Thank goodness I have my weekly hair appointment with Walter tomorrow because as Adriene had noted earlier in the day, my "do is just about through."

I'm in no mood for the Bruckheimer blow-'em-up shoot 'em-dead movie tonight, but one of my hot young actors, twenty-year-old Jared Greenway, has his first major part in this flick. It's a good role for him. Jared dies in the movie, but he dashes through enough frames with his shirt open so that we're sure to start receiving more movie offers, maybe a guest spot on *Will & Grace*, a Gap commercial, a TRL appearance . . .

Just as I pull out of the garage, I see Amaya's name on the screen of my cell.

"Check your BlackBerry," she says when I pick up. "I forwarded you a copy of a new Industrywhispers.com email."

"You know I don't read that nonsense, Amaya," I say impatiently.

"I know, diva, that's why lucky for you I read it for you. There's an item listed in the Hot Water section that sounds like it might be about you."

"Thanks, I'll check it out." I promise to hit her back, and pull the car over to read.

HOT WATER!!!!!

What agent on the go-go was spotted tap dancing like something out of "All That Jazz" during a tense breakfast meeting at a swanky-and-swell BH hotel trying to keep her superstar client from bailing? This agent better snag some golden glory for her star's recent "death-defying" performance to keep her happy . . .

Great, there's no way no one knows that's not me. *All That Jazz* was Cassidy's first major movie and death-defying performance refers to her character in *Emma* beating cancer. I act like I don't read this stuff but everyone in town reads it. Maybe the partners are above reading internet gossip. No such luck. A new message pops up on my screen.

TO: Gordon, Trista
FROM: Banks, Hunter
RE: FW: Industrywhispers.com Buzz Report
    See below. Hope there's no truth to this bit in Industry-whispers.com . . .

                                                    HB

I toss the BlackBerry back into my bag and speed out of the parking lot, sure that Steven was only too glad to share this news with his uncle.

WHEN I GET TO the theater I see Jared's limo making its way to the hot spot in front of the red carpet. There's a swarm of teenage girls packed into bleacher seating behind the press and photographers' bullpen. Viv is jockeying for position in the front row next to *Access Hollywood*'s Shaun Robinson. Viv knows TV trumps print on the red carpet, so she's staked out a prime spot next to Shaun so that when stars complete their *Access* interview she can grab them and get a few quotes. Good. This is the perfect storm for Jared to arrive in. They go bananas as soon as he steps out of the limo. He's brought his mom, publicist Sloane Sedgewick, and the homely fiancée, Heather, who looks like she made the shapeless dress she's wearing herself. Is that rayon? Poor girl. Unfortunately for her, "married Jared" isn't as marketable as "single bad-boy Jared." I suspect that Sloane will send Heather back to the cornfields before *Game Over* makes it to DVD.

As the five of us make our way down the red carpet, Sloane chooses which reporter Jared should speak with. She wields her power discriminately, her icy-blue eyes casting daggers at reporters who have written negative stories about her clients. I know Sloane's had it out for Viv ever since she ran an exclusive interview with the Salvadoran hotel maid who claims she's having the child of one of Sloane's biggest clients, so I know I'll have to step in. Just as we're about to pass, I loop my arm through Jared's and take him over to Shaun and give Viv a wink to indicate she should get ready to speak with him next. Sloane glares at me while tapping one of her razor-sharp Jimmy Choo heels impatiently. I feign innocence.

As I continue to scan the non–red carpet crowd, I see Garrett. He's hard to miss. A "pretty muthafucka," as Amaya likes to call him, he's tall with toasted cinnamon-color skin, a close crop of dark curls, muscular build and piercing brown eyes. He carries himself with the unmistakable manner of someone who's used to going anywhere and being in charge. Too sexy. The guard at the door must have thought so, too, because when she can't seem to find his name on the guest list, he smiles with a row of perfect teeth, leans in to whisper something in her ear that makes her laugh, and she waves him inside.

I smile in anticipation of our dinner tonight and then rejoin my group as they make their way into the theater. It's showtime.

As I approach Garrett after the premiere ends, he's talking to another handsome black man wearing dark blue jeans and a tight black V-neck sweater.

"Trista, baby," he says in my ear as he kisses me on the cheek. I get a little tingle in my stomach, feeling his arms around me.

"Garrett, so good to see you," I say just as our lips meet for a quick kiss. We must have embraced for a moment too long. The stranger clears his throat.

"My fault," Garrett says, pulling away from me. "Trista, this is my boy Mike. We go way back."

"Hi, Mike," I say as I reach to accept his outstretched hand. "Nice to meet you."

"Nice to meet you, too," he says with a smile full of perfect white teeth and one sexy dimple. Viv's a sucker for chocolate skin and a great smile. I wonder if he's single. I casually glance down at his left hand but can't see if he's wearing a wedding band.

"Mike's wife, Tamika Taylor, was a makeup artist on *Game Over*. We ran into each other inside," says Garrett.

"Oh, that's great," I say, trying not to show that I'm bummed to hear he's married. Sorry, Viv.

"Well, it's nice to finally meet you," Mike says, smiling again. "I've heard a lot about you." Garrett playfully punches his friend on the shoulder as if Mike has said something he shouldn't. I half-smile back and put my arm through Garrett's.

We chat a bit more before Mike says he has to go find his wife so they can head over to the premiere party. Garrett and I walk over to his black Range Rover.

"So, what did you think of the movie?" I ask as he steers the truck into traffic.

"I think when we get to Koi we're going to celebrate your hit movie and new star with a bottle of wine," he says, reaching for my hand and stroking my fingers. The good thing about dating a man like Garrett is that he can appreciate the challenges of my job but he's established enough that he doesn't need to use me for connections.

"Yeah, I'm excited for Jared," I say leaning in to stroke his arm. "This project should really be good for his career. I spoke to a lot of producers tonight that want to talk about creating vehicles for him. The partners should be pleased."

"This will help when it comes time to be considered for partner." As Garrett talks about what other things I need to do to position myself I think about how wonderful it feels to be with someone who supports my ambition and isn't threatened by my success.

"Those are all great points, Garrett," I say as I lean over and kiss him on the neck. "But that's enough about business, honey. Tell me how much you missed me."

"I did miss you, Trista," he says huskily as he brings my hand up to his lips and kisses it softly. "Hey, what do you think about skipping dinner?"

"You're not hungry?" I ask.

"Not for food." He grins and places his hand on my thigh. We make it to his house in the Hollywood Hills in twenty minutes. I walk around the sunken living room and take in the breathtaking view of the city while he gets us some wine.

"So are you at least going to still feed me tonight?" I say jokingly as I take the glass of merlot from him.

"Of course I am," he says, pulling me down next to him on the black leather sofa. "I just thought we could start with dessert." Garrett takes the glass from my hand and puts it down on the coffee table and then kisses me. My whole body begins to warm up. The tingle that was in my stomach earlier begins to move lower. I pull his face close to mine and slip my tongue into his waiting mouth. I lean back on the sofa, pulling him down on top of me. He slips one hand underneath my shirt and uses the other to work his way along my thigh and up my leather skirt.

As he kisses my neck I pull his shirt from out of his pants and begin to unbutton it. He sits up slightly, takes his shirt off and then lifts mine over my head. When he lies down again on top of me, the cool skin of his chest feels warm, sensual. He slips his hand between us and unhooks the clasp on my bra in one fluid motion. Then he begins massaging my left breast with one hand and kissing the other one, sucking on my nipples lightly.

"You like that?" he asks huskily in my ear.

"Oh, yeah," I say and arch my back. "Please, don't stop." He pushes my skirt up and begins to grind his hips into mine on the sofa, hitting just the right spot. He rains kisses down the length of my body, and when he arrives at my panties he throws one leg over his shoulder and slips his tongue inside and begins to lick me softly. I sigh and close my eyes in anticipation of what's about to happen. As I begin to lower my panties to give him easier access to my goodies, he moves back up to my neck. Damn, is he done? Don't tell me he's one of those brothers that doesn't put in the work, head down south for two seconds, licking around here and there.

I am too heated to not get mine tonight, so I decide to take matters into my own hands. I push against his shoulders and we roll over until I'm straddling him. Reaching down between my legs, I loosen his belt, pull it through the loops, and then toss it across the room. Then I unbutton his pants and stand over him to pull them, along with his boxers, down his legs. When I look up between his legs I nearly lose my breath. Brotherman is working with some serious equipment. Perhaps all is not lost. Damn, he looks good enough to eat.

Before I finish what I've started, I reach for my handbag and pull out a condom and slip it on him. Then I lower myself slowly. He moans with appreciation.

"You like that?" I ask him teasingly as I lean down and lick his earlobe.

"Oh, yeah, I like it," he says as he grabs my hips and pushes into me. Bracing one of my arms against the shoulder of the couch, I close my eyes, rotate my hips, and move slowly up and down until I get into a nice rhythm. One of his hands squeezes my breast as I slip one of my hands between my legs and begin to rock back and forth. As I feel my body start to pulsate I quicken my pace. We climax together and then collapse against each other on the sofa.

"So, can a sister get something to eat now?" I ask playfully.

"Baby, after that you can get anything you want," he says as he laughs.

5

AMAYA

No, I'm sorry, Amaya isn't home right now. Yes, ma'am, I'll be sure to give her your message as soon as she returns from her trip . . . 'The All American Collection Agency, 888-797-0000, twenty-four hours a day'—got it. You have a nice day now."

If I receive one more phone call from these damn collection agencies, I'm going to scream. Every single day at the same ungodly hour the phone rings, and it's always the same ol' shit. Give me a break! Don't they think that if I had the money to pay them off, I would have done it by now? Jesus. I'm not sadomasochistic, just broke. The worst part is, I don't even know how things have gotten this bad. Okay, yes I do. As a matter of fact, I'm sitting on one of the reasons right now. My Le Corbusier chaise longe was simply a must-have according to *Elle Décor*, and who am I to argue with the experts? I just wish that damn Dead Straight check would hurry the hell up.

I don't know how much longer I can do this. It's been a month since my audition for the lead role in the new Soular Son film, *The Black Crusader*, and I still haven't heard squat. Normally, I refuse to stress over anything (my L.A. hair stylist says worry makes my hair brittle), but this one has kept me up the past couple of nights. For the first time I wasn't called in for the token black girl role—the maid, the nanny, the neck-twizzling angry best friend, or even the crack ho. This character has integrity, a career, a purpose—shoot, she even has a last name. This role has the potential to rocket-launch my name right up there next to Halle. Okay, more like under, but still. I hate Holly-wood.

The phone rings and I don't want to answer it, but it could be Clarence with news about the part, and I'm going to be too through with myself for missing the call. I can guarantee he'll leave a vague message with instructions to call back as soon as possible instead of simply say-ing whether or not I landed the part.

"Hell-lo?" I finally answer in my most seductive voice.

"And just who may I ask do you got the extra-sexy voice going for this early in the morning?" playfully teases Viv.

"Oh, hey, girl," I say, disappointed. "Why didn't your number pop up?"

"Just the latest tactic in the celeb wars," she explains. "We can call out of the office without the newspaper's name popping up and giving us away."

"True . . ."

"Anyway, it's been three weeks since anyone has even heard a peep from you and all I get is, 'Oh, hey'?" she questions with her signature Vivian-is-the-mama tone of voice.

"Shoot, you're lucky I even answered the phone," I retort. "You know how I feel about folks calling me from blocked numbers!"

"Well, excuse me, sunshine," she responds.

"My bad," I apologize flatly. "I've just been a little distracted."

"Distracted? That doesn't sound like our everyday knucklehead Negro problem. Let me guess—still no word on the part, huh?"

"Nope. Not a peep," I respond despondently.

"Hmmm, that's weird. It shouldn't take this long," she muses.

"Honestly, I really don't feel like talking about it," I try to answer diplomatically.

"Okay, but I still think . . ." she insists.

"So, how's my little man doing in school?" I interject, desperately trying to steer the conversation away from my career.

"Humph, acting just as grown as you and Trista have him thinking he is," she answers, switching gears easily to her favorite subject in the entire world.

"Wait a minute, what happened?"

"Chile, apparently when he's not bouncing off of the furniture and breaking down the walls in my house, Corey is breaking little hearts in his class," she laughs.

"Shut up!"

"Girl, yeah. He had two little girls fighting during recess over who was going to be his girlfriend," she giggles. "By the time the recess monitor arrived, the poor things were in tears and ya boy was talking about why can't they *all* be his girlfriends!"

"Oh my goodness," I laugh for the first time in days.

"If you ask me it's that dang ol' Irish Moss cologne you bought him for Christmas. Ever since he first smelled it, he's been asking me to dab it on him every time he leaves the house. It's crazy!"

"Ha! I told you that scent was the truth. That mess will make a grown woman catfight in an alley over the bum wearing it," I boast.

"All I know is your little wannabe Casanova will only be wearing Auntie Amaya's present on very special occasions from now on."

"I hear ya, sister. But remember, don't hate the player, hate the game," I remind her as I slowly stand up and stretch my back.

"Trust me, ain't no game going down as long as I rule 2201 High Ridge Road."

"I know that's correct." I cosign on her declaration of parental control. "Shoot, I wonder if Damon was wearing some on the night of Elise's engagement party . . ."

"Ouch, that's cold. You wrong for that one, Amaya."

"What?" I question sheepishly.

"Don't you 'what' me," Viv chides playfully.

"I'm just saying. There had to be a really good reason for Trista to cut up like that, is all," I persist.

"Amaya, if you don't stop!"

"Okay, okay," I giggle. "I'm going straight to hell in a handbasket. I know."

"You, my dear, are a trifling mess and need Jesus in your life forreal, forreal. But seriously, I was calling to see if you'd checked your email recently. Your girl sent us some homework and wanted to know if we were free for dinner tomorrow night at our spot. It's about time we catch up and trade war stories . . ."

"Ugh, Trista stays trying to give somebody some damn instructions," I grumble as I amble over to my Dell laptop.

"Stop complaining and check your email," she instructs.

"All right, all right, I'll do it now," I concede.

"By the way, why didn't I see you at the Bruckheimer premiere last Wednesday? I worked the red carpet, and Trista was there with her new boy Jared Greenway. Shoot, seemed like all of Hollywood was there except you and your weirdo agent . . ."

"Girl, if you don't leave Clarence alone! Actually, we discussed attending but decided that it wasn't an event that would really help my visibility, so we opted out and had dinner with a couple of indie producers who submitted a script for me to review." I lie, hoping that Inspector Gadget will accept my answer and not force me to admit that once again I hadn't been in the loop to be invited to a major premiere.

"I hear ya," she answers suddenly distracted. "So what's up for today? Wait, let me guess, you're going to get yet another facial, or maybe have your entire body waxed?"

"First of all, don't hate on my flawless skin. Secondly, I don't do wax—that's so five years ago. It's all about permanent removal now. Electrolysis. Third, my schedule is much more hectic than you think."

"Poor thing, I can only imagine how you find the time to breathe between all the spa treatments, Kabala for Dummies courses at the temple, workout sessions with your fine-ass trainer . . ."

"Phillip's gay, Vivian."

"He's a man."

"Give me a break. I'm lunching with Benita at the Four Seasons this afternoon."

"Aww, well, why didn't you say so? I love your mom! She is so great. How sweet are your little monthly mother-daughter lunches? You two are so cute together . . ."

Humph, if she's so damn cute, then please feel free to take her yourself, I immediately think. As far as I can see, there is nothing even remotely cute about my mother. In fact, ruthless, calculating, demanding, gold-digging bitch are adjectives far more likely to come to my mind when I think about Benita.

"I wish my mother was as cool as your mom," Vivian sighs.

"Whatever—now I see how you do! Benita gets preferential treatment over Phillip," I joke. "So much for the fair and unbiased reporter in you, huh?"

"Um, how did you put it? 'Phillip. Is. Gay.' He can't do shit for either of us."

"Actually, I beg to differ. Between my thighs is a much better place to be now that Phillip is a part of my life. And if you would just sign your lazy butt up, he'll gladly do wonders for you . . ."

"Ugh, Amaya. You know the last thing I want to hear from you is about the condition of my thighs, thank you very much," says Viv, quickly cutting short all conversation about exercise.

"Dang, don't be so sensitive, Viv. You know I love your shape. But the reality is that all the big booty that you could get away with down in the dirty South is just not cutting it here in LaLa-land," I insist in what has become a recurring riff between us since she moved to Los Angeles.

"Anyhoo," she responds, refusing to acknowledge my last remark, "tell your mama I send my love."

"The only thing I'm going to tell her is that you made me late for lunch if you don't let me get off this phone," I retort as I glance at the clock.

"Oh no, don't you blame me for your inability to motivate! Stop worrying about the role and get cracking. Don't forget to check your email, and I will talk to you later."

"Hugs and kisses, hot mama," I answer lovingly as I hang up the phone.

I take a deep cleansing breath and exhale; talking to Vivian can be exhausting. Regardless, she's right. I don't have anything to be concerned about. That Soular Son role is in the bag. As I start to log onto my computer, my Sidekick vibrates in its cradle. Without even bothering to look I already know who the caller is—Keith. Since getting stood up in Atlanta, I have refused to answer any of his calls or return his insistent 911 pages. As far as I'm concerned, I've had just about enough of Keith and his worthless words; it's time to put his sorry ass on time out. I've decided to let my silence speak volumes. And if the daily bouquets of fresh lilacs, lilies, and yellow roses, not to mention the jewelry—so far I've received a pair of black pearl earrings, emerald chandelier earrings, a matching emerald ring, a pair of diamond hoops, and a platinum charm bracelet with our initials together on a charm—are any indication, Keith is getting my message loud and clear: Playtime is over.

As THE VALET at the Four Seasons opens the door to the silver E-series Mercedes Benz Keith bought me for our last so-called anniversary, I run a quick last-minute appearance check. Skin glowing, check. Eyebrows arched to perfection, check. Makeup flawless, check. Although it seems on the outside that everything is in place, I can't help but feel sick to my stomach. Lunch with Benita is a mandatory monthly torture that I dread like a pimple on my back. To make matters worse, I'm twenty minutes late. Now, in addition to her usual rants about my inability to find "a nice, wealthy man to take care of me," I'm going to have to hear about my tardiness. Just great.

It's not that my mother doesn't mean well. After all, she is the main reason I'm so driven to succeed. When she became pregnant at the age of fifteen and my father refused to claim me, she made a conscious decision never to allow herself to be screwed over by a man again. To say my mother is bitter is an understatement. But I can't knock her hustle, because so far she's managed to keep that promise. I can still remember every single one of her lectures about the shortcomings of the opposite sex . . .

"Men are only capable of accomplishing one thing on their own, Amaya. You know what that is? Well, let me tell you what that is. Making a baby. That's right. Shooting out semen is about the only thing that men can handle on their own—and, quiet as it's kept, they're barely able to do that right. For everything else, it takes a woman to lead them around by the nose. So if you're going to spend your entire life raising someone else's grown-ass child, he better have the money to make you comfortable. Do you hear me? You don't need to be with any man that can't take care of you as much as you're going to have to take care of him. Don't believe that love bullshit, it's for broke motherfuckers. You are gorgeous and you should never have to work or want beyond what your man brings home. So you better get you a very wealthy man. And if you're really lucky you'll land yourself two. The more the merrier, dammit, 'cause ain't no man ever going to be faithful. Fuck feelings, look out for yourself."

Over the course of the years, her daily diatribes stuck with me. As I watched her go from wealthy man to wealthier man, from Section 8 to suburbia, I started to understand the method to her madness. Eventually, instead of trying to block out her rantings, I committed them to memory and depended on them as much as my Bible.

As I was graduating from UC and preparing to permanently move out to Los Angeles, my mother was in the process of finalizing her third divorce. Caught up in her immediate need to distance herself from everything that reminded her of her latest "no-good, tired-ass, lame-game but extremely rich ex," she decided to follow me out to L.A. for a fresh start. Upon arrival on the West Coast, she dyed her hair strawberry blond, got a breast lift and tummy tuck, and requested never to be called "mother" again. None of which bothers me quite as much as the newfound free time that Benita has on her hands. Since work is a non-issue (her alimony payments keep her covered), Benita has now taken up managing my social life as a hobby. Many a night I'll receive the midnight call that consists of her check on the status of my love life and her not-so-gentle reminder that with every day, more of my eggs are dying. As if I don't know. Yet all of the phone calls combined are relatively painless compared to this mandatory monthly assessment—or, as she has affectionately dubbed it, our mother-daughter tea. It's at these face-to-face meetings that, without fail, Benita will break me down both mentally and physically under the guise of ensuring that I am on the right track to my "Mrs." title. However, with each passing lunch, it becomes increasingly clear that regardless of what I accomplish, nothing will ever satisfy her.

I zip up my bag, jump out of the car, and snatch the parking ticket from the valet. Enough procrastinating—it's time to meet monster dearest. As I rush into the leaf-covered entrance of the hotel, I run smack into a very chiseled set of abs.

"Whoa, whoa, take it easy, ma. The hotel ain't goin' nowhere," laughs a strangely familiar voice.

I step back and remove my dark tinted Christian Dior sunglasses so that I can take a better look at the owner of this rock-hard midsection and find myself locking eyes with the hot new rookie and starting center for the Los Angeles Stingers, Troy Bennett.

"Oh my, please excuse me. I certainly didn't mean to hurt you," I reply coyly, taking in his flawless butterscotch complexion and soft curly hair.

"Aww, it ain't nothing, pretty girl," he quickly replies as his eyes appreciatively travel up and down my body and get stuck somewhere between my breasts. "In fact, I should probably be thanking you for providing a reason for us to speak."

"Oh yeah?" I ask, suddenly very glad that I decided to wear my low-cut mango Diane von Furstenberg wrap dress.

"Yeah, yeah, yeah," he enthusiastically replies with a sly grin on his adorable face. "So, Speedy Gonzales, my name is Troy. And yours?"

"Amaya," I answer and slowly run my fingers through my hair. In the blink of an eye, I forget all about my waiting mother and go full throttle into seductress mode. This man is simply too fine for his own good in his white Brooks Brothers oxford shirt, khaki slacks, and Todd's driving moccasins. I easily envision wrapping myself around him like a chocolate-covered pretzel.

"Amaya, huh? That's a beautiful name. It fits the owner perfectly," he says softly as he reaches out and pushes back a stray hair from my face. "Have we met before? You look so familiar . . ."

"Why, thank you, Troy," I respond without breaking our gaze. "Perhaps you've seen some of my work, because you would remember if we'd already met."

"That's it! You're that Dead Straight hair chick! I see you in the hair commercials all the time. And weren't you in that movie *Bad Chicks* or something?"

"You mean *Bad Girlz*," I correct him, pleased he recognized me. And if he saw that bullshit, then he *has* to remember my prison shower scene. He's hooked.

Just then the valet pulls a shiny black Porsche Cayenne up to the entrance, hops out, and looks over toward Troy.

"Well, Amaya," he starts slowly, "since you bumped into me, it seems only right that you make it up to me by accompanying me to dinner tomorrow night."

"Well, if it'll make us fair and square . . ."

"Well, let's just say it'll be a nice first step toward restitution," Troy smirks.

"And just so you know, I'm all about providing full restitution for my wrongs," I toss back.

"I like that. Here's my number," he says as he hands me a business card and walks toward the truck. Before he gets into the driver's side, he stops and says, "I look forward to tomorrow."

"As do I," I reply without a moment's hesitation, and pivot on my gold sandals. As I slowly walk into the lobby of the hotel (to give Troy a lasting and ample view) I remember Trista and Vivian's request for dinner tomorrow night at Koi. Shoot, Trista's going to trip, because I already emailed her my confirmation. Oh well, they'll simply have to understand. I'm already in the heat of my battle.

Still thinking about how to diplomatically back out of my dinner plans with the girls to get with Troy, I hear my mother call out, "Amaya you're late! I was just about to leave you."

"I'm so sorry, Mom . . ." I start, but she cuts me off.

"Didn't I tell you about calling me that? My name is Benita. I've raised my child, I ain't nobody's mama no more."

"My bad, Benita."

"'Your bad'? Why must you insist on speaking like that? Just because you came from the ghetto doesn't mean you still have to act like it," she snips as she examines her freshly done manicure in her signature Ballet Slippers color.

As I stare at her chiseled caramel-colored face, perfectly dyed hair, Tahitian pearl set, and Chanel tweed suit, I am reminded again of what a stunning woman my mother is and just how far she's come from our days of dressing like sisters, instead of mother and daughter, in Miami's Magnolia Keys projects. "You're right, Benita," I apologize and settle back into the plush banquette, "we've both come a very long way."

"Well, I don't know about the both part, but that's neither here nor there . . ."

I shake my head and signal the waiter. Once we place orders for our cantaloupe soups and goat cheese and arugula salads, she gets right down to business.

"So how are things?" she inquires with a tight smile.

"One day at a time. Still waiting to hear back about that Soular Son film," I answer cautiously.

"Hmmm. Well, I certainly hope you didn't go in there looking like you do today," she responds. "I can see your roots from a mile away, and what's going on with your skin? Is that a pimple on your cheek?"

"No, Benita," I sigh. "Jean-Claude straightened my hair the day before the audition, and you can trust that my face was flawless."

"Well, good. At least we know you got one thing from me . . ."

"Oh, and just what might that one thing be?"

"Don't get smart, Amaya," she answers as she locks her almond-shaped eyes on mine in the deadly stare-down that I never win.

I avert my gaze to my own neatly manicured hands and nervously play with the coral and twenty-four-karat rose-gold bracelet dangling from my wrist.

"That's what I thought," she gloats. "Like I was saying, at least we know you got my good skin out of the deal, since you damn sure got your father's black-ass complexion."

Although it isn't the first time I've received an unwarranted lash about my undeniable resemblance to my father, it hurts nonetheless. "Benita, you should really spend less time worrying about my skin and more time applying sun block," I coolly reply. "I hear skin cancer is killing you old high-yella ladies in droves nowadays."

"And who, may I ask, are you calling old?" she questions, glaring across the table.

"If the shoe fits . . ."

At that exact moment, our waiter arrives with our appetizers and we retract our talons, put our public smiles back into place, and thank the man. "Anyway, enough about that acting nonsense," Benita starts after a couple sips of her Pellegrino and a minor adjustment of the cuffs on her jacket. "How was Elise's wedding? Did you and Keith have a good time?"

One night my mother called after I'd had a particularly heated argument with Keith and, in a fit of absolute despair, I spilled the beans about our clandestine relationship. To my surprise, instead of berating me for my scandalous behavior, Benita totally supported me. In fact, she encouraged me to keep seeing him. As she so eloquently put it—"You don't know Keith's wife or her kids, so you don't owe her anything. There's a reason that Keith comes to you, and only time will tell what God has in store for the two of you." As much as I'd like to believe that my mother simply had a moment of pure unadulterated love and caring for her only child's happiness, I'm much more inclined to believe that her recently seeing Keith's picture on the cover of *Black Enterprise* had more to do with her unusual empathy for my situation.

Either way, since that fateful night, she's been the third party in our relationship. In truth, she's probably done more to talk me off the ledge each time I threaten to leave than he has. Benita is Keith's one-woman cheerleading squad. Which is all good and fine except, last time I checked, she was my damn mother.

"The wedding was fabulous. I looked stunning, as did Elise," I reply. "But as usual, at the last minute Keith stood me up."

"Stop being dramatic. Did he call you before the wedding started? You have not been stood up if he calls and informs you ahead of time."

"Fifteen minutes before he's supposed to arrive?" I ask incredulously. Even a cold-hearted woman like herself had to agree that this was not entirely acceptable.

"You know he's a busy man, Amaya. Things come up and he has to handle them. What are you going to do when the two of you are married and he has to go out of town at the last minute? Are you going to act up and be ungrateful then?"

"Who the hell says we're getting married?" I snap, my patience all but evaporating.

"Darling, please, it's obvious that Keith loves you. And if you'll only be a little more patient and give him a chance, he'll prove it."

"Benita, I'm tired of the both of you," I sigh. "I'm not speaking to Keith."

"Big words from someone who doesn't have man the first to claim . . ." she mutters as she dabs at the corners of her mouth with the linen napkin.

"I'll have you know that I'm dating quite a few men at the moment," I shoot back. "In fact, I just made plans to get together with Troy Bennett tomorrow night."

"Oh, really?" My mother squeals like a little girl. "Didn't he just sign a huge endorsement contract? I just read about him in the papers—so handsome and rich!"

I watch as the wheels start turning in her head and a cold beam enters her eye.

"I take it that you're familiar with Mr. Bennett," I say with a slight sneer.

"Familiar enough to know that Troy will make the perfect date."

"I should think so," I reply between bites of my salad.

"Not just for tomorrow, Amaya. What about Thursday night?" she impatiently replies.

"What's Thursday night?"

"You're so out of the loop it frightens me," she sighs. "Thursday night is the biannual Rap Renegade party at El Centro. Everyone in that whole hip-hop music industry is going to be in town for that thing."

"And just what does that have to do with me?" I pout, realizing that in all three hundred of the unreturned pages and phone messages that Keith has sent since I left Atlanta, he never once mentioned this event, let alone invited me to join him.

"Well, considering Beat Down Records is a major sponsor of the event, I'm going to assume that Keith will be there," she explains slowly, as if I were mentally challenged. "Why not light a little fire under Keith's butt by showcasing the competition?"

No one could ever say that my mother didn't have a good idea once in a while.

"Who knows," she continues. "The party might be the perfect place for the two of you to start up a new conversation, if you catch my drift."

Where my mother's suggestion ends, the race in my mind begins. I can see it now: I'll show up on the red carpet wearing a dazzling low-cut Richard Tyler mini-dress on the arm of Mr. Bennett. Naturally we'll be the evening's most talked-about couple and the paparazzi will eat us alive. Forced to watch Troy fawn over me all night long, Keith's mouth and heart will drop to the floor. In fact, the sight of me in another man's arms may drive him to declare his love for me right in the middle of the party.

"You know, Benita, you might actually have a good point," I grudgingly allow.

"Thank you, my dear," she says, graciously accepting my compliment. "And you know, in retrospect, you might actually be on to something with this silent treatment. There's nothing like freezing a man out to make him want you more. And we want that boy to have icicles hanging off him when he sees you with Troy."

"Now that's what I'm talking about!"

I'M ON MY way home from lunch when I make a last-minute decision to swing by my agent's office to find out why I've missed yet another premiere, see if he's heard anything about the role, and secure my entry to the Rap Renegade party. Clarence's office is located in the heart of downtown L.A. and completely out of my way. I hate going there. But a missed premiere and a thirty-day wait to hear back about an audition requires an immediate face-to-face.

The first thing I notice when I step into the office is the trashy-looking receptionist. With each step I take toward the front desk, I feel my nose crinkling and the far-upper-right corner of my upper lip rising as if something smells really bad.

"May I help you?" she asks with a roll of the eyes.

"I'm here to see Clarence," I start to answer impatiently.

"Err—um, why don't you just take a seat over there and I'ma see if his people can find him," she answers with a simultaneous smack of her chewing gum before I can even finish my sentence.

As I head over to the old, cracked brown-leather couch against the far wall I make a mental note to donate money to the Robert Kelly Adult Literacy Foundation as soon as I make my first million, because I cannot stand ignorant people.

"Amaya, my angel," Clarence exclaims as his sour-looking assistant finally shows me to his office.

"Do you always make your angels wait so long, Clarence?" I ask sarcastically as I stride past her into his spacious corner office.

"Aww, don't be like that. You know I'd never purposely make you wait. I was tying up some loose ends, sweetie," he oozes as he emerges from behind his black-lacquer desk.

"Don't 'sweetie' me," I retort, giving his knockoff Gucci suit and run-down Italian shoes a scornful once-over. "Where was my invite to last week's *Game Over* premiere?"

"Come on, Amaya, you know how those things are. They weren't inviting anyone except the A-listers," he hesitates.

"Oh really?" I retort. "And didn't you promise me that by now I would *be* one of those A-listers? Huh, Clarence?"

I can't believe how naïve I was when I first moved to Los Angeles. To think that I actually believed that this fool was really somebody in the Hollywood hierarchy—and even worse, that he really cared about me. The only damn thing he cares about is getting his percentage of whatever little check I manage to finagle and an occasional cheap feel. But, quietly, even that would be just fine with me if he helped me land this role.

"I-I-I, um . . ." Clarence lamely stutters in response.

"Because according to my calendar, it's been damn near a month since I auditioned for that Soular Son project and I still haven't heard anything. So just what are you doing?"

"I've been pulling in all my favors, Amaya. I swear I have," he squeaks.

"Cut the bullshit, Clarence! I'm tired of making nice. I want this goddamn role!"

"I kn-kn-know," he starts to stammer.

"And excuse me if I'm mistaken, but have I *not* paid my dues? Have I *not* been extremely accommodating?" I ask.

"Y-y-yes, yes you have been more than generous," he squeaks, trying to loosen the tie that suddenly seems to be choking him.

"Well, then, don't make me regret it," I warn between clenched teeth, "because I don't think your friends, or should I say men whose asses you lick, would appreciate a blind item on Industrywhispers.com with details of all of my so-called meetings with them."

"N-n-no, we don't need that."

"Oh, Clarence," I say, softening my voice and suddenly switching gears, "what's done is done. I know you're trying your best."

Thinking that the worst is over, Clarence starts nodding his head like one of those godforsaken bobble-head dolls. "Of course, you know I am."

"You know I would never do anything to hurt you. It's just that I absolutely *need* to know what's going on. I simply can't handle the uncertainty." Tossing my hair over my face, I dramatically fall into the couch. "You know I would do anything to get that role," I hint seductively as I bury my face in the crook of my arm.

Like Pavlov's dog to the bell, Clarence hurries over to the couch and tries to console me. "Amaya, you know that I'm working as hard as I can to get you this role. I've pulled out all the stops and I won't rest till you're the star you deserve to be."

And until you get the nice fifteen percent that you convinced my silly behind to sign away, you low-life bastard, I think as I silently fume. "You know, I haven't worked on a new project in weeks, Clarence."

"I know, I know," he says, and his beady little eyes hungrily devour my breasts. I watch in pure disgust as he literally licks his lips.

"So I was thinking maybe you could help me out. You know, just a little something to hold me over until we hear back . . ."

"Amaya, you know my policy about lending clients money, but for you anything. Just consider this a gift," he says as he draws my hand on top of his minuscule erection. "After all, one hand washes the other."

No more than ten minutes later, I'm walking out of his office, fifteen hundred dollars richer and needing to wash my hands. "Um, I assume you plan to make up for last week by getting me on the VIP list for the Rap Renegade event this Thursday night, correct?" I state more than ask Clarence from the open doorway.

"Absolutely," he mumbles from his crumpled position on the couch.

"Good."

As I pass by his sorry-ass assistant, she shoots me one of her knowing glances, which I return with a "kiss my ass" cut of the eye. Those
who can, do. The last thing I plan to worry about is what she thinks of
me. She is more than welcome to sit there and screen Clarence's calls
while I shop for Thursday with his money.

6

VIVIAN

Being an entertainment reporter sucks. You're on all day, every day—constantly thinking about story concepts, interview questions, how you'll pitch it to your editor, how to work the publicists to get access to the entertainers, how you'll frame your piece, which quotes you'll use, whether the other papers—or the slick white boy on the rise who sits next to you—will steal your feature, or, worse, scoop your exclusives. My friends think it's a glamorous life. I did, too, until I found out what it's really like to cover Hollywood for one of L.A.'s top tabloids. Er—um, I mean newspapers. You have to stay up on the latest crappy music fads, read mediocre books, watch TV shows and movies that aren't worth the paper their scripts are written on, interview celebrities who barely know how to spell s-m-a-r-t, much less say something remotely like it during their sputtering, self-serving interviews, and go to overhyped parties and events full of self-important, self-absorbed, C-list "celebrities" who act like their Botox treatments, head-to-toe lipo, silicone implants, dye-jobs, and overpriced, made-in-Taiwan, paid-for-on-Rodeo duds make them capable of parting the Red Sea. Weeks will go by where my days consist of coming in at ten A.M., getting sent out on assignment, coming back and writing on deadline, arguing with my editor over all the ridiculous changes and mistakes he's edited into my story, then shoving something down my throat as I head over to whatever premiere/party/schmooze fest I've been suckered into covering instead of being allowed to write more serious pieces that delve into

the business of entertainment, or the smart, thoughtful cultural-criti-
cism pieces I've always dreamed of writing.

Some days I think working in a factory would be more glamorous
than this, which is exactly what I'm thinking as I wheel my Saab out of
the *Los Angeles Daily News* parking garage and down La Brea toward a
small Beverly Hills studio where my latest occupational hazard is about
to show his face. Today my editor socked me with a profile of Young
Daddy MC, an aging nineties rapper who, despite not having had a hit
since MC Hammer was flapping at the top of the charts, is attempting a
comeback as some kind of ladies' man of hip hop. His new single, "All
This Love," is somewhere on the Top 200, and getting semi-decent play
on the pop stations, thanks to MTV2 and some extremely corny white
DJs who think they're cool for knowing who Daddy is. But he's no
Tupac. And he certainly doesn't deserve any play in the *Daily News*.

I tried to explain this to my editor, Joel. He's such a star-fucker—
goes to more parties and gets more Hollywood ass than any journalist
should be allowed. But he's the golden boy at the *Daily News*, mainly
because he's managed to create titillating celeb coverage that's got the
other major tabloids struggling to keep up. Unfortunately, he's also my
assignment chief. Did I mention that he's delusional, too? "Come on,
Vivian," he said, leaning a little too close to my face as he loomed menacingly over my desk. His breath stank. "It's Young Daddy. You know—
he did 'Pop It,' and 'Work,' and 'Hit That,'" he said all excited, before
trying to bust a tune. "*Love the way you work that / wanna get at that / baby
keep moving that / hit that, hit that, hit that, hit that . . .*"

"Just, no . . . stop—that's, that's just so unbecoming of a man of your
stature," I said, wincing and shaking my head at my boss. "Please.
Stop."

"I'm just saying," Joel laughed, "that this is one of his best songs,
and he's about to go big time—so I'm doing you a *favor* by handing you
this scoop."

"Um, I refuse to believe that my career is going to take this great
leap forward from writing a four-hundred-word story on a forty-year-

old rapper—unless you're privy to some information you're holding back from me," I said dryly.

"Come on, Viv, it'll be fun . . . or at least funny. He's posing for *Playgirl*."

My gasp was audible. "*Playgirl*?!" I said, incredulous, taking a moment to let the image of Daddy naked settle into my head. Ugh. "You're sending me to a *Playgirl* shoot to watch some old-ass rapper show off his limp penis for a few record sales?"

Joel looked at his watch. I could tell he was getting annoyed. "Viv, the shoot is at Sea Studios at eleven," he said. "You need to get moving. I promised his publicist you'd be there to talk to him during makeup and hair—I don't think he'll want you there after the photo session starts. I've gotta go to the morning edit meeting. Have fun."

I rolled my eyes at Joel as he walked away. I was tired of him dumping the scum interviews on me. If it was a piece on an actress who had a minor part in a movie that didn't stand a chance at the box office, I got the assignment (and she was usually a bitch). If it involved doing something completely ridiculous, like showing readers what it's like to try out for a spot as a Lakers Girl, the story was mine (I looked a straight ass in that story; every picture showed me flapping and tripping all over myself while the other eight hundred girls auditioning did the moves they were supposed to do). The only time I got to profile white artists was when it was a surly actor the white boys in my office were too scared to talk to, like Robert DeNiro (Joel said he was sending me because DeNiro "likes black chicks, and he'll probably be more comfortable talking to you") and Harvey Keitel (thank goodness he stood me up—Keitel is notorious for being a shit in interviews). And all the big stars—Cruise, Roberts, Hanks, Gibson, Pitt—were off limits to me, as were, sometimes, the black ones, like Poitier and Lena Horne. I had to fight to get the Halle Berry, Sam Jackson, and Laurence Fishburne profiles; and the only reason I even got to say Denzel's name in my office was because Trista knew his agent and hooked me up. Shoot—one of my coworkers is still refusing to talk to me after I accused her of stealing my Angela Bassett interview (a profile, by the way, that ended up on the cover—which happens for black celebrities only when a white reporter gets the byline).

So let's just say that it doesn't surprise me that I am on my way to see Daddy's wrinkled dick. But I'm not mad (anymore). At least I'll be able to hammer out my story and be done by six P.M., with no other obligations than to go home and see my son. By the time I pull into the studio parking lot, I've already figured out what I'm going to say in my story, as well as the quotes I need to get out of Daddy to make it happen. He is about to get the Vivian autopilot special, a technique that involves not really caring what my subjects have to say, just what I want them to say. As soon as I hear it? Interview over.

Which is the attitude I have before I even walk into the Sea Studios door. But the dramaless interview I'm hoping for is shot to hell when Daddy's publicist, Breena Scott, heads me off at the door. I have to stop myself from saying "Damn" out loud; Breena Scott is one of the aging dinosaurs on the Hollywood circuit who most recently made a name for herself spinning the stories of young, hot music artists on the scene back in the mid-nineties. Just as West Coast hip-hop took off, so did Breena's career; her legendary parties made her a staple of the tabloid gossip columns, and there was hardly a rapper quoted who didn't speak to her before dialing a reporter's number—and she made sure everyone knew it. If you weren't on Breena's hot list, you got no play, and no play meant no story.

But as her clients either died off, went to prison, or fell off the charts, Breena spent a bit more time puffing her chest out, and promoting mediocre artists, while she refashioned herself into a self-help guru of sorts. Her book *Guilty Pleasures: Enjoying Life When You're Forty and Fabulous* is a staple on the *Essence* best-seller list, and earns her enough exposure on morning radio to convince her she still has "it." And still having "it" gives her license to think she can still treat reporters like shit.

"Breena! Long time no see!" I say with all the enthusiasm I can muster, reaching in to give her an air kiss and a half-hug. And, bitch that she is, Breena tries to pretend she can't quite place where we've met before.

"Tell me your name again, love," she says. "You look familiar, but . . . "

"Vivian Evans? The *Daily News*?" I say. "We worked together on profiles I did on Nia Smalls, Bella Strong, and Aussie?"

She pauses for a moment, then squints her green contact-filled eyes like she needs to take a moment to process what I've just said. "Ah, yes. Vivian Evans," she says, still acting unsure as she runs her fingers through her wavy, jet-black weave. Then she just moves on. "You'll have about fifteen minutes with Daddy before the shoot starts. You are not to ask him about his personal life, his split with his old record company, the child-support lawsuit, and especially not his rumored relationship with the pop singer Nikki Spare."

"Well, you've effectively limited the story to a piece about Daddy and his goods," I say half-jokingly, making a mental note to ask him about everything she says is off limits at the end of the interview, after I've got all the general quotes I need and have nothing to lose if Daddy and Breena get mad and kick me out.

Breena rolls her eyes. "Let me show you inside," she says, unamused.

I've barely gotten into the cavernous, stark-white studio before Daddy is all over me—literally. He is in a white bathrobe and flip-flops, swirling ice in a glass full of what I'd venture is some kind of liquor, to judge from the tint of red creeping into the whites of his eyes. Before I can even think about extending my hand to greet him, he reaches for my back with his free hand and pulls me close to him. He smells like a bar at last call—musty, stale, sticky. I fall stiffly into his arms and try not to inhale while he greets me with his vodka breath. "How you doing with yo' fine self?" he asks, pushing me back to get a better view. I want to wash. "Come on over here so you can get your interview on. Yeah," he says pushing me ahead of him, no doubt so he could stare at my ass.

Within fifteen minutes, he manages to tell me about the "triflin' ho" who successfully proved he was the father of her child, deny that he ever raised his hand to any of the various "birds" he's "tapped," proudly proclaim that "I takes care of my kids," and admit that he released rats and snakes in the offices of his former record label, where they'd be "right at home with all the sneaky cagey muthafuckas up in there stealin' people's money." All without my prompting, and much to the horror of Breena, who is so disturbed by the prospect of what might turn up in tomorrow's paper that she tries (unsuccessfully) to cut off the interview several times, only to be told to "step off" by Daddy. She comes back with the photographer, who effectively ends the interview just as Daddy is going into detail about what it means for his career to put his penis on display in a smut magazine that caters to white girls. Saved by the shutter. "I'm sorry, but we'll have to end the interview here," Breena snips. "The shoot's about to begin."

"You gonna stick around for the goodies?" Daddy says, tugging at the knotted belt that held his robe together. He has a gleam in his eyes when he says it.

"I'm sorry but it's a closed set," Breena says to no one in particular.

"Come on—who's it gonna hurt if she stays?" Daddy says. "I want her to."

I am curious to see how one goes about getting buck naked, knowing that a bunch of nasty women are going to plunk down four dollars for a glossy picture of his dick. "Fine, if that's what you want," Breena says. "Is that okay?" she asks the photographer.

"Sure," he shrugs.

Daddy has the photographer's assistant bring him another drink. He offers me one, too. I accept bottled water and settle back in my chair as Daddy alternately sips his drink and bounces around in his robe like a prizefighter before a championship brawl.

"Nervous?" I ask.

"Nah," he says, but his voice isn't as confident as it was during the interview. "It's just body parts, right? Everybody's seen one."

"But not yours," I smirk.

"Yeah," he says quietly, before he turns and walks slowly toward the set.

It's a poetic moment for me—here he is, an aging rapper so desperate for a second run that he's willing to trick himself out for a last shot at the attention he craves. Even if that attention means embarrassment. Just tragic.

I am mentally editing the lead for my profile when the photographer instructs Daddy to open his robe. I look up in time to see the wrinkles form like pools around the corners of Daddy's eyes. He looks like he's aged twenty years in just the last five minutes. "Okay, champ—nice and easy. Don't take it totally off—just open it a little. I want you to feel comfortable. Relax and pretend you're in your bedroom, with your lady."

Daddy forces a grin onto his face. "You got what you need?" he asks me.

"Um, yeah, I guess," I say slowly. "Everything but the money shot."

He chuckles. The photographer shifts uneasily. Clearly, he's ready to get the party started, and all the extra convo is holding up his art. Daddy doesn't seem to give a damn.

"Listen here, reporter lady. Why don't we meet up later tonight so we can finish what we started?" he says, his voice regaining a bit of the cockiness I'd seen earlier.

"I have enough for my story," I say, quick to add that the piece is due by four P.M.

"How about tomorrow? You'll want to write part two after we hook up," he says.

My silence is heavy, but he presses on. "Come on, reporter lady—loosen up, come have some fun with me. There's a party at the *Globe*. Let me buy you a drink for being so cool. It's the least I can do, you know—you made this a lot easier for me."

"I don't know about making it easier," I answer, nodding toward his robe, which is closed tighter than a nineteen-year-old virgin's knotted-robe belt on honeymoon night.

He looks down and lets out a hearty laugh. Then, in one fell swoop, he unties his belt and lets the mound of terry cloth fall behind him. I try not to look, but my eyes instinctively focus on the part my mind told me not to look at. Even limp it is quite impressive. I try to hide my shock. No such luck. He looks down, and then up just in time to meet my eyes. He laughs again. Damn. Busted!

"Come on, reporter lady," he says, still chuckling. "No strings. Just come out tomorrow night. If you're down, meet me at the Warner Music party on Thursday. It's going to be all the way live. I'll buy you a cosmo, a berry martini, whatever you want. A-yo, Breena—hit my girl off with my cell and two-way. The *real* numbers, Breena."

And with that, he chucks the robe across the room and splays his lanky but muscular body across the red-velvet chaise longue that serves as his stage. He is on.

I am out.

"Girl, you better go to that party!" Amaya practically screams into the phone. "For real—it's gonna be *the* party. Erykah Badu is performing, and I heard Will and Jada were cohosting with Lena Floyd. OH MY GOD!!!"

"What?" I yell. "Amaya—what's wrong? You okay?"

"You know what?" she stage-whispers. Lord, Amaya and her dramatics.

"You scared the shit outta me," I say, looking around my work pod to make sure none of my coworkers are listening in. I'm supposed to be writing Daddy's story, but I had to tell Amaya about his proposition. "What the hell are you yelling for?"

"You want to know why I'm yelling?" she asks.

"Yes, why are you yelling?"

"You really wanna know?"

"Amaya," I say, my eyes darting around my office. "Spit it out. I've got work to do."

"You're right about that," she says, "and I'm going to give you a helping hand."

"Amaya, come on, girl—work with me."

"Okay, Lena Floyd is cohosting the party tomorrow night, right?"

"That's what you just told me."

"Well, do you know who Lena Floyd's plastic surgeon is?"

"Um, no," I say, exasperated. "You gonna tell me anytime this afternoon?"

"Don't get cute," Amaya shoots back. "I'm trying to help you out here." She skips a beat, then continues. "Lena Floyd's plastic surgeon is yo baby's daddy."

"Um, okaaayy," I say, not getting the point, which annoys Amaya even more.

"So, if Lena Floyd is hosting the party, and yo baby's daddy is her main scalpel squeeze, he'll probably be in the house tomorrow night," she says. "Now, do I have to spell the rest of it out for you?"

"Go on," I say, leaning into the receiver a little.

"So if Sean is at the party, what better way to get his attention than to show up in the arms of a rich, well-known man?" she says with an extra heap of Amaya dramatics.

"Well, I don't know if he's rich, and if he was still well-known, he wouldn't be getting naked for *Playgirl*. But that's besides the point," I say, understanding instinctively where Amaya is headed with this. "I show up to the party looking extra cute, bump into Sean with a celebrity on my arm, and he's got to look twice, right?"

"Exactly," Amaya continues. "What you wearing?"

"Whatchu mean, 'What am I wearing?'" I say defensively—partly because I haven't even considered it yet, partly because I know I don't have anything in my closet worthy of draping over the arm of a celebrity or attracting the attentions of a (hopefully) jealous ex-lover, and partly because I know Amaya is going to give me grief for not having a few standout standby outfits to whip out for occasions such as this one.

"Come on, honey, you know I love you and all, but you can't tell me you're going to wear your standard-issue reporter wear to a hot party," Amaya insists, disgusted. "Let me paint a picture: The man you're trying to marry within the next year will be at the bomb party with a bunch of fly people. You want to show up looking like eye candy, not eye boogers. Remember the Vow. Work with me."

I decide to ignore that. "Ooh, I know," I say excitedly, hoping if I put a little pep in my voice she will buy into the outfit I am about to describe. "I have a pair of low-cut jeans I can wear. They hang just a little too low on my waist for comfort, but I have a baby-T I can pair with them, and a nice Banana Republic jacket and Pumas—though I also have a nice pair of red sandals I can put on if you don't think sneakers are appropriate."

"Oh my," Amaya huffs. "We've got work to do, don't we?"

"No, *I* have work to do, and if I don't hurry up and write this story, I won't have time to head out to the store to get something new. Not that I'll find anything anyway, seeing as there isn't a designer on earth who recognizes that real women have curves, not trainers and plastic surgeons."

"Um, we're in L.A., darling—everybody's exercising and getting cut. Don't hate," Amaya shoots back.

"Well, I don't, dammit, and I don't feel like killing myself trying to squeeze my ass and hips into some ill-fitting outfit that'll cost me a mortgage payment."

"Viv, hold on," Amaya says before abruptly putting me on hold. I type my story slug into the computer and then my headline, and have already started the story when Amaya comes back on the line. She isn't alone.

"Trista? Get your girl," Amaya seethes.

"Vivian? It's me!" Trista says.

"Hey, girl," I call back. "What's happening, hot mama?"

"Nothing nearly as exciting as what's going on with you. And here you were complaining about doing a story on Young Daddy MC, and turns out you might get to hit that, hit that, hit that, hit that with your own baby daddy!"

"Oh God, Trista—please, don't," I laugh at her attempt to sing the lyrics from Daddy's last hit. "Stick to the smooth jazz station. Rap *so* doesn't become you."

"Well, it sure is going to become you tomorrow night if Amaya and I have anything to do with it," she shoots back, laughing. "Listen, you've got a dilemma, but we're going to handle this right quick. First, you're going to go get something cute to wear—not tonight but tomorrow, after lunch. Tonight you're going to lose five pounds."

"Trista, what the hell are you smoking over there at TA?" I laugh. "What are you talking about losing five pounds tonight?"

"See?" Amaya chimes. "I told you she wouldn't listen, even if you were the one to suggest it."

"What the hell are you two talking about?" I say, a little annoyed. I hate it when the two of them conspire to gang up on me; they'll walk into the conversation with a clear plan to shut me down, and start talking over me like I'm not in the room.

"What am I not going to listen to?" I ask again.

"Oh, you're going to listen, because the Vow depends on you listening," Trista states firmly. "We need you to focus, Viv. Sean. Hot party. Pretty women. And you, swooping in to get your man. Amaya—tell her what's up."

I sit back in my chair and wait for the grand plan.

"Okay, first you're going to go see my girl Shahirah, over at the Heal Thyself Spa and Retreat in Beverly Hills," Amaya says. "She owes me a favor, and I already scheduled your appointment with her for tonight, so get someone to watch Corey."

"I just got my toes done yesterday, and I'm in no mood for a massage," I say dismissively.

"You're not going for a pedicure or a massage. You're going there so that you can lose a quick five pounds, so that when we go shopping tomorrow you can fit into something super-sexy," Trista explains. "Amaya swears it works."

"I don't understand," I say back.

"Shahirah is going to give you a colonic tonight, and tomorrow you're not going to drink anything but water until you get to the party. I know it sounds crazy," Amaya says, rushing through her words to counter what she thinks might be my onslaught. "But trust me, after she gets finished with you, your stomach will be so flat you'll think you've had my personal trainer on your ass for the last three months."

"And once you get all that gunk out of your system and refresh your body with nature's elixir, you'll be at least eight pounds lighter when you float into that party tomorrow on Daddy's arm, ready to reclaim your own baby's daddy," Trista finishes with a flourish.

"Your appointment's at six-thirty. And don't be late—Shahirah's booked, and I had to do some fast talking to get you in."

"And make sure you've got your calendar cleared for lunch tomorrow—we've got a date with my shopper at Fred Segal," Trista adds.

"A colonic? Fred Segal? God, this all seems so expensive."

"And necessary," Trista says. "Just trust us on this, honey—don't fight it."

"Colonic, six-thirty. Lunch, noon. See you tomorrow, beautiful," Amaya chimes.

And with that, they hang up.

I'M NO COW, but I'll be the first to admit that I'm slightly juicier than most of the silicone sticks strutting around L.A. Okay, "slightly" may be too delicate a word. I'm a full-figured girl, with hips, ass, and boobs for days—but I more than make up for it all with a tiny waist that accentuates my curves, so I don't look fat. At least that's what Amaya claimed when she forced me to try on that beautiful pink floral Diane von Furstenberg wrap dress—the $478 pink floral Diane von Furstenberg wrap dress—at Fred Segal. I have to admit that had she and Trista not been there, I would never have thought to try it on (hell, I wouldn't have been in Fred Segal!). My instincts are always to hide my assets with flowing, oversized shirts, skirts, dresses, and jackets, not squeeze them into outfits I fear will expose all my flaws. "Girl, hips and ass ain't flaws—ask Beyoncé or J-Lo," Amaya said. "Shoot, most people like Trista's skinny ass would pay good money for a little bit of what you got."

"And then *you'd* pay good money to cut it off," I said, twirling in the dressing room mirror, admiring how well it fit.

"Well, just remember that it's white Hollywood producers who like the anorexic bitches. Everybody else who counts—that means black men—wants a little somethin' somethin' to hold on to," Amaya said, adjusting my collar and inspecting me from all angles. "Girl? You look good! That colonic you had yesterday did you wonders!"

"It did me wonders, all right," I said, my lips twirled up the side of my face. Just before my colonic, I had the librarians at the *News* pull some clips for me on the procedure, so that I'd know what I was walking into. Most of them were pretty straightforward: colonics clear your digestive system of the food and toxins it's held on to. None of them mentioned it would hurt the way it did—it made me think that much less of the celebrities who use it (and the cocaine diet) to lose a quick few pounds before special events. What kind of fool would knowingly put herself through that torture to fit into a dress? As if they all aren't bony enough. Freaks, I tell you.

"I feel like I haven't eaten in days," I told my girls, "but I'm scared to put anything in my stomach, lest it slide right through my body and out every available orifice before I have the chance to make it to the bathroom."

Amaya tried to ignore my complaints, but she couldn't help putting her two cents in. "I'm going to pretend I don't hear you complaining about losing seven pounds in less than twenty-four hours so that you can look fabulous for the party. What do you think, Trista?"

She was working her cell phone and BlackBerry, but she looked up long enough to give me a thumbs-up and a mile-wide smile. "Beautiful!" she mouthed.

And that's how I feel pulling my car up to the valet and stepping out onto the red carpet that leads to the front door of Bella. Sure, I've spent the equivalent of a quarter of my mortgage payment, and I'll have to go without lunch for at least two months, and consider eliminating one of Corey's after-school activities, and wear my hair in a natural for the next few weeks instead of going to the hairdresser for my seventy-five-dollar press and curl. But the dress, the snake up my behind, the hunger pains, the faceful of greasy makeup Amaya made me slather all over my mug, the frantic phone calls to get on the guest list—all of it was worth it if it catches the attention of two men in the room—the self-proclaimed greatest rapper of all time, and the man of my dreams.

I am sipping a cranberry spritzer and practically stalking the guys with the mini–crab cake and chicken caesar wrap platters (I'm hungry, okay? And now I'm not thinking about no colonic) when I spot Sean walking through the crowd. He looks splendid all in white, his locks sweeping past his shoulders, making the perfect frame for his face. He is alone. I am in heaven. I carefully dab my napkin at my lips to wipe away any telltale signs of my hors d'oeuvres. But just as I am thinking of the perfect line to say to my future husband, Sean stops walking and turns to look behind him. And that's when he grabs her arm and whispers something in her ear.

She is tall. And blond. And white all over. And whatever he says to her is obviously quite pleasing, because within seconds, she is all molars and veneers. Before she can say a word, he grabs her hand and starts pushing through the crowd some more. Had I not already swallowed that crab cake, I might have choked.

Just as I am struggling to get my bearings, I spot Daddy's entourage—he is traveling light tonight; only four burly bodyguards, and six homies with various responsibilities, like procuring groupies and fetching drinks—making its way through the crowd and over toward the stairs that lead to the VIP area. I'm hoping that Daddy will find it in his heart to mingle with the common folks, because I haven't got clearance for the VIP section from the event's publicist. I hadn't hooked up with Daddy beforehand. I called his cell and left several messages, but he never returned my calls. I'm hoping he at least remembers his invitation when I catch up to him. Otherwise, my chances of making it to the VIP room are slim to none. I make a point of positioning myself near the stairs early on, so that I can catch him before he disappears into an inaccessible part of the club. I alternately try to keep an eye on Sean, the blond bimbo, and the dozen or so men of unclear purpose surrounding Daddy, who are rudely clearing a swath on the part of the crowded dance floor that leads to the staircase. All of them seem to be approaching at the same time. Perfect.

I run my hands over my dress and adjust the belt one more time, then put on a wide grin as Daddy walks up. Just as I step forward, three other tall, slinky women in tight dresses and weaves down their backs step in front of me—one of them over me and on my foot—and begin calling Daddy's name. I instinctively reach down to rub my violated pinky toe, which is throbbing after being stabbed by the groupie's razor-sharp stiletto, but instead I lose my footing and stumble forward onto the floor, taking one of the groupies with me. We end up in a heap of chiffon and silk—when I look up, Daddy is being ushered up the stairs by VIP bouncers, while some of his boys, straggling behind him, fall out in hysterics. I'm so embarrassed I wish that I could turn into a pool of liquid and melt into the parquet floor.

"Damn, Daddy—get your girls," one of his boys says to no one in particular.

"They ain't none of Daddy's girls," another says, looking down and shaking his head, barely containing his giggles.

I scramble to my feet and adjust my dress. "Actually, he asked me to come here," I say, trying my best to be charming in such an awkward situation.

"Please, he asked all of us to be here," counters one of the groupies, a stunning light-skinned sister with hazel eyes and long auburn hair, as she steps in front of me. "How about we go get to know each other better?" she says slyly to Daddy's boy.

He looks her up and down, and then does the same to me, as if we are on an auction block and he is considering whether to bid. "Turn around, let me see something," he says, raising his chin to the groupie roadkill. She happily obliges—with a damn smile. By now, my mouth is agape. "Dih-zayum! Ay, Lou! Baby got back!" he yells, signaling to his friend. "Yeah, why don't you come on up here to Daddy's house and make it a home," he says, grabbing her hand. She practically skips up the steps toward him, and tosses me a wink for good measure. "Maybe next time," she offers.

"Damn, girl," another one of the groupies calls out to me nastily. "Watch where you goin' next time—ruined my VIP move. Shit, now I gotta wait for Snoop or somebody to roll up in here. Damn."

My mouth still open, I watch her slink off with the other groupie girl in tow. I hadn't noticed it, but once I look around and make note of who is standing in the area, I realize that I've positioned myself near the bar, in what can easily be taken for the groupie bench—where all the women who want to hook up with celebrities stand, hoping to get "chosen" for VIP treatment. I mentally picture myself kicking my own ass for not thinking of that before I stood over there. For not getting confirmation from Daddy before I showed up at this godforsaken place. For even coming. I could be at home, watching *Law and Order* and having a bag of Pop Secret popcorn. But no, I'm here, being embarrassed and dismissed like I am one of the dregs of the L.A. party scene—nothing but a buy-her-a-dinner-at-Roscoe's-and-get-all-the-ass-you-want groupie ho. My bad, I'm not even that in Daddy's boys' eyes—I'm the fat friend of the groupie ho. Nothing worse than that. I don't know whether I should be grateful or pissed. I settle on pissed.

"Um, everything okay here?"

My eyes follow the voice, but I know already who it is. As if Daddy's boys haven't already practically painted a neon FOOL across my forehead, here is the man I've gotten all gussied up for, standing in front of me, presumably having seen me get played. With the blonde. I am speechless. But what was I gonna tell him—I used a chunk of his child support on an overpriced piece of cloth and left my child at home with a sitter and a frozen pizza dinner so I could come out and make him jealous? I had no words.

"Viv," Sean said, leaning in a little closer. "Everything okay?"

"Um, yeah," I mumble. "Everything's fine."

He looks me up and down like he is checking me out, but his eye-brows are furled, so it isn't a "good" checking me out. It's a "damn—what the hell is going on with you" checking me out. "Was that Young Daddy MC going up the stairs?"

"Yes," I say, hoping that one-word answers will make him disap-pear.

"You know him?"

"Not really," I say.

"Why were you trying to go upstairs with him—you working on a story or something?" he asks. Just as he does, the blonde reaches for his hand and signals to him that there is an opening at the bar. I guess the trick wants a drink.

"Why are you with her—you looking for another client?" (I know, I know—perfectly venomous, but hey, he took me there.)

She shoots me a look (clearly, white girls in L.A. are getting bolder by the minute—I know this heifer didn't just roll her eyes at me), and I shoot her one right back, then focus again on Sean.

"I don't think that's really any of your concern," Sean says tartly.

"Well, what I'm doing here is really none of your concern either, but that didn't stop you from asking, now did it?" I respond nastily.

"Whatever, Viv," he says, signaling to the blonde to head with him back over to the bar. He doesn't say another word; all I see is his back. I am so livid at how horribly wrong everything has gone I actually con-sider walking over there and beating her ass—you know, as consolation. Just as I'm debating whether showing up in tomorrow's gossip pages is worth my chance to show this blonde how we get down in the 'hood, someone taps me on my shoulder.

"What!" I say nastily, before I even turn around to see who it was.

"Reporter lady," Daddy says, a smile spreading across his lips. "You made it!"

I was so busy focusing on Sean and the blonde that I hadn't seen Daddy come back down the stairs, and so he kind of took me by sur-prise. I am not quite in the mood to talk to him, particularly since he'd left me hanging while his boys summarily dismissed me. My greeting is tepid at best. "Hey," I say, uninspired.

"My assistant tried to ring you up but she said she couldn't get through," he says, still enthusiastic and not quite catching on to my attitude. "I knew you'd get your way in here, though. I'm glad you came."

"Oh really?" I ask. "Didn't seem like that when you pushed through here and your boys snatched up some of these girls to give you some VIP company," I respond, nodding to the bevy of beauties who had started to crowd us while we talked. One actually put her hands on his shoulder in an effort to get his attention. To his credit, he doesn't pay her any mind. He focuses only on me.

"Why don't you come upstairs and have a glass of champagne?" he says. "It's getting a little crowded down here, if you know what I mean."

His mentioning liquor makes me look over toward the bar and I remember the reason I'm standing in the middle of this club on a Thursday night in the first place. The beauty of it all is that Sean is staring dead in my mouth when I finally spot him curled around a Heineken, his bimbo trying her best to get him to focus on her. I milk my moment for all it's worth.

"Sure, sure, let's go upstairs for a drink," I say.

"Okay—I just have to go to the bathroom before we head up. I hate that about this club—no bathroom in the VIP. What's the point of VIP if you gotta break up your buzz and run the groupie gauntlet to take a leak?" he shrugs.

"Yeah, awful design," I say, trying to pretend like I know what he's talking about and am actually paying attention. I'm really trying to see whether Sean is still watching us. He is. "How about I wait for you by the bar until you come back? They're not going to let me up in VIP unless I look like one of the groupies you invited up."

"Fo sho," he says, "but you ain't no groupie, so let's get that straight right now."

"Yes, let's," I shoot back.

"But you sure wearin' that dress," he says. "Not in a groupie kinda way, though," he stammers, trying to back off the oomph he gave his remark, which made my brows furl. "I meant it's beautiful, and you look tasteful, not like some of these other birds."

"Birds, huh? I'm just going to go over here and wait by the bar," I say, laughing at his attempt to get back into my good graces. "You go on ahead and do what you have to do. But do it quick; I'm thirsty."

"Yes, ma'am," he says, saluting me before walking away.

I saunter over to the bar and squeeze in a few bodies away from Sean and the blonde. I have to keep telling myself not to look over in his direction, but my peripheral vision is in full effect. Sean is burning a hot hole in my profile, and the blonde is burning a hot hole in his ear, no doubt trying to get him to stop looking at me. Finally, he gets out of his seat and walks over toward me. I brace myself and try to come up with something to say. But he doesn't stop. He just stares at me as he walks by, the blonde following close behind. He's halfway out the door when Daddy returns, a group of girls in tow.

"Reporter lady—you ready?" he asks. "Let's get outta here."

And with that, I follow him up the stairs.

If Amaya were standing in front of me, I would plant a sloppy wet one square on her cheek.

7

TRISTA

I snap my cell phone shut and tuck it back into the plastic clip attached to the waistband of my nylon running shorts, then kick my Nike Cross Trainers up in the air.

"Yes!" I squeal. A pair of joggers making their way along the Santa Monica pier turn to look at me. I raise my water bottle in a mock toast to myself and take a long sip. If I wasn't so rhythmically challenged I'd break out in the running man right now.

I had been in the midst of my morning run when a call came in from one of the guys at Paramount. They were trying to attach talent to a new action picture about a Secret Service agent who gets framed for the assassination of the president and must find the real killer to avert a nuclear disaster of apocalyptic proportions. Admittedly the plot is a stretch, but it's the perfect starring role for Jared. The overseas receipts alone would cement his future—and my partnership. Paramount wants him to come in and read with the already-cast female lead, Kimberly Springfield, to test their onscreen chemistry. I wasn't psyched to be working with Cassidy's Oscar competition, but this is the type of action role that could make Jared's career, in a Will Smith—*Men In Black* kind of way. Ka-ching! Almost makes working on Saturday worth it.

Just as I finish stretching my legs on one of the weathered wooden benches and cue up my favorite song on the iPod strapped to my arm, Jeff Redd's "I Found Love," my cell vibrates. I answer the phone without looking at the caller ID.

"Trista?" It's my sister Tanisha.

"Oh, hi, Tanisha." Shit, I wasn't in the mood to go twelve rounds with my sister today. My call with Paramount had gone well, and I'm scheduled to meet Viv and Amaya for a spa date this afternoon. Turning around on the pier, I head back toward my condo, and brace myself for hurricane Tanisha.

"Hey, yourself" she says as she coughs into the receiver, her voice husky from her morning Newports. A strained pause rests uncomfortably in the silence.

"Is anything wrong?" I ask. "Did you get the check?" I hope the only reason she's calling is because the monthly check I send her and Daddy to cover the mortgage and expenses on the new house I bought them two years ago has not appeared in her mailbox.

"We got your check," she snaps between drags on a cigarette.

"How's Daddy?" I inquire, ignoring the absence of a thank-you and hating myself for not using caller ID for its intended purpose: to send unwanted calls from people like my sister straight to voicemail.

"I know you're busy," she says mockingly, "so, I'll get to the point. The doctor says Daddy needs some tests and Medicaid don't cover 'em." Our father has been battling prostate cancer, and over the last six months his health has started to deteriorate.

"Did you make an appointment with the specialist I told you about last month?" I ask with exasperation, knowing the answer to the question already.

"We don't need no damn specialist; the clinic is fine," she snaps. "We just need these tests so Dr. Wills can get his diagnosis together."

"Tanisha, he needs to see a specialist," I say through gritted teeth. I'm fed up. I've been telling my sister that the doctors down at the South Central clinic don't know what they are doing half the time, and the other half they're just getting rich off of poor black people by running bogus tests to collect insurance money. Tanisha thought that my giving her the name of the top oncologist at Cedars Sinai, whose name Viv got from Sean, was my way of flaunting my success in her face.

"Look, Tanisha, Daddy isn't going to get any better unless we get him the appropriate medical care. Dr. Wills is just giving you guys the run-around," I snap back. "He probably doesn't even need any tests."

"Well, well, well, you a doctor, now, too?" she snorts into the phone.

"Of course not." I rip out the elastic band holding the ponytail on top of my head in frustration and rake my fingers through my hair. "All I'm trying to say is that he needs to see another doctor. A specialist. We can arrange for all of Daddy's records to be sent over to Dr. Tanya Irby, at Cedars Sinai, and she can give us a more thorough assessment."

"And I told you, they done all that and more down at the clinic. But of course you know best. I don't know anything, I'm just your ignorant sister who takes care of Daddy by my damn self while you stop by every once in a while, so don't tell me what he needs."

"Tanisha . . ." I try to interrupt her rant but she cuts me off.

"Forget it, I'll call Aunt Brenda and them and get the money. We don't need your help." She slams down the receiver and the sound makes me jump as if struck.

Snapping my phone shut, I realize that while arguing with Tanisha I've made it back to my condo. I leave my dirty sneakers outside before unlocking the French doors and stepping into my living room. I take a deep breath. This beachfront condo I snapped up in a foreclosure auction last year is my sanctuary. Normally, just walking into it puts my mind instantly at peace. It's been renovated from top to bottom and meticulously decorated with the help of Viv—that girl has a serious eye for what works. My broker tells me I've more than doubled the value with the work I've done. And the natural palette of soothing creams and beiges, with burnished gold accents, has a calming influence. I run upstairs to my bathroom and turn on the shower, in the hope that its multiple heads will relieve the tension in my neck. As I step inside, I slip on my shower cap, and then flop down on the cold terra-cotta seat built into the shower. No, those powerful jets won't work their magic today. Tanisha has struck a nerve.

Though born just three years apart, my sister and I were never what anyone would call close. In fact, Mama used to say we didn't have the sense God gave us to appreciate each other. By the time I came along, TeTe was used to being the only child. She threw a fit every time Mama made her bring me with her when she went out to play. Didn't matter to me, though. I would just read a book outside until it was time to race home to beat the streetlights coming on.

By the time she hit sixteen, Te was the neighborhood fly girl, sporting a sandy blond asymmetrical bob copied from a Salt 'n' Pepa video, and with a body shaped like a Coke bottle stuffed into too-tight jeans. Girls envied TeTe and could be heard sucking their teeth and muttering, "She think she cute," whenever she walked by. Not to mention all the threats to jump her. But the guys? Brothers couldn't get enough of my sister. They were always buying her presents, so much so that she had a Members Only jacket in damn near every color yet never let me borrow any of them. Guys used to come to pick her up and snicker when they looked at my skinny frame, asking, "You sure you TeTe's sister?"

When Mama's drinking got really bad, Daddy (who had never been able to stand up to his wife, let alone his fast-ass daughter) watched as Tanisha used her frequent absences as a license to run wild. She barely graduated high school, and instead of getting a job, she rolled with the Crips in our neighborhood. And then, to no one's surprise but her own, TeTe got knocked up by her boyfriend Darnell at age nineteen. When my mother found out about the pregnancy, she threw Tanisha out, over my father's protests. So Te moved in with Darnell's family. Once my nephew Tyquan was born, Tanisha begged Darnell to quit the gang life, but he wouldn't listen. When he got shot over some beef with the Bloods, Tanisha moved back home. She threw out all the blue bandanas and got a job at the post office. She straightened up just in time to watch Mama drink herself to an early grave (she died during my freshman year in college).

I immersed myself in school and only came home occasionally. This served to further piss off my sister, who never missed an opportunity to rag on me. Over the years we've managed to remain civil enough to be in the same room on holidays, but nothing more. When Daddy got sick, our relationship became even more strained, as a bleak prognosis, the stress of the clinic's ineffectiveness, and the complexities of Medicaid policies threatened to overwhelm us both.

Tanisha knows that Aunt Brenda, my dad's sister, and her broke-ass twin sons Jason and Jamel—thirty-nine years old and still living at home—don't have a dime to spare for the tests. She knows I'll send the money.

Washing up quickly, I wrap a towel around my damp body and walk into my bedroom, where I snatch my purse off the bed. I write out a check for $5,000 to Tanisha Gordon and stuff it into an envelope before I can change my mind.

PULLING UP TO Le Meridian, I see my girls standing in front. Amaya, dressed in a short denim miniskirt, a yellow tube top sprinkled with pink rhinestones, and huge Dior sunglasses, tries to angle her body in different poses in the hopes that the gaggle of paparazzi staked out in front of the hotel will snap her picture. Doesn't she realize by now that unless you're one of the sexy six—Halle, Beyoncé, Gabrielle, Nia, Vivica, or Jada—photographers don't care about shooting black actresses? Viv, dressed in khaki pants and a crisp white linen blouse, waves as I stop in front of the valet stand.

"Hey, y'all. Sorry, Tanisha called," I say, by way of explanation for being late for the spa date I hooked up at the invitation-only Saks Fifth Avenue/Jimmy Choo Awards suite. As the Golden Globes, SAG Awards, and Oscars, approach, Hollywood kicks into full-on get-fabulous mode and companies host luxury suites in hotels so stars, stylists, and other A-listers can stop by for treatments and to shop for gowns and accessories.

"How's your dad?" asks Viv as we make our way into the hotel's bustling lobby.

"Well, I'd love to tell you, but I can't convince my sister to take him to see the specialist that Sean recommended, so I really don't know," I say, rolling my eyes. "She called because the doctor at the clinic wants to run some tests that Medicaid just happens not to cover, and, of course, we got into it."

"That has to be so frustrating," says Amaya as she pushes the elevator button.

"This Dr. Wills character has been screwing us around for months. Remember I told ya'll about that time I found that $19,000 charge for a mastectomy on my daddy's bill and when I confronted him he said it was just an accounting error?"

"I don't know why your sister won't listen," says Viv. "That would make a heck of a story: Medicaid fraud in the 'hood.'"

"So why don't you write it, little Miss L.A. *Daily News*?" I ask.

"Because I'm too busy blowing the lid off of world-changing events like who wore what nail polish to whichever party, teen-star eating disorders, paternity test results, and botched Botox procedures," she says, only half-joking. Viv's been threatening for years to quit her mind-numbing beat and write serious features.

"Well, *I'd* rather read about all that fluffy stuff than some Medicaid craziness," says Amaya, pushing her shades up into her hair. "Too much of a downer." Viv and I both shake our heads.

When the elevator doors open, we step into the spa's elegant reception area and I start to relax. This is just what I need. As we approach the desk, the receptionist, who is on the phone, glances up at us and then continues her conversation.

"Oh, I know she isn't trying to ignore us," says Amaya. The receptionist flips her peroxide-blond ponytail in our direction and turns her back.

"Uh . . . excuse me." I try to get her attention but she continues what sounds like a chat with a friend about an audition.

"After I read my scene he said he thought I could be the next Kimberly Springfield," she giggles, her hand caressing a script with TA's red cover-sheet. Viv rolls her eyes. Fed up with the lack of respect threatening to kill my beauty buzz, and still bent out of shape from my sister's phone call, I'm in no mood for games. I reach across the desk to disconnect her call. She continues to blather on until she notices my finger on the phone.

"What the hell . . ." she exclaims as she swivels around in her chair; an angry flush stains her cheeks. She stands up as I remove my finger from the phone. Her anorexic frame shakes in her tight jeans with the indignation that only a white woman could muster when faced with three angry black women. "Did you just hang up my . . ."

"Yes, uh . . ." I squint to read the nametag pinned to the pink polo shirt that strains against her surgically enhanced breasts and then set my wait-list-only navy Hermès Birkin bag on the desk. "Yes, Jessica, I did disconnect your call. Now call Parker Jamison and tell her Trista Gordon, with The Agency, and her party are here."

"Chop-chop." Amaya claps her hands in Jessica's face to punctuate my statement.

"Ms. Gordon?" she says sheepishly, her face registering my six-thou-sand-dollar handbag, my name, and, most important, my affiliation.

"And party," snaps Viv, clearly enjoying Jessica's discomfort.

"I'm so sorry, Ms. Gordon," she says, rushing from around the back of the desk. Just as she seems to be about to kneel down and kiss our feet, I see Parker crossing the reception area in our direction.

"Trista, darling," says the always flattering spa manager as we exchange air kisses. She then removes a tiny bell from the pocket of her black Mandarin-collared jacket and gives it a slight ring. Suddenly a muscular waiter in tight white T-shirt and jeans appears by her side, holding a tray with flutes of champagne.

"Trista, I'm so glad you and your lovely friends could join us today," says Parker as she hands each of us a glass of bubbly. "Is Jessica taking good care of you?" We all turn expectantly toward the flummoxed receptionist, who is now hiding the script behind her back and looking down at the floor. I decide to use my powers for good today and spare her dreams of fame, and this little minimum-wage job.

"Yes, she was just perfect," I say, smiling brightly. "And, Parker, we're ready to get the works." As nothing escapes Parker's attention at her spa, she raises a razor-thin eyebrow at Jessica as we head back to our private cabanas to change, a clear indication she'll be back to discuss our reception. Jessica slumps back down in her chair, still holding the script.

As WE SIT IN our private treatment room, in fluffy white robes with fragrant avocado and mint masks on our faces, three nail technicians begin our paraffin pedicures, our final treat for the day.

"Girls, I could get used to this," says Viv, sipping her glass of Pellegrino and adjusting the massage setting on her chair. In the past three hours we have been plucked, waxed, buffed, rubbed, and polished to within an inch of our lives. "Shoot, I'm not even mad at that little girl at the front desk anymore."

"I know that's right—although you really should have slipped her Sean's card so he could fix those sad little lopsided silicone sacks," offers Amaya.

"You are so wrong for that," I say, laughing. As Amaya's C-cups runneth over naturally, she loves to pick on the less fortunate of us. But she has a point. There's nothing more unattractive than bad plastic surgery. Poor girl probably got them down in Tijuana with a coupon. Some things you really just shouldn't skimp on.

"If I could hang out like this every month, I'd never need a man," says Viv.

"Shit, why do you think we're doing all of this stuff?" asks Amaya, leaning forward in her chair. "You think I got my coochie waxed in the shape of an arrow for my own viewing pleasure? Shit, somebody's got to see that and show some appreciation."

"You got a *what?*" I ask, positive I can't have heard her correctly.

"You heard me, an arrow."

"What the fuck for?" asks Viv.

"Exactly for that. To fuck!" The nail technicians exchange glances under lowered lashes and giggle softly.

"Girl, what are you talking about?" I ask.

"Don't you know that nothing makes a brother drop to his knees quicker than seeing your coochie all done up with a special design. Shows that you were thinking about him and you wanted it to be nice and smooth for him—and his tongue."

"Eww, girl, you so nasty," says Viv as she takes a slice of cantaloupe from the glass plate of fresh fruit resting on her lap and slips it in her mouth.

"Shit, you need to ask them if they can wax your stuff into the shape of a scalpel to get Sean to pay some attention to you!" Amaya says. We all burst into laughter.

"Hold up—seriously, though, you mean to tell me you two don't wax?" she asks.

"I wax," I answer defensively. "But I just have them clean up the sides so it's nice and neat, but none of that crazy Brazilian shit or whatever X-rated thing you got going on down there."

"What about you, Viv? You still running around here looking like a bush baby?" Amaya asks with a challenge in her voice.

"That's none of your business," she says, sliding down deeper into her seat and closing the robe tightly across her thighs.

"I guess I just got my answer. Look, y'all, if you want to compete with these other women out here you got to up your game, show the brothers that you got something special to offer. And for me, ain't nothing more special than my coochie-coo."

"Then why are you always giving it away?" I snap. Viv reaches across Amaya and gives me a high five.

"Don't be jealous, girls. There's nothing wrong with having a healthy sexual appetite and sharing the wealth with a deserving gentleman. I keep my men wanting me at all times. Surprises in the bedroom, videos, lingerie that'll make a porn star blush, and a little text sex."

"Text sex?" Viv and I say in unison.

"Yes, my little innocents," she says impatiently, clearly growing bored with our lack of knowledge. "Phone sex is played. You've got to get with the twenty-first-century technology, ladies. Text-messaging my man dirty little thoughts throughout the day, and sometimes attaching a naughty little picture with my camera phone makes sure that Keith's thinking about my pussy at all times. When we finally hook up after I've been sending him messages during meetings, you best believe it's off the chain, because he's been thinking about sliding between my thighs all day."

Amaya reaches for her silver cell phone from the pocket of her robe, punches a few buttons, and then passes it to me. Viv leans over and we scroll through a series of saved messages that appear to be an exchange Amaya and Keith had a while ago. We're both speechless. Much of the text reads as if it came straight out of the script of an X-rated movie. Thankfully she doesn't show us any photos.

"Uh, okay," I say, handing back the phone. And while I make a mental note never to borrow her cell phone, I can see why Amaya keeps her men coming back for more.

"You better get with it, ladies," she says. "Plus, you got to compete with what these other hos out here will do."

"What are you talking about?" Viv asks.

"The white girls. You know, brothers think they are freaks and will do anything in the bed. And the Latina girls ain't much better, with all that *'sí, papi'* bullshit."

"You need serious help," Viv says, shaking her head and smiling at the giggling nail technicians, who are trying to act like they aren't listening. I'm not really worried, though, as Parker would personally eviscerate any employee found gossiping about clients. Le Meridian is the model of discretion.

"I'm dead serious, Viv. You need to know what you're competing against out there. And use everything you've got to get what you want."

"It's not a competition," says Viv.

"Right, and you sound like your mother now," I say, chiming in.

"Are you two kidding me? The brothers out here in L.A., at least the ones worth giving a shit about, are getting prime, grade-A pussy thrown at them by chicks that will fuck them every which way. And please don't even get me started on the DL brothers—those switch hitters are just messing it up for everybody. It's gotten so bad that falling in love with a gay man is like a rite of passage. I'm telling you, if you two don't get it together, you won't make it. Shoot, you guys are the first ones to roll your eyes when you see a good-looking brother walking down the street with some J-Lo type, but did you ever ask yourself how it is she's got him? It's because she's giving him what he wants, what he needs."

"So you're saying if I wax, Sean will come back to me?"

"Not just wax, girl, you got to give him something special in the bedroom. Spice it up. You got to put it on him like a porn star."

"Amaya!" I exclaim, grabbing her arm, hoping that will make her lower her voice.

"Look here, I'm just telling the truth. Especially to you, Viv. You can't even imagine the type of freaky shit those groupies have begged Daddy MC to let them do to him. You guys can keep doing the same old stuff if you want to, but I'm taking the Vow seriously—I'm in it to win it."

"And who are you trying to win now? Still going after the married man with the hopes that he's going to leave his wife?" I ask sarcastically.

"By the time I am through with Keith, you bet he's leaving her old dried-up ass."

"All because of the arrow?"

"It's not just the arrow, ladies. I'm the total package."

"Total package?" Viv asks.

"Yes, sweetheart, the total package. You got to learn what your man wants, the freaky shit he'll only whisper in your ear when he's about to come, the stuff he doesn't really want you to know he's into. And once you show him you're down, he'll be yours."

"And just where, pray tell, did you learn to whip it on the brothers so well?" asks Viv, only half-joking.

"Some of it I must admit is a gift," Amaya answers as she adjusts the robe across her ample breasts and raises her champagne glass in a toast to herself, "but most of it I picked up in classes."

"Classes?" Viv and I exclaim in unison.

"Yes, girls, classes. I guess it would be too much to expect that you two would know anything about the Pleasure Principles Center in West Hollywood."

"Uh, can't say that I'm familiar," I answer. At the same time I try to raise a brow, but the avocado mask won't let me.

"The PPC is an institution dedicated to the arts of pleasure and intimacy. They offer classes on everything—self-stimulation, tantric sex, BJs, S&M workshops, even private couples sessions. I can't believe you guys haven't heard of this place. Lots of people go there—first wives, second wives, of course all the third wives, stars, singers, gay men. Girl, *everybody* goes there."

Viv and I both stare at her with open mouths.

"And what happens in these, uh, classes?" I ask, afraid that the answer to my question is the disgusting orgy of writhing body parts I can't get out of my head.

"It's not what you think, silly. Actually, it's kind of like a regular class we took at UC. Like, there's a small group of students and usually one instructor, or two, depending on the course and the type of demonstrations needed, and you're encouraged to take notes. Although there's no final exam. But I guess you figure out if you passed or failed by your man's reaction," she says, laughing.

"And what classes have you taken?" asks Vivian.

"Just a couple. Uh, let me think. I took the BJ one—got to control those gag reflexes—Self-Stimulation for Maximum Pleasure, Bondage for Beginners, and Totally Tantric. I think that's it . . ."

"I guess I can understand why you'd take the BJ class," I remark, "but why self-stimulation? You don't strike me as the type that needs help getting in the mood."

"It helps you figure out what you like so you can help your lover turn you on and achieve maximum pleasure. I'm about to sign up for the Blow and Get Low class."

"Why Blow and Get Low?" asks Viv.

"Because my girl Pam told me her husband Paul bought her a new candy-red XJ-6 after she whipped something she learned in that class on him. Want to join me?" she asks, daring us. Viv and I look at each other.

"Forget it, I'm just going to sign all of us up," she declares. "It's just the thing you two need to jump-start your missionary-only groove thangs."

"Okay, well, sounds like that's solved," I say, worried about what may happen but also a little excited at the thought of what we may learn. And who knows, maybe I can pick up some tongue techniques for Garrett in the process. Maybe I should give him a PPC gift certificate for his birthday . . .

By Tuesday the spa treatments I enjoyed with my girls have lost their luster. Work is kicking my butt. And as the conference room empties out from this afternoon's meeting, I scoop my portfolio up off the table and practically sprint back to my office on the other side of the building. Lots to do. When I walk past Adriene, who is sitting at her desk with a curly black bob today, she reminds me that I've only got a couple of more hours before Garrett will pick me up for a Valentine's Day fundraiser.

Scrolling through my email messages, I forward most to Adriene with instructions for her to handle them, and then open one from an unfamiliar address and an intriguing subject line.

TO:Tgordon@TA.com
FROM: Dreynolds@GMF.com
Subject: I'm moving to L.A.
Trista,

Before you delete this email, please read it all the way through. I'm moving to L.A. My firm is opening an office there. I want to talk to you. Please give me a call at 816-555-5245 or

email me back. I really want to explain what happened in
Atlanta. Hope to hear from you soon.

—Damon

    Damon Reynolds

    Vice President

    Global Investments

I slump down in my chair. Is he serious? I can't believe he had the
nerve to email me. What does he want? Real estate advice? A smack
upside the head? Another romp in the sheets? Well, whatever the hell
he's selling, I'm sure not buying. I start to delete the message, but first
I need to forward it to the girls. I need witnesses to this bullshit.

After clicking send, I drag the message to the trash with my mouse
and immediately empty it to make sure the message is permanently
gone. I'm on a roller coaster right now, with a couple of weeks of pre-
mieres, parties, and a bunch of important meetings ahead of me. Not to
mention, I'm excited about seeing Garrett tonight. I shake my head to
erase the memory of the night Damon and I spent together. I will not
allow myself to get sidetracked over an insignificant email from someone I no longer care about. I have moved on.

8

AMAYA

"Well, ladies, did I or did I not tell you that it was going to be the truth?" I ask Trista and Viv as we head into the Pleasure Center's deserted steam room to unwind after our two-hour private Blow and Get Low class.

"I feel like a porn star," Vivian laughs. "Who knew my big ol' booty could twist like that. What was that move called where we flip over and grab our ankles, again?"

"I believe that one was 'the jackhammer,'" I reply.

"Yeah, well, just call me the queen of the jackhammers, because that bad boy is about to become my signature move," boasts Viv with a wicked grin.

"What about all the different ways to give great head?" Trista chimes in. "I might have to start including 'Good Head Girl' on my résumé from now on!"

"Yeah, you were definitely doing your thing, Tris. But did you see how wide ol' girl opened her mouth during her demonstration?" Vivian asks, tightening the towel around her body. "She must've unhinged her jaw to get that entire dildo to fit in there . . ."

"All I can say is, meet your competition," I answer seriously. "It's women like Joy—friendly, fairly attractive, good bodies, and with the jaws of a python—that are taking all the good men right from underneath our noses. And I don't know about you, but I want to learn every last thing that she knows, even if it costs me a couple hundred a pop."

"Truth be told, she kind of reminds me of the bimbo I saw Sean with," grumbles Viv.

"Well, please believe, I got my money's worth today," Trista states firmly.

"I know that's right. I saw you in the corner getting your deep throat on," I tease.

"Jesus, Amaya!" exclaims Vivian.

"Amaya, what?" I respond, tossing her a look that dares her to say something smart. "Vivian, you more than either of us needs to be right up in here with me, especially now that you know Sean is sleeping with the enemy. White women don't play."

"I don't even want to think about it," she replies softly.

"You need to be doing more than just thinking," I retort. "You need to be plotting, planning, and figuring out what you have to do to get your man back."

"And just what do you think I have been doing, Amaya?" she says defensively.

"I don't know, but from the looks of that tired-ass ponytail and baggy sweatsuit, it doesn't look like much to me," I sigh, turning over onto my stomach.

"Excuse me, I didn't realize that I was here to audition for a spot on the catwalk, Amaya," Vivian continues as she turns away in the opposite direction with a huff.

"Amaya may sound like she's being a bitch," Trista interjects as she cut her eyes at me and gently turns Viv back around to face us, "but unfortunately she does have a point, Viv. Every aspect of your life needs to be on point 24/7."

"I've been trying, y'all," she states, clearly overwhelmed, "but I'm so busy working, taking care of Corey, and halfway keeping up my house, I just don't have a moment to think about myself."

"If you need help, Viv, just ask," I reply, in a much softer tone. "But you've got to get serious. I'm talking a new haircut, a new wardrobe, and a new attitude."

"And don't doubt our connections," Trista said, cutting Vivian's pity party short. "I know an amazing trainer who owes me a favor for a walk-on I got her in the last Ben Stiller flick. You can work out with her. Not only will Monica come to you, morning or night, but she guarantees to tighten and tone in three weeks."

"Hold up, what does my shape have to do with anything? When I first met Sean I was full figured and he loved every single inch. So what if I've put on a couple of pounds? Hello? I gave birth to his only son. Unlike Amaya," she hisses, cutting her eyes at me, "my livelihood isn't based on my jean size. I ain't about to go on no goddamn diet for no man!"

"Woah, woah, woah. Viv, ain't nobody asking you to go on a diet. We just want you to take better care of you so that you can handle your bizness, girl!" Trista responds.

"I'm-I'm-I'm just saying . . ." she stammers.

"Just saying what? Just saying that you're so glad we're here to help you stay focused, correct?" I immediately counter.

"I hate it when you guys are right," she finally concedes. "All right, I'll work with the trainer. We'll see."

"Yes, you will," says Trista and we quickly share a look of victory.

"Okay, that's more than enough about me and mine," Viv says, suddenly switching gears, "I want to know whatever happened at the Rap Renegade party. Last I saw, you were looking extra fabulous on the red carpet with that fine basketball player, then I lost you in the crowd. Break it down. I want details!"

"Oh, that's right!" Trista exclaims. "We sure haven't heard what happened at the party. Come on, Amaya, spill the beans."

"Well, let's just say that the way things are going, your girl might have two proposals before the end of the year," I hedge.

"What?!" they screech in unison.

"Listen, you guys can keep playing if you want," I say with a smirk as I stand up and wrap my towel around my body. "I'm 'bout handling my business."

"Whatever, gangsta boo, just break it down," sarcastically answers Trista as she follows me out of the sauna and into the showers. "What the hell went on at the party?"

"Okay, okay, you know I'm not one to kiss and tell, but here's how it went down: So Troy and I arrived at El Centro right in the middle of all the red carpet frenzy. And just like I planned, the paparazzi went bananas. Chile, I don't know if it was our spiritual connection or the low-cut, sheer Richard Tyler dress, but your boy was sporting me like a new winter coat . . ." I laugh from inside my shower stall.

"The only connection I could sense was between everyone's eyes and your breasts," Vivian interrupts. "Tris, your girl had on the hottest dress of the evening. Even Beyoncé's little satin B-Wear number was suspect next to Ms. Thing."

"I saw all the photos on Industrywhispers.com," Trista responds dryly.

"Er-um, like I was saying, we must have spent at least twenty minutes just trying to get down the carpet and into the actual party. In fact, I was having such a good time that I didn't even notice Keith until we ran up into him and his little raggedy entourage."

"I can't believe I missed that!" screams Vivian.

"Yes sir, literally ran up into them. Why, Troy almost knocked one of Keith's little bugaboo boys over by mistake! It was too funny. But not as funny as the look on Keith's face when he realized that Troy and I were together."

"I know he was sick," Trista mocks.

"Girl, that ain't even the half! 'Cause you know that it's basketball season, so everyone is sweating Troy like a fever. Even Keith's posse was trying to get him to come sit at their table in VIP and what not."

"So were you like, 'Let's go'?"

"Hell no, I wasn't like, let's go," I respond sarcastically, turning my shower off. "I was, like, it's whatever. I just kept smiling and holding Troy's hand like I was supposed to do. Keith might've saved those dirty looks for the woman he has at home."

"Amaya, I know you're crazy but please don't tell me that you were sitting up at the Beat Down Records table with Troy," Trista questions, concern filling her voice.

"I'm crazy but not retarded," I laugh. "Troy reserved a table in VIP exclusively for us. But it really didn't matter because we spent the whole night on the dance floor. Kid Capri and Biz Markie were on the turntables, so the music was bananas. Considering how tall he is, Troy was working it out. I don't think I've had that much fun in years."

"So, okay, you had a blast with Troy and pissed off Keith. What makes you think that's going to get you two proposals?" Vivian interrupts as we sit down to dry off and dress in the green-marble locker room.

"May I finish?" I answer with a quick eye-roll. "So right before we left the party, I went to the ladies' room to freshen up my makeup and this fool Keith followed me. As I'm coming out, he steps directly in my face and asks me if I'm satisfied."

"Satisfied? What kind of ridiculous question is that?" Trista inquires with a huff.

"Girl, that's the same thing I was thinking. And I assume the expression on my face reflected it because before I could respond he grabbed my wrist and dragged me into some random nook under the stairs to the Blue Smoke Room."

"You mean to tell me he *dragged* you?" questions Vivian incredulously. "Come on now, Amaya, I can't see anyone dragging your loud behind anywhere quietly!"

"For real, he was holding my wrist so tightly, I just shut the hell up. Of course when we finally got into the corner, I snatched my wrist back and was like, 'What in the world! . . .' He got all up in my space again and was like, 'I will not tolerate seeing you with anyone else.' At this point, I'm catching a major attitude. I mean, I'm not the chick that you can just drag around. I haven't spoken to Keith's dumb ass in over two months, and this certainly was not scoring any points in my books. So I said to him, 'You made your choice. She's at home waiting for you.' So he said, 'I promise you, that shit is a wrap. Seeing you with money tonight almost made me murder son for no reason. Stop playing with me, Amaya. You know you belong with me!'"

"Now, I'm going to keep it real. I really love Keith, and he's the one I want to be with at the end of the day. But I've been down this road too many times. So I told him not to be mad because I've found someone who wants to be with only me. I was like, 'I told you I don't do number two.' Next thing I know this Negro is kissing me so hard I thought I was going to suffocate. And his hand is up my dress. PS, I wasn't wearing panties. So you figure it out!"

"Omigod, you are the worst!" Trista says with a mixture of disgust and glee.

"On the real, I didn't know whether I was going to die from the orgasm or the lack of oxygen. Either way, just as suddenly as he started, he stopped, straightened up his clothes and left my ass standing there."

"Shut up!" they both scream.

"I promise you. It was a mess. My dress was twisted, lipstick was smeared, hair just looking crazy, I still can't believe no one saw what happened, but that's L.A. for you . . ." I ended with a shake of the head.

"What the hell did Troy say about you being gone for so long?" follows Vivian.

"Thankfully he was talking to some ball players and barely noticed I was gone."

"Jesus, Amaya, your shit is crazy! You gotta be careful," cautioned Vivian.

"Who are you telling? And the worst part is, after that encounter with Keith, I was so horny I scratched all my good intentions to make Troy wait for the booty. I put it on him like Heather Hunter," I say with a sly grin. "It jumped off as we were sitting in his car outside of my apartment. One minute we're talking, the next he's lifting me out of my seat and I'm on his lap—in his 745i, mind you—getting my dry grind on like a damn teenager! Just like that, the Richard Tyler was down around my waist and he was sucking my nipples so hard I thought milk was going to squirt out."

"Thank God for tinted windows," Trista interjects sarcastically.

"You said it, not me. So we're kissing all crazy and I can feel his erection pressing on my inner thigh. I pry myself off of him and hop back in the passenger seat. Then before he can say anything, I drop down and suck his little man like my nickname is Hoover 2000. All he could manage to say, was, 'Oh shit, oh shit.' Then right as he was about to come, I stopped, pinched the tip and told him that I wanted to take it upstairs. You should have seen his eyes bug out, but I was dressed and out of that truck before he could string a sentence together. And thank God I got a head start, because as soon as he got inside, Troy had me pinned up against the wall in the hallway. Honestly, I don't remember my feet even touching the ground the entire time we were doing it. One thing I do know is that his shit is so damn long he was tickling my tonsils with each thrust. From there it was a freaking marathon, we sexed in damn near every room in my crib. When I woke up the next morning, my lil' girl was swollen and hanging out. Luckily, Troy was more than happy to provide an early-morning mouth-to-mouth, if you know what I'm saying."

"Aww, damn," says Trista as she zips up her pants in the full-length mirror.

"Say what you want, all I know is that Troy has been at my house damn near every night since. We do all the corny things, like go to the L.A. Zoo, take drives up the coast to Santa Barbara, watch the sunset at the pier, and I still can't get enough of him."

"What about Keith?" Viv questions as she pulls her hair up into a neat ponytail.

"Ah, Keith . . ." I answer with a sly grin. "Yeah, well, the reason that Troy and I are together every *other* night is because when it's Troy's night *off*, Keith is *on!* A couple days after the party we got together, talked everything out, and your boy has been making it his business to spend quality time. As a matter of fact, we've even been house hunting for his new spot when he moves out. Can you believe it?"

"What I can't believe is that you're just now telling us," exclaims Trista.

"Oh, please, between juggling the two of them and all these little nickel-and-dime jobs I've been auditioning for, I barely have time to breathe."

"Wow, clearly I need to get on my job," Trista admits as we leave the Center.

"That's what I've been trying to tell you," I respond, while digging through my gym bag for my shades. "Speaking of jobs, I got to run and meet my little hookup at the Armani showroom. I gotta pick out my outfits for all the Awards Week after-parties."

"Mmm, Armani . . . very nice. I remember seeing Gabrielle Union in a hot black Armani dress at the BET Awards once," Trista comments. "Now, who's this hookup?"

"This stylist Amber that I'm cool with. She's actually really good friends with that new designer Yana K."

"Yeah, well, it must be nice," Viv sighs. "The overseer only granted me the first half of the day off, so I've got to get back to the plantation. What about you, Tris?"

"I'm headed into the office my damn self," empathizes Trista. "By the way, with all your juicy gossip, I almost forgot to tell you that I saw that new Pyrotech cookware infomercial you did last night after Leno. As always, you were gorgeous."

"Thanks, babe," I say with a wistful grin as I hand the cute little valet a ten-dollar bill and jump into my car. "Hopefully it will be one of my last."

As soon as I pull out of the Center I call my girl Amber to let her know that I'm on my way. I met Amber at one of the first open calls I'd answered shortly after moving to Los Angeles. We were both painfully new to the scene. So when all the more-experienced actresses and models refused to even make eye contact with us, we instantly gravitated toward each other and bonded. An Alicia Silverstone look-alike, she's one of the most down white girls I've ever met. For the first couple of years, whenever I couldn't convince Trista or Viv to come out on a weeknight and hang, Amber and I were an unstoppable duo in the club scene—there was no party too exclusive for us, no VIP we couldn't infiltrate. We went through men and their money like water. Like me, Amber was a natural hustler; while I continued pursuing acting, she landed an exclusive styling contract with Robot Films for all the Chris Robinson videos, and hit it big in the fashion game.

"Hey, chica! Just wanted to let you know that I'm on my way," I inform her as soon as Amber picks up the line.

"Okay, babe, I'm in the middle of fitting someone now. Hopefully, she'll be out of here by the time you arrive. Either way, it's cool," she responds.

"Bet. Hugs and kisses," I answer before hanging up.

Since she started styling in L.A., Amber has really made a name for herself among the "it" urban crowd. I guess that's because her lily-white complexion grants her easy access to designers and the pick of the collections, while black stylists with the same amount of experience are left to beg for the scraps. Yet it's hardly a surprise, considering most designers really don't see the benefits of loaning their items to black actors and actresses to begin with. At the end of the day, the photographers are only going to shoot so many photos of the black talent before moving on to the next white thing sashaying down the carpet—even if she only has a five-minute cameo under her belt.

I wondered who Amber is working with, since she didn't bother to mention a name. Armani is an acquired taste for most of the younger urban crowd, who normally go straight for the Gucci, Versace, or Louis Vuitton. Knowing how fast the good dresses can disappear, I pick up the pace and arrive at the showroom in a mere fifteen minutes.

The parking gods are working in my favor and I land a spot in the parking garage right across the street from the Armani entrance. As I wait for the light to cross the road I overhear two young women who really should have been in somebody's high school discussing my favorite Marc Jacobs jeans.

"Ugh, like, I cannot believe she has those MJs on. I waited an entire season for that wash and they totally never came in stock," complains the willowy brunette.

"Like, omigod, don't even worry about it. She probably works in a stockroom and stole a pair," her ash-blond friend offers.

Works in a stockroom? Who the hell were they referring to? I was so tempted to turn around and read the little trust-fund babies from head to toe that my palms started itching. But instead I decide to ignore them and keep it moving. Besides, with my luck, they'd turn out to be the daughters of some important film executive. Speaking of which, I haven't received my daily update call from Clarence about the Soular Son film. I make a mental note to call as soon as I finish with Amber.

When the light finally changes, I make sure to put a smile on my face and swing my hips extra hard because I know that those hateful girls are watching as they walk behind me. Then just as we arrive at the corner and start to go our separate ways, I reconsider my decision of silence. When I blow up, it's going to be so big a couple of whiny, hungry-looking white girls won't be able to stop me. So I say over my right shoulder, "Pathetic bitches," without breaking my stride or my smile. As I continue walking away, out of the corner of my eye, I can see them standing there in disbelief. Touché, wenches!

Once inside, I watch the spring '05 Armani fashion show and flip through a recent copy of British *Vogue* until Amber walks up.

"Are you ready, beautiful?" she asks with a grin. As usual she looks great—her long blond hair is pulled up in a simple twist. She has on a sheer black tank top with low-slung black-and-white print skirt and fire-engine-red Gucci pumps.

"You know I'm always ready," I say playfully.

"Cool," she says, then gives me a quick hug and points toward the door we need to walk through. "FYI, my other client is still trying on her last piece, so just look around while I finish up with her. I shouldn't be long. She knows that I can't have more than one client running around in the showroom at a time, so . . ." she explains as we enter the huge room where the samples are hanging.

"Okay, Amber, that's like the third time you've called her 'my client' instead of using a name," I finally blurt out. "Who the hell is it? Angela, Jada, Nia, for Christ's sake?"

"Close," she smiles and then whispers, "It's Trixie Cooper. But you can't tell her that she's not Angela or better. Honestly, I try not to say her name, because I swear the woman has bionic ears and can hear through walls."

Trixie Cooper? As in Trixie Cooper the drop-dead-beautiful, award-winning actress and, more importantly, wife of the love of my life Keith Cooper? My ears start ringing. I've never been this close to Trixie before. The only time I ever see her is in a movie or on the pages of *People* with their kids. She never hangs out with Keith and his entourage. She's the black Erika Kane—untouchable and not to be crossed. As these thoughts run through my head, Amber stops speaking and looks at me strangely.

"You all right? Do you know her or something?" she asks.

No, we haven't met, I'm just fucking her husband, is what I really want to say, but instead I simply squeeze out a very strangled "Oh no, I'm just a huge fan of her work."

"Hmmm, if you say so," Amber finally concedes after about ten seconds more of staring in my face. "Either way, I'm just going to try and rush her up out of here."

"No, really, it's fine," I insist, struggling to regain my composure. "And I've got all day."

"You're such a sweetheart," she coos. "If you see anything you like, try it on."

Considering there's only two tiny changing rooms in the space and they're right next to each other, I'm tempted to grab the first thing I spot in my size and head over there. But on second thought, I don't want her to see me in something crazy-looking. She'll assume I have absolutely no taste. So I take my time and pick out three sleek full-length dresses to start with and head over to the dressing area.

Each step feels like an eternity, and when I finally reach the stalls Trixie is headed back in to change her clothes, so I only catch a glimpse of her small, caramel-colored back. It's just enough time for me to pick out the spot where I'd stab her if murder were a legal option.

"Let me see what you've picked," requests Amber, interrupting my criminal reverie.

"Oh, I just grabbed the first things I saw," I lie smoothly.

"Oh yeah, these are great. I absolutely love your taste," Amber says as she strokes the soft silk material. I hope that Trixie's heard every last syllable.

"Yeah, well, you know, I do what I can," I casually reply as I take the dresses into the available dressing stall and close the curtain with a decisive snap.

Not even a moment later I hear her voice for the first time. Clear as a bell, she's very soft-spoken but direct in tone. I can tell she is a woman accustomed to getting everything she wants. Chills run up my spine and I freeze with one leg still in my jeans and the other in midair.

"Darling, can you please zip this up for me," she requests.

"Of course I will," Amber answers.

"Hmm, think I like this one, what about you?"

"I'm not sure that I like it quite as much as the last dress. However, both look fabulous, darling," Amber responds appropriately.

"Well, in that case I'll just take both," she laughs.

"Now, Trixie, you know it's Awards Week," Amber starts gently. "It's really hard to take two dresses right now . . ."

"I know it's hard," Trixie responds without missing a beat, "but be a dear and make it happen, will you?"

I use the awkward silence as my opportunity to come out from behind the curtains and not only rescue my girl but finally meet my nemesis face-to-face.

"You like?" I question as I make a complete turn in the breathtaking satin-and-silk strapless peach-colored dress.

"Wow, it's gorgeous," Amber answers as she moves away from Trixie to finish zipping me up. "And you won't need the seamstress to adjust a thing."

"Oh my, isn't that *interesting* on you," is the only comment from Trixie.

"I'm being so rude," apologizes Amber. "Trixie, this is Amaya Anderson. Amaya, this is Trixie Cooper."

"Pleased to meet you," I say and offer my best fake smile as I extend my hand.

"Hmm, I'm sure," Trixie replies as she uses the sudden vibration of her cell phone from within the dressing stall as an excuse to ignore my outstretched hand. "If you'll excuse me," she says and darts behind the curtains.

I turn and look at Amber with one raised eyebrow. She simply shrugs her shoulders in response and mouths, "Crazy." We burst into laughter.

"Girl, this dress is perfect. Don't even bother trying on anything else. Go change and let's go. We need to get the hell over to Yana K.'s before there's nothing left," Amber says as soon as she's able to catch her breath.

"True . . . I'll meet you out front in five minutes."

"Trixie, sweetie, I've got to run," Amber calls over the top of the stall. "When you finish changing, please bring your selections out to the front."

"Oh yes, that's fine," she answers, clearly distracted.

As I duck back in my stall and start to undress, a wave of relief washes over me. Now that I've stared the beast down, I'm no longer concerned about measuring up. I am just as beautiful—and, more important, I'm younger. She may know more people, but once I land this Soular Son role, I'll be everywhere. That woman's days are numbered, and she doesn't even know it.

The soft sound of schoolgirl giggles interrupts my mental celebration, and I realize that Trixie is still on the phone. Despite her obvious attempt to use a hushed tone, I'm still able to hear every single word of her conversation.

"Oh, *stop*. You're being too nasty. Just wait until I get my hands on you!"

Nasty? I crouch down close to the space on the floor just below the curtain that seperates us and hold my breath to try and get a better listen.

"Only for you, baby. You know I like it when you punish me for being a bad girl."

I know this woman is not having phone sex with Keith right here in the showroom. My throat starts to clench up. That deceitful bastard told me that he barely spoke to her anymore. As I turn to grab my cell phone and call his lying ass, I hear her say—

". . . it's Sam's. All Sam's."

Hold up! Who the hell is Sam? I almost swallow my tongue. Trixie Cooper is having an affair with someone named Sam? For two years Keith has been treating me like shit and putting us on hold because he can't find it in his heart to leave his picture-perfect wife, and now I find out she's screwing around with some other dude? And I heard it out of her mouth? I want to laugh out. This is priceless.

"Yeah, yeah, I love you, too. I'll see you tonight." With a snap of the phone it's over. I wait until I hear her pull back the curtain and leave the showroom before I dare to breathe again. As I hurry to pull on my clothes, my mind is whirling. I snatch the dress I've selected and rush out to the front to meet Amber.

"Girl, what took you so long?" she asks when I finally join her in the lobby. "I already filled out the delivery forms for you."

"Oh, my bad. I just didn't want to run into your client again," I answer coyly as I hand the gown over and give my information for next-day delivery.

"Whatever, that's your girl," she quickly retorts. "But, quite honestly, just now was probably a better time to meet her than in the back, earlier."

"Oh, really," I say, feigning ignorance as we step into the elevator.

"Yeah, girl, don't ask me why, but she waltzed out of here grinning from ear to ear," Amber says with a shake of her golden head.

"Hmm, maybe it had to do with the phone call she took while we were in the showroom," I hedge as we head out into the bright sunshine.

"Oh, oh, I don't even want to know," giggles Amber as she runs ahead of me across the street to the garage.

"Yes, you do you little liar," I laugh as I easily catch up with her.

"Okay, okay, what did you hear?" she finally relents.

"Well, turns out little miss holier-than-thou was in the stall having phone sex."

"What?!" Amber screams as her eyes became wide as saucers.

"Yes, girl, and wait, let me tell you, it was with somebody named Sam," I continue with an evil grin as we reach my car. "Now, correct me if I'm wrong, but the last time I read *People*, Trixie was happily married to Keith Cooper of Beat Down Records."

"Uh, that would be correct," Amber agrees. "But, you know, I heard that she's really out there."

Now it was my turn to scream.

"Like for real, and I've heard that from several reliable sources," Amber confides with authority. "But, Amaya, promise you won't say anything. And if you do, you totally didn't hear it from me!"

"Okay, Amber Littleton, I'm officially about to put you out of my car for lying!"

"I swear on my mother's life," she asserts as she turns up the radio and starts bobbing her head to Biggie like a certified thug.

Once again my mind is reeling. This could really be the key to releasing Keith from Trixie's iron grip. But how do I tell him and avoid him lashing out at me? 'Cause you know no man wants to hear that his woman has been stepping out on him. If I confront him with words, he'll never believe me. He'll just say I'm being hateful and probably cut me off. Bottom line, I need irrefutable proof. I have no choice but to call in a professional.

When I first moved to L.A. and was super strapped for cash, Clarence's boy at the LAPD hooked me up with a decoy gig for a young private investigator named Lisa Smith. She was working on a couple of adultery cases and needed someone to distract a musician's bodyguard so that she could get in his room backstage and nose around. It was an easy assignment that paid well enough to cover my rent and utilities for a month. Lisa and I had hit it off immediately, and she promised that if I ever needed help, I should give her a call and she'd hook me up with the "friend-of-the-family discount." I haven't spoken to her in over a year, but I'm sure her number is somewhere in my apartment. As soon as Awards Week ends I'll be sure to give her a call.

AFTER AN ENTIRE day of running around with Amber I'm exhausted. After we left the Yana K. boutique we headed over to Showroom 65. I must have tried on at least fifty different dresses. I swear the next time I take this outfit off, I'm going to throw it away! Just as I'm about to jump on the freeway, my pager starts to vibrate. It's Keith. He wants to know if I'm busy . . . suddenly I'm not so tired anymore. I make a hard U-turn and head back into the city, to the Beat Down Records office. Time to go pay my baby a little visit.

As soon as I enter into the reception area my ears are accosted with an extra-loud mix of Young Daddy MC's new music video and BET's *Rap City* with Tigger blasting from the two monitors on the wall. As I wait for his assistant to come out and get me, I listen to the receptionist dishing all the latest rumors about some gay rapper with whomever she's talking to on the phone. The entire space smells like weed and I just pray that Keith's assistant hurries the hell up. Just as I was about to send Keith a nasty page for making me wait in the lobby when he knows I hate the smell of smoke, a small Japanese guy beckons me in.

"What up, Amaya?" Andrew asks as he quickly gives me a peck on the cheek.

"Hey, Andrew," I answer sweetly. Andrew, a Harvard student who came to intern at Beat Down after his freshman year and never left, has been with Keith the entire time we've dated; he usually coordinates our secret rendezvous.

"Ah, now I see why his bad mood just changed so suddenly," he joked. "I didn't realize that you were coming to visit."

"Actually, this is a last-minute decision but I'm flattered that you think I make that much of a difference."

"Hey, I know my boss, and trust me when I tell you—you make a difference," Andrew answers with a chuckle as he knocks on Keith's door.

A gruff voice from within calls out, "It's open."

I slide in and close the door firmly behind me.

"Yo, be sure to lock it behind you," Keith instructs as I walk into the large corner office. Keith's office is ghetto fabulous to the max. Hard-edged glass tables and a buttery black-leather sofa with a couple of club chairs are set off to the side of his massive glass-and-chrome desk. The state-of-the-art Bose sound system, which covers the entire back wall, plays a remix of Killer's new single. From his position behind the desk he exudes the aura of a very powerful businessman.

"*Please*," I remind him with a sigh as I turn back and lock the door.

"My bad. Please," he chuckles. "You still trying to school a brother, Amaya."

"That's better," I say as I walk over and make myself very comfortable in his lap. "So what's up, baby? I'm happy to see you."

"Nothing. I just wanted to feel you near me, is all. I'm having a shitty day and I figured I'd try and turn the tide back by spending a quick minute with my favorite girl," he answers, enveloping me in his muscular arms and nuzzling his head against my breasts.

As I look down at his bald head and chocolate-brown skin I am again amazed at how wonderful Keith can be even when he's not trying. As I enjoy the pressure from his strong embrace and listen to the rhythmic rise and fall of his breathing, I want nothing more than for this moment to go on forever. I kiss the top of his head softly to get him to look up at me. I'm immediately drawn into his big brown eyes.

"Yo, you know you make me happy, right?" he asks sincerely.

"I know, sweetie," I answer leaning in to kiss him softly on his full lips. If only I could believe the words coming out of his mouth.

"Thank you for coming out of your way to let me hold you for a minute," he continues.

"Keith, if you'd get it together, we could always be like this," I respond honestly.

"I told you that that situation is a wrap," he cuts me off sharply.

"Okay," I reply with the sarcastic smirk that always grates on his nerves.

"What's that supposed to mean?" he asks as he now holds me at a distance.

"Nothing," I sigh as I break his embrace and stand. "But let me ask you this—if it's a wrap, why are we still looking over our shoulders, double-locking doors and what not?"

"Please don't start," he counters as he stands.

"Just forget it, Keith. I already said okay."

Before we can pursue the issue any further the special phone line that Andrew uses when there's an artist in the office starts to ring. "Damn, that's Killer Dun. I want him to do something with Young Daddy MC but he insists that he's just not feeling it. These fucking artists have a little bit too much opinion nowadays for my liking," he grumbles, his mind already moving on to the next issue at hand.

"Okay, well, I'm gone," I tell him. I know from his tone that it's going to be a very one-sided conversation with Killer Dun.

"All right," he replies distractedly as he walks me to his office door. "Give me a call tonight before you go to sleep."

"Okay, babe." As I walk down the hallway filled with platinum plaques, I'm amazed at how much Keith has accomplished since his days selling bootleg CDs and promoting parties. He's so focused. He's just the type of man I need in my life. And with a little help from Trixie and Troy, that's exactly what I'm going to have!

9

VIVIAN

Amaya, step away from the potato salad," I say cautiously. "I'd move away if I was you," Trista says, laughing. "You know she'll jack you up if even one of those potatoes doesn't taste just right."

"But potato salad needs paprika," Amaya says, reaching for the seasoning. I looked at Trista, and then switch my focus back to Amaya. She catches the glare in my eye and, punctuating her action with a "Well, damn," very gently places the bottle back on the counter. "If you ask me, you shouldn't be serving up all these carbs, anyway. Can't catch a man in L.A. if you're wearing potatoes on your hips."

"Whatever, bitch," I shoot back. "Drop the paprika."

I don't care about Amaya's feelings today. It's Corey's seventh birthday and I'm putting the finishing touches on a bash he won't soon forget. We've been planning it for months—he asked for a fish theme, so we looked up some ideas on the Internet, checked out a few *Parenting* magazine articles we found at the library, and *voilà*, created an "Under the Sea" extravaganza for fifteen, replete with shark cupcakes, a fish-shaped piñata, a boisterous round of "Go Fish," and goldfish—both the crackers and the real thing—for party favors. And every party I put together comes with a spread fit for my little king.

Of course I had ulterior motives; despite the fact that we hadn't spoken since the unfortunate club run-in with the blonde, Sean agreed (through Corey) to come by the house to celebrate his son's birthday, along with his sister Jalene and his mom—so I knew I had to put my whole foot in it. And to do that properly, I needed to pick up a few last-minute accoutrements from Wal-Mart, which got me to thinking about what it would be like to walk down the aisle. It was the dress on the cover of *Modern Bride* that made me float over to the store's magazine rack and run my fingers over the cover. By the time I made it to the checkout, I was halfway through the magazine, and had already imagined how I'd change that satin, floor-length, off-the-shoulder wrap dress the model was wearing to suit my taste. Maybe I'd switch up the color to ivory, for an old-world, antiqued feel, and rim the train with cowry shells instead of rhinestones to make it Afrocentric. By the time the attitudinal checkout chick finished tossing around the groceries of the customer in front of me and announced to the woman behind me that she was the last customer because it was "way past time for her break," I'd worked out how much it should cost to reproduce the dress (about $500 if I let my mom sew it), what style shoes would look best with it (slingbacks, for sure), how my hair should be styled (textured afro, for the Afrocentric theme), and what color the bridal party should be wearing (bronze with ivory accents). I was still torn between whether we should exchange our vows by the beach at sunset or if we should keep it black and get married in a formal ceremony in the New Hope Baptist church in Compton.

Hey, I'm a firm believer that positive thinking begets positive results, and if I just envisioned my wedding to Sean, it would happen. It wouldn't hurt, either, to show him what he's missing by being somewhere other than with me. If throwing my son a slamming birthday party can help facilitate that, then a slamming party it's going to be. And Amaya wasn't about to mess it up by mis-seasoning my food.

"Why don't you sit with your hands on the table, where I can see them?"

"Why don't you tell me why there's a bridal book over there on the counter?" Amaya shoots back. "Or is Trista the only one in the room who's going to get the blow-by-blow of your hot date with Daddy? Did he ask you to marry him yet?"

I give Trista an "I know you didn't tell that girl all my damn business" look.

"I got a big mouth, don't I?" she laughs, raising her hands in surrender. "Totally guilty."

"I want the dirty details. Let's go," Amaya says, rubbing her hands together.

I turn back to my sink full of chicken parts and continue to shake Lawry's Seasoning Salt over them. "Nothing really happened," I say. "I think that Negro's catching feelings or something, though."

"That's what I'm talking about," Amaya says, jumping out of her chair to high-five me. She thought better of it when she saw grease and chicken fat on my hands. "Um, I'm going to take a rain check on the high five. But, girl, you know you got to give the kid some details. You whipped it on him good, huh?"

"I went out with him a few times, but I insisted he take me to places without VIP rooms and without all his little men," I say. "When he's around the circus, he likes standing center ring and performing for anyone who'll watch."

"That's what stars do, Viv," Amaya says matter-of-factly.

"But I don't like Daddy the rapper. I like Jerome Houston the man, who happens to be quite sweet, much smarter than his public persona would have you believe, and not at all the thug lover you see in all those videos running up and down the BET schedule."

"Yeah, yeah, yeah—get to the juicy part," Amaya rushes. "Did you whip it on him like a porn star or what?"

"Amaya!" Trista says, shushing her. "Lil' man might hear you!"

"My bad," she whispers, giggling. "But seriously, did you put some of those tricks you learned in the Blow and Get Low class to good use?"

I suck my teeth. "Amaya—how would it look, me giving a blow job to a man I have no intention of marrying? Unlike some of us in the room, I'm saving my bag of tricks for the person who'll accompany me down the aisle."

"But you just said you're whipping it on ol' Daddy-o," she shoots back.

"Not on purpose," I say. "I like him, but I've only got eyes for my baby daddy."

"And your baby daddy is coming to the party today, right?" Trista asks.

"That's what he told Corey," I say.

"Ooh, one big happy family!" Trista says dryly.

"That's what I'm hoping," I said, ignoring her. "So everything has to be perfect."

"Tell me this," Amaya says, calling out from the next room, where she's folding napkins. "How much did your little interlude with Daddy have to do with Sean's renewed interest in his baby's mama?"

"Amaya! Keep it down before my godson hears you!" Trista says.

Amaya tips back to the doorway and sticks her head into the kitchen. "Hey, he's *my* godson, too. But for real, what's up with that?"

"You know what? It hasn't come up. Sean and I never talked about it; in fact, the only communication we've had with one another has been through our answering machines, because we keep missing each other," I say. "I was sure he was going to call and say something about it, but he didn't."

"That doesn't mean it wasn't on his mind," Amaya says.

"Well, I'm sure that it probably was, which means that your plan worked, right?"

"Yup, it sure did. Who knows how to play a player?" Amaya asks, before turning on her heels and heading back into the dining room to resume her napkin duties.

"Well tell me, playa playa," I say, as I toss the chicken into my Hefty bag full of flour and then my frying pan of hot cooking oil. "How exactly do I handle Daddy? Because that boy's acting like he's in love or something."

"In love?" Trista asks incredulous. "Love would require a bit of sensitivity and emotion. I figured he was pouring all that into his latest booty single."

"Ha ha," I say, mocking Trista. "He's definitely sensitive and emotional. In fact, he was quite upset that I couldn't make it to his video shoot today in San Francisco. I don't know, you guys—he's not the man the image stacks him up to be. He calls when he says he's going to call, and he hasn't so much as tried to kiss me, even though we've actually gone out a few times. If he'd be just a little bit more sincere and drop the bad-boy thug thing, he might actually be able to revive that career of his."

"Never mind the sensitive-thug crap—you turned down a chance to be down in a Daddy video?" Amaya calls from the dining room.

"Um, I'm throwing a birthday party for my son," I deadpan.

"And her baby daddy is coming over—not that that's any improvement over a Daddy video," Trista says sarcastically. "Ms. Thing's trying to be Martha Stewart up in here, not the lead video ho."

"Hey," I shoot back at Trista, "don't be hating on Sean, and don't be throwing negative energy on my Vow," I say. "As hard as it may be for you to do it, think only positive things about me and Sean, okay?"

"I'm just saying—you're a beautiful woman, and I'm not quite sure why you're going to waste the ten months you've got to find a man on a man who hasn't given anyone reason to believe he's worthy," she says. "I'm just looking out for you."

"Trista, save the drama for your mama and worry about getting your own man," I say quietly. "I'm not trying to go through this with you today."

"Right, right, true," says Amaya, "but the next time you get invited to a video shoot, you need to holla at your girl."

"I'll be more than happy to let you have him for yourself. I've got to focus my attention on what's real, and the only thing that makes sense for me right now is Sean and Vivian and Corey together again," I said. "Daddy's going to have to get his brown sugar from somewhere else. This deep throat is taken."

"I know that's right!" Amaya laughed.

M<small>Y</small> <small>MOTHER ARRIVED</small> first—came with her homemade biscuits, a yellow-bellied watermelon, three elaborately wrapped presents for her grandson, and a bunch of questions about why that damn bridal magazine was on the counter. I forgot to move it, so it served me right that I'd have to explain that, no, I wasn't getting married and, no, Sean and I hadn't gotten back together. I'd brought it on myself but I was still in no mood to hear her lecture about how I was going to get my heart broken chasing after a man who didn't have the sense of a billy goat to stop running from what was tangible and real: the ready-made family he had in me and his son. "I honestly don't understand why you don't just get you somebody who's going to appreciate all the love you and my grandbaby have to offer," she'd say whenever she sensed I was fretting over Sean, which was often. "You can't make a man love you, but you can walk away and find you a new man who's willing."

She was right, but mostly the venom she reserved for Sean came from two things: for one, he got her only child, the first in the family to attend college, knocked up in her senior year, just as she was preparing to be somebody; and, for two, his mother acted like Mamie Evans' daughter was some ghetto bitch who purposely got pregnant to trap Lily Jordan's well-to-do-and-going-places son. If there were two things my mother couldn't stand was the idea that her daughter wouldn't live a better life than she, and that Sean's mom, who didn't have two nickels to rub together until her son became a prosperous doctor, dismissed her child as nothing more than a lazy 'hood rat looking for a meal ticket. When the two of them were in one room, it was always hotter than the Fourth of July. I'd started preparing myself for the show the moment Sean said he and his mother were coming to the party.

"So," my mom says, picking up my platter of fried chicken and placing it gingerly on the dining room table between her basket of biscuits and a bowl of cucumber and tomato salad, "Sean and you getting cozy enough for you to be buying bridal magazines?"

I try to sound as measured and even-toned as I possibly can. "We're quietly working some things through and taking our time to figure out where we go from here," I say simply. I toss a "save me" look in Amaya and Trista's direction, but I see through the kitchen window over the sink that they've both ducked out back and left their girl hanging.

"Well, where else is there to go? You done had his baby, and that obviously didn't mean anything to him. What else you going to put yourself through to get him to realize where his butt shoulda been all along?" Just then the doorbell rings. Saved.

"I'll get it," I shout as I practically sprint for the front door. What I find on my front stoop leaves me dizzy.

Sean clears his throat. His mother stands there with her lips pursed, like she smells something foul. His sister, Jalene, waves a weak hello. I don't really register the words coming from anyone's mouth—I just remember the blonde extending her hand as if she actually expected me to shake it, and Trista stepping in to help me as she invited my "guests" in. My mother, unaware of the drama that is unfolding at my entryway, but sensing by the look on my face that something is wrong, is all loud with her inquisition. "Vivian? What ails you, girl?" she calls out as I rush past her. Amaya, having peeked around the corner to see what all the fuss is about, widens her eyes, takes one look at Trista, another at me, and lets it rip: "Oh, somebody please tell me he didn't bring blondie to the party!"

"Amaya! Shh!" Trista mouths, pushing her finger to her lips.

"He wrong for that," she stage-whispers, shaking her head. "Dead wrong."

I walk calmly over to the sink, not quite sure what to do as I process what's unfolding in my foyer and brace for the showdown that's sure to come. I turn on the water in the kitchen sink and squirt a few drops of dishwashing liquid into my hands. I start rubbing—first my palms, then my fingers. But I can't really feel them. Tears well in my eyes. I can't see. My mother's voice is what I hear first. "Well, ain't this nothing?" she says, disgust ringing her words as the foursome settle in the kitchen.

There's silence. I can't see her face, but I know her eyes are shifting back and forth between Sean, the white girl, Jalene, and their mother. "And she got the nerve to treat us like garbage when her own son drags trash into other people's houses."

"Now, hold on a minute, Mamie Evans," Lily says tightly. "There's no need to be disrespectful."

"No, honey," my mother says, shutting her down with a quickness. "What there's no need for is your son bringing strange women to my daughter's home, my grandbaby's party—around family. This here is a private affair for Corey, not a high school house party for your son and his little friends."

"Who says she's not family?" Lily shoots back.

"Well, she damn for sure ain't no kin to me," my mother says through her teeth.

Amaya lets out a snort, but quickly covers her mouth. Trista, ever the politician, steps between the two women and tries to settle things down. Jalene tries to help, too.

"How about we all go into the dining room, have a cool drink and remember what we're all here for," Trista says.

"Ain't but four people in this house confused, and they just walked in the door," my mother says, nodding toward the foursome. The doorbell rings. More guests are arriving. Just what I need—a pack of seven-year-olds walking into the middle of the Evans-Jordan family feud. The tension is palpable; my son's voice shatters the silence.

"Mommy! Mommy! Daddy's here!"

For the first time since I opened my door for him, I look Sean in the eyes. He stares right back at me; defiance and disgust settle around his brows. I swear, if I could reach into my good knife drawer and grab my biggest Cutco stainless steel and stab the shit out of him—*and* get away with it? . . . He'd be in a bloody heap in the middle of my kitchen by now. The blonde and his mama, too. But I've no more time to consider such folly; my child is calling my name.

"I know, sweetie, he's in here," I say, trying to control the quiver in my voice, my eyes still locked with Sean's.

"No, Daddy's here, and he brought me a car!" he says, running out the front door.

Now my brows are wrinkled. This Negro bought my child a car? What the hell? I push past Sean (making sure to brush his shoulder hard with mine) and make my way to the foyer, my eyes searching for Corey. "Baby, what are you . . ."

For the second time in a matter of minutes, what I see on my front stoop leaves me speechless. There he is, Daddy the rapper, slapping my child five and grinning from ear to ear. Just beyond the porch, sitting on the brick overlay leading to the front walk, is a shiny-yellow child-sized Corvette convertible. C-O-R-E-Y is painted on the door; music is blasting from what appears to be a radio in the dash.

"Yeah, little man. Happy birthday," Daddy says. "It's good to be seven, huh?"

"It sure is," Corey says, fingering the steering wheel.

"You got your license?" Daddy asks.

"No!" Corey giggles. "I'm too little to have a license!"

"Maybe I can pull some strings down at the DMV. In the meantime, check with your moms to see if you can take it for a spin, all right, little man?"

"Okay," Corey says before he turns to me. "Can I get in, Mom? Pretty please?"

I force a smile, and toss a look at Daddy before I move in to give him a hug and a proper greeting. "I thought you were in San Francisco today."

"My video shoot got postponed—something about the director not having the right permits to shoot on the bridge or some madness. We postponed it until next week," he says. "I hope you don't mind me crashing the party."

I don't say anything, just stare for a minute.

"Um, can I come in?" he says, half-joking.

"Oh, no, no—it's okay, come on in," I say, taking one last look at Corey and his friends crowding around the Corvette before turning around to open the door. Sean is taking it all in—standing in my way. I shoot him the evil eye and push past him. "Daddy? Sean. Sean? Daddy." Then I turn my attentions back to my thug love. "You hungry?" I ask.

"It smells good up in here—is that fried chicken?" he says.

"Sure is," I smile. "Been slaving over the stove all morning for my baby."

"Beauty, brains, and a good cook, too? Somebody better snatch you up quick," he says, walking into the kitchen to a waiting audience.

Amaya speaks first. "Well, if it isn't Young Daddy MC," she says, extending her hand for a shake. "Viv has told us so much about you. Welcome. I'm Amaya."

"Hey, Amaya, and don't hold anything Viv told you against me, okay?"

"Not a problem," Amaya says. "This is Trista, Viv's mom, Miss Mamie, Jalene, and some other guests of Corey's," she says, dismissing Lily and the blonde. By now, Sean is in the kitchen, too. He's seething.

"We're going to go out back," he says.

"Bye," I say without hesitating.

"Yeah, bye," Amaya says just as quickly.

Lily sucks her teeth and turns on her heel. Sean shoots a look at the blonde and signals her with his chin to head for the door. Daddy watches them walk out, still oblivious to the showdown at the Evans corral. "All right, man, I'll holla at you later," he says to Sean. Sean doesn't say anything back—just pushes right past him.

"Girl," my mother says. "You got something on your hands right there."

Jalene grabs my arm. "Can I speak to you for a minute?" she asks.

"Jay, I have to get the food on the table and get the games together," I say, sure that she was only going to try to make excuses for her brother bringing the white woman to the house. Jalene, with whom I'd become fast friends while I was dating her brother in college, has a kind of power over me; no matter what Sean and I were going through, she'd willingly jeopardize her friendship with me, and her kinship to her brother, to try to get us to reach some understanding. Usually it helped. But today I am in no mood to have her try to explain why I shouldn't be mad about the white girl.

"Just for a minute," she says. "And then I'll help you put everything out."

"Jay, not for nothing, but I'm not interested," I say.

I walked into the dining room. "How about we call the birthday boy into the house so we can eat?"

AFTER THE HOT mess that unfolded at my son's birthday party, I couldn't begin to explain in any kind of sane, rational way how Sean and I ended up in the sack. My mind's settled on believing that after his second run-in with Daddy, my boy just came to his senses and realized he couldn't, like, live without me. The circumstances behind our reconnecting with one another—between the sheets, that is—certainly didn't hurt things.

It happened on the night of the Golden Globes, which is ironic because it's the one night of the year that I'm most evil. I know, I know—there are entertainment reporters across the land who would *kill* to get all shined up and stand front and center on the red carpet, rubbing elbows with Hollywood's glitterati. Thing is, if you're covering it for a newspaper or a small-time or out-of-town TV station, you're rubbing a lot more than just elbows. Indeed, the area where they have those reporters—which, including me, totals at least four dozen each year, if not more—is all of twelve feet by twelve feet, which means that we're practically smelling each other's asses as we shout perfectly ridiculous questions at the stars making their way into the Beverly Hilton Hotel for the night's festivities. Covering the pressroom wasn't any better; in fact, it was a snore. I mean, how many times can one ask a celebrity where they're going to put their statue and expect an original, smart, clever answer? I'd grown so bored of the whole affair that mostly I just hung back by the re-

freshments table with a hot cup of coffee in one hand and my tape
recorder near the speaker. If I heard anything remotely interesting, I'd
check the tape counter and make a notation in my notebook, so that I'd
have something to call in to the rewrite desk that was waiting breathlessly
for me to give them star quotes to fill out the *Daily News*'s lousy stories.
But mostly I just sat back and watched the action—the photographers
jockeying for the shot that would make the cover of tomorrow's papers,
the reporters trying to finesse the flaks for celebrity access, the security
detail alternately flirting and scolding the blondes who were trying to use
their feminine wiles to get this close to the celebrity presenters, who
never really had much to say and made it clear they weren't up for the
prying questioning. Truly, the one highlight of the night was when Cassidy St. James won for best actress, and that was only because I knew how
hard my girl Trista had worked to drum up publicity and support for her.
I knew she'd be handsomely rewarded for her efforts, at least by her
company, if not by Cassidy, who is notorious for treating the people who
work for her—Trista included—like minions and hangers-on who don't
deserve respect or thank-yous for their hard work. My girl wasn't thinking like that, though. When Trista finally made it back to the pressroom,
she practically floated over to me.

"We did it!" she screamed, jumping up and down and hugging me all
at once. Trista hardly ever lost her composure—she's the epitome of
even-toned civility—but tonight was her night and all that prim and
proper stuff went out the window.

"So does this mean that you finally get to calm down and take a
break—treat yourself to some much-needed time off?" I asked as I
pulled back from our embrace.

"Time off?" Trista laughed. "That's cute. No, darling, my work is
just starting. I have new clients to sign up at TA. I have partner to make.
I've got . . ."

"A man to get," I said, cutting her off. I tapped my watch. "Time's
a-ticking, my dear. Don't forget the Vow."

"Yes, indeed it is," Trista said, "but I'm not going to let that steal my joy right now. I'm going to bask in this victory, if you don't mind. I'll think about the boys tomorrow." She paused for a moment to listen to Cassidy wow the journalists with a teary speech about how wonderful it was to "be accepted at this age as an actress with real chops," and how she couldn't have done it without a "great team" behind her. I could tell Trista was bothered that the actress never once mentioned her by name; I made a mental note to grab Cassidy's quote off the tape, and be sure that the rewrite team attributed the win to Trista's award campaign efforts. Trista politely clapped when the publicist ushered the newly minted winner off the stage and back to her seat in the awards ceremony audience, and then she turned her attention back to me. "So which party are you hitting tonight?" she asked.

"I have a few I have to stop by. The Jacob Lawrence Agency is having their annual bash, and then there's the *Esquire* after-party. And Amaya made me promise to go over to Beat Down Records' party, but I don't know if I want to be bothered, because Daddy'll probably be there, seeing as he's on the label and all. I'm in no mood for his boys and the groupie-ho element he always seems to attract. Besides, I'm tired already, just thinking about covering three parties in one night. I didn't even do that in college, and I sure as shootin' wasn't an old lady then!"

"I know that's right," Trista said, throwing me a high five. "You know I'll be stuck traipsing behind Cassidy. If we don't hook up later at one of the parties, then I'll catch you tomorrow at the class."

"Oh yeah, the class," I said, rolling my eyes for emphasis. "I can't believe Amaya's got us stripteasing in front of complete strangers this time."

"Actually, I kind of like the idea of knowing how to peel it off," Trista laughed. "Now all I need to do is get up enough nerve to do it in front of Garrett."

"Well, after you're finished with that one, you might want to sign up for another BJ course—the advanced class is even freakier than the beginner's course we took before," I giggled.

"Vivian Evans!" Trista said, covering her mouth with her hand and widening her eyes. "Tell me you did not sign up for another Blow and Get Low class!"

"Shhh! Before someone hears you," I said, my eyes darting around while I laughed. "I'm not going to front—I needed some extra help in the oral pleasure department. And, might I add, I've gotten so good I can take practically an entire small banana in my mouth without gagging or drooling. My tongue game is kind of sick, if I say so myself," I added smugly.

"Eww—tongue game?" Trista said, all at once disgusted and fascinated.

"Tongue game, girl," I said. "Remind me to show you what I learned."

"Okay, now you're scaring me—you sound just like Amaya."

"Maybe. But that girl might be on to something, no matter how pitiful it sounds," I laughed. "Just do me a favor and keep this between us. I'll never hear the end of it if Amaya finds out I'm a member."

"Your secret's safe with me, trust," Trista said with a flick of her wrist. "Okay, I have to get back to my seat. Maybe I'll see you later?"

"Maybe," I said, giving her kisses on both cheeks. "If not, enjoy your night. You deserve it."

"Thanks, baby," Trista said, before sashaying out of the room.

I never did see Trista that night. Instead, I found myself twirled in the sheets with my son's father, putting my BJ secrets to the best use in all of California that night.

I'm still not really all that sure how I got there. All I know is that I was at the bar, sipping on a cranberry and orange juice, trying to get up the nerve to go over and reintroduce myself to Brian McKnight, whom I'd interviewed and profiled a few months earlier, when I felt a wet kiss on my left cheek. Startled, I fixed my mouth to give whoever slobbered on my cheek a good tongue-lashing. Imagine my surprise, then, when I looked up and saw Sean. "You working or enjoying?" he said flatly.

Unsure of exactly how I was supposed to react (the devil on my left shoulder said to roll my eyes and toss him a little attitude; the angel on my right kept saying, "The Vow"), I didn't say anything immediately. I went with indifferent. "Unfortunately, I'm working," I said.

"Doesn't look like you're working too hard over here by the bar," he said, teasing me. "I will tell you, though, that you're certainly looking good standing here doing nothing."

I'm sure I blushed. Was he flirting with me? Was he over the Daddy/birthday party incident? Where was the blonde? I literally had to bite my tongue to keep from asking the last question. I quickly surmised that it wouldn't hurt to be cordial; let the bitch walk up and see her man having a civil conversation—a downright pleasant one—with the mother of his child. "Why, thank you, Sean," I smiled. "I was hoping Brian over there noticed, too. Alas, no action. What brings you out on this lovely evening?"

"Well, it sure wasn't Brian McKnight," he said, wrinkling his nose. "I got an invitation from Jacob Lawrence."

"Jacob Lawrence, huh?" I said, surprised. "How'd you get that hookup?"

"He's a client," Sean deadpanned.

"Who? Jacob Lawrence?"

"Yup."

"Let me get this straight: Jacob Lawrence, the head of one of Hollywood's largest talent agencies, and the youngest player in the game, goes under your knife?"

"Yup."

"Well I'll be damned—he's what, like, thirty-seven, thirty-eight years old? And he's a dude. Since when do men get work done?"

"He's thirty-eight, and he's not the only man I've performed corrective surgery on. A good thirty percent of my business comes from men looking for a little tweaking. But you didn't hear that from me, Ms. *Daily News*—I don't want to wake up tomorrow with that in the paper, Viv," he said, getting all serious.

"But . . ."

"Uh, but nothing, Vivian Evans. If you want to keep getting that child-support check, you better keep that one to yourself. The moment my clients think their confidentiality has been violated, my business goes down the tubes—and so do those lovely checks I drop off every month. So, please, babe, keep it to yourself."

"Oh, fine," I said, feigning disgust. "Go on ahead and ruin my chances for a Pulitzer. I coulda been a contender if my baby daddy wasn't blocking my story."

Sean cracked up, and held up his finger to signal the bartender. "Yeah, um, let me get a Heineken," he said, then turned to me. "What's your poison?"

"Nothing for me. I'm still working on this cranberry and orange juice."

"Cranberry and orange juice? Come on, Viv—it's an awards night, live a little!"

"I can tell you it's not all the fun it's cracked up to be," I said. "And it'll help to be sober if I'm going to put the moves on ol' Brian over there."

"Okay, first of all, I'm not going to be taking too much more commentary on Brian McKnight. He's corny anyway. Second of all, if you have something stronger than juice, you might be inspired to stop hugging the bar and actually get to work."

"For your information, I'm working quite hard right now, and I need to stay just as sober when I'm working as you do. Why you so worried about the *Daily News*'s quotes all of a sudden? Or is it that you're just trying to get me drunk? Where are your drinking partners, anyway?" I asked, the closest I got to inquiring about the blonde.

"Mmm, now there's an interesting prospect—Vivian Evans, looking sexy and feeling tipsy. You know, a brother might be tempted to take advantage of a good-looking drunk woman on a rich night like this," Sean said, leaning in closer to me. "I came alone. You drink. I'll watch."

I have to admit, I wasn't exactly expecting that compliment, but I was quick on my feet—I knew an opportunity when I heard it. My man was moving toward a proposition. Damn if I wasn't going to hear it and take advantage. A little play was in order. I frowned, smirked, and then let out a definitive, "Negro, please. What in the world has gotten into you—you been drinking?"

He laughed heartily, ran his fingers over his locks, and shook his head. "Can't pull the wool over Vivian Evans' eyes, can I?" he said.

"No, Negro, you can't. No matter how much I love me some Sean, I think I can smell a con job coming and going. I know you much too well to know that there are plenty other women in this town who would be more than happy to keep you company—a few of them to whom you'd probably like to return the favor, so cut the Billy Dee act."

"You're absolutely right, Vivian Evans—you do love me, and you know me well," he said, laughing some more.

"Nice try, though. Keep that up and one of these days you might just win an Oscar of your own."

"You know what, Vivian? That's what I love about you—you never hesitate to put 'em in their place." He was quiet for a minute, as was I. Our eyes scanned the room, neither of us sure of what to say next. A waiter broke the silence when he sashayed over to us with a tray full of sushi—part of the Asian-fusion theme the Jacob Lawrence Agency had created for the evening. "Uni roll?" he practically sang. I was tired of the finger foods, and I definitely was in no mood for raw fish that had been circulating around a party for hours, so I passed. So did Sean. "I'm hungry, and this sushi isn't getting it. Want to go get a bite to eat?" he said.

I was beside myself but unsure of how to respond. Here I was with the love of my life, who was inviting me out for some one-on-one, presumably to spend some time together—and not to discuss child support, or get into an argument over the care of our child, or what went wrong at Corey's birthday party. But where was the blonde? And why was he all of a sudden asking me out? And where was this sudden interest coming from? Did my rendezvous with Daddy have anything to do with this?

I had to ask—hey, I ask questions for a living, and damn if I wasn't going to get the 411 on that chick.

"How would your friend feel about that?" I said.

"What friend?" he said, looking at me quizzically.

"Your friend who crashed Corey's birthday party."

Sean looked perplexed, then sheepish. "You know, Viv, she isn't who you think she is," he said.

"Oh, really? Seems like the two of you were pretty friendly at that record-release party, and she was practically clinging to your arm when you showed up on my front stoop," I said quickly.

"Viv—she's my publicist," he said simply.

"Your publicist?" I said. My eyes widened. "What does a plastic surgeon need with a publicist?"

He sucked his teeth and tossed his head back. "Come on, Viv—I just told you Jacob Lawrence himself is a client. How do you think I get high-profile people like him to bring their business my way?"

I didn't say anything, just raised my eyebrow and nodded. So she wasn't what I thought she was, huh? Well, that certainly changed things.

So what's a girl to do on a starry night with a half-drunk ex she's still got the hots for who's asking her out for a meal that will likely end up hotter and steamier than any plate we could get at a late-night eatery? A half-drunk ex I had to convince to propose and marry me in the next ten months? Not for nothing, but this could jump-start my Vow. I had to force myself not to jump at the invitation. You know, play it cool. But not too cool. "Actually, I probably should be getting back to the house soon," I said, turning him down but trying to add just the right mix of reluctance so that he'd know I was interested. I didn't want to sound desperate, but I did want to go out with him. "My mom will be bringing Corey home pretty early tomorrow so he can get ready for school, and I'll need to get his things together before I turn in, so . . ." I said trailing off.

"Um, okay, well, are you sure? It's still early yet," he said, searching his watch. It was just after midnight.

"I've been at it for a while, and I really want to get out of these shoes. I love them, but they don't exactly feel like sneakers," I said.

"Hmm, sounds like the lady could use a massage," he said.

"You offering?" I asked. It just slipped out—I certainly didn't mean to make it seem like I was throwing myself at him. But Sean was the foot massage master. He'd taken a few courses in college when he was a freshman studying to be a sports trainer, and I was the happy recipient of many a foot and calf rub, particularly when I was carrying our child and could barely feel my legs and feet from the pressure of the pregnancy. Dr. Jordan (what I started calling him when he switched his major to premed) even prescribed yoga therapy for me to help stretch my limbs and make me feel more comfortable and relaxed in the final days before I gave birth. It worked. Not that it didn't still hurt like hell, but my labor was only three hours, and it took only ten minutes of pushing to bring our son into this world—unheard of for a first-time mom— and my OB-GYN assured me that it was due in large part to my exercise and massage regimen.

"I'll make a deal with you: you make me some of those delicious banana pancakes of yours, and I'll give you a massage you'll never forget."

And, yes, I worked him out like a . . . what did Amaya say? A porn star. But even though our tryst on the living room floor at my place was exceptional, what happened after our hot and heavy session was by far the more interesting part of the evening—well, morning. After we'd finished making love, Sean, like the gentleman he is, got up and got a sista a cool drink, a pillow, and a blanket so that we could cuddle on the couch while Donny Hathaway's voice filled the room. And we just got to talking about Corey and what we wanted for him, and how hard it must be for him to live with his daddy in one place and him in another and how lucky we had it growing up with both our parents in the house and how we were going to work really hard to give him as normal a life as possible. "Wouldn't it be something, though, if he could have a mom and dad in the same house, though?" I'd said after we grew silent, each of us lost in our thoughts of our son.

"I guess," Sean said quietly. "But there'd have to be a solid foundation, with a lot of love and very little conflict for it to work. Who's to say that could happen with us?"

"Who's to say it couldn't?" I asked, turning to look him in his beautiful eyes.

"It hasn't worked for us in a long time," he said quietly. "We were kids when it last did."

"And now we're grown, and we've lived and dated and loved enough to know what it takes for it to work, haven't we?"

"One would think so," he said. "One would think so."

Donny sang some more, and now Sean was singing with him as he slowly stroked my hair. And Donny was absolutely right: for all we know, tomorrow is made for sun.

After our birthday party blow-up, I tossed that bridal magazine into the recycling bin; I was sure that the white girl was signal enough that Sean didn't love me anymore. But now, as I lay in the arms of the love of my life, I made a mental note to retrieve it the moment Sean pulled his car out of the driveway.

10

TRISTA

Waking up in Garrett's arms feels heavenly. I burrow deeper into his warm embrace, our naked bodies a puzzle of tangled limbs. I kiss him softly on the lips as he sleeps. I wish I could stay here in his arms a little longer but I need to get to work. But before I go into the office I've got to go home and change clothes. I can't exactly roll into the office wearing the white satin Dolce & Gabana pantsuit and the Blahnik Swarovski-crystal-studded sandals I wore to the awards last night. Although I must admit, this suit, with the single diamond-cluster button closure that Amaya convinced me must be worn without a top, was so fierce I'd dare somebody to say something about it.

It had been quite a night. Cassidy won the award for best actress and I was on top of the world. I was a little miffed that she thanked the firm in her acceptance speech and not me personally, but the thumbs-up I got from Mr. Banks reassured me. And watching Steven seethe while standing next to his uncle was the icing on my cake.

After the awards, Garrett and I got into one of the limousines The Agency had hired for the night and headed over to the *In Style* party. Just as Garrett broke open a bottle of Cristal in the back of the car to celebrate, my father called on my cell to congratulate me. When he tried to pass the phone to my sister, I heard her say she needed to go check on Tyquan. I told my dad I'd make it over this weekend to tell him all about it. I refused to let Tanisha's nastiness get to me that night.

The *In Style* party was a lavish affair. The candlelit room had been

transformed into a beautiful vineyard. Arbor-like structures were sta-
tioned around the perimeter of the room, framing the rich, jewel-toned
linens on the tables. The intoxicating scent of the towering floral
arrangements hit us as soon as we walked in the door.

Most of the major category winners were there and Cassidy glowed
center stage. When she saw me making my way into the party, she
screamed my name and ran over as quickly as possible in her form-
fitting, Grecian-style, one-shoulder gown in the exact same shade of
gold as the statuette she clutched to her breast. Carefully orchestrated
tears streamed down her face. Before I could tell her that this was only
the beginning of the things I foresaw for her career she was yanked away
by her publicist to take pictures. No matter, I was high on winning. That
night, studio heads—people whose "people" I could normally only talk
to—came up to me to offer their congratulations. I also fielded a lot of
interest in Jared's career and in some other of my clients as well. By far
one of the biggest highlights was when some stars I knew were shopping
for new representation dropped thinly veiled hints that they would be
open to the idea of lunch. I ducked into a corner and whipped out my
BlackBerry to email Adriene, asking her to schedules dates as soon as
possible. It was my night. I had made it. And I was sharing the spotlight.

Wearing a black tuxedo that would've put James Bond to shame,
Garrett stood by my side the entire night. We flowed seamlessly through
the crowd. I liked the feel of his hand at the small of my back as we
moved through the party. He knew quite a few of the people there and
introduced me to his colleagues as his "girlfriend." I really liked the
sound of that. When we talked, it felt as if no one else was in the room.
And I'm never like that at a function where I could be making contacts.
But it seemed like everyone else just faded into the background and all
that mattered was being in this moment with Garrett. As the night went
on, and the drinks kept flowing, I got high on winning, and on Garrett.

A bathroom break would change all that.

After I made my way back into the party I heard someone calling my
name. When I turned around, I saw Damon striding toward me. What's

he doing here? I considered bolting in the other direction but thought better of it. This is *my* turf. Besides, I'd had just enough champagne to tell him off.

"Hey, Trista," he said when he made it through the crowd, "you look amazing. Congratulations." As he leaned in to kiss me on the cheek I pulled back.

"Thank you," I said icily. Damn, he looked good. The tailored tuxedo fit him very well, but I was determined not to give him the satisfaction of a compliment.

"Did you get my email?"

"What are you doing here?" I asked testily, looking around the room for Garrett.

"I came with my boss, who sits on the board of one of the studios, hoping to see you. Look, I owe you an explanation about what happened in Atlanta." I cut him off before he could continue.

"Damon, what happened in Atlanta is long forgotten. This is the best night of my life and the last thing I want to do is rehash a mistake I made months ago with you," I said as I took a sip of champagne. As I tilted my glass, some of the champagne spilled onto the top of my breasts and ran down between them. I saw his eyes follow the path and I felt a surge of power. "So what is it you want, Damon?"

"I just want to say I'm sorry. That woman, Alicia, was someone that I broke things off with right before I came to the wedding, but she flew out to try to surprise me."

"Well, you looked surprised all right." I laughed bitterly.

"Yes, I *was* surprised by her appearance, but more important," he said as he took my hand in his, "I was surprised by all the old feelings when I saw you again."

Just as I tried to snatch my hand back, someone stepped between us. Standing a bit too close, it was evident in the way Steven slurred his words, and from the smell of his breath, that he'd had a lot to drink. I stepped back to escape his foul breath.

"Well, Trista, congrats," he said with mock sincerity, as he took another swig of the amber-colored liquid in his glass, spilling some on his tux. He was clearly drunk. I could see his adult acne flaring up in response to his frustration. I thought about suggesting a topical ointment.

"Thank you, Steven," I answered coolly.

"Guess you just got lucky," he said. I felt Damon stiffen beside me.

"Yeah, Steven, whatever . . ."

"Well, don't get too cocky and think you're automatically making partner," he sneered, his eyes narrowing into little angry slits.

But now I didn't care who the hell his uncle was. I was ready to get straight South Central on his ass.

"I think we're finished with this conversation," interrupted Damon as he took me by my elbow to lead me away from Steven. As he turned to make his way past, he brushed Steven hard enough to knock him down into one of the potted trees. Steven dropped his drink and spilled the rest of the contents in his lap. All I could do was laugh at the sight of the waiters trying to help him out of the tree.

"Hey," I tried to protest but Damon kept moving through the crowd. I saw Garrett looking around the room for me, but he didn't see us. Damon led me into a deserted room.

"Trista, what the hell was that all about?" he asked, as he loosened his bow tie.

"That was just a guy I work with who's not happy about me winning tonight. And what does it matter to you?"

"It matters to me because I didn't like the way he was talking to you."

"Oh, I'm sorry, did you think he was disrespecting me? Well, that was nothing compared to the way you disrespected me in Atlanta! And the way you've always disrespected me and what I want."

"I told you what happened there. I tried to find you to explain, but you took off just like you always do when you're faced with something you don't want to deal with."

"Damon, the only thing I don't want to deal with anymore is you.

You don't owe me any explanation. I'm not trying to hear anything you've got to say. This is so typical of you. Can't you see? I've done it! I've done everything I said I was going to do. And you know what? I did it without you!"

"Trista, I'm proud of you. More than you'll ever know. But I don't know why you felt like you had to do it on your own."

"Well, I'm *not* on my own anymore, Damon. I'm with someone who completely supports me and isn't threatened by my success." He seemed surprised at this last statement.

"Is that what you think? That I'm threatened by your success? Trista, is that all you think is still between us?"

"But that's just it, Damon. I don't want there to be anything between us. It's over. Let's just let it go, Damon. It's over." At the sound of someone opening the door we jumped apart.

"Oh, excuse me," apologized a waitress as she quickly backed out and shut the door behind her. I took this interruption as my chance to escape and bolted from the room. I heard him calling my name behind me but I moved through the crowd until I found Garrett.

"Hey, baby. Did you get lost?" he asked as he wrapped his arm around my waist to pull me close and kiss my forehead.

"No, there was just a really long line in the ladies room," I answered trying not to sound as flustered as I felt.

"Are you about ready to go?" he asked.

"You read my mind. I think I'm ready for a private celebration," I whispered seductively in his ear. "Let's get out of here." When we got outside we had to wait for the attendant to call for our car. Just as it pulled up, I saw Damon step out of the party and light a cigar. When he looked up he saw us standing under the awning.

"Trista, are you leaving?" he asked, his eyes searched mine.

"Uh, yes, Damon. It was nice to see you," I said, as I tried to sound casual. What more could I say to have him get the message that we're over? Then I got an idea.

"Damon, this is Garrett James, my boyfriend. Garrett, this is an old friend from college, Damon Reynolds." I watched Damon as he absorbed my words and thought I saw a flicker of surprise, but then it disappeared and he shook Garrett's extended hand.

"Nice to meet you, man," Garrett said. "What brings you to L.A.?"

"I just moved here to open an office," Damon said.

"What line of business are you in?"

"I work with Global Investments."

"GI? Oh, wow, I've got a meeting with you guys next week to discuss representation. I'm a managing partner with Williams, Nave, Townsend and James." I couldn't believe my ears. Did he just say what I think he said? This can't be happening.

"Cool," said Damon. "Look forward to it, man. See you around, Trista." Damon winked at me, shook Garrett's hand again, and told him he looked forward to talking to him next week.

I SLIP OUT of Garrett's bed and begin to pick up my clothing from the floor but can't seem to find my thong. I blush with the memory of how it came off last night. To rid my mind of thoughts of Damon, I initiated a little foreplay in the limo. When I tuned the radio to my favorite station, the DJ must have known what I had in mind because Prince's "I Want to Be Your Lover" was playing. I thought Garrett would get off on the thought that the driver could be watching us, so I left the tinted partition down halfway and then climbed on his lap. I figured right. As I loosened the button on my blazer, I could feel that he was already aroused. Luckily it was a quick ride to his house in the hills. Once we made it to his bedroom, I decided to try something from the Blow and Get Low course. The finale for my little show was removing my thong and tossing them onto his head, but I'm not sure where it went after that. I crawl around on the floor and reach around under the bed with my hand, hoping it got kicked under there.

"Good morning, beautiful," says Garrett as he yawns, stretches, and sits up in his bed. He pushes a button on the nightstand and the blinds open to reveal a breathtaking view of the Hollywood hills.

"Good morning to you, too," I say as I abandon my search and climb back into the bed. I straddle his body and lean down to kiss him. "How are you this morning, baby?"

"Mmmm . . . I'm doing real good now," he says sleepily as he grabs my hips.

"What you got going on down there?" I ask as I lean down and begin to kiss his lips and flick my tongue along the side of his neck.

"Watch yourself, girl. You know that's my spot."

"Oh, I know that's your spot. But right now, it's all mine." I laugh softly as I continue to work my way down his hard body.

"Now that's how I'd like to be awakened every morning," he says as he pulls me up by the shoulders and kisses me long and deep.

"Every morning, huh?" I say, teasingly tracing the outline of his mouth with my tongue. He's right, this is a nice way to start your morning, wrapped in the arms of someone special. Sharing the most important night of my life with Garrett had felt like the most natural thing in the world.

"Don't start anything, 'cause I've got to go," I say, deciding that I better get my clothes on before we start making love again. Smiling, I slide down the length of his long, hard body, and off the end of the bed to resume the search for my missing underwear.

"Gotcha," I say as I pull out something from under the bed. But when I get it in the light I see that it's not my black thong but a large purple polyester g-string.

"What the fuck?" I say, eyes flashing as I stand up and hold the offending object in two fingers, then fling it onto his naked chest. I don't even want to think of the type of woman he was fucking that would wear that mess.

"What's this?" he asks as he looks down at the wrinkled ball of purple spandex.

"Why don't you tell me, you sorry motherfucker." I hunt desperately around the room for my clothes, hoping I can make it out of there before I totally lose it.

"Trista, please let me explain," he says and jumps up out of the bed, wrapping the sheet around his waist.

"No explanation necessary. I think I know all I need to know. You've been fucking some cheap, fat-ass ho." I decide to skip looking for the thong—let some other woman find my underwear next time—and quickly pull on my pants and jacket. In the harsh light of day, the single-button clasp feels ridiculous, but I close the jacket as much as I can over my breasts and stuff my feet into the crystal-studded shoes.

"Trista, please. It was a long time ago."

"Whatever, Garrett." I grab my satin clutch off the nightstand and storm out of his bedroom. When I get downstairs I suddenly remember that we came to his house in the limo. How am I going to get home? Fuck, it's not like I can just walk home. I pull my cell phone out of my handbag and call the one person I know is up this early.

"Vivian Evans, *Daily News*," says Viv when she picks up. I can hear the sound of her typing on her computer in the background.

"It's Trista," I say, breathing heavily. "Look, I know you're probably on deadline but can you please come get me from Garrett's house?"

"Sure, but just one question—are you okay?" she asks, her voice immediately filling with concern.

"Yeah, I'm fine. I'll tell you what happened when you get here. I'm at 1603 Valley View Drive. Please hurry." It only takes about thirty minutes for Viv to get there, but it feels like forever as I lock myself in one of Garrett's bathrooms to avoid talking to him. He sits outside the door, trying to explain that the g-string was from a long time ago and how much he really wants us to work this out. I keep flushing the toilet to drown him out. When I hear Viv blow her horn outside I stomp past him and slam the front door behind me.

WHEN I CLIMB into the passenger seat of Viv's Saab, I see that Amaya's in the back, drinking a cup of Starbucks, wearing dark glasses, no makeup, and a wrinkled T-shirt and shorts. Jesus, is that a banana clip in her hair? She obviously just woke up as she never leaves the house without full makeup and hair.

"Did you have to bring her?" I sigh, realizing I'm about to get the third degree.

"I had to bring backup because I didn't know what I was walking into," says Viv as she whips the small car down the winding canyon roads.

"You should appreciate me. Vivian woke me up out of a dead sleep to come save your ass," says Amaya as she passes her cup of coffee to me so I can take a sip. "And you know I didn't get in from the *Essence* Black Hollywood party until a couple of hours ago."

The events of the past twenty-four hours finally catch up with me and I burst into tears. By the time I finish telling them the whole story, we arrive at my condo. We pile out of the car and make our way inside. I head upstairs to take a quick shower and change my clothes.

When I come back down, hair in a ponytail, wearing shorts and a T-shirt, I see that Viv has made scrambled eggs, bacon, and toast. We all sit down at the table.

"Can you believe this mess?" I ask no one in particular as I butter my toast.

"Girl, this is some *Days of Our Lives* shit you got going on right here," says Amaya, munching on a slice of turkey bacon.

"She's not the only candidate for an episode of *Days of Our Lives*," says Viv. "I mean, one day Sean is romping around town with a white woman, the next he's opening the door to a possible life together. Then he simply stops calling except when he needs to ask me something about our son. Not to mention the thing with Daddy, a man who, professionally, stands for everything I rail against. I'm so confused, I don't know which way is up."

"Damn, y'all are both a mess," says Amaya. "Personally, my love life is right on track. Yours truly has hooked up with the hottest forty-two-points-a-game rookie in the NBA, and now that Keith gotten a whiff of the competition, I'll be marching down the aisle before you know it."

"I just can't believe Garrett is seeing someone else," I say.

"Are you serious?" asks Amaya. "No disrespect, but you haven't actually been faithful. I mean, are you and Garrett even in a monogamous relationship?"

"That's true," says Viv. "I'm not saying you don't have a right to be upset, but you did sleep with Damon while you were seeing Garrett—admittedly, I guess, that was the early stages of the relationship."

"So are you saying I don't have a right to be upset?" I ask indignantly.

"I'm not saying that at all," says Amaya. "I just don't understand why you're getting all worked up over Garrett's stuck-up behind if you're doing your own thing, too. And besides, you look too good to be crying over his behind. You got to get yours, girl."

"I feel that Trista should look at some of the things she's done but I also think she should dump Garrett," says Viv. "You don't know who that g-string belongs to or how long it's been there."

"Does it matter how long it's been there?" I ask as I stab at my eggs, wishing they were Garrett's eyes.

"Not in this day and age," says Viv vehemently.

"I hear you, but we're perfect together," I whimper. I hate myself for sounding so whiny, but it's true. Garrett and I are made for each other. Was finding some underwear that he said was from long ago a reason to throw it all away? Besides, we're together practically every night, and when we're not, he's with his boys or at work. When would he have time to hook up with someone else?

"Well, he did say it was from a while ago. And he was introducing me last night as his girlfriend. We never did have a formal conversation about where this relationship was going and I guess I always knew he could technically be sleeping with other women—but I just didn't want to think that he actually was."

"Does he get a pass for this?" asks Viv, cutting to the chase.

"I'm not saying he gets a pass . . ." Amaya starts to say, but stops when the doorbell rings.

"Who could that be?" I mutter, walking to the front door. Looking through the peephole, I see Garrett. I can't believe he has the nerve to come here. I run back into the kitchen and tell Amaya and Viv that he's here.

"So what are you going to do?" asks Amaya as the doorbell rings again.

"I don't know. What should I do?"

"Look, girl, at least talk to him and see what he has to say," says Amaya, clearing the dishes from the table and setting them in the sink. "Just keep in mind what *you've* done and haven't told him about." Amaya and Viv hug me, give Garrett the evil eye as they pass him, then let him in the house on their way out the door.

I BOIL SOME water for a pot of tea, mostly to keep myself from having to face Garrett immediately. I grab a wicker tray and place the teapot and two cups on it to bring it out onto the deck, where he's waiting. Garrett stands up and takes the tray from me and sets it on the glass table.

Dressed in a pair of faded jeans, white T-shirt, and brown leather driving moccasins, Garret absentmindedly massages the back of his neck.

When he doesn't say anything for a few minutes I jump up full of nervous energy and begin watering the flower boxes hanging along the railing. As I walk past Garrett he reaches out and pulls me back toward him. With his face buried in my back, he holds me tightly as I try to twist away.

"Trista, I'm so sorry," he says, his voice slightly muffled by my T-shirt.

"For what? You don't owe me anything." As soon as I say the words I feel like I've said them before. It reminds me of my conversation with Damon.

Suddenly I feel tired. I stare out at the surf as it washes up against the shore. I'm so sick and tired of the games. Black men can have any woman they want. They've got women throwing themselves at them all the time, willing to do whatever they want, whenever they want. But I don't want to compete.

"I'm so sick of this shit," I say, dropping the half-empty watering can. Some of the water splashes onto my bare feet and Garrett's shoes.

"I know, I know," he says.

"No, Garrett. I don't think you do know." I decide to be totally honest for once. I pull away from him and turn to face him. "I'm through with this bullshit, Garrett. The bullshit of dating black men. Of dating people who clearly don't have my best interests at heart. Of dating people for whom all of this is just a game, just another conquest." I think I may be scaring him, but I don't care and just keep going.

"I'm sick of playing games with you guys, acting like I don't care. I don't want to play games anymore. I don't want to worry about who my man is sleeping with. I want to be in love and want somebody to love me back. To share this, the best time of my life, with this person. For real. We've been seeing each other for a few months now and I realize we haven't discussed a commitment or anything, but would it be reasonable to expect that you weren't fucking anybody else?"

"Trista, that happened a long time ago, and I swear it's not going on anymore," he says pulling me onto his lap.

"Garrett, I don't know if you are or aren't seeing her anymore, but I can't do this." Again I try to pull away from him, but he still won't let me go.

"You're exactly right. I'm tired of playing games. When we're together I just don't want to be anywhere else. We're made for each other, Trista." He strokes the side of my cheek and kisses me softly on the lips. I want to believe him. I want this to be it. For him to be the one. But how can I be sure?

"Trista, I'm not going to lie to you and say that I've been perfect, because I haven't. But what I can say is, I want to be honest about my feelings today and going forward." He takes my face in his hands and stares into my eyes. "Trista, I think I'm falling in love with you. I've

never felt this way before." As I look at him I want to believe in what he's
saying. Could he be the one? He is the first person I've ever been with
who seems to get me. He's the first person to encourage and support my
ambition and not be threatened by it.

"I want to believe you, Garrett, I really do," I murmur softly.

"Then believe me, Trista," he says, kissing me on the cheek and
neck. "Believe in us." He slips his hands under my T-shirt and caresses
my back.

"How do I know you won't hurt me?" He never answers my question, just picks me up and carries me back into the house and up to my
bedroom.

ON SUNDAY I attend the early service at church and then go to see my
father. "Daddy," I call out as I let myself into the house with my key. I
walk into the small living room, hoping to see him sitting in his favorite
recliner, but when I hear the sound of a television coming from the back
of the house, I head to his bedroom. Knocking softly on the door before
I walk in, I see my father propped up in bed watching *Wheel of Fortune*.

"Hi, Daddy," I say, walking into the room and sitting down on the
side of the bed. I look around the small room. The cherry furniture still
looks brand new, as Tanisha dusts it nearly every day to keep the dust
from bothering Daddy. The walls are decorated with family photos. The
only thing that looks out of place is the portable oxygen tank standing by
the bed. He lifts his oxygen mask when he sees me so he can give me a
kiss on the cheek. He's thinner than the last time I saw him.

"Hey, pumpkin," he says and smiles. I dump out the contents of the
shopping bag I'm carrying on the bed and his eyes seem to light up a bit.
There's a DVD player and a collection of John Wayne movies, plus a few
kung-fu movies for my nephew.

"Thank you, baby," he says as he squints at the box but can't seem to
make out the words. I place his glasses on his face so he can see.

"No problem, Daddy. Tyquan can probably hook up the DVD player
to your TV for you. Where's Te?" I hope she's gone to the store or some-

thing so that we won't have to see each other today and argue over Daddy's medical care.

"She's out in the back messing with the tomatoes."

"What about Ty?"

"He spent the night at a friend's house." He pulls himself up slowly in the bed.

"Daddy, did you eat today?" I ask. I see a plate with a sandwich and a bowl of soup resting on a tray table, but it doesn't look like he's touched it.

"Oh, I ate a little earlier, but you know I got to watch my figure for the ladies." He chuckles at his own joke and pats my hand reassuringly. I know it's useless to try to make him eat. I start to fold the clothes sitting in the laundry basket on the floor.

"Did you bring the statue with you?" Daddy asks.

"No, Dad," I say. I explain that even though I don't get the actual statue, I do get the recognition at work.

"That's great news, pumpkin. Your mother would be so proud of you." As I glance at the picture of my mother from their wedding day on his dresser, I bristle. Actually, I don't think Mama would be proud at all. In fact, she probably would have been too drunk to acknowledge my accomplishment. It's not worth arguing over.

"How are you feeling these days?" I ask, to change the subject.

"Oh, you know. Good days and bad." This is a change, as usually my father says he's doing fine and never lets on if he's feeling poorly. We talk for a little while longer, and when I finish folding his clothes I turn around to find that he's fallen asleep. Tucking the blanket up under his arms, I adjust the oxygen mask on his face, then kiss him on his forehead. I turn off the television and then pick up the tray and head to the kitchen. I see my sister, dressed in sweatpants and a T-shirt, is at the sink, rinsing off some tomatoes. Tanisha turns around at the sound of my footsteps.

"Oh, I didn't know you were here," she says.

"I was in with Daddy." I set the tray on the table and take a few bites of the sandwich. "He didn't want his lunch."

"Yeah, that's pretty much how it goes these days. I try to get him to drink fluids to stay hydrated, but now even that's becoming a challenge." She glances at the clock over the stove.

"Is it time for Daddy's medicine?" I ask, reaching for the plastic basket in the middle of the table overflowing with prescription bottles.

"Yep," she says as she pours a handful of colored pills into her hand. When she returns from Daddy's room she sits back down at the table.

"So, I see you got Daddy another new toy," she says. I can't tell if she's baiting me or she's just making an observation.

"I also brought you a little something." I gesture to an overflowing shopping bag stuffed with beauty products, cashmere pajamas, a Swiss Army watch, pearl earrings, and other goodies from the gift baskets TA had sent out to all our nominated clients.

"Thanks," she says, not even glancing at the bag. "Daddy should like that DVD player. Tyquan can hook it up when he gets home from Isaac's house this afternoon."

As she puts the pill holder back in the basket, I notice the envelope that I sent with the check for the tests is underneath. I pull it out and see that it's unopened.

"You didn't even open this?" I ask, holding up the letter.

"I told you that we'd get the money," she says gruffly.

"Tanisha, you know Aunt Brenda doesn't have the money. Now, why don't you take this money and get the tests that the doctor claims Daddy needs?"

"I worked out a payment plan with the clinic so we didn't have to come up with the money all at once. They ran the tests last week." I am seething at the thought that she didn't even call to tell me all of this, let alone inform me of the results of the tests.

"Well, what were the results?"

"We don't have them back yet," she snaps.

"Gee, what a surprise," I mumble under my breath.

"If you've got something to say, Trista, just say it."

"I don't have anything to say about the tests since I don't even know what the tests were or what they were for."

"As soon as we get the results I'll be sure to fax them over to your office."

"Tanisha, please don't try to act like I'm too busy to be concerned with my own father's health."

"Oh, yeah, right. You just pop over whenever you can with your expensive little toys and that's supposed to mean you care."

"I do care!" I say through clenched teeth. I had hoped we could talk rationally about Daddy's treatment but I should have known better. What did she think I was trying to prove? As if getting the best medical care for him was somehow going to be a bad thing. I decide to try another tactic.

"Look, Tanisha, I'm not trying to say I'm here as much as you are. You're right, you do most of the work when it comes to caring for Daddy, but I help the best way I can."

"Here we go again," she says, rolling her eyes and gesturing around the small kitchen. "Yes, Trista, we know you bought this damn house and practically everything in it, to say nothing of your little monthly checks."

"Yes, Tanisha, I do pay the bills, but I never throw that in your face. You're the one that's always bringing it up."

"You don't have to bring it up because it comes up every time I call you and you ask if I got your check, or when every time you come over here and you bring some expensive new thing or gadget for Daddy or Ty and brag about your job."

"Jesus, Tanisha," I exclaimed, "this isn't even about you. This is about Daddy. Can you focus on that for once?"

"For once? Are you serious? Who do you think I'm focused on every damn day of my life? Don't you dare tell me to focus!" She stands up, knocking over her chair.

I attempt to lower my voice to what I hope is a reasonable tone to penetrate her thick skull. "What would it hurt to have Dr. Irby at Cedars Sinai look at Daddy's records?"

"It's not about me not wanting to take Daddy to Cedars Sinai," she says putting her hand on her hip and shaking her head. "Daddy doesn't want to see a new doctor. Trista, he's old, and he's scared."

I'm too worked up to really hear her and am determined to make my point.

"But, Tanisha, we need to get him to see a specialist. Someone that really knows what they are doing." I pick the envelope up off of the floor, tear it open, and remove the check. "Please think about the specialist. And in the meantime take this check to pay for the tests. I don't want you guys worrying about the bill."

When I hold out the check to her she walks over to me and snatches it out of my hand and rips it in half and lets the pieces fall to the floor.

"I told you we don't need your money." She turns around and walks out of the kitchen. I don't even know why I bother. I'm too old to be fighting with my sister like we're still little kids. I'm sick of her acting like I'm the uncaring daughter and she's the sainted angel there to take care of Daddy's every need. Doesn't she know I want to be here more, but I do what I can to make sure he's comfortable and well cared for? Why isn't that good enough for her?

My cell rings when I get in the car. When I answer I hear Viv on the line.

"Hey, Viv, what's up?" I ask, happy to have a distraction from my sister's drama.

"Hi, I'm just calling to check in to see how you're doing," she says. "What happened with you and Garrett the other day?" I give her an abbreviated replay and tell her we're still together. There's silence on the line. "What? You think I did the wrong thing?"

"No, it's not that. It's just that . . . are you sure you can trust him?"

"About as much as you can trust Sean!" I snap back at her. Who is she to judge what I'm doing when she can't even stand up for herself with the father of her child?

"What's that supposed to mean?" I can hear the hurt in her voice.

"Nothing, forget what I said. I'm sorry. I just had another fight with my sister, so I'm just lashing out."

"It's okay," she says. "I was also just calling because I ran into Damon last night."

"Damon? Why would I care that you ran into Damon? You could run over Damon for all I care." Dammit, if he told her what happened at the party, he was going to wish he'd never moved to California. "That man is officially out of my life. Uh, did you forget about girlfriend showing up at Elise's wedding?"

"No, but you know that boy still loves your evil ass," says Viv. "Although, I have to admit, I don't know why. I could see it in his eyes that night, and now he's living in L.A., too. Shit, girl . . ."

"Whatever, ain't nobody trying to hear that nonsense," I say with what I hope is a tone full of finality.

"Look, I ran into Damon last night when I was covering a party at CroBar, and he told me the whole story about what happened in Atlanta. And seriously, you know I've got NASA-certified radar for bullshit. I believe him when he says he was broken up with that girl."

"Look, what happened in Atlanta was a mistake," I snap. "I'm happy with Garrett." What was Damon doing at CroBar, anyway, I wondered to myself. He hadn't been in town all that long and already hanging out at the hottest club in town. With all those hoochies up in there, I'm sure he didn't go home alone. When Viv tries to protest again, I cut her off quickly before hanging up the phone.

"Look, Viv, I don't want to be with Damon. It's over. Let sleeping dogs *lie*."

11

AMAYA

Today is the day. According to the tip that I got from my girl Candy, whose cousin, Sharonda, is temping in the Soular Son office, the execs are making offers this morning, and word is, the actress selected for the role is a relative unknown (hello, me all day long). The muscles in my stomach tighten involuntarily. I gotta get up. I'm way too nervous to try to go back to sleep. I slip out of my bed, grab a robe, and head downstairs to my living room, leaving my overnight guest soundly snoring in the bed.

I grab the cordless off the base and curl up on the chaise. Ring, dammit, ring! Any other day, this freaking phone would be off the hook, but now that I actually want someone to call, it's dead-ass quiet. Okay, I'm officially panicking. What if I don't get the role? What if I'm just not good enough? I've been telling myself that if only I could just catch a break, I'd show them all. And now look, I finally got my big break and I probably don't even have what it takes. How will I face everyone? I won't be able to blame it on anything but a lack of talent. I can just see the looks of pity now. My friends say that they're completely behind me, but I know that they've all had doubts about my ability to make it as a certified actress . . . especially Trista. Shoot, her ass wasn't even willing to take me on as a client back in the day, before she started landing the real A-listers. Let's not forget about Benita. Jesus! More importantly, how can I really expect Keith to leave Trixie for a wack-ass B-list actress? If I'm even that, truth be told, sometimes I'm not even sure. So on top of everything else, I'm also going to lose my man. As my throat starts to clench up, the receiver rings. I inhale deeply, promise to get right forreal, forreal if God hooks me up just this once, and answer the phone.

"Hello," I answer hesitantly.

"Amaya, wow, am I glad that I caught you," Clarence's nasal voice greets me. "You know, normally you never pick up your home phone when I call . . ."

"Yes, yes, Clarence, I know," I snip, cutting his attempt at small talk short. "But I did pick up this time, so what's going on? Do you have something that you want to tell me or are you just calling to hear the sound of my voice?"

"Well, now that you mention it, I do so love the sound of your voice . . . especially when you're saying those nasty things to me. And considering I haven't seen you in the office in a while . . ." he begins with the bullshit again.

"Jesus, Clarence! I'm so not in the mood for it this morning," I respond, getting increasingly pissed off by the second. "Do you have something to tell me or not?"

"Okay, okay, you don't have to be mean," he huffs. "I was just calling to tell you that I finally heard back from the Soular Son office."

"O-o-omigod . . ." I stutter.

"And they want you, Amaya! This is it. Babe, you're officially going to be a star!"

I felt the phone slipping from my hand as his words registered. I got it! Oh my Lord, I got it! After six and a half months of waiting, praying, and literally sweating it out, I've landed the lead role in the Soular Son film. Woo-hoo, watch out, Hollywood, I'm about to be a starra!

"Hello, Amaya, are you still there? Hello? . . ." The annoying sound of Clarence's voice in the receiver jolts me back to the conversation.

"Yes, yes, I'm here," I quickly answer as I try to stop my hands from shaking so I can pick up the phone from the floor. It takes everything in me not to scream for joy in his ear.

"So, like I was saying," he continues, "they were totally blown away by your call-back performance. Apparently, you beat out a number of very established veterans, my dear. And I don't have to tell you what costarring with Carter James is gonna do for your career! See? Just like I promised, you're cracking the A-list. Now all you'll need to do is come down to my office next week to look over the script draft and discuss what you want in your rider, okay?"

"I'll be there bright and early on Tuesday morning," I reply gleefully.

"And you know, after you sign the papers, perhaps we can have a little private celebration of our own," Clarence hints in what I'm sure he considers to be a very suggestive voice. Unfortunately, it nauseates me more than anything else.

"You're so bad, Clarence. I'll see you on Tuesday," I coo in my fakest voice and hang up on him before he can start with the phone-sex nonsense.

Humph, private celebration my behind. Luckily, I'm so ecstatic about the news, even Clarence's crassness can't ruin my moment. I remain motionless in my living room, savoring the moment. *They want me! They really, really want me!* From out of nowhere, the tears start rolling down my face. All these years I've been talking a good game but it isn't until this moment that I realize that my dreams are really coming true. I look in the mirror over the fireplace and I can see the reflection of the defiant little black girl from down bottom who refused to let anything stop her. She's finally going to get her shot at the big time. Time to call my girls . . .

"This is Trista," Trista tersely answers her direct line.

"I got it! I got it!" I start in immediately.

"What? Who is this?" she asks irritably.

"Trista, it's Amaya! I got the role of Tatiana Le Shay in the new Soular Son film," I practically scream into the phone as I jump around the living room.

"Omigod, yeah! I am so happy for you," Trista shouts back. "I told you, Amaya, I told you! Oh, sweetie, I am so happy for you! You are about to blow up!"

"I know, I know, I just can't believe this," I say in disbelief.

"Well, start believing it! And you're working with Carter James? *Humph*, some of our clients would kill for this opportunity," she joked. "You better watch your back!"

"Girl, I swear I can't feel any of my fingers or toes I'm so numb," I laugh as I wipe away the tears that continue to fall.

"Since your fingers are acting up, let me call Vivian. But please don't think that just 'cause you about to have a little bit of money that I'm your maid," she sarcastically replies. "Hold on."

As Trista clicks over to conference in Viv, my mind runs over her last comment—I am about to be rich . . . or at least a hell of a lot better off than I am right now. I was easily looking at a cute little $250,000 after taxes. I start mentally listing all the bills I'm finally going to be able to pay off, as well as all the shoes, handbags, and designer duds that I've been depriving my closet of. But first things first: I want a new place. As I survey my simple but chic one-bedroom apartment, I imagine everything I could do with about two more rooms and three more closets. As much as I love tossing around the 90210 area code, I could certainly live without it for twice the space.

"You still there?" Trista asks as she clicks back over.

"Barely," I giggle.

"This is the *Daily News*, Vivian Evans speaking," she finally answers after the fifth ring.

"Girl, what the hell took you so long to pick up the phone!?" Trista explodes before Viv finishes her greeting.

"I was conducting an interview on the other line," Viv snippily answers back.

"Stop fronting, you know you were just talking to Young Daddy," Trista teases.

"Yeah, okay, whatever you want to think," she laughs guiltily. "So what's up, what's the emergency, Tris? You calling about my Memorial Day barbeque?"

Unable to hold back any longer, I blurt out, "I got the part!"

"Huh, you got the part?" Viv questions as she slowly wraps her brain around the idea. "You got the part! Oh Lord, my girl is about to blow up!" Vivian shouts.

"I know, I know, I can't even believe it! I thought I was going to vomit when Clarence finally told me! I am so excited!"

"We're so proud of you," Trista says sincerely.

"Yeah, you busted your chops and earned this opportunity all on your own. You completely deserve every blessing that you're about to reap," seconds Viv.

"Aww, y'all are just going to keep me crying, huh?" I ask as I remember all the nights spent on the phone complaining to Viv about one bad audition or another.

"I'm serious, Amaya," Viv states.

"Well, if you're that proud, slip a mention in tomorrow's buzz page," I hint.

"Girl, please, you know how my editor is—Joel could care less about the cast of a black movie. Unless you're degrading yourself or just got out of jail, he is not studying you," she replies sarcastically.

"Please, please, please," I resort to begging. I know that once a leak gets out in the *Daily News*, my juice on the scene will increase tenfold.

"Oh, all right. I'll try, but no promises," she finally relents.

"Thank you, thank you," I gush with full faith that my girl is going to pull it off.

"Did you tell your mom yet?" inquires Trista.

"Naw, you guys were the first people I thought to call."

"Well, then, get off the phone with us and call Benita right now," barks Vivian.

"Okay, okay," I say grudgingly. "Celebratory drinks at my house later on tonight?"

"I'm there," Trista answers immediately.

"Count me in, too," chimes Viv.

"Cool, see y'all then," I say as I wipe away my tears and hang up the phone.

Instead of calling my mom, I head back upstairs at top speed and leap on top of the curled-up body in my bed. Whooping with glee, I bounce around until Keith finally pokes his sleepy head out with an extremely confused expression.

"Okay, Amaya, stop, I'm up. What's up," he asks, rubbing sleep out of his eyes.

"Baby, I got it, I got it!" I shriek.

"You got what?" he asks, still looking confused.

"I got the lead in the new Soular Son film, *The Black Crusader*! I won the role of Tatiana Le Shay," I excitedly explain as I continue bouncing around like a hyperactive five-year-old. "Your girl is about to be a cer-tified movie star!"

"*The Black Crusader*? A Soular Son film? Oh shit, that's hot," he says as he nods his head in appreciation of my accomplishment. He looks at me with a huge smile. "You know, I'm real proud of you right now. Real proud."

I finally fall down next to him on the mattress. "For real, you're proud of me?" I ask quietly as I start to play with my hair. I can feel my heart swelling. "You know, this is the best day of my life and I'm just glad that you're here with me."

"I know you've been on the grind for a minute now. I know how crazy those open casting calls can be, I see the hundreds of so-called actresses and pretty faces all vying for the same two spots they give to black girls around here. I love that you're so focused on what you want. You've got a real take-no-prisoners attitude that turns me on. And it makes me feel good to see you get everything you want," he says, stroking my arm.

"Don't you mean almost everything?" I gently correct as I stare at him, trying to find an honest answer in his eyes.

"Naw, I said what I mean. Everything—the looks, the smarts, the movie, and you know you got me," he states simply as he pulls me toward his body and kisses me deeply.

"I love you so much, Keith," I answer breathlessly without thinking. As soon as the words slip out of my mouth, I regret my statement. Things have been so great between us lately that I totally let my guard down. How could I have been so stupid as to let that slip out? I know the rules, and that four-letter word is totally taboo with this man. Keith stops for a moment and examines my face carefully. If he doesn't say something in the next ten seconds I'm going to freak out. One-two-three-four . . .

"I love you, too, baby girl," he replies huskily and pulls me in for another kiss.

Keith just said that he loves me! My mind is completely ablaze. In the two long years that we've been together, not once has he uttered those words. On the contrary, every time I start to hint around them, he'll instantly shut me down with his patented "Stop stressing, I got you ma." It had gotten to the point where I'd given up. For the second time in one day, I feel as if I've just hit the lotto.

Without uttering another word, I slowly pull my sheer nightie over my head and straddle his torso. My body is supercharged. I begin slowly sucking on his earlobe and rubbing the top of his head. He massages my lower back. "So you love me," I whisper.

Keith groans in response as he starts to squirm underneath me. I can feel his penis standing at attention as it brushes against my ass. I trail my way down to the nape of his neck with my tongue and slowly start nibbling.

"Say it again, say you love me." As he attempts to lift me off of his chest I tighten my thighs around his torso and go for his secret weak spot—the nipples. As I suck on the right one and trace circles around the left with my nail, I watch his tormented face. Keith roughly grabs my ass, places his penis between the cheeks, and starts to slowly lift me up and down his shaft. Before I lose control of the situation, I pull away and slide down to face the waistband of his gray boxer shorts. After gently placing the penis back in his drawers, I tug the front down with my teeth while pulling the back off with my hands. As soon as they're off, I look up and meet his gaze dead on.

"Say it."

"Oh baby, you know I got you," he whimpers.

I push apart his legs and crawl up between them. As my lips reach the tip of his penis, I give a quick lick. "Say it," I repeat as I softly blow on his quivering member.

"Damn, Amaya, okay. I love you. I love you," he answers urgently while simultaneously lifting his hips. In that moment, I finally see what I've been waiting all this time for—Keith surrendering himself completely to me and our love. I victoriously proceed to put all the skills I learned in our Blow and Get Low class to good use.

"Good afternoon." As usual, my mother answers the phone on exactly the third ring.

"Good afternoon, Benita," I reply as I brace myself for her sour reply.

"Well, Amaya, what a nice surprise," she replies, totally throwing me off guard with her unexpected pleasantries.

"Oh, okay. Well, I'm just calling to share some news with you," I begin as I start to gear up to inform her about the movie.

"That's so funny, because I have news of my own," she replies with a giggle.

Immediately suspicious, I put myself on time out and zero in on what Benita has to say. "By all means, you go first," I coax warily.

"Well, my dear," she begins and inhales an extended breath for dramatic effect, "your dear mother is moving back to Florida."

Mother? Moving? Who is this giggling imposter and where is my real mother, bitter-ass Benita? "Excuse me?" I sputter.

"Amaya, I've met the most wonderful man and I'm leaving Los

Angeles to be with him," she continues as I do my damndest not to drop my phone.

"It's barely been three weeks since our last lunch and you're in love?" I ask.

"Honestly, I don't know what to say," she answers, uncharacteristically at a loss for words. "From the moment we met at the Midnight Mixer event at the botanical gardens, we felt a connection. We've been together ever since."

I couldn't tell whether I was more sickened by the idea of my mother having a fairy-tale romance or the implications of her being with some man "ever since."

"Regardless, darling, aren't you just thrilled to pieces for me?" she insists. "I'll be moving to Miami as soon as I can get my things all packed up."

"Just as thrilled as I was the last two times you met Mr. Right, Benita," I reply with a little more sarcasm than intended.

"Oh, Amaya," she sighs softly, "I know it's probably difficult for you to believe but Gerald is the real deal. He has an amazing heart. In fact, he's a personal-injury attorney. Perhaps you've seen the commercials for Williams, Miller and Burke? Well that's his firm. He's opening a new office in Miami in the fall, so we're headed down to start organizing and get things in order."

"Oh Lord, not a cheesy ambulance-chaser, Benita," I sigh.

"I really resent that, Amaya. You haven't even met Gerald. He happens to be very successful at what he does."

"Why am I not surprised," I mutter under my breath.

"Excuse me?"

I wonder to myself, could that new tone in her voice be sincerity? Impossible. "I'm just saying. I've been down this marriage road with you before. At least before you were clear that it was about the money. Now you're talking about some real deal and it's all happening in the next three weeks," I respond, unwilling to relent.

"I see. Hopefully, when you meet him you'll understand. I haven't felt this way since I met your father and . . . well, I'm sure you can understand—there's nothing like being head-over-heels in love," she says softly.

Benita was head-over-heels in love with my father? Whoa. I couldn't remember ever hearing a kind word pass her lips about my father in my entire life. This Gerald guy must be something special. "Listen, Benita, if you like him, that's more than enough for me. But I was actually calling to inform you that I've landed a lead role in the new Soular Son film, *The Black Crusader*," I say, steering the conversation back my way.

"Well, I must say, that's certainly not what I was expecting to hear, but congratulations nonetheless. I'm pleased to see that all that money you've been spending on your so-called acting classes have paid off," Benita replies.

"Thank you, I think."

"So, how much money will you really make from this project? And an even better question, how long will it last you?"

Aha, now *there's* the Benita I know and . . . I *knew* there was a reason I didn't call her first. She can never be completely happy for me—there's always something with her. "I'll make a decent amount for a first-time lead, Benita. But more important are the doors that will open for me after this film. It has the potential to really take me to the next level," I explain with as much patience as I can muster.

"Yes, well, I'm just concerned about how you'll maintain yourself, Amaya," she continues. "You know, you're not going to be thirty-something forever. You really should find yourself a more stable situation."

"I assume you're talking about a partner with a substantial income," I answer, completely exasperated at the direction the conversation has taken.

"Well, I'm just saying. How are things with Keith going? Has having Troy around as live bait helped at all? I've seen the two of you on the buzz pages a couple times. You do make a handsome couple."

"Actually, I think I'm really making progress. Keith actually told me that he loved me this morning. So I guess having Troy around has helped. Although, I must admit, I'm enjoying Troy's company way beyond him being live bait for Keith."

"Hmmm, I'm pleased to hear that Mr. Bennett is good company, but I hope you're not losing focus. An 'I love you' is nice, but it's nowhere near signed divorce papers."

"No, I am not losing focus. But do tell, whatever happened to patience?" I ask sarcastically, happy to have an opportunity to throw her words back at her.

"With me moving, I'm just afraid that you won't stay on track, my dear. I certainly don't want to look up and have a forty-year-old spinster on my hands."

"Don't worry, Benita, that's not going to happen. Not only do I plan to be extremely successful and self-sufficient, I have no doubt that I will not be alone," I answer with much more confidence than I feel.

"If you say so," she concludes. "Well, my darling, let me go. Please don't forget to make the reservations for our final brunch. I'll talk to you then. Smooches."

"Smooches," I reply as I slowly place the receiver back on the base and fall back listlessly into my pillows, devoid of all my earlier excitement. No matter how much I try to fight it, Benita always manages to snatch the wind completely out of my sails.

As I PULL out of my parking garage an hour later, my mind is still scrambling to process all this new information. Benita in love? Not only in love but about to move back to Miami (a city she swore never to return to, come hell or high water) for some man named Gerald she just met three weeks ago? How is it that one woman can find so many men willing to love her and I can't even convince one to take me seriously? Shit, my sorry ass just got an "I love you" for the first time, and I've been with Keith for *how* long? I silently fume as I head over to G. Garvin's to meet Troy for our lunch date.

Clearly spending time with Troy and Keith's sudden good behavior has thrown me off my Vow game plan for a couple of months, but thanks to Benita's little revelation the blinders are off. It's time to get back on track. I can't have my mom manage to get yet another proposal before I even get my first. And not for nothing, there are only four months to go until the end of the year. I pull my cell out of my gold Louis Vuitton bag, dial information, and ask to be connected to the Eye Spy Surveillance Company as I pull out onto the 405. I make an appointment to swing by their office at six P.M. Keith can keep talking all that love shit till the cows come home, I'm about to get some proof on Trixie to help light the divorce fire up under his behind.

As I PASS BY a young white woman in her early thirties with an engagement ring the size of a baby's fist on her hand waiting at the entrance of the restaurant for the valet to pull her car around, I become even more irritated. As much as I hate listening to my mother, she's right: I'm not going to be thirty-something forever. I need someone to share the rest of my life with. As far as I'm concerned I've been more than patient, and right about now I need a bit of instant gratification.

As soon as I walk inside, I sense all eyes on me and my green-jersey backless Chloe halter dress. It was just one of those dresses that make it good to be a black woman with tight curves. As the maître d' leads me over to Troy's table in the back, I notice that, as usual, he's not alone. It seems like more and more, Troy is finding it impossible to separate himself from his cronies. Unless we're attending an invite-only event, I can guarantee that he'll be accompanied by two or three of his clown-ass teammates. Rookies who don't know how to act with all that new money. I don't get it—don't they spend enough time with each other at practice, on the road, and during the games? I swear, they're like high school boys. Always making crude jokes about women and discussing sports. It's one of the only things about Troy that works my nerves. I really wish he would try to act older than his twenty-two years and cut them short. Thankfully, he dismisses the crew just as I'm seated, then starts in with his usual round of compliments. Not that I don't appreciate hearing what he has to say, but today I'm on a mission.

"Sweetie, we need to talk," I blurt out, interrupting him mid-sentence.

"What's up?" he asks, cheesing from one diamond-studded ear to the other.

"Basically, it's two things," I begin. "First of all, I just found out today that I got that part in the Soular Son film."

"Amaya, that's so hot! I'm so happy for you," he exclaims as he reaches over to kiss me. "I can't wait to see my girl kicking ass on the big screen!"

"Wait a minute, Troy," I say as I struggle to untangle myself from his embrace. "Let me finish!"

"My bad, babe, go 'head, then," he apologizes.

"Well, this film also means that there are going to be a lot of changes in my life," I start again once I straighten my dress. "I'm going to be traveling for long periods of time to the different shoot locations. I'll be meeting a lot of new people, and my personal life is about to become a lot more public."

"Okay, so what's your point?" he asks, sounding slightly confused. "I mean, it's not like everyone doesn't already know we're dating."

"That's my point right there—we're dating. As far as I can see, there's no commitment in that. At the end of the day, you can very well turn around and be with some random chick and you wouldn't even owe me so much as an explanation, Troy."

"Yo, you know I would never do that to you, Amaya. My word is my bond. You're the only woman that I'm seeing. You're like my wifey," he says defensively.

"I don't want to be a wifey, Troy. I want to be a wife," I implore as I grab one of his huge hands in both of mine. "I know it's only been five months, but I'm sure about the way I feel about you. And we spend all this time together, anyway . . ."

"Aww, man. Come on now. What's wrong with the way things are going?" he questions suspiciously as he gently pulls his hand away.

"Not a damn thing," I spit back, changing up my needy-nice-girl tactic mid-flow. "As a matter of fact, forget I even brought the shit up. Let's just eat."

"Whoa, whoa, ma, hold up, now." Unlike Keith, Troy had never witnessed my queen bitch side before. He immediately starts to back-pedal into safer territory. "You ain't got to get mad like that."

"I ain't mad, it's cool," I say, blocking my face with the menu.

"Naw, for real," he says and gently moves the menu from in front of me. "If it's that serious to you, fine. I hear you."

"And just what does you 'hear me' mean, Troy?" I inquire frostily.

"It means, it might not happen tomorrow or even next week but you'll have a set of keys to the crib and whatever else you need to be happy before you step one of your pretty toes on that set, okay?" he says with a resigned grin.

I suppress my urge to jump on his lap right there in the restaurant and simply say, "I don't want you to do anything you're not comfortable with, Troy."

"Trust, I'm not doing anything I don't want to, Amaya," he answers. "Now let's stop discussing and start celebrating because my baby is about to be a supa-dupa-star!"

ONE DOWN AND one to go, I smugly think to myself as I sit back on the cool black leather couch in the enormous reception area of Eye Spy Surveillance. The cute gay receptionist informs me that Ms. Smith will be out shortly and offers me a glass of water. I politely decline and continue to fidget with the strap of the gold Rolex Troy bought me last week. The sound of CNN on the flat-screen drones in the background as I debate whether I should even bother spending all this money to trap Trixie. I mean, I did hear the woman with my very own ears, and my word should be golden right about now. If Keith doesn't want to believe me, fuck him. I still have Troy. Just as I rise to leave, Lisa enters the room. As soon as I see her, I change my mind—one can never be too safe. I greet her with a quick hug and follow her down the hall. A striking brunette in some bad-ass Sergio Rossi pumps, Lisa looks like she'd be more at home on a runway than a stakeout. Raised in a family of cops and private eyes, she runs this thriving business with her older brothers. Although her client list is strictly confidential, from the single case that I helped with, it's obvious to me that Lisa works with some big dogs.

After catching up for about fifteen minutes, I candidly explain my situation. I tell her everything from how long Keith and I have been dating to the day in the Armani dressing room to Keith's declaration of love this very morning. Shoot, it's better than a damn therapy session. Lisa listens wordlessly, nodding her head and taking notes, interrupting only once or twice for a clarification. When I finally finish, she reviews her notes again and assures me that it sounds like a pretty standard case. The only obstacle would be if Trixie were working on a film out of town. From the sounds of it, this Sam guy is in Los Angeles. I agree and promise to do some research to find out whether or not she's going to be filming anything within the next couple of months and get back to Lisa as soon as possible.

With that out of the way, Lisa proceeds to explain a few "extra" options available with her service: photos or video, phone tap or list and length of cell-phone calls, credit-card receipts . . . it went on and on. As much as I would like to get the works on Trixie, I know that my friend-of-the-family discount is only going to carry me so far. I don't possess nearly the amount of money necessary to make those dreams come through. So I simply settled for color photos, digital and print. I make out a check for $900, and make a mental note to swing by the post office to check my PO box for this month's Dead Straight check. As I rise to leave Lisa's office, I can feel my good mood from earlier return. Maybe speaking to Benita wasn't such a bad thing after all. Thanks to her needling, I'm back on track with my private-investigation plans for Keith, and I've even forced Troy to step up his game. Score another for the little black girl; it's full steam ahead!

12

VIVIAN

I walk into Young Daddy MC's house, fully expecting to find the standard rapper decor: black leather couches; bland white paint; cheap, gold-trimmed étagères filled with insignificant mementos and sports memorabilia; a framed poster of Al Pacino from *Scarface*; a full collection of blaxploitation DVDs. You see a couple of episodes of MTV's *Cribs* or BET's *How I'm Living* and you've seen 'em all. But Daddy, with whom I've been spending a lot of time lately, continues to surprise me in the most unusual ways: he isn't the irresponsible, party-hard rapper desperately trying to hold on to his last two minutes of fame. In fact, over the past few months, he has virtually cut off the deadbeat hype crowd that used him to get into parties and pay for their drinks, and has started spending more time thinking seriously about his career—and spending quite a bit of time with me. We get along easily; he told me a few weeks ago that he likes hanging out with me because I am unpretentious and didn't seem phased by his fame. Plus, he said, he trusted me—if I, a reporter, hadn't spread his business in the tabloids by now, I was a friend worth keeping. I'm by no means one of those writers who gets her rocks off hanging around with the stars; no, there is something different about Daddy's actions when he isn't around the lights and cameras. I like what I see—a smart, thoughtful man who is attentive, sweet, and ambitious. Indeed, he's begun to plot and plan his debut on the big screen—a career change that follows that of rappers-turned-actors Ice Cube, Queen Latifah, and LL Cool J. At the very least, the move will boost his waning rap career—and it might well mean a new source of income for him. He grows excited every time he talks about his big changes with me.

He lives in a tasteful condo in Beverly Hills, beautifully outfitted with plush neutral sofas, chairs, and settees, colorful artwork, and an impressive collection of artifacts he says he hand-picked during his travels through Europe, Africa, and Asia. He doesn't even have a television in his living room— "I don't really watch it much," he confided. "I'd rather study scripts and write rhymes than waste my time watching reality shows and bad made-for-TV movies." And get this: the boy cooks. Loves to, he claims.

Which is why I find myself sitting in his condo on a Tuesday evening after work, wishing I'd bothered to dress up for the occasion. Everything is so incredibly lovely—silver place settings sparkle against the ruby table linens that cover his ten-seat dining room table. Candles flicker all around the dimmed common areas; his CD player dances through a mix of classic and contemporary R&B—Stevie Wonder's *Songs in the Key of Life* flows easily into Alicia Keys' *Songs in A Minor*, into Mary J. Blige's *My Life*. I'd just finished eyeing the collection of Senegalese tapestries he'd artfully hung in the hallway just off the kitchen when Mary starts singing the title track from the hit album; I was humming to Mary's scats, about two seconds from catching the Holy Ghost, when Daddy walks into the dining room, a plate of food in each hand.

"You got a nice voice—you sing?" he asks, startling me out of my off-tune flow.

"I have shower concerts at least once a week," I joke. "I can't give away tickets."

"Shoot, by the time they finished pushing buttons in the studio, even Mary J. Blige wouldn't be able to tell the difference between you and her singing," he laughs. "But seriously, you have a nice voice."

"Why, thank you, sir," I say, taking my seat at the table. I lean into the plate and breath in deeply. "Mmm, I'm hungry as heck. This smells absolutely delicious."

"Steamed monk fish in a caper butter sauce, shrimp risotto, and broiled asparagus," he says.

"Um, okay—tell me that you ordered this from some fancy restaurant somewhere and had it delivered. Or that you hired some chef to cook it for you and then discreetly slip out, so I'd think you really cooked this meal yourself. Because I just refuse to believe you can burn like this on the regular, and this is the first time I'm being invited over to witness your skills."

"Nope—it's not takeout and there's no little Italian guy running around in the kitchen. It's all me," he says, taking a bite. "Eat up."

We talk easily about everything imaginable—the upcoming gubernatorial elections, which car is better, a Benz or a BMW, the state of Hollywood and how rappers are replacing black actors on the big screen. Our conversation just flows without pretension—even when we disagree, we manage to find some common ground and learn from one another in the process. Funny thing is, we never ever talk about relationships—ours or any that we'd had with anyone else. Somehow, we've taken an interesting turn and ended up in the friend zone, I'm sure at my own doing, seeing as I am consumed with moving my relationship with Sean out of the ex-sex category and into the winner's circle. The sexual tension is there, for sure—we'd talked before about racier subjects, like who our firsts were, who did it best, the kinkiest things we'd ever done with the opposite sex. But I get the distinct impression that he knows not to push me. Besides, Daddy has his choice of ass, I'm sure, and probably isn't starving for my affection, not with all the groupies who regularly turn a simple trip to places like Baskin-Robbins into *here's my number/can I get your autograph on my breast/what you doing later tonight*—and who turn my stomach, and sometimes even make me ashamed to be female. I do know that all their shenanigans make me even more appealing to him: I'm the nonjudgmental, safe, non-celebrity-obsessed "mom"—the closest thing to normality he could possibly get. Maybe he wants to keep the relationship unmolested. Ass he can get anywhere.

Which is why I feel totally comfortable telling him about the Vow while we sit eating dessert and sipping wine on the sofa.

"So, hold up, let me get this straight: you three plan on finding men who will meet you, propose, and marry you before New Year's Eve—in, like, six months?" he says, his mouth agape, enough for me to see the chocolate mousse in there.

"Well, we all have prospects, so it's not like we actually still have to *find* the men," I say casually.

"And you're going to try to coax a commitment out of him in less than a year."

"But see, that's just it right there: I don't understand why we have to 'coax' someone—particularly a black man—to marry us. We're three beautiful, strong, educated black women who just want to fall in love with someone who will love us back. Maybe you can explain to me why you guys are so afraid of commitment."

"Wait—hold up: you and your girls have set some arbitrary timetable to rope a brother down and make him dedicate the rest of his life to you after being together for only a matter of months, and you're wondering why brothers are afraid of commitment? Can you say, type-A personality—run?"

"What would you prefer—a fifteen-month deadline, a five-year one, fifteen? What's the difference, if you love the person you're with, whether you get married in seven months as opposed to seven years? You love each other, you get married. Why stall the process?"

"Maybe he needs to cross the street to make sure the grass really isn't greener," Daddy laughs. "Can't rush those things."

"So is that what Corey's dad is doing—taking his time?" I ask. "Should I be prepared to wait until my child goes to college before I expect an 'I do' out of him?"

"Sean is the target of your Vow?" Daddy says, staring into my eyes. I don't know if I'm reading him right, but he looks disappointed, if only for an instant.

"He's not a target—he's Corey's father and the man I've loved since freshman year in college," I say quietly. "And, quite honestly, I'm at my wits' end trying to figure out what we're doing. On any given week we can be thick as thieves, showing up together for school functions, talking about Corey's progress, taking him to interesting places, making plans for his future. We even have a set game night—I cook, Sean helps me with the dishes, Corey picks the game, we put our son to bed, and we cap the evening with mind-blowing sex. But then days will go by where I don't hear from him unless it's a voicemail, or a quick phone call—and sometimes I don't even get that. I just can't figure out what we're doing."

Daddy is quiet, contemplative. He takes another spoonful of mousse. "What do you think you're doing?" he asks.

"I'm trying to get my man to see that he doesn't have to look any further—that I'm that smart, hardworking, God-fearing, beautiful woman he's been searching for all his life. But then again, I'm not really clear on why I have to do all this convincing. That's the dilemma of the black woman in America. We're in crisis."

"Crisis?" he laughs. "How you figure?"

"You Negroes have worked yourselves into such a tizzy, what with rap videos and pop culture, and these big-boobed silicone mannequins with their weaves down their backs dancing all up in our screens, and these lyrics screaming to everyone that sex is a commodity, not something special shared between two people. You're always hunting for the next hot chick ready to sleep with you in exchange for a ride in the front seat of your expensive cars, while the rest of us normal girls—the ones who'll cook your dinner, wash your clothes, take care of your kids, bring home some cash from our little jobs, and make sure we sex you up proper—we don't get a second glance. Ask me why."

"I don't have to, I'm sure you're going to tell me," he laughs.

"It's not funny, Jerome," I say, getting serious, and a little mad. "The reason why is because black men have been deluded into thinking that if they have a five spot, a shiny car, a fresh line-up, and a hard dick, then they're somebody black women are supposed to be fighting over."

"That's only because you all put black men on a pedestal like we're hot commodities," he says.

"So if I started treating Sean like shit, then he'd marry me? How does he win with a woman who mistreats him?"

"That's just it, though—it's not about winning—it's about being able to feel like a man . . ." he starts to explain, but I cut him off.

"But cooking, cleaning, and taking care of him doesn't make him feel like a man?"

"Let me finish," he says. "It's about being able to feel like a man and being able to make the decision about when and how you're going to fall in love—and that doesn't involve timetables and clocks and schedules that you didn't have any part in. And if you start making them think that their life is going to be reduced to putting the kids to sleep, watching Leno, having sex, then falling asleep—all at the same exact time every night, then they really won't want to have anything to do with it. It's the loss of freedom and variety and the fear of boredom that men are running away from. And you can say all you want about the video hos and body image and all that, but men are literal creatures and they want to have what they see."

"And every black man on the planet just happens to like the same thing: the red-boned, long-haired, thin, hour-glass vision of perfection flooding BET?"

"Well, that's not my particular preference, but I can see how someone could be attracted to that," he says nervously, scratching his eyebrows.

"Well then just what is your type? Because if your dating history serves me correct, the high-profile chicks you used to saunter around town with all fit that bill."

"You should know by now not to believe everything you see in the gossip pages," he shoots. "Just because you saw it and somebody gave their interpretation of what they thought was happening doesn't make it true."

"Well, if that's not your type, then what is?"

Daddy is quiet for a moment. He takes a sip from his wineglass, then lifts his napkin from his lap to wipe his thick lips and goatee. The flickering candles make his eyes dance. "Actually, if I had a type, she'd be a lot like you," he says, leaning in.

Whoa. The birds stop chirping. The DJ scratches the record. All noise ceases. That sounded like a come-on. Was that a come-on? Yes, Viv, that was a come-on. What to do? I don't say a word. He keeps going.

"She'd be smart like you. And loyal, like you. And pretty like you. And thick and juicy, just like you . . ." he says before leaning in. And, after a beat of silence, he plants a soft, warm kiss on my lips.

I move my head back just slightly, making our lips disconnect. He's caught me off-guard and I am not so sure I want to take it there. But his lips taste so good. And the wine has me buzzed. This time it is I who move in. I fall into his lips, soft as pillows. And then I kiss him again. And again. When I lean in for another, he parts his lips and licks my tongue. We sink into each other's embrace, our tongues probing the insides of each other's mouths—a make-out session that would make two junior-high kids, skipping seventh period to perfect their make-out game, sit up and take notes. I am grateful, though, when he pulls back and starts planting soft kisses on my neck and my cheeks, and my forehead, and my ears (that's my spot!). But his tongue is quickly becoming too wet—one thing I couldn't ever stand was a sloppy kisser, and Jerome is fast becoming the king of the slobbery tongue game.

But that makes no never mind, particularly when I feel his palm on my breast. My nipples harden almost instantly—and my clit swells at the same pace. I reach up and run my left hand over the back of his head and gently guide his lips toward the left side of my sweater; I run my right hand across the muscles on his shoulders, down to his rock hard biceps, which I give a little squeeze. I'm still not sure if it is his muscles or his tongue that made me moan, but I know the moment he lifts my sweater, pushes my bra aside, and takes my nipple into his mouth that I was going to ride his ass into the sunset.

"You are so sexy," he says, between mouthfuls of my breast, as he starts tugging at my belt. "I've been waiting to feel those legs wrapped around me."

I don't say anything back—I haven't, until that very moment, allowed myself to think about what it would be like to fuck Daddy. Sure, I'd probably considered it fleetingly back when he was at the top of his game and I was actually into his music—but this? This wasn't something I came prepared to do. I actually considered putting a stop to it all—how would it look, me talking about trying to marry my baby's daddy in one breath, and then letting some rapper nail me to his sofa the next. It is my libido, though, that was calling the shots—not my common sense. So instead of getting up off that couch and taking my ass home to my child, I lean back into the plush fabric and pull Daddy closer still—pushed his head into my breast, and then my stomach, and then giggle as he loosens the button to my jeans, and pulls the zipper down, his tongue and lips doing all the talking they needed to get me to settle in for the first sexual escapade I'd had with a man other than Sean in, shoot, God knows how long. Years.

I'm not sure it hadn't been that long for Daddy, too, or if he is just a zealous kinda lover, because he is pretty hasty—almost forceful—when he pulls my pants and panties off and dives into my vagina like it is his last meal. I'm not quite prepared for his tongue to jam onto my clit so quickly—normally I need to work up to direct contact to get the kind of sensation it takes for me to come, and this time is no exception. I lift my thighs into the air and wriggle a bit to get him to move his tongue down a little, and he complies, but he is still chomping on me like I was a bucket of Popeyes. His front teeth are digging into my skin so hard that I consider either pushing his head away or asking him to stop, but then he sticks his tongue deep inside my vagina and starts to lick all around and makes me feel so good that I lift my thighs to him, this time for doing it right. I slowly rotate my ass, meeting each one of his licks with a thrust of my hips, going faster and faster still, until it seems like he was fucking me with his tongue. "Oh God," I moan, opening my legs wider to give him full access to my clit. Just a few more strategic licks and I am going to come—hard. "Yes," I say softly.

Just as I felt myself about to climax, he jams his finger into my ass. "Ow," I say, unable to hold back my displeasure. He doesn't seem to notice, though; he neither realizes that his anal intrusion hurts, nor that it's messed up my high. In fact, he moves his tongue action from my vagina down to my ass—is licking and sucking like someone'd spread his mousse all over it. He rubs my clit with his thumb, which I guess feels kinda good, except that I wanted more tongue there, instead of in my asshole. Just as I was about to work my vagina back into his mouth, he reels back, spits on me, and jams his finger in again. "Jerome!" I call out, a frown on my face.

He doesn't look up, just keeps fumbling his fingers all over my vagina and ass. "Feels good, baby—go 'head, call Daddy's name," he mumbles as he puts his tongue back on my clit. That eases the pain a bit, but damn—did he just spit on me? Ugh. And why is his middle finger still jammed in my ass?

Just as it starts to feel good again, and I am hiking my hips back into the air to meet his tongue thrusts, he stops altogether, stands up, pulls his pants down and hops on top of me. His penis is hard—he wriggles it around on my thigh as he tries to stick his tongue in my mouth. I don't play that—there's nothing more nasty to me than a man who tries to stick his tongue in my mouth after he's just finished licking my ass and vagina. So I turn my head in time enough for his tongue to land in my ear, which isn't what I mean to do, considering he had a face full of my bodily juices, but it is better he gets them on my cheek and ear (well, I really prefer he wipe his mouth on a towel or washcloth or something) than my lips.

But that is the least of my worries. Before I can really grasp what's happening, he jumps up, snatches off his pants, climbs back onto the sofa, and thrusts his penis and balls into my face. His dick slides up the side of my cheek—his balls across my nose. It was like he is fucking my skin; I'm not sure if I'm supposed to be enjoying the sensation, or if he just can't really navigate his dick into my mouth, but the thrusting goes on a little too long for my comfort. Finally, I crane my neck just a bit and take his penis into my mouth (silently thanking Amaya for inspiring me to take the advanced Blow and Get Low course to learn how to practically swallow a super-sized penis whole). Daddy's dick is wide and impressively long—what he lacks in tongue game I sure as hell hope he can make up with in thrusts, because right about now he is coming up short. I lightly tap my fingers up and down the vein on the underside of his penis as I suck and lick it and suck some more. I grab it tight with my right hand and massage it as I stick it deeper into my mouth and suction-suck it on the way back out. With my left hand, I rub and gently pull his balls, which make him thrust his penis even harder into my mouth. Damn, even with my extra lessons, I can hardly handle his dick going that deep into my mouth, but I relax my throat muscles and let him go deeper still. "Yeah, suck it baby," he says, thrusting harder. "Suck it. Suck it. Yeah, suck it, suck it—suuuuuuuuuuuck it! Aaaaaaargh!"

No, this nigga did not.

I try my best to seal my throat and turn my head to the side so the liquid can run out of my mouth, but by now he is in full come mode, grabbing onto the arm of the couch and fucking my mouth like he was riding ass. I gag as his sperm hits the back of my mouth and struggle not to swallow. I try to push him off of me, but he is still resistant; his body is still jerking and shivering as the last of his sperm trickles out. Finally, he pulls out and moves from over top of me; I shoot up and grab the dessert napkin to relieve my mouth of his liquid.

"Goddamn, girl—where you learn to suck a dick like that?" he says, smiling and completely oblivious to my spitting fury. "If I didn't know any better, I'da thought you were a white girl!" he chuckles, reaching down and massaging himself.

Just as I fix my mouth to tell him not to ever, ever, ever do that shit again, my cell phone rings, jarring both of us. I consider not answering it but then I think better of it; the only somebody who would be calling my cell phone at this hour is my mom, who is watching Corey.

"Excuse me," I say curtly, pushing myself up and around him, "I have to get that." I reach into my purse, pull my cell out, and check the number; it is my mother. She is calling me from her cell phone, which is weird, seeing as she is supposed to be at my house, getting Corey ready for bed. Why doesn't she just use the house phone? "Hey, Mom," I say into the receiver. "What's up?"

"It's Corey," she says. I don't really remember much after she tells me something is wrong with my baby. I was bending over and collecting my panties off the floor within a millisecond; everything in the room goes black, except for my clothes and the door. I think I hear "not well," "ambulance," "hospital," and "working on him," but I definitely hear "Cedars."

"I'll see you there," I said, shutting the phone and grabbing my keys.

"What's wrong?" Daddy asked, the terror in his eyes mirroring mine.

"It's Corey," I say, rushing to the door.

Daddy grabs his coat and follows me out.

It takes only about ten minutes to get to Cedars-Sinai, though it feels like ten hours. I say a silent "Thank you" to God for Daddy, because I know my car would have been wrapped around a pole within seconds of my getting behind the wheel if I had tried to drive. Daddy takes my keys and commandeers the car, while I alternately try to get my mom back on the phone and find Sean. Alas, I can't reach either of them, which makes me even more terrified. How am I to be sure that my child is even alive? I feel so vulnerable. I want to claw my heart out.

"Viv, you gotta calm down," Daddy says, reaching over to rub my hand. I don't want to feel his touch, or hear his voice. I just want to see my child. How would I ever live without him? How could I breathe? "Everything is going to be all right," he insists.

"What if it's not?" I say, tears streaming down my face. My wet mascara is fire in my eyes. "He's only seven, Jerome. Seven," I sob. "He's my baby. I haven't had a chance to raise him, to watch him grow. I never watched a sunset with him, or showed him the Big Dipper, or told him all about girls, or unconditional love. I'm not finished being a mom yet—he can't be finished being a son. There's so much more."

"Viv—you're talking crazy," Daddy says. "You don't know what's happened, and you're already leaping to the funeral. Your son is going to be fine—you have to believe that for it to be true."

I nod. But the thought of my son dying without his mother by his side makes me cry harder still.

I don't immediately see my mom when we burst through the emergency-room doors, but as soon as I tell the nurse my name, Daddy and I are ushered into a room just off the lobby. My child is hooked up to several machines—one is giving him oxygen, another monitors his heart rate, another pumps some kind of clear fluid into his arm. A doctor and a nurse stand over him, talking quietly to my mom.

"Mommy? What's wrong with Corey," I say frantically, bursting into tears as I rush over to him. He is pale and limp. "What's wrong with my baby?"

"Vivian, calm down, honey. Be calm," my mother says, hugging me and trying to pull me away from Corey.

"No," I say firmly. "You tell me what's wrong with my child right now!"

Daddy rubs my arm. "Viv, come on, you have to calm down," he whispers quickly in my ear. "You're going to upset Corey. He needs to see you with a level head. Talk to the doctors."

I really have to will myself to focus enough to hear what the doctor is saying and actually comprehend it. Corey, he says, is suffering from acute respiratory failure, triggered by allergies that caused him to have an asthma attack. He'd fallen asleep from the trauma surrounding his not being able to breath—that and the medication. The plan is to admit him so that his bronchial tubes could be drained and he could be treated with medication that would ease his breathing.

"Does your family have a history of allergies or asthma?" the doctor asks. His nameplate says Houston. I look at my mom, and she shakes her head.

"No," I answer quickly.

"How about his father's side?"

That question is jarring—not just because I'm not sure of the answer, but also because it is the first time I realized that Sean still hasn't returned my frantic phone calls or shown up at the hospital to see about his son. I immediately see red.

"I don't know," I say quietly. I see Dr. Houston shoot a look at the nurse—they immediately surmised that because my child's father wasn't in the room that I probably don't even know who the daddy is, much less his medical history. Which means that I am either going to be dismissed as some poor, uninsured patient who can't afford the good treatment, or I am going to have to set them straight this instant to make sure my child gets the best care possible. I'd come up against the single-mom stereotype before, but this isn't the time for me to have to prove myself to these people. I just want my son to get better.

"His father, Dr. Jordan, will be here any minute," I say, nodding and wiping tears from my eyes. "He'll tell you about the other side of Corey's family health history. In the meantime, is he going to be okay?"

"We're going to have to admit him for observation. We'll know a little bit more in the morning," Dr. Houston says.

"He's going to have to stay here?" I whimper.

"Ms. Jordan," he says, assuming my last name is the same as Corey's, and talking to me like I couldn't understand the words coming out of his mouth, "your son suffered a severe asthma attack. Had your mother waited for the ambulance to arrive, he may not have made it. Keeping him here is the least of your worries right now."

I try not to pay attention to the condescending attitude; Corey is all that matters now.

"We'll have him in a room shortly," Dr. Houston says before scribbling something on Corey's medical chart and leaving the room, the nurse on his heels. Moments later, she reappears.

"Ms. Jordan, do you have health insurance?"

I shoot daggers into her oversized frame. "Of course," I say, digging into my purse to get my card. "Here."

"We're going to need you to fill out some paperwork," she says, taking the card from my hand.

"Fine—but I'd really like to spend some time with my child before I do. I just got here, and he needs me." The nurse nods, turns on her heels, and walks out. I lean over Corey and give him a kiss on his forehead. He looks so helpless; I feel so helpless. I burst into tears again. My mother and Daddy jostle to console me. I shake them both off.

"How did his breathing get so labored?" I demand.

My mother, instinctively understanding that this would not be a good time to give me shit for giving her shit, just answers the question.

"I'm not sure how it happened," she says simply. "He was breathing that way when Sean brought him home after dinner."

"Did Sean say anything about it?"

"No," my mom answers. "He barely said two words to me; he was too busy running out the door."

"Did he say where they'd been?"

"Sean didn't, but Corey said they'd had dinner over at one of his friends' houses, and that he was scared because she had two cats and one of them kept hissing and clawing at him."

"What?" I say. "What woman's house did he have my child at?"

"Corey said it was the woman from the birthday party—the white girl."

"He took my son over to that heifer's nasty-ass, cat-infested house for dinner, and then dropped him off at my place like he was some sick puppy he was leaving on the side of the highway?" I ask, incredulous.

My mother says nothing. Daddy stands quiet, staring at the floor.

"I can't believe that bastard. Where is he, anyway? I tried his phone, his two-way, called his office, his voicemail—every number I have for his stupid ass. Why hasn't he called back? And why isn't he here?" I ask no one in particular. Just as I'd worked myself into a complete frenzy, the nurse comes in.

"We've got a room all set for him," she says. "If you'll follow me, we can take care of the paperwork while we prep your son for admission."

THE MACHINE they'd hooked Corey up to is noisily pulling what appears to be green and yellow snot out of my son's throat. A monitor just to the left of his bed beeps steadily every few minutes, reassuring everyone within a two-mile radius, it seems, that the boy was breathing and his heart was pumping. Though the doctor making rounds and the nurse both assure me that Corey was a fighter and would pull through, I can't take my eyes off my son for fear that if I close them, he would leave me forever. I ache for sleep, but it just isn't an option. I even refuse to let the nurse show me how to convert my visitor's chair into a pullout bed (Cedars had them in each of the children's rooms to accommodate parents who just couldn't bear leaving their babies in the hospital). I have no intention of using it for anything other than watching after my child.

My mother left about two hours ago; Daddy arranges for one of his boys to drive her home back to Chino—my mother hates driving at night, and isn't all that familiar with the roads. (In fact, I know she is working on pure adrenaline and willpower when she navigated her Celica through the streets of West Hollywood to the hospital; if she didn't think her grandson was dying, she would have waited for the ambulance to give them a lift.) She leaves the car for me so that I can come and go as I please, but Daddy stays on to comfort me and provide support while I watch my child's chest heave in and out from his labored breathing. I cry, Daddy listens. "He keeps me honest," I say, nodding my head for emphasis, wiping tears from my cheeks. "He's a good boy. What would I do without my child?" I ask, bursting into tears again.

In the two hours that I stand sentry at Corey's sickbed, I alternate between extreme anxiety over my son's condition and extreme anger that his father is probably the one responsible for this mess. Not that either of us had known that Corey had asthma or that he might have been this severely allergic to animals (neither Sean nor I have allergies, and though he'd get the sniffles if a cat rubbed on him just a little too much, he'd never suffered such a severe breathing attack before), but I can't understand how he can be so busy to get back to whatever he is plotting and planning with Brittany that he can't see that his child is ill. I mean, how could a person *be* so inattentive and self-centered that he doesn't notice his child is having problems breathing?

But that is just like his ass—self-centered bastard! Everything is about Sean—what Sean wants, what Sean needs, what Sean's got to have this very minute. Been that way from the moment I met him in college. He's a spoiled brat—got it from his mama. That became clear when we were planning to have our baby and were pondering a future together.

"I'm just saying," he'd said slowly, "you, me, and the baby will all be better off if we postpone the wedding until I finish my studies. After the baby's born, you graduate, and I get my residency, then we can revisit it."

"Sean, what the hell are you talking about?" I said, water welling in the corners of my eyes. The baby shifted in my belly and stuck his butt out, forming a huge, hard lump just next to my belly button. Ordinarily I would have gently rubbed my tummy and talked to my little one to coax him into shifting his tiny body so that I could feel more comfortable, but I couldn't move my hands, or any of my limbs for that matter. My fiancé, the father of my unborn child, was telling me, his seven-months-pregnant girlfriend, that we needed to put our life together on hold, with seemingly no guarantees that we would pick up where we left off once he finished whatever the hell he thought he had to do without me and the kid. "What exactly does 'revisit' mean?"

He cupped his hands together and dropped his face into his palms. His locks hung long and low. I couldn't see his face, but I sensed that he was searching for the right words to say to me to keep me from going postal on his ass. I beat him to the punch.

"If I'm hearing correctly, you're saying that you want me and this baby to wait around four years while you build a life for yourself," I said, my voice getting louder, but still quivering. "What exactly are me and the baby supposed to do without you? Are we to simply sit back and be comfortable being statistics—another single mom and a baby boy without a daddy around? Is that what you have planned for our lives? Has my input suddenly become irrelevant? Because up until now, I thought we were in this together."

"We are, babe," he said, exasperated. "But there's just no way that I'll be able to focus in med school if I'm worried about working to make ends meet. I can't concentrate on my studies and change diapers at the same time. All I'm asking for is four years."

"Negro, do you know what can happen in four years?" I said, incredulous. "Our baby will be getting ready for kindergarten. Taking care of a baby alone can force me to postpone completing my studies and take a job outside of my career, which could mean the end of my dream of being a journalist. You could find someone else and . . ."

Sean cut me off.

"Viv—you're reading too far into the future," he said.

"You're forcing me to!" I said.

"You choose to be a pessimist about it," he said quietly. "I'm going to be optimistic and trust that in four years, we'll be just as much in love with one another as we are this moment, and that our son will grow up to know that his dad made this decision for his own good."

"You mean for your good," I shot back. "The only one who benefits here is you. Who put this in your mind, anyway—your mother? What, did she lock you in a room and preach to you about how my baby and I are going to ruin her dreams of having a doctor for a son? Does she think I'm going to steal your money? Is that what's going on? She's all but said so to my face!" (I wasn't exaggerating; Mrs. Jordan summoned me to her home one Sunday afternoon, sat me down, and, under the guise of telling me what I "needed to hear," proceeded to accuse me of using my pregnancy to trap her child.)

"My mother has nothing to do with this," Sean insisted. "I just think this is a sound decision. The moment I graduate from med school, we can talk about a wedding."

"Well, I have news for you, Sean Jordan," I said, snatching my engagement ring off my finger and tossing it into his lap. "You can keep your damn ring. You can keep your damn wedding plans. And you can forget about me marrying your selfish ass. I don't want to be married to a man who thinks it's okay to make a baby and not care for it or its mother."

And with that, I stomped out of the college dorm we shared, and out of Sean's life. Though he was there for the baby's birth, and did a decent job of supplementing my income with cash to buy diapers and food, the primary care of my child came from me, with help from my mom, and an occasional check from Sean's mother (though I refused to cash them after we got into an argument about what I should be spending it on: I mean, if I know the baby needed Similac and I needed rent money, why should I spend the much-needed cash on baby clothes he was just going to grow out of?). By the time he graduated from med school, I was so busy being a mom, freelancing at various newspapers, and trying to build a name for myself as a credible journalist, and he was so busy trying to become a cosmetic surgeon, that love and weddings never came back up. In fact, I didn't start thinking about building a life together with Sean until my child was old enough to ask me why his dad and I weren't together.

And now I'm wondering why I even bothered. I can finally see who Sean really is. As I hover over our son's sickbed, I realize that his actions couldn't have spoken any louder. He's ignored all of my desperate phone calls, pages, and voicemails because he doesn't care to answer them—clearly, whoever he's with is much more pressing than me and his son.

I reach over and stroke my son's hair. "You're going to be all right, baby."

Just then, Sean comes bounding into the hospital room, eyes red and bucked, breathing like he's just run a marathon. "Oh God, Corey—are you okay?" Sean says, rushing over to the bed.

"Hey, Dad," Corey says weakly. Even though he has an oxygen mask on his face, I can tell he is trying his best to smile. He'd been asking for Sean; I was way tempted to tell him his father wasn't shit and didn't come to see him because he was holed up with some heifer somewhere, but because my son needed to keep up his strength—both physical and mental—I simply told him his dad was on his way.

Sean touches his son's hand gingerly, then looks up to meet Daddy's gaze. He grinds his teeth, making his temple and jaw vibrate—something Sean does when he is most angry. He stares pensively at Daddy, and then he turns his attention to me.

"Viv, what happened?" he says quickly.

"I think I should be asking you that same question," I say, crossing my arms.

"Viv, now's not the time to give me a hard time," he snaps. "What's wrong with my son?"

"Well, my son suffered a severe asthma attack, probably brought on by whatever animal you had him around yesterday before you kicked him out of your car."

Sean screws up his face and turns his whole body toward me. "Vivian, what the hell are you talking about?"

"I'm talking about the diagnosis the doctor gave me last night when I was here and you were, well, wherever it was that you were that you couldn't answer my emergency phone calls, voicemails, and pages letting you know your child was rushed to the hospital and hooked up to a bunch of machines to help him breathe," I seethe. "If you weren't around your animal, you would have gotten the scoop on what was up with your child last night, when he needed you to be here most. Don't worry, though, we've got it under control."

"Who the hell is 'we'?" he says, looking at Daddy, who is trying his best to focus on Corey so as not to be drawn into the drama, and to protect the kid from it, too. "You talking about thug passion over here?" Then he directs his ire at my friend. "You may be called Daddy, but there's only one Daddy in my son's life and that's me—please believe that, money."

"Hey, man . . ." Daddy starts. But I raise my hand to cut him off.

"How about *you* start acting like one, then?" I say to Sean, standing up.

"What?" Sean says, incredulous. "Let me tell you something, Vivian Evans. You don't have a monopoly on being a good parent, and you've definitely become way too comfortable giving me less credit than I deserve. If telling you where I was last night will get you to focus on my son instead of my whereabouts, then here goes . . ." he starts.

"You know what, Sean? I don't give a damn where you were, frankly," I say.

"No! I'm going to tell you so you know," he says, holding his hand up and talking quickly. "I took Corey with me to my publicist's place so we could start making some media planning for my practice, and then after I dropped Corey off I stopped off at Starbucks to get a cup of coffee, but I parked illegally and a cop came by and towed my car, with my cell phone and pager in it. It took me all night to get my car back, and I didn't get your messages until a half-hour ago."

Just as I am thinking of a verbal assault to launch back, I catch sight of my son out the corner of my eye. When I look at him, he is crying softly. Realizing how jacked it is that his mother and father are practically clawing each other's eyes out in front of their sick son, I stop myself from saying anything else, and walk toward his bed to comfort him. Just then, the doctor comes in.

"Good afternoon, Mrs. Jordan," he said.

"Actually, my name is Ms. Evans," I say, still staring at Corey and patting his hand. I mouth "I'm sorry," to him, but he continues to tear. "My son has his father's surname. This is Dr. Jordan," I say, pointing the doctor in Sean's direction.

"Nice to meet you, doctor," Sean says, extending his hand.

"Pleasure," the doctor says. "I've read the X rays we took of your son's chest earlier this morning and it looks like the Albuterol is working well. I don't like to have kids his age on it for too long, but as soon as his levels are back to normal, which should be over the next day or so, we'll take him off of it and send him on home."

"So he's going to be okay," Sean asks. The smile in his eyes mixes with the mist of his tears.

"He's a trouper," the doctor says. "He'll be back to homework at the kitchen table by the end of the week."

"You hear that, champ?" Daddy says, grabbing Corey's hand and giving a thousand-watt smile. "Homework's just around the corner!"

Corey wipes the tears from his eyes, and smiles.

Disgust washes over Sean's face. He glares at Daddy, but turns his attention to the doctor. "Hold up, Doc—I'd like to talk to you some more about his condition. Do you have a minute?"

"I'm actually on my rounds, Doctor," he says. "Can you take a walk with me?"

"Sure," Sean says. He turns to Corey. "I'll be back in a few minutes, son," he says. And with that, he shoots a final look at Daddy and me, turns and follows the doctor out the door.

Daddy stands up. "Hey, Viv, can I holla at you for a minute?"

I screw up my face even more. Not that he's done anything wrong; Daddy has been a critical support for me as I wondered whether my child had taken his last good breath. But I am in no mood to have to coddle Daddy over Sean's rude behavior, and I am sure as hell not ready to recap the disastrous couch episode of a few hours earlier. I have no words for it anyway; I need to focus on Corey.

"Can it wait?" I say as I kiss Corey's hand and stare into his eyes.

"Actually, it would help if I could talk to you now," Daddy urges. "It'll just be a minute."

I look at my watch, then back at Corey. "Baby, I'm going to turn on the Disney Channel. Watch it until Mommy comes back into the room. I won't be long." I give him a peck on the cheek and head for the door, Daddy on my heels. "So, what's up?" I ask.

Daddy looks down at his feet, as if the words he is searching for could be found in the laces of his Air Force Ones. I could barely hear him when he finally does speak. "You know, nobody should spend a lifetime trying to make someone love her," he begins. "You deserve someone who's going to appreciate and respect you—take care of you . . ."

Aw, damn. Not this. Not now.

"We've been having a good time together over these past few months, and I've gotten pretty attached to you and Corey . . ."

"Look," I say, cutting him off, "I don't know if this is such a good . . ."

"Let me finish," he says, holding up his hand. "Please, I've waited a minute to tell you how I feel about you."

"And standing in the hallway outside my son's hospital room is a good time?" I snap.

"Come on, Viv—I can't think of any better time," he says. "Love doesn't wait for the right time, it just happens. Just like it did back at my place tonight. And I've fallen in love with you . . ."

Just as Daddy is launching into his soliloquy, Sean walks out of a room a few doors down. He is looking at what appears to be a brochure, but as he approaches us, he looks up. A thousand daggers would have felt better than his icy stare. The nerve to toss me dirty looks? Please. I stare right back, making my eyes just as steely. I suck my teeth as he passed. When he hits the double doors leading out of the children's ward, I turn my attention to Daddy.

"Look, this isn't really a good time to talk about this. And even if it was, I don't think our being more than friends is a good idea. I really do like you, but I think I made a mistake tonight. I've always made it my policy not to mix business with pleasure," I say, trying desperately to let him down easy, quickly. I hold back on the part about how bad the sex was. For a rapper who brags about his ability to hit that, he missed my mark on every level.

"Viv, I'm not asking you to marry a brother. I'm just asking you to give me a chance to get to know you better, and we can see where it goes from there. Can you at least give that a try?" He licks his lips; his dimples were deep enough to fit a small fist. I smile at him nervously, and then look up the hallway again. I look back at Daddy, and lean in slowly. I kiss his cheek. He smiles.

"Yeah, that's what I'm talkin 'bout," he says.

What he doesn't realize is that my kiss is the beginning of a polite send-off.

Fuck the Vow, fuck Daddy, and especially fuck Sean. It's time for me to live life for me and my son, because, clearly, we're the only ones who love us for who we are—straight, no chaser. From now on, I'm going to focus on nursing my son back to health and making myself happy, without Sean. It's time for some changes around here.

13

TRISTA

Sloane Sedgewick sweeps into The Ivy cursing loudly into her cell phone. The power publicist's large pink leather Jimmy Choo tote knocks one of the diners in the head as she weaves her way through the maze of tables in the popular see-and-be-seen eatery. From the sound of all the "goddammits," some reporter must have written something nasty about one of her clients. Her tiny cream leather miniskirt with laser-cut detail along the bottom skims the tops of her thin, ghost-white thighs, her tight black cashmere tank top showing off skeletal arms. In a town where tanning is considered a birthright, her pasty white skin stands out. She stops at several tables to exchange kisses with a few stars but pointedly ignores a Brazilian supermodel she represented until a bootleg video surfaced on the Internet of her blowing some random guy in a nightclub bathroom (rumor has it Sloane dropped her after telling her that if you have to get caught on film with someone's dick in your mouth, at least make sure it's someone important). After she reaches our table, she waves a hand with an eight-carat pink diamond engagement ring in a platinum setting, beckoning one of the waiters.

"Did you get engaged, Sloane?" I ask coyly, after she snaps her phone shut. I, along with the rest of L.A., know full well that she got engaged last week to Harry Bolton, a powerful three-times-divorced big dog at Disney. She smiles and pushes large Gucci sunglasses up into her cascade of blond shoulder-length waves and extends her left hand so I could get a better look at her ring.

"Yes, darling, and it's serious bling," she says and purses her freshly enhanced lips. Like most white girls in L.A., Sloane peppers her conversation with hip-hop slang to show how cool they are. I hate when they do that.

"Congrats, you must be so excited," I say, knowing she no more loves that man than I do. A well-preserved thirty-something (read: cosmetic surgeon on speed dial), Sloane had been on the husband hunt for a while. This marriage would probably last long enough for her to get pregnant and insure a hefty divorce settlement.

"So, let's talk about Jared," says Sloane, briskly switching gears. I hope she gets to the point of this lunch so I can get home in time to change before I have to meet Garrett tonight.

"Okay, what's up?" I ask, as I squeeze a lime into my glass of Pellegrino. "The Paramount screen test with Glenn went well. I'm confident he'll get the part. We should be ready to formally announce next week."

"There's no doubt he's getting the part. He's perfect. I want to talk about pushing him up into the twenty-million-dollar territory, up there with Cruise, Smith and Clooney."

"What do you have in mind?" I ask.

"Jared Greenway and Kimberly Springfield," she says and traces the rim of her glass with her finger.

"Jared and Kimberly? What do you mean? Are they seeing each other?" They just met on the set, and as far as I know he is pretty devoted to his fiancée.

"Well, they aren't seeing each other yet, but by the time I finish working my magic they will be," she says mischievously.

"What are you talking about, Sloane?" I say, beginning to get irritated. The waiter returned with our chopped salads and Sloane waits until he departs to answer.

"What I'm saying is, Jared and Kimberly are going to start seeing each other," she says with a hint of exasperation. "*People* magazine will be begging for the exclusive! It will create an avalanche of buzz for the project when they're seen around town together, and that, I assure you, will translate into stampedes at the box office on opening day." Her icy-blue eyes gleam with the thought of all the press hits.

"Hello? Sloane? Jared's engaged," I remind her. "I know you've kept it out of the papers that they are actually planning to get married."

"You mean *was* engaged. By the time Heather gets finished reading in the *Star* and *Us Weekly* that her high-school sweetheart is fucking Kimberly Springfield, she'll be on the next plane back to Idaho. Don't worry, I'll make sure she flies first class, to soften the blow."

"That's insane," I say, and I look at her like she's lost her mind. She actually wants to plant these ludicrous stories about a fake romance.

"Oh, grow up, Trista," she says. "This is how the big boys do things."

"I'm not going to be Jared's pimp," I said. I am also concerned because Kimberly was Steven's client, and I didn't want to be part of something that would bolster the visibility of the client of my main competition for partner. No way.

"Well, luckily I'm more than willing to do it. All I have to do is explain to Jared what this will do for his career."

"The only thing that Jared needs to do for his career is focus on acting. I won't be a part of destroying his relationship." I know that sometimes publicists planted fairly innocent items about clients hooking up, or tipped off paparazzi when clients were getting away together, to fuel interest in a project, but this was manipulation. I had avoided the sleazy rep that a lot of agents had in our business; I focused on signing talented people and working hard to get them the right deals. I wasn't down for *this*.

Reaching into her bag, Sloane removes her cell phone and places the earpiece in her ear and stands up to leave. "Look, Trista, the wheels are already in motion; check out the *Star* on Wednesday. And either you get on board with this or you don't, but it's going to happen," she says with a hard glint in her eye.

AFTER MY MEETING with Sloane I make it back to my condo in record time to get ready. Fresh from the shower, I plop down on the chair next to my bed and readjust the heated roller that's digging into the nape of my neck. I look around at my room and survey the damage. My duvet is barely visible under the weight of half my closet. I've tried on every outfit I own. A pile of shoes rests against the side of the bed, and I kick a stray black Marc Jacobs tote across the room, stubbing my toe on the heavy hardware.

I usually don't get nervous, but tonight is different: I'm meeting Garrett and his parents at an art auction for one of their charities at the Corcoran Gallery. Look, I say to myself as I rub my big toe, happy to see I didn't chip the glossy red polish, get it together, girl. You can do this. And while I've never formally met his parents, I certainly know who the Jameses are. Garrett's father was the first black L.A. County district attorney and recently retired from the bench. His mother, Barbara, a former ballerina, is the doyenne of black L.A. society, sitting on several prominent boards and committees. They belong to the old-black-money crowd in L.A., with a gated estate in Hancock Park.

Things have been going pretty well with us. Ever since our "talk" at my condo a couple of months ago, we'd been seeing each other more frequently and getting to know each other better. If I wasn't staying over at his place, he was over at mine. We enjoyed doing simple things, like taking long walks on the beach, going to the movies, and staying up late talking into the night. And always work the room together at work events. I even told him about Sloane's plan and he had given me some good ideas about how to maintain control of my client. I felt like we were really connecting. I felt for the first time in a long time like I was falling in love.

My self-imposed panic attack is interrupted by the sound of the telephone ringing.

"Hello?" I answer.

"What's up, girl?" asks Amaya. "Getting ready for your fancy dinner with Cliff and Claire Huxtable?" She laughs into the receiver.

"Ugh . . . Please say you're calling to make me feel better?" I whine.

"No, I was just calling to let you know that Corey had a good checkup this morning. In fact, Viv said he should be getting out of the hospital tomorrow," says Amaya.

"Thank the Lord," I say. "Viv must be so relieved."

"Yeah, girl. She's got a new attitude. And Jerome's been over at the house a lot. This is the type of thing that changes your perspective on a whole lot of stuff."

"Amen to that. So what else is up?"

"I was also calling to see what you're going to wear today."

"Girl, please. I'm sitting here in my underwear, trying to figure that out. Hey, Garrett gave me an extra ticket for tonight. You should come." I start holding outfits against my body and looking in the mirror.

"Maybe I'll do that. Since you're meeting his parents—a pretty serious step, I might add—I suggest something slightly conservative, but you want to be sharp 'cause you wanna let his Mama know you ain't no joke with a pair of fly-ass shoes."

"Okay," I say. "What do you think about that little black Prada dress with the satin piping along the bottom and those gold snakeskin pumps you always like to borrow—assuming you didn't stretch those bad boys out the last time you wore them."

"Whatever, girl. You know I didn't stretch out your shoes. I think I remember that dress . . ." Her voice trails off as she tries to recall it.

"You know the one, I wore it to your *Bad Girlz* premiere," I say. "One of the worst movies in the world—aside from your scenes—of course!"

"Don't hate . . . Just pray that this Soular Son film keeps me from having to be a part of the sequel. Anyway, I remember that dress. It was real cute."

"Cool. See you there?"

"Maybe. Toodles, girlfriend."

Problem solved. I walk into the bathroom to begin putting on my makeup when I hear the phone ring again. Looking at the number on the bathroom extension, I don't recognize the digits but answer anyway.

"Hello," I say as I rub foundation into my skin with a small sponge.

"Hi, Trista, it's Damon." Damn, what does he want? The conversation I had with Viv last week replays in my mind. There's no way he still has feelings for me. Did Viv give him my number?

"Hi, Damon. How'd you get my number?"

"Uh, information. Look, I was just calling to say I'm sorry for what happened at the Oscar party. Look, I see you're in a relationship with Garrett, and I can respect that. I was just hoping that we could be friends again. We've been through a lot together. Seeing you again has just made me remember we were good friends back in the day. With my firm working with your boyfriend's firm we're bound to keep running into each other. Let's just put the past behind us."

I pause as I take in his words and drop the makeup sponge on the tray. The past is the past. Why are brothers always trying to be friends? Can't we just be sworn enemies forever? But if he can try to be mature about it, I certainly can, too. He won't outdo me.

"Yes, you're right, I *am* happy with Garrett. He's a great guy," I say, a bit too brightly. "Of course the past is the past, and we're both moving on."

"That's great," he says, releasing what sounds like a breath of relief. We chat for a few more minutes about how he's getting settled in L.A., the crazy traffic, and his new job. When I glance at my watch I see I'm really late now.

"Hey, Damon, I've gotta go. I'm supposed to meet Garrett soon."

"At the DARE reception at the Corcoran?" he asks.

"Yeah, how did you know?" Damn, Damon. I know we're trying to be friends and all, but do I have to see you every time I'm hooking up with my man?

"Garrett sent an invite over to my office last week with a note saying he thought this might be a good way for me to meet some people. Guess I'll see you there."

We hang up the phone and I stare into the mirror. Quickly I dash some soft gold shadow along my lightly outlined eyes and finish with a slight dusting of bronzer on the cheeks and my cleavage. Then I pull the heated rollers out of my hair. I pull a wide-tooth comb through the warm curls and then fluff it up with my fingers until it frames my face. I take a bottle of Narciso Rodriguez fragrance and spritz some on my neck and between my breasts. I dress quickly and then grab my hand-bag and the invitation with gold-leaf lettering from the bureau and head downstairs.

"Get it together, girl," I mutter to myself. "It's time to meet the parents."

WALKING INTO the gallery, I stop at the reception table to check in. The room is filled with black L.A.'s who's-who. As I turn to make my way into an area of the exhibit labeled "Harlem Renaissance," I see Keith Cooper in the far corner of the room with a beautiful woman. It's his wife, the actress Trixie Cooper. With her smooth, honey-brown skin, cheekbones that could cut glass, and long dark brown hair that frames her famous face, she's even more beautiful in person. I hope Amaya knows what she's doing with Keith, this doesn't look like a couple that's getting divorced anytime soon.

Glancing down at my program, I notice that Keith and his wife are cohosting this event with Garrett's parents. Suddenly Amaya's phone call makes sense. She knew Keith was cohosting this event with his wife and she was hoping I'd invite her. She better not be planning to show up up here and act a fool.

Stepping into the dining area, I see Garrett in a dark suit, standing at a podium. I can't help but smile. He's talking to an older man in a pinstriped suit, and the two bear a strong resemblance to each other, so I assume that must be the Judge. Garrett sees me and says something to his father, who turns and looks at me. Suddenly I feel like I'm one of the pictures hanging on the walls here tonight, to be evaluated by a poten-tial buyer. Garrett's father pats him on the shoulder and then walks back behind the small stage. Garrett makes his way over to me.

"Hi, gorgeous," he says and plants a warm kiss on my lips. I get that tingle in my stomach as he leads me out of the room to give me a tour of the gallery. We stop at a couple of the prints along the way, and he jots down his bid on a hauntingly beautiful 1940s image of a black woman and child sitting on the stoop in front of a tenement. As we're concluding our tour he tells me that his mother is a painter; she has pieces at the auction. He leads me over to a collection of watercolors with scenes of rolling countryside.

"Your mother is very talented," I say, looking at the pictures. "Where did she paint these? This sure doesn't look like L.A."

"At our house in Tuscany. She goes there every summer and paints. So what you're looking at here is our backyard."

"That's some backyard," I say, laughing, as I mentally compare it to South Central.

"Well, hopefully you'll let me show it to you in person," he says as he pulls me close to his body. I look up and giggle at the thought of running off to Italy with this man.

"Italy, huh?" I say, smiling.

"Yes, that would be a perfect way for us to celebrate after you make partner," he says, then whispers something softly in my ear in Italian. I have no idea what this man is saying, but whatever it is it sounds pretty good to me.

"Stop it, Garrett," I say, only half serious. "You're embarrassing me."

"Yes, Garrett," says a woman's voice mockingly from behind me. "You're embarrassing the *poor* girl." I turn away from Garrett's embrace to see a woman facing me with tight skin the color of roasted toffee, sharply arched eyebrows and flawless makeup. Her dark brown hair, streaked with auburn and gold highlights, is pulled back in a sleek chignon at the nape of her swanlike neck. This must be the mother. She is channeling Diahann Carroll from her Dominique Deveraux days, in a white Chanel suit with gold buttons as big as my fist and the same gold snakeskin pumps I'm wearing. I shift one leg behind the other to hide my shoes, as I doubt she's the type who would find that a charming coincidence.

"Mother," says Garrett, as he kisses her, "I want you to meet Trista Gordon."

"It's a pleasure to meet you, Mrs. James," I say as I extend my hand. She offers a limp wrist, as if she expects me to kiss her hand.

"Likewise, Trista," she says as she looks me up and down. Her eyes narrow when she reaches the tips of my shoes.

"Garrett, darling, where is your father?" she asks. She's finished with me.

"He's talking to the DARE people about the program," he answers. Garrett turns, puts his arm around my waist as if to pull me into the conversation. "I was just showing Trista your work, Mother."

"Oh, really?" she says and turns back to me. "So, tell me, Trista, what do you think of my little paintings?"

"They're lovely," I say. "I've never been to Italy, but from what I see in your work I can't wait to go."

"Planning a trip soon?" she asks frostily with a raised, sculpted eyebrow.

"I told her we should go over to the house sometime," says Garrett. I can tell by the way her body stiffens that Mrs. James isn't actually interested in that proposition.

"How nice. Well, it was lovely to meet you, Trista. I must now go find Garrett's father." She gives me a lukewarm smile before leaving.

"That couldn't have gone worse," I say, releasing the breath I've been holding.

"What are you talking about?" asks Garrett as we begin walking back into the dining room. "She loved you." When we make it to our table, I look up at the stage and see that Garrett's parents are sitting up on the dais with the DARE director and Keith and his wife. When Garrett makes the introductions around the table I see his college friend Mike and meet his wife, Tracey, and another guy from Garrett's office. The two other women at the table, Ché Bendel and Desiree Downey, eye me frostily. Moments after meeting me, one whispers something to the other that makes her laugh when they think I'm not looking. I hate them already.

The program begins with a short speech by DARE's director, Joe Petty, thanking everyone for coming to support their program to keep children off drugs. He then turns and introduces two teenagers, who appear by his side as if someone said, "Cue the cute inner-city kids," and explains to the audience how their generous contributions today will go to help kids like these, trapped in a neighborhood rife with drug dealing, to make the right choices in life. I hate these types of events where rich black people trot out poor black people to make themselves feel good. Mrs. James and Keith's wife, Trixie, then announce the winning bids in the silent auction. The waiters serve the first course.

"Have you met Bunny?" asks Ché, as she checks her glossy black shoulder-length curls in the reflection of her gold Versace compact. She then adjusts her stylish leopard-print dress with its daringly low neckline. Desiree, wearing a beautiful gold suit with a lacey camisole underneath, talks to Bryan.

"Bunny?" I ask, not sure who she's referring to.

"Yes, Bunny, Garrett's mother," Ché says, raising a perfectly shaped eyebrow at me as if I'm totally clueless. "Everyone calls her Bunny."

"Oh, I didn't know," I say.

"Yes, Bunny," says Desiree, joining our conversation. "Aunt Bunny is simply the best. We love, love, love her." It is clear by her use of "Aunt Bunny" that she's trying to send a message to me that they are close. Desiree prattles on about how they all grew up together, took family trips together, and have known each other forever. I signal the waiter to refill my wineglass. This could be a long night.

"Well, I just met her a few minutes ago," I say, taking a sip of wine. "She seems quite lovely." Ché and Desiree exchange glances and smile at each other.

"So, what do you do, Trista?" asks Ché.

"I'm an agent at TA," I answer. I pick up my fork to begin eating my Caesar salad.

"Oh, that must be fun," says Desiree, wrinkling her little button nose (it really is the size of a button). When I ask them what they do,

Ché says she owns a little boutique on Melrose, and that Desiree designs jewelry. They are typical L.A. BAPs—"Stepford sistas," as Amaya likes to call them. Girls who grew up with privilege, are always dressed perfectly, hair impeccable, and if they work it's more like a hobby. They are more familiar with the South of France than South Central. There's a lot of inbreeding in their circles and they don't like interlopers. Still, I decide to try to play nicely.

"Oh, I love your store," I say to Ché, trying to forge some sort of bond, to make this evening bearable. We talk fashion for a little while when Desiree tells me about her latest buying trip to Italy in which she took Ché with her for a few weeks. She casually mentions that they stayed at the Jameses' villa.

"That's so nice," I say sweetly as I take another sip from my glass. "I look forward to going over with Garrett next month." I stab the last leaf of lettuce on my plate with my fork and plant it in my mouth. Take that, heiffa.

"Are these seats taken?" a deep voice says over my shoulder. I look up and see Damon standing with Amaya. She looks at me expectantly, dressed in a light-blue thin dress that hugs her body. I gaze up at the dais and see that Keith is also aware of her presence. He does not look happy. Ché and Desiree give Amaya the black-girl once-over, throwing serious shade all the while checking her out under lowered lashes. They might as well have said, "Bitch, who the fuck are *you*?"

"Hey, Tris," Amaya says as she kisses me on the cheek before slipping into the empty seat next to Garrett. Damon sits down beside her. Garrett makes the introductions around the table. Ché and Desiree turn their full attention to Damon. Bryan, who is seated, tells Amaya that he recognizes her from somewhere but can't place her. Ordinarily Amaya would take this as an opportunity to flirt with a brother—but she's got her eyes on another prize tonight. Garrett continues to talk to his friends, so I ask Amaya to come to the ladies' room with me. We need to talk.

"What the hell is going on?" I hiss when we get to the ladies' lounge.

"What do you mean? I ran into Damon in the lobby and we walked in together," she says, removing her lipstick and lip brush from her small beaded clutch for a touch-up.

"Don't be coy, heiffa. I'm not talking about Damon. I'm talking about Keith. You knew he was cohosting this event with his wife. That's why you're here."

"Is he?" she asks. I give her a look to let her know I'm on to her.

"Look, what you do with Keith is your business, but don't get your dirty laundry mixed in with mine. I don't need the fireworks tonight."

"Girl, please. I've got this all under control." She reaches down and reties the silver straps of her sandals around her ankles, then rises and smooths down the front of her dress. It's apparent from the look of the sheer material that you can't wear undergarments with this dress.

"Nice dress," I say sarcastically as we turn to leave the powder room.

"Thanks, girl. Just a little something I picked up." As we make our way back into the dining room, it's as if Amaya were walking a red carpet. She smiles and blows kisses at people she recognizes around the room. I glance up at the dais again and see Keith is staring daggers into her backside. His wife seems oblivious to her entrance as she chats with the DARE director's wife, Tracey Petty.

"Hey, baby," says Garrett as he holds my chair and I take my seat at the table. "Damon was just telling us that you guys all went to UC together." I stare pointedly at Damon. There was no need to let everyone know any more than that.

"Yep, that's right," Damon says as he cuts into his breast of chicken. Ché, not satisfied that the attention is shifting away from her, jumps into the conversation.

"Oh, that's so funny. Garrett and I both went to Stanford together."

"Is that right, honey?" I ask, not sure what the point of her comment is.

"Yep," Garrett shifts uncomfortably in his seat, but before I can ask another question Mrs. James appears behind her son. She greets Ché and Desiree with kisses, while pointedly ignoring me and Amaya.

"Garrett, will you join your father and me for a cocktail afterwards?" she asks. "We'd like to chat."

"Of course, Mother. Trista and I will see you later," Garrett said. I can tell by the look on her face she was hoping I would be going home instead of joining a family conversation. I wonder if what she wants to talk about is me. When I turn around in my chair to ask Amaya what she thinks I should do about mommie dearest, I see that she's slipped away from the table. Without even looking back at the stage, I know that Keith's chair is empty as well.

AT THE CONCLUSION of the reception, Desiree and Ché ask Damon if he wants to join them for a drink in West Hollywood. I am surprised to hear him say yes.

"Sure, sounds good," he says. "Are you guys going to join us?"

"Oh, no thanks," I say, looping my arm through Garrett's. The Stepford sistas' faces perk up at my answer. "You three have fun."

"Cool," Ché says as she whips out her compact to check her flawless makeup yet again before departing. As I turn to ask Garrett if we're going to his place or mine I overhear Ché inviting Damon to a dinner party later in the week and giving him her business card. He smiles at her and puts the card into his jacket. When he looks up, he catches me observing their conversation. He winks at me, stands up, and then, smiling down at Ché, helps her up from her chair. I can't believe he wants to go out with her. Since when is she his type?

Ché loops her arms through Damon's and walks out of the reception. At least if he's hanging out with her I don't have to worry about him getting into my business. The room empties out quickly and soon the only other people left in the gallery are those on the planning committee, who are now sitting at the reception table, cataloguing the auction results and writing up shipping receipts under Trixie's watchful eye.

When Garrett's parents come over to the table, his father gives me a warm embrace.

"So nice to meet you, young lady," the Judge says. I smile brightly and catch a glimpse of Bunny's face, which looks like she's sucking on a lemon. Love, love, love the father; hate, hate, hate the mother.

The Judge asks me to accompany him through a final sweep of the gallery so he can show me some of his favorites. Garrett and his mother follow behind us.

As we all reach the end of the exhibit we hear whispered voices and a woman's giggles coming from a roped-off area in the back of the room. Suddenly Amaya walks out adjusting the top of her dress to cover nipples on high-beam and Keith follows behind her. Her face wears a self-satisfied smile until she sees me and Garrett's family.

"Uh, Trista, I'll call you later," she mumbles in my ear as she rushes out of the gallery.

I'm furious. I feel a hot flush rush up my neck. Keith tries to play off getting busted. He shakes the Judge's hand, thanks him for working with him. When he steps over to Mrs. James to try to kiss her on the cheek, she turns her head just out of his reach. He heads off, presumably to find his wife. "Wasn't that Trista's little friend?" Mrs. James asks, pointing over her shoulder, her eyes narrowed into little slits, her jawline tight.

"Yes," mumbles Garrett, looking at me quizzically.

"Tsk, tsk. We have to stop just letting anyone into these events," she says dismissively. After an awkward silence, Garrett says our goodbyes to his parents and we head out of the gallery. I can't believe Amaya. How could she be messing around with that man, and his wife is in the next room?

"So, WHAT'S UP with your friend?" Garrett asks as we wait for our cars to be brought around. I don't want to get in the middle of Amaya's mess, so I play dumb. I explain that I had invited her with the extra ticket he had given me and pretend to know nothing about her connection with Keith. Luckily he didn't pump me for details. Suddenly his friend Mike comes bounding out of the gallery.

"Ready to go, man?" he asks, slapping Garrett on the back. I look at Garrett quizzically as I was just about to suggest we go back to his place.

"Uh, yeah," he stutters. "You don't mind, right, honey? Mike's getting some of the guys together tonight. Cool?"

"Sure," I say, trying to mask my disappointment. "Will I see you Saturday?"

"Well, actually we were kinda planning to play golf that morning, and then catch up with some other friends." Mike looked at me expectantly, almost with a challenge in his eye. I didn't want to come between the two friends hanging out.

"No problem," I say with false brightness. "I'll probably just go see my dad."

"Thanks for understanding, Tris," Garrett says quickly. He kisses me goodnight and then helps me into my car. As soon as I merge onto the bumper-to-bumper traffic on the 405 freeway I dial Amaya's number and adjust my earpiece.

"Damn you, Amaya! Pick up the phone!" I yell as I weave in and out of traffic. I hang up and redial repeatedly. When I get her voicemail for the fifth time I throw the cell phone onto the passenger seat in disgust. I can't believe she dragged me and my man—and his family, for that matter—into her bullshit. I'm going to kill her.

I'M STRESSED. It's Monday and Cassidy hasn't returned my repeated calls to set up a meeting to discuss a new Miramax project, and now there's drama with Jared and Kimberly. Just as Sloane predicted, the *Star* came out with an item about Jared and Kimberly's alleged canoodling on the set. The other tabloids picked up on the story and began following them both around town. Apparently it was all more than Jared's fiancée could take. But instead of slinking back to Idaho, as Sloane had predicted, Heather swallowed a bottle of sleeping pills. My latest update from one of Sloane's assistants said they had pumped Heather's stomach and Jared was with her. Sloane is working desperately to keep it out of the papers. If she doesn't fix this, Jared will come off looking like a bastard who has driven this girl to try to kill herself. Audiences wouldn't like that. Our Paramount contract will be history. Jared's career will be over before it even started.

I call Viv to check on Corey before heading over to Garrett's office to pick him up to go to another client's premiere.

"What's up, Viv," I ask when she answers the phone.

"Nothing, girl. Just frying some chicken for dinner," she says. Damn, I wish she hadn't said that. Just the idea of Viv's fried chicken makes me want to drive over to her house. Just to torture myself I ask her what else she's making.

"Oh, just some of Corey's favorites. Mac and cheese, collard greens, some sweet potatoes, and some corn bread. It's our special 'eat what you like night.' The rest of the week we're not eating this mess—strictly veggies and baked or roasted meats for us."

"Damn, you're killing me. I know you put your foot in it, too."

"I need to since I've had to work late the last two nights, chasing around the new 'it' couple, Jared and Kimberly. My editor, the star-fucker, officially has a hard-on for the two of them and basically has me staking out their every move."

"They don't call it Hollyweird for nothing, sista," I say. I want to tell her about Heather's suicide attempt but I can't. Thankfully she drops it.

"Hey, why don't you come over? Jerome's coming over to watch the basketball game with us, but there's more than enough."

"Oh, Big Daddy's coming over, huh?" I say teasingly. "He's been spending a lot of time over there. Anything you need to tell me?"

"No, silly. We're just hanging out. He really likes Corey, and we're just going to watch the game. You know ain't nothing jumping off over here. It's not even like that. We're just friends, girl. Besides, I'm focused on making sure Corey stays healthy, and writing pieces as the culture critic for that online magazine I told you about. My third story runs next week."

"Can't wait to read it," I say. "I'm glad you're pursuing the type of writing you really love to do." I hope Daddy can get Sean out of her head.

"If you aren't coming over here, what are you doing tonight?" she asks. The sound of the grease popping in the skillet makes my stomach growl.

"Going to pick up Garrett to go to the *Washed Up* premiere," I answer.

"Oh, sounds like you two are inseparable. Although now that Damon's in town . . ." her voice trails off suggestively.

"Let it go, girl," I snap. Why does she have to keep bringing him up?

"You know, I don't think you really know what you want," she says.

"What do you mean by that?" I ask impatiently. "I'm looking for a relationship. I'm looking for someone who respects me, isn't threatened by my success, someone who can contribute to our financial security, someone supportive."

"Trista, what is wrong with you, girl? It doesn't seem like you're looking for a relationship as much as you're looking for a business partner."

"And what makes you the expert? You know what? Never mind. I don't even want to get into this with you. I gotta go."

"I'm just telling you this 'cause I love you and I may see something you don't."

"Whatever," I say. Now I'm annoyed. "Look, I'll call you tomorrow to find out what happened with you and Daddy."

"Well, hopefully I'll be reporting the same ol' thing: Nothing happened," she says as she hangs up the phone.

THE NEXT MORNING when I turn on my computer, I see a new email. I stop highlighting clauses in a contract and open a message from Amaya with an e-vite. I click on the link and a cartoon Elvis in a white pantsuit starts singing "Viva Las Vegas." Pink text appears below it on the screen:

YOU'RE INVITED TO: Amaya's 26th BIRTHDAY BASH
WHEN: September 24–26

WHERE: The Palm Hotel, Las Vegas

WHAT TO BRING: ABC—attitude, bikini, and condoms!

I'm still steamed at Amaya for her little performance at the Corcoran, but just looking at the invite piques my curiosity. I ask Adriene to conference in Amaya and Viv.

"Did you get my e-vite?" asks Amaya when we all get on the line.

"Aww, yeah. Vegas!" says Viv. "You know, that's just what I need after all the drama with Corey and Sean. Hot damn, it's on now!"

"Hold up, are you sure your other man is going to let you go? Maybe you should ask your Daddy first," I say as I laugh at my own joke.

"Listen, I go wherever I want to go," she replies tersely.

"Whatever, we're going to celebrate my birthday," says Amaya, jumping in. "And as the slogan goes: What happens in Vegas, stays in Vegas!"

"Oh, look here, I see on the invitation that it's your twenty-sixth birthday . . ." Viv says, laughing. "Didn't we celebrate your twenty-sixth last year?"

"And the year before that?" I offer.

"As far as casting agents and nosy reporters like yourself are concerned, I'm twenty-six. Look, this is going to be three days and two nights of fun in Sin City. I even convinced Elise to fly out. And I haven't even told you guys the best part."

"Well, don't hold back," I say. "What's the deal?"

"Keith bought all of us first-class tickets and booked us a luxury suite at the Palm," she says, her voice full of excitement. Does accepting Keith's generosity make me an accomplice to ruining his marriage, I wonder.

"Trista, I know you're already overthinking this," says Amaya. "Let's just go to Vegas and see Elise and hang out together. I promise it will be drama-free. And hopefully I'll have another surprise to share with you guys when we get there."

"All right, then, that sounds like an offer we can't refuse," Viv says.

"C'mon, Trista, let's get away for a weekend. Although I doubt I'll be bringing a bikini, and I damn sure won't need any condoms, but I've got plenty of 'tude."

"Well, I'm sure Amaya's packing enough condoms for all of us!" I say as I think about this little getaway a minute longer.

"Whatever, heiffa," shoots back Amaya. "You know you want to go."

"Sounds like we're going to Vegas, ladies," I say. "Besides, what's the worst that could happen?"

14

AMAYA

Go, Amaya, it's ya birthday! I sing along to my *Uncle Luke's Greatest Hits* CD as I hurriedly pack the red Tumi suitcase on my floor. Go, Amaya, go, go, go! I pause to break it down—humph, seems to me I can still pop my coochie with the best of them.

We're finally heading off to Vegas for my "twenty-sixth" birthday extravaganza, and I can barely wait for the opportunity to kick back with my girls and clear my head. Since I landed the Soular Son role, it feels like I've been running nonstop. Thanks to Viv's little leak, I've been caught up in a whirlwind of press. In the last two and a half months, I've been invited to more events than in the entire time I've lived in Los Angeles. Before I could consider calling Amber to hook me up with some decent outfits to be seen around town in, Clarence's phone was ringing off the hook with folks offering to send me samples. They aren't the big boys, like Gucci or Versace, but it's free! I swear, this industry is a trip. One day you're trying to beg, borrow, and steal just to show up and the next moment everybody loves you and it's not an event without you. Oh, and did I mention that one of the veteran actresses I beat out for the role was Keith's wife?

But nothing compares to the juggling act that I've got going on with Keith and Troy. Now that Keith's officially "in love," he's on a mission for me to dump Troy. But I'm sticking to my guns—I am not doing a thing until I see the signed divorce papers.

"Get 'em, girl," Troy says with a grin startling me from my thoughts and dance as he emerges, naked and dripping wet from my bathroom, rubbing his curly head with a towel.

"You like that, huh," I ask seductively.

"I don't know," he answers appreciatively. "I'm not even sure it's safe to let you out of my eyesight for a minute, let alone to roll to Vegas for an entire weekend."

"Don't worry," I answer as I saunter over and start licking the water drops from his chiseled chest. "My girls won't make me do anything your boys wouldn't do to you."

"Mmmm," he mumbles into the back of my head, "somehow that doesn't make me feel any better."

I look him in the eye and ask innocently, "What, you don't trust me?" He just looks at me and replies, "Yeah, I trust you all right. I trust you as far as I can throw you."

I gasp in mock surprise and dramatically pull away. Before I halfway spin around, he scoops me up in a bear hug and carries me to the bed where he unceremoniously drops me on my butt. Before I can sit up, he playfully falls on top of me and pins me down.

"Promise me you're not going to cut up in Vegas," he whispers in my ear as he licks and kisses my earlobe.

"Troy, stop playing. You're going to get my hair wet," I squeal, squirming beneath his slippery body.

"Promise me, Amaya," he insists as he pushes away the thin straps of my camisole with his mouth and sucks on my already hard nipple. Lord have mercy, this little boy is good. With just a couple of licks, I'm more than ready to give up the center of my tootsie roll. It takes every ounce of willpower in my body to push him off and sit up.

"Baby, it's almost time for you to take me to the airport. Please go get dressed," I plead as I stand up and straighten out the delicate top.

"Yo, for real, what's up?" he asks as he finally sits up. "Why can't you promise? Is there something I should know before you leave here?"

"Give me a break, Troy," I answer, a little annoyed by his insistence. "I'm not about to go to Vegas and do anything that I'm not already doing right here in Los Angeles. I just don't believe in wasting my word."

"Yeah, okay, whatever, Amaya," he answers with a noticeable attitude and strides over to the dressing room, where his clothes are laid out and waiting for him.

As I watch him walk away, I consider chasing after him to try and smooth things over but quickly decide against it. As much sneaking around as I do in Los Angeles with Keith, Troy's never batted an eye or suspected a thing, but now that I'm going out of town with my girls on a trip that he knows about—*that's* a problem? Isn't he constantly on the road? Refusing to spoil the mood of my day, I turn up the stereo and keep packing. Fifteen minutes later, Troy emerges from the dressing room and breezes right past me. "I'll be downstairs," he tosses over his shoulder.

I really need to thank Troy. His behavior this morning is going to make it much easier for me to enjoy the all-expense-paid trip that Keith has given me as a birthday gift totally guilt-free. For a moment there, I'd become confused. I'd started to think that maybe Troy had real potential. Clearly I need to stick to plan A: Troy is a decoy, not my goal. Not to mention, I'm not stupid. I know what this kind of suddenly possessive shit really means—he's cutting up. I'm willing to bet that he's done something on the road that I don't know about *yet*. Now his nerves are bad because he knows how it can go down. Whatever, Negro, I conclude as I run a quick last-minute and head downstairs to inform him that my luggage is waiting upstairs for him to carry out to the truck.

The entire ride to the airport is silent except for the sound of Troy's Jadakiss CD. As he pulls the Cayenne up to Delta's curbside check-in, I immediately look around for Trista and Viv. As I turn back around to unfasten my seatbelt, I catch Troy staring at me.

"What?" I ask irritably. "Are you not finished ruining my birthday?"

"I'm so sorry, babe, I don't know what came over me," he apologizes softly.

You know what came over you, fool, I think. *I'm the one that you think doesn't know.*

"Can you please forgive me? I don't want us to fight, especially over your birthday weekend," he pleads, reaching out to stroke my hair.

"Oh, Troy," I sigh slowly as I quickly consider my options—play hard, refuse to accept his apology, and risk losing my bait; or . . . play nice, accept the apology, and pray that Keith hurries up. Either way, I'm putting the pressure on Keith when I return to L.A.

I decide to keep my eyes on the prize, "I don't want to fight. I would never do anything to jeopardize what we have." Each word burns my throat as I swallow my pride.

"That's my baby girl," he says with a cocky smile as he leans in for a kiss. Thankfully, at that exact moment, the traffic cop knocks loudly on the car window.

"Either you're unloading or you're moving," the overweight, pimply-faced man screams as spittle decorates the pane of glass.

"Jesus, I hate those motherfuckers," Troy exclaims as he pulls away from me and starts to get out of the truck.

"Hardest-working force in the war on terror," I mumble in consent as I pull down the visor to retouch my gloss. As soon as I finish, I jump out of the truck and walk over to where Troy has placed my luggage on the curbside. People immediately recognize Troy's striking six-eleven frame, I can hear the buzz of the basketball fans growing behind us.

"Okay, ma," he says as he bends down to give me a quick kiss on the mouth. "Let me go before people start asking for a bunch of autographs and whatnot."

"Sure," I reply evenly. "So you're picking me up on Monday night?"

"Actually, I may have a late practice, so I'll probably send a car," he replies a little too quickly, "but I'll definitely come through the crib with all your gifts afterwards."

"I hear ya," I answer distractedly as I spot Trista getting out of the back of a Mercedes car service wearing a yellow-and-white strapless Theory sundress.

"Be good, babe," he calls as he jumps back into his truck.

No, nigga, *you* need to be good. Talking 'bout some late night practice, I curse mentally yet simply reply, "Will do."

"Is THIS THE life or what?" I sigh contentedly to Viv and Trista as we relax in our first-class seats on the direct flight to Vegas.

"I know that's correct," Viv quickly agrees.

"Personally, I would like to propose the first of many toasts to Amaya, the birthday girl," says Trista as she raises her glass of champagne. "May her thirty-second—ahem, I mean twenty-sixth—year be better than any of us can imagine."

"Hear! Hear!" seconds Viv.

"Thank you, thank you very much," I say as I jokingly cut my eyes at Trista and take a sip. "In turn, I would like to toast my beloved best friends, Trista, Viv, and Elise—even though she won't be with us for a few more hours. You guys are my inspirations."

"Yeah, yeah, whatever, drama queen," replies Trista with a slight hint of sarcasm.

"Damn that, I know I love you. Since Corey's hospitalization, shit done changed. I'm new and improved and down for living life to the fullest," answers Viv.

"I agree that this getaway couldn't have come at a better time, but don't thank me, girl," I correct her, ignoring Trista's little comment. "Thank our benefactor, Keith Cooper. Not only did he hook your girl up with this beautiful Balenciaga tote I've been dying for, he was also kind enough to bankroll this little first-class getaway for the four of us."

"I'll drink to that," laughs Trista.

"I don't know how you do it," giggles Viv, already visibly feeling the effects of her two vodka and tonics in the Platinum Flyer Lounge and now this glass of bubbly.

"If I tell you, I'll have to kill you," I whisper menacingly and then fall back in my seat, laughing. "Girl, please, as much mess as I put up with, this trip is the least."

"Well, please let the choir sing," agrees Trista in her church-lady singsong voice as she reclines her seat back and closes her eyes.

"Tris, I know you're not going to sleep," Vivian whines. "We're only a hop, skip, and a jump away."

"Yes the hell I am," she answers, pulling the blanket up around her neck. "And if you knew what was good for your little tipsy behind you'd do the same."

"Trista's right, Viv. You better get what little rest you can now because as soon as we land it's going to be on and popping!'"

"Fine, you old spoilsports, but, for the record, I'm not even tired," Viv grudgingly relents and reclines her seat as well. Within minutes both Trista and Vivian are sound asleep.

As I sip on my glass and watch my girls sleep, I realize just how grateful I am that they're all coming together to share my birthday weekend—especially Trista. Things haven't been right between us since that little incident at the Corcoran Gallery. I mean; I know I was dead wrong for pulling that stunt with Keith, but sometimes I act without thinking. She knows how I am. Matter of fact, she was there when I keyed our chemistry professor's Cadillac after he turned one of my low exam scores into a class joke.

Granted, I've come a long way since college, but it's like, when I saw Keith sitting up there with Trixie, something just snapped in my mind. I needed to prove to myself that he would do whatever I wanted despite his wife standing only a few feet away. I had no idea Trista and Garrett's entire family would walk in on us like that! I was so mortified I ran straight out of the gallery and even left my phone behind. Whenever I try to discuss what happened with Trista, she insists everything is fine— but I know better. That girl holds a serious grudge. I just hope that we're able to finally patch things up in Vegas.

Speaking of Keith, I still haven't figured out what I'm going to do with the dirt I learned about his beloved wife. About a week ago, I finally heard back from Lisa. Despite our original delivery agreement, she insisted that I come into the office to discuss her findings. I assumed it was gonna be a scandalous situation, but I had no idea . . .

"Thanks for coming, Amaya," Lisa said as she shut the door and walked back over to her desk. "You look great as always. Loving the top—is that Catherine?"

"Malandrino it is. And thank you, so do you. Now please correct me if I'm wrong but I thought we agreed that you'd just email the photos and then mail me the proofs. What gives?" I asked from the edge of my seat, practically salivating.

"True, true. However, as I'm sure you'll see, this is some shit," she replied with a raised eyebrow as she slid the envelope across her desk toward me.

"Really . . ." I responded, wondering what could possibly be shit to an experienced PI like Lisa as I ripped open the envelope's seal.

As I review the forty-eight crystal-clear shots of Mrs. Trixie Cooper getting it on with a beautiful blonde woman in a hotel suite, I want to fall to my knees and start speaking in tongues—thank you, Jesus! Thank you, Jesus! Not only has the Lord heard my prayer, he hooked a sister up! Come to find out, not only has Trixie been turning tricks for someone other than Keith, but "Sam" isn't even a man!

Since that afternoon, at Lisa's suggestion, I've been super-tight-lipped about the whole thing—it's taken all my willpower not to mention it even to Viv and Trista. She made a very important point about how this information is too hot for even the best of friends to be expected to keep silent on. Keith's been in Chicago for the past two weeks, so I definitely haven't spoken a word to him about it. But we're having dinner on Tuesday night, when he returns, so I'm thinking that I'll check on the progress of his divorce then. If it seems like things are moving along smoothly, then maybe I'll save the photos for a rainy day. You never know how Trixie is going to act after she finds out that the two of us are together. Better safe than sorry, I think smugly.

JUST AS I'D EXPECTED, from the minute our flight lands at the Vegas airport we are off and running. From the baggage claim, a stretch limo whisks us through the thick desert heat to the Palms, where we're all rooming together in a luxurious four-bedroom penthouse suite. As we cruise down the crowded strip, I can feel my body absorbing all the energy from the lights and drama that only Sin City can provide. Upon our arrival at the hotel, we quickly change into our bathing suits and head straight out to secure a couple of poolside lounge chairs. A little over an hour later, Elise, who arrived on a separate flight from Atlanta, joins us.

"Guess who's here!" exclaims Elise as she sneaks up behind our chairs.

"We thought you'd never get here!" we cry, scrambling to greet her with hugs and kisses. The ten months since we've last seen her suddenly feel like ten years.

"Y'all ain't the only ones," she replies with a sigh and falls into a fourth lounge chair that we've been reserving for her. "Whew, it's hotter than hell out here. Where's the damn waitress? I need some water ASAP."

"Okay, you look amazing," starts Trista admiring Elise's sexy one-piece suit.

"Married ten months and you haven't put on a pound," Viv complains. "I thought you were supposed to put on at least fifteen pounds during your honeymoon!"

"Girl, please. With so many deranged and desperate single women out there, I have no choice but to stay looking right if I want to keep my man."

"Hey, hey, hey," I laugh, pretending to be hurt as I sit up and carefully adjust the triangle top on my skimpy red string bikini. "You happen to be talking to some of those deranged and desperate single women."

"I know that's right," seconds Viv.

"My bad," Elise quickly corrects herself. "But y'all don't know nothing about these ATL girls. They're educated, stay looking right, and are always ready to throw together a good-ass home-cooked meal. I swear, if you blink your eye for two seconds too long they'll be right up in your damn kitchen feeding your family!"

"Maybe," says Trista as she turns over onto her stomach. "But we do know that Will loves your dirty drawers, so don't bother trying to sell us that little sob story!"

"I hear ya," Elise replies with a half-hearted shrug as she stands up and walks over to the bar to get her water, ending the conversation abruptly and leaving us all looking at each other over the tops of our sunglasses with raised eyebrows.

We lounge between the pool and the bar for the remainder of the afternoon, drinking martinis, catching up, and wading in the water—'cause you know we weren't about to get our hair wet. By the time the sun starts to set in the sky I'm almost drunk, and couldn't be happier.

"Well, I don't know about y'all, but I'm ready to go in," I say, steadying myself on the back of my chair as I attempt to stand and tie my sarong around my hips. "Because bottom line is, as much as Keith Cooper loves my chocolate skin, he sure as hell doesn't want me coming back from Vegas blue-black from too much sun."

"As black as his behind is, he got the nerve," Elise smartly answers from behind her huge Jackie O—esque sunglasses.

"Girl, you know how color-struck some black men can be," responds Viv. "Between that and the obsession with long hair, they'll keep a sister insecure."

"Or in a cheap weave," I laugh.

"I know that's correct," laughs Trista.

"I say we all take a little disco nap, and just choose a restaurant to eat at when we get up," Elise finally decides. "I don't know about you ladies, but I'm exhausted!"

"Cool," I respond.

NEEDLESS TO say, our little "disco nap" turns into a full-blown siesta. By the time I wake, it's well past ten o'clock and I am completely ravenous. I decide to run out and grab a snack without waking up the girls. Lord knows those three sleep harder than rocks, and it'd take at least twenty minutes before I'd be able to motivate them.

Before I slip out of the suite, I scribble a quick note to the girls on the pad on the hall table, letting them know that I'm headed down to the café and inviting them to join me if they wake before I return. Although by the sounds of the snoring coming from the rooms, I'm certain to return well before any of these three even bats an eye.

Although the elevator car is empty when I begin my descent, it goes without saying that by the time I arrive at the lower levels it will be jam-packed. The Palms is a notorious resting spot for the real-deal ballers and shot callers when they come to town. There's never a shortage of eye candy and potential connections—if you know what I'm saying. No sooner do I reach the café and become comfortably seated in a booth, when I spot an all too familiar face—Jamal. Lord have mercy. I haven't seen him since last December, at Trista's company Christmas Eve party, and he looks better than ever. As we make eye contact, a slow smile spreads across his face. I inhale deeply as he turns and heads over to my table. I exhale as the memories of the party flood back into my mind.

Every year Trista invites me. One of the most highly anticipated affairs of the year, it was an amazing event—held at the home of The Agency's CEO, there were trapeze artists, fire eaters, and an array of burlesque dancers, in addition to a five-course buffet. This year Jay-Z and Madonna both performed a couple of sets. It's understood that this is one of the few L.A. parties left in existence where there will be no VIP section—because everyone is a VIP. Everyone, from Governor Schwarzenegger to the Olsen twins, was in attendance. Even though it was her own holiday party, Trista still had to work the room and make sure that all her clients were being accommodated. So I was left pretty much to my own devices for the majority of the night. About five glasses of Veuve and two shots of Patrón in, I lost track of Trista completely and met Jamal on the dance floor. The newbie male model who just landed a Sean John underwear billboard on Sunset was the sexiest dancer I'd come across in a while. Long story short, we ended up leaving the party together. And we brought in Christmas with Jamal bringing me to climax after climax.

Unfortunately, bad timing and the shows in Paris kept us from reconnecting, so we mutually decided to just let it go. Occasionally I'll see his face on a new billboard, in a video, or in an ad in *XXL* and reminisce about our one-night. And now, out of nowhere, here he is, in Vegas, of all places. This is starting out to be a banging birthday weekend . . .

"Hey, sexy," he growls in my ear as he bends down to kiss me on my cheek.

"Not me," I coolly reply from behind my lowered lids. "You're the sexy one."

"Whatever, Amaya," he grins as he slides into the booth next to me. "So, congratulations on landing the movie. I'm happy to see that you're blowing up."

"Why, thank you," I reply, sipping the water that the waitress placed on the table.

"Shouldn't you be in a VIP section somewhere with your ball-playing boyfriend?"

"Glad to see you're following my life so closely," I answer, secretly thrilled that he's been keeping up with my whereabouts. "Actually, it's my birthday weekend and I'm here in Vegas kicking it with my girls. What are you doing here, nosey?"

"Oh, just trying to get my little side hustle on. I'm the principle male in the new Foxy Brown video that they're shooting," Jamal replies as he gently plays with my hair.

"Really?" I respond as my skin starts to tingle from his close proximity.

"Yeah, we've been out here for a couple of days," he says and continues to stare at me from behind the most perfect set of eyelashes I've ever seen on a man. "We're actually finishing up tomorrow. If you and your girls are feeling up to getting into some mischief, you should definitely come through our wrap party at the Hard Rock Hotel."

"Hmmm, sounds interesting," I murmur, thinking about all the mischief I'd personally like to get into with Jamal.

"Well, my pager number hasn't changed," he says, finally breaking his gaze.

"I hear ya," I casually reply with a sideways grin.

"Hear what?" a voice behind me loudly inquires, and I turn to find that Elise has snuck up on me once again.

"Oh, hey, girl," I greet her. "This is my old friend, Jamal. Jamal, this is Elise Jacobs-Johnson. She's one of the girlfriends that I was telling you about earlier."

"Very pleased to meet you," replies Jamal as he gives Elise the once-over.

"Same here," she answers, shifting slightly to offer him a better view of her butt in the skin-tight Joe Jeans. "I certainly hope that I'm not interrupting something."

"Oh, no, beautiful. I was just inviting Amaya to this wrap party at the Hard Rock tomorrow night," he easily explains. "I thought you guys might want some company while you're helping Amaya celebrate her birthday."

"Is that so? Well, I've never been one to turn down a gentleman's offer of assistance," Elise replies coyly as she fingers her diamond-studded heart pendant. Once again, I find myself staring at her with raised eyebrows.

"So I guess we'll be seeing you tomorrow, Jamal," she continues ignoring me.

"I look forward to it," he replies as he kisses us both on the cheek and walks away. "Good night, ladies."

"Good night," Elise replies, breaking her neck to get a good look at his butt.

"Elise Erin Jacobs-Johnson," I hiss. "What in the world are you doing?"

"Oh, Amaya, relax. I'm just having fun," she casually responds as she signals to the waitress to bring her a menu. "Can't a married woman test out her skills a little?"

"Okay, if you say so," I answer hesitantly. "You've been acting crazy since you got here. Just don't get in trouble trying to be cute."

"No trouble," she replies as she turns back around. "No trouble at all."

"HAPPY BIRTHDAY to you, / Happy birthday to you, / Happy birthday, dear Amaya, / Happy birthday to you," the girls sing at the top of their lungs. After spending our entire day shopping and window wishing, the girls surprise me with a huge strawberry shortcake and champagne when we return to the suite Saturday evening.

"I am so blessed to have you guys in my life," I sniffle. "I love you guys!"

"Aww, we love you, too, knucklehead," says Elise as she gives me a tight hug.

"And we all know that it's only a minute before you blow up," continues Trista, "so don't be trying to shake a sister when you do."

"I will never be like that," I answer truthfully. "You guys are practically the only people in this world who really know my heart, and I would be totally lost without you."

"Yeah, well, just don't forget me in your acceptance speech, that's all I have to say," laughs Vivian.

"And risk getting cursed out every day for the rest of my natural-born life? Not."

"Best believe that," cosigns Elise.

"Well, since you guys were kind enough to drop what you were doing and help me celebrate my birthday, I have something for you as well," I grin slyly as I head into my bedroom to grab the birthday gift that Clarence surprised me with a couple of days ago—an advance copy of the October issue of *King* magazine. It'd taken damn near six months of stalking, but right before I found out about the film, Clarence finally managed to convince Datwon Thomas, *King*'s editor-in-chief, to shoot me for one of his coveted cover spots. Only the sexiest chicks in the game grace the cover of *King*: Gabrielle, Kelis, Ashanti, and now me. Humph, I'll bet Datwon is super-geeked that his publication is the first to have me on the cover. Personally, every time I think about how much more exposure I'm going to get from this cover, I break out in a Kool-Aid grin. The article is a sexy read, while the photo spread, which riffs off the shower scenes from my *Bad Girlz* performance, is off the chain. As for the cover, well, I really did my thing. From the hot-pink rhinestone-studded bikini to the S-shaped profile pose, let's just say that I earned the cover line—"Amazing Amaya!"

"More surprises?" says Viv gleefully as she rushes to see what it is that I have hidden in my room.

"God, Viv, you're like a little kid," chastises Trista, but she follows close behind.

"I was going to wait until our dinner party tonight, but oh well . . . Ta-*dah*," I exclaim as I turn around with the front cover facing them. "Have a sneak peep at my very first magazine cover!"

"Oh my," is Viv's only reply as she stops dead in her tracks, her mouth agape.

"Wow," Elise states, her eyes wide as saucers.

"Amaya, why would you . . ." Trista trails off.

"Why would I *what*?" I ask immediately defensively. "You guys think I look crazy or something?"

"May I see?" Elise asks as she takes the magazine from my hand and starts to flip through it.

"Not crazy," says Viv gently. "It's just that . . . your breasts are kinda hanging out."

"My breasts are not hanging, they're standing out," I correct her. "And for your information, I like the way I look. There isn't even any airbrushing involved. Not for nothing, it's a huge accomplishment to be chosen for a *King* cover!"

"Hanging or standing, it really doesn't matter. Love you to death,

Amaya," Trista says matter-of-factly, "but unless you're an established star like Vivica or Tyra, this cover was not the move."

"Thanks a fucking lot, Trista," I say from between clenched teeth.

"Actually," Elise starts thoughtfully as she turns to the article, "I think you look amazing, Amaya. It takes balls to do something like this, and, personally, I think it's hot."

"Well, if there's anyone with the balls, it's Amaya," Viv offers as Elise passes her the issue.

"From what I can see, the photos are going to turn a lot of heads—but in your quotes you come across as young, sexy, and smart. Not at all like an airhead or some cheap video girl," Elise assures me with a huge smile. "Let me be the first to congratulate you on your first cover, hot mama."

"Thanks, E," I say as my eyes throw daggers at Trista. "I appreciate your support. I'm really excited about it."

"Hey, I'm not saying I don't support you," Trista says in a lame attempt to backtrack. "I'm just being real about the professional implications of the cover."

"I hear ya, but can you do me a favor and keep your 'realness' to yourself right now?" I respond as the tension in the room continues to build.

"Whatever, Amaya," she mutters as she turns and heads back into the living room. "I'm going to get in the shower."

"Okay, settle down, tiger," Elise jokes as she tries to defuse my obvious annoyance.

"I'm fine," I insist as I turn away to move over to the window. "I'm just sorry that I bothered. I should've just showed it to people that will be as excited as I am and let y'all find out about it when it hits the news-stands."

"It is actually a very well written piece," Viv gently inserts. "And, quite honestly, I'd probably do the same thing if my breasts could still stand up . . ."

Elise walks over to where I'm standing by the window and gives me

a tight hug. I bury my face in her shoulder to stop the tears. "Yo, don't worry about what Trista thinks. You know how manic she is about keeping up appearances. It's her job, for Christ's sake. Let her worry about what everyone is going to say, you enjoy making people talk. That's what got you this far, didn't it? So what if it's a gamble? You're that chick. If anyone can pull it off, you can."

"I'm sorry I spoke so quickly," Viv apologizes as she comes over to hug me. "You look great and I'm very proud of you."

"It's cool," I say as I dry my tears. "I just hate when I think I've done something right and it blows up in my face."

"You don't have to apologize, we all go through it," Elise continues. "Shoot, don't nobody have to tell me about shit blowing up in my face."

"Huh, what are you talking about, E? Your life is freaking perfect," I counter.

"Girl, please, there's nothing perfect about my life," she sighs, falling onto the bed.

"Okay, what the hell is going on? You've been acting real shady about Will and how married life is going ever since you arrived. Is everything all right?" Viv demands as she walks over to the bed and sits down beside Elise.

"I just don't know, y'all. This marriage thing isn't what it's cracked up to be—at all. It's like, now that we're married, Will's developed this really nonchalant attitude about everything that concerns me. He's so focused on his political ambitions, it's as if he has no energy left for our marriage. I really feel like I have no identity except for being his wife. And, to make matters worse, my period is late," she responds softly.

"What the hell . . ." I start as I head over to the bed.

"Oh yeah, girl, I've been going through it. This whole time I'm thinking that I'm so lucky because I'm finally out of the game and come to find out that winning isn't nearly as sweet as I imagined. And now that there might be a baby involved, I just don't know which way is up," Elise continues.

"Have you tried talking to him?" asks Viv gently.

"Of course I have, but it just falls on deaf ears. I even tried talking to his mother, but her attitude was simply, welcome to the club. Apparently this is how all the men in his family behave," Elise states simply. "To make matters worse, his mother made it very clear that if I don't like it, there are a whole lot of women who will gladly take my place. So now I'm all paranoid, thinking that there's someone out there trying to replace me."

"Damn his mother and her doomsday attitude. You don't have to deal with that shit," I respond sourly. "Even if you are pregnant, you still have choices."

"Girl, now you know," she laughs bitterly. "About two weeks ago, I told William that if he didn't have the energy to dedicate to keeping our relationship going then we should consider a trial separation. And, girl, he about freaked out. He knows the deal—not only will I leave, but I won't look back once I'm gone. When I get home, we're starting couples therapy. I'll probably tell him about the baby then."

"Wow," Viv exhales loudly. "I'd have never guessed. I just assumed that since you weren't like the three of us, struggling to make our Vow a reality, you were better off."

"Yeah, well, hopefully we *will* be. I love my husband and plan to do everything in my power to work things out. I don't need the moon and the stars to be happy with him. But the bottom line is, I'm not going to be the only one doing the work, especially if we have a little one on the way," Elise states simply as she pulls herself up and forces a smile. "But we're not here to worry about that or what some random people might say about your devastatingly sexy cover. We're here to celebrate, so let's get it popping!"

"I know that's right," I say, refusing to let the entire mood be spoiled. "E, you call room service and order another bottle of Veuve for us and some fruit juice for you. I'm about to jump in the shower and start to get ready. Viv, you go see if Trista is out of the shower yet. We're about to turn this party out!"

"Okay, well, just remember y'all asked for it," Viv responds with a grin.

"Bring it on, hot mama, bring it on!"

Two HOURS LATER we pile into the limo and head over to the Hard Rock. I'm still salty with Trista for being so judgmental, but I decide to concentrate on having a blast. I'm with my girls, about to see a cute boy, and feeling good. There's an unbelievable crowd of beautiful people milling around the lobby of the hotel. It's showtime, baby!

The promoter at the entrance immediately recognizes me and whisks us inside. The entire space is filled with photographers' flashing lights, half-naked video girls, slightly familiar-looking male models, and Foxy's Brooklyn crew. The music thumps loudly in my ears and with each step my adrenaline rushes higher. I feel like a total ghetto celeb as people stop, stare, and whisper. When we finally reach the roped-off VIP area, I spy Foxy and her girls laughing in the right corner. Out of respect, I head over and offer a quick hello while the girls settle into our booth. Turns out, Foxy is familiar with my last indie film, *A Bad Bitch Rides in Harlem,* and invites us to join her rowdy crew. I momentarily pause, thinking of Trista. In the cutthroat world of Hollywood everyone is subject to judgment by association: I'm sure rappers and hip-hop heads are not the type of company she wants to be photographed hanging out with. But then again, I'm the damn actress. Her place is behind the scenes. If I don't care, then neither should she! So I graciously accept Foxy's offer, turn, and signal to the girls to come on over.

Turns out that Elise is actually a huge fan of Foxy's, and Viv had what was one of the few decent interviews Foxy has ever given, so they are more than happy to keep the party going in the larger booth. Trista, on the other hand, looks totally annoyed and refuses to sit. She insists on heading out to the dance floor to wander around on her own.

"What is her damn problem?" I angrily inquire.

"Girl, please," Elise again tries to smooth everything over as a super cute Latin guy comes and pulls her up to dance. "She's probably just going to go call Garrett and complain about how undignified we're all behaving. Don't even worry about it."

"Elise is right. Trista will be just fine," seconds Viv as she nods her head at the cutie at the other booth raising his champagne glass in obvious appreciation of her fitted fuchsia dress. "Now, if you'll excuse me, I'm about to go get friendly with the natives."

As annoyed as I am, the sight of Vivian sauntering over to talk to a dude she wouldn't give the time of day to if she were sober gives me a fit of giggles. Suddenly, a pair of very large hands cover my eyes from behind. "How you doing, miss?"

"Mmm, just fine, thank you," I purr as I remove the hands and turn to face Jamal. He looks good enough to eat in his blue-and-white button-up and dark-blue jeans. Whew, I love it when black men get their grown and sexy on!

"What's really good, birthday girl? You planning to play the booth all night or you trying to shake that ass for a player?" he dares me.

"You know, this just so happens to be my jam," I answer, rising to follow him out on to the dance floor. As I pass Elise and Viv, I nudge them to let them know that I'm headed out to the floor. They're both so caught up dancing and having a good time, they barely notice. As we enter the crowd, I quickly scan to see if I can spot Trista. Mad as I am, I certainly don't want her to get caught up in some shit without any of us around to help. Noticing my roving eye, Jamal spins me around to face him.

"Scared your man might show up?" he jokes.

"Actually, I was looking for one of my girls," I correct.

"Don't worry, Amaya. If she's remotely like you, I'm sure she's up in here having herself a great time," he assures me as he pulls me close and runs his fingers down my back. Before too long, I completely lose consciousness of everything around me except for the heat from Jamal's rock-hard joint on my butt.

I have no idea how much time has passed when I feel a hard jabbing sensation on my shoulder. Shaken out of my private-dancer mode, I spin around to confront whoever the hell is poking me like that. "Excuse you," I ask.

"We're ready to go," Trista states nastily with a hard eye roll for emphasis.

"Trista, we just got here, why don't you relax," I sigh, annoyed by her intrusion.

"Look, Amaya. It's damn near five o'clock in the morning, I have a splitting headache, Elise is grinding on some dude that looks like he just got released from jail, and Viv is in a bathroom stall about to vomit. Please say good night to your little friend and come on," she snaps as she cuts her eyes at both Jamal and me.

Jamal takes one look at Trista and chuckles softly, "Go head, ma. You got my number and I know where you're staying. We'll definitely get up."

"Fine," I turn around, give Jamal a long-ass good-bye kiss and whisper, "I will see you later." Then I brush past Trista to go collect Viv and Elise. It was time to go all right.

The next morning the sound of steady knocking at my door jars me out of my slumber. "Amaya! Come get the phone," insists Trista from outside my door.

I'm so groggy, I can barely form the words to tell her that I'm on my way. As I attempt to sit up, I'm suddenly pulled back onto the bed. What the hell? Oh shit, my right wrist is tied to the freaking bedpost with a slipknot.

"Amaya, will you please come on. Keith's on the telephone," Trista continues.

"Just a second," I answer, trying to sound as normal as possible while struggling to untie my wrist. I can't believe this shit. After a few seconds I realize it's simply not coming undone. "Um Tris, do me a favor and please just bring the phone in here," I ask trying to cover myself with as much of the sheet as I can reach with my free hand.

As soon as Trista steps through the door and sees me tied to the bed-post her look of annoyance turns to disgust. Ignoring it, I motion for her to pass me the phone so that I can cradle it between my head and shoulders.

"Hey, baby," I whisper softly into the phone, desperately trying to sound sleepy.

"Hey, birthday girl, what took you so long to get to the phone," Keith questions. "I sure hope that you weren't up late celebrating with no nigga."

"Aww, naw. I'm just dead-ass tired from last night, that's all."

"Hmm . . . if you say so. I just wanted to be the first to wish you a happy birthday. I know it's early but I'm going to be tied up in the stu-dio all day with Young Daddy."

"Oh, okay," I whisper. "And babe, thank you so much for every-thing, I'm having a blast. I just wish you could be here with me."

"Next time, sweetie, next time. I'll holla at you later, okay? I love you."

"I love you, too, Keith."

As soon as I hear the phone click, I drop the receiver into my lap with a sigh of relief. That was too close. I call out to Trista to come back into my room. Trista walks back in with a super stank look on her face.

"What?" she demands.

"Ugh, what is all that for? I was simply going to thank you for help-ing me out and ask you to please pass me the pair of scissors that are in the desk in the living room."

Wordlessly, Trista turns and walks back out. When she finally re-turns with the scissors, she's mumbling under her breath. She drops the scissors on my lap, rolls her eyes and walks back out. As I cut the silk headscarf that's holding my wrist captive, I can feel the heat from my anger rising through my body. I have officially run out of patience.

I can't believe that Jamal left me tied to the bed. I mean, don't get me wrong, from what I can remember, last night was definitely the jump off—Jamal came up to the suite about an hour after we left the party with a bucket of ice, a bottle of Moët, and a rock-hard penis. I know what we did about the dick, but from the look of the slightly damp sheets, I can only guess what happened with the rest. But did he have to leave a sista hanging?

Either way, that was the least of my worries right now. Now, Trista, on the other hand . . . As soon as I free myself, I grab my robe and head over to her bedroom. I knock with the same urgency that she used earlier at my door. She finally opens the door.

"May I speak to you out here in the living room?" I ask between clenched teeth.

"Can this wait?" she replies snottily.

"No, it can't. So either you grab a robe and come out here or I'll come in there with you," I respond, staring her down.

"Fine. I'm coming," she answers and closes the door in my face.

As I sit down on the couch, my body is trembling with anger. Trista is really on some next-level nonsense right now. "You know what, Trista?" I start as soon as she crosses the threshold of her bedroom, "I don't know what the hell has crawled up your ass, but you really need to get over it! 'Cause this bitchy attitude you've got is for the birds."

"Fuck you, Amaya. The only one that's acting up is you. Maybe the reason you recognize the attitude is because you've been acting like a trick," she angrily retorts.

"You guys," says Viv, who appears in the entrance to her bedroom, looking green around the gills. "Please stop yelling, it's not that serious."

"Actually, Viv, I think it is," Trista snaps. "First, Amaya, you totally embarrass me at the gallery and fuck up any chance that I may have had with Garrett's family, then you have the nerve to cop an attitude when I give you honest feedback about the soft-porn cover that's about to end your half-assed career. Last night you were acting like a stripper in the middle of a huge party with photographers everywhere, and this morning I had to help you out of some bondage shit that God only knows who

left you in," she continues. "I'm sick of your thoughtless and irresponsible behavior."

"First of all, let that be the last time you ever speak to me that way or
I will slap the taste out of your mouth," I hiss jumping up to stand
directly in her face. "I have apologized a thousand times for the incident at the gallery, but the bottom line is I am a grown woman. I'll do
whatever the hell I feel like when and where I want. And that happens to
include having sex on my birthday! PS, I don't give a damn about what
you think about my *King* cover. You don't even have a clue how hard I
had to hustle to get that shit. In case you haven't noticed they're not
handing out magazine covers to black actresses these days. Oh, but how
would you notice since you refuse to work with anyone but white folks?
Or is it that you're just mad that I'm the one that's on the cover and all
you'll ever do is beg to get others put on? Either way, I don't give a
damn. Those are *your* issues. Just know that Garrett's family isn't acting
up because of me. It's because of you! Garrett's family doesn't want you
around their son because they can smell your fraudulent behavior a
mile away."

"You don't know what you're talking about," she retorts, stepping
back slightly.

"I'm talking about the way you front like your shit don't stink and we
all know that you ain't nothing but 'hood. Bitch, you're more ghetto
than any of the four of us in here, and you've got the nerve to look down
on someone? Please. You need to get your life together."

"Umm, excuse me but my life is together. Unlike some who are
dependent on a piece of dick to provide, I'm handling my business
standing up, not lying down!"

"But you didn't have enough of a problem with the way I'm living to
accept the free trip out here, huh? Not for nothing," I add the final
twist, "the time you take to worry about me, you'd figure out why your
own sister can't stand the sound of your voice."

If looks could kill, I'd have died as soon as the words escaped my
lips. Trista's face immediately turned a deep red, and her normally

expressive eyes narrowed to mere slits. "To hell with this, I'm out of here," Trista mutters and brushes past Elise, who has just come out of her bedroom and slams her bedroom door.

WHEN I FINALLY emerge from my room later in the afternoon, Trista and all her things are gone. I can't believe that she really left, but I'm still too angry to care. What was supposed to be a celebration of friend- ship, success, and happiness has turned into one of the worst weekends of my life. Best friend, my ass—it's obvious that Trista wants someone to blame for all of her personal issues. Well, I'm not about to be anybody's scapegoat. So what if I've had to rely on the men in my life to provide? She's a hater. I deserve that shit and more. And as far as I'm concerned, Trista can keep it moving, because I damn sure don't need it.

15

VIVIAN

The hot sweet coffee sprayed out of my mouth, droplets landing all over my morning paper, my computer screen, the edge of my desk, and on the back of my pod-mate's Mac. I reached for a napkin to wipe my mouth and cover up my cough, trying my best to stifle it so my coworkers couldn't hear me choking. Not that it would have mattered, mind you; they'd probably already seen for their own eyes what made me lose my double mocha latte: a picture of me cursing out Daddy in front of Mr. Chow's in the gossip section of my newspaper's chief rival, the *Los Angeles Herald.* In color. With a completely fabricated blow-by-blow account of what the columnist said went down.

"Rapper Young Daddy MC may be the suave ladies man in his super-hot videos, but when it comes to handling a *Los Angeles Daily News* entertainment scribe named Vivian Evans, he's not so smooth. The two were spotted outside the trendy eatery Mr. Chow's engaging in verbal fisticuffs after Evans apparently busted her celeb paramour for scribbling a statuesque model's number on a piece of scrap paper while he thought she was out of sight. 'She called him everything but a child of God,' said one of our spies, who witnessed the Thursday-night altercation at the valet stand just outside the restaurant. With the bevy of beauties vying for his attention—particularly now that they'll be able to see his goods, both on the big screen in his soon-to-be-lensed flick *Metro* and in an upcoming *Playgirl* spread—perhaps Plain Jane Evans should focus on covering her hip-hop honeys instead of dating them . . ."

I buried my head in my hands and peeked at the item a few times, half-hoping that, if I stared at it long and hard enough, my name, in bold, and my face, contorted in what appeared to be anger, would fade off the page. They didn't. Still splayed across my desk was an inaccurate account of a dinner date I'd had with Daddy, in which I playfully laid him out for using my business card to write down some broad's number while he was out with me. But trust me when I say: I didn't give a damn that he was walking around collecting numbers like he was a rep for the Yellow Pages. We're just friends. I've made that clear to him a few times since his declaration of admiration at the hospital. And he's finally got it into his thick skull that (a) I'm on a man break and (b) he and I can't ever be more than just friends. So friends he settled for. On the night that picture was taken, we were engaged in a not-so-serious argument—like friends who get into a heated debate, then change subjects and voice pitches as if the disagreement never happened. "Verbal fisticuffs"? "Plain Jane"? I was mortified.

The ding of my email account snapped me out of my stupor; it was Joel summoning me into his office. He didn't say what he wanted, but I knew, and I'm sure that he knew I knew. I was going to be reprimanded—or worse—for making myself scandalous gossip-column fodder for the competition. Hell, I wanted to put my own foot in my ass. I could definitely see him wanting to plant one of his square-toe Gucci's there. I dragged my behind into his office like a child who'd just been ordered to walk outside and break a switch off the front-yard tree, in sure knowledge that she was about to be damn-near skinned alive.

"So, tell me you've got something on Young Daddy MC that you can write to justify your being out with him at Mr. Chow's in front of paparazzi," Joel said. He was tapping his pencil on his desk, which just happened to have the *Herald*'s gossip pages spread out across it. "Just tell me that."

I wiped my brow and kept my mouth closed. I hadn't quite figured out what to say.

"Come on, Viv—give me something," he said, his voice getting louder as he hopped out of his chair and walked over to the door. He slammed it shut, adding, I'm sure, to the low murmur of drama among my coworkers that hung like a fog out in the newsroom. Then he made his way back to his chair, talking without missing a beat. "Young Daddy MC is about to star in an action flick opposite some of the biggest names in Hollywood. He's spread all over the pages of *Playgirl*. He's being talked about on every celebrity gossip show imaginable. And now he's in the pages of the *Herald*. With you. Tell me that I have an exposé you can write up today that I can crash onto the Sunday cover with so that I can justify why one of my top reporters is on a date with him and shows up in the comp's gossip pages. I want exclusives on the projects he's working on, how much cash he wastes on cheap diamonds, what he washes his ass with in the morning, whether he's got the goods in bed . . ."

"Whoa, whoa," I said, cutting him off. "First of all, that picture of me with him isn't what you think. Second of all, even if we were an item, you can't be serious when you say you actually want me to write a story telling people intimate details about my love life, like I'm some cheap prostitute selling her story to the *National Enquirer!*"

"A prostitute, I'm going to presume, can't write a cover story," he said, slamming his hand on his desk for emphasis.

"And neither can I," I yelled back. "I'm embarrassed enough that some gossip monger put an inaccurate version of my personal business in the newspaper for the entire world to see. I will not be pimped by you or anyone else for dirt on what I do when I leave these offices."

"You will if I tell you to," he seethed.

"You know what? Go ahead and insist I do that, then," I said, going for the door. "And make sure you call Human Resources to let them know what you're planning. I know I'm going to.

"Ain't this a bitch?" I said as I slinked through the newsroom, grabbed my purse, and walked out to the lobby. I lit up the arrow on the down elevator display and stood there, desperate for one of the doors to open so that I could escape the office without having to actually talk to any of my coworkers. After what seemed like an eternity, the door to the left car opened—and who should be in it but Annie, the new young chippy intern that Joel had become quite smitten with over the past few months. She practically begged to cover parties into the wee hours of the morning; he loved that she could go out and mingle with the celebrities and come back with enough trash to fill the gossip pages to the brim. In my heyday, I would have felt threatened. Now I was just glad someone else was doing the dirty work, so I could focus on working my industry connections to pitch long, serious magazine pieces about culture, entertainment, and politics, the reason I became a journalist in the first damn place.

"Good morning, Vivian," she smirked. She held a copy of the *Herald* in one hand, a cup of coffee in the other. I didn't say anything—just looked her up and down and put my hand on the elevator doors.

"You coming out? I'm in a rush," I said.

"From the looks of the paper, I can see why," she said. "So, is Daddy as good as they say?"

"I'm sorry?" I said, wrinkling my entire mug. No, this heifer was not asking me this.

"Daddy. The story says you're dating him. I hear he's incredible in bed."

I stared daggers into her eyes, but, unashamed and seemingly emboldened by the newspaper article in her hand, she stared right back. This was a DEFCON 1 situation. The bitch is going down. "I'll tell you what: after you finish wiping what's left of Joel's cum from the corners of your mouth, why don't you set up an interview with Daddy and find out for yourself? You seem to be really good at that. I hear you usually are. I hope it tastes good going down. Now, if you'll excuse me."

So stunned was she by my blow that the only thing that moved on her body was her bottom lip. It was quivering. I had to stop myself from laughing. She wasn't moving, so I got onto the elevator, never once taking my eyes off her after I pushed the down button. Just as the doors began to close, she squeezed between them and scurried down the hallway. I shook my head, then watched the lights as the elevator descended.

I burst out the front doors and out into the cool air. It smelled like rain. I jammed my hand into my pocketbook, pulled out my cell phone, and scrolled through my numbers until I got to Jerome, and then I hit send. His cell phone rang twice before he picked up. "Well, if it isn't Plain Jane," Daddy said cheerfully.

"I can't say I'm glad you're amused," I sneered as I walked into a Starbucks just down the road from my office. I sat on a stool by the window. "Can you please explain to me where the hell the *Herald* got that damn picture from? We haven't been to Mr. Chow's in months."

"Why you upset? At least they got your good side—you looked good, girl," he joked.

"I'm not laughing, Jerome," I said through clenched teeth. "I'm a reporter, in case you forgot. I've been an entertainment reporter for five years, and never once have I ever considered dating the people I interview, precisely for this reason. I know plenty of writers who sleep their way to exclusives, but I can honestly say I never did that—I've always taken pride in being able to get my stories the right way. So it sucks that even though I hooked up with you well after I covered you, my career is about to go down the toilet over a silly-ass gossip story that's nowhere near truthful."

"Damn, Viv—that's a little dramatic, isn't it? Your career going down the toilet?" Daddy said, incredulous. "Over a picture? You and I both know we were just chillin' that night and nothing went down."

"It's my credibility on the line," I shouted into the phone, drawing the attention of a Botox victim sipping an iced latte on the stool next to me. I rolled my eyes at her; she knew not to say shit to me. But I did lower my voice. "Look, you have to make this right," I whispered.

"I know how to make it right," he said quickly. "I can make an honest woman out of you. That way, you can just cop to being my girl, your boss will crawl out your ass because he'll know not to mess with the girlfriend of a hardcore rapper, and you'll be proud to be seen in the news-papers with your man."

"Jerome, what the hell are you talking about?"

"I'm just saying, Viv, you never gave a brother a chance. And I understand that you were focusing on getting your son healthy and all, but I deserved a shot at your heart. I know I'm not Sean, but I figured not being his ass would give me an in. Why can't you cut a brother a break and give him some love?"

I didn't quite know what to say. Perhaps I'd confused him by turn-ing him down at the hospital but accepting his offers to hang out "like friends should." We'd talked a lot during those dinners, including the night at Mr. Chow's, about the reasons why I felt like I needed to take a break from dating. He knew not to push the issue. But it was looking like he needed the "we're just friends" reminder.

He wasn't trying to hear it. "I just don't understand black women," he said, sounding annoyed. "You all stand on your soapboxes and tell the world your Terry McMillan can't-get-a-good-black-man stories, and then when a good brother comes along, you just toss him to the side for the guy who's not interested in doing the right thing."

"Jerome, I know you're not sitting here stereotyping black women with this nonsense," I said, sounding equally annoyed.

"I'm not talking about all black women—I'm talking about you right now," he said.

"Me? How you figure?" I said, incredulous.

"Come on, Viv—you're the queen of the chase. You been running after a brother who don't want you for almost a decade, and the more he pushes you away, the more you chase him. What's up with that?"

"I like to think that I, like a lot of my sisters, am simply focused on what I want. And unlike you doggish men, we women feel no need to string a bunch of random men through a smorgasbord of unnecessary dates, sex, and false commitments, especially when we've settled on who should be our main course."

"And what happens when you eat your main course and you're still not satisfied and hungry as hell?" he asked. "A man gets up and goes to another restaurant if he's still hungry. Black women? They sit there and stare at the plate, wondering if someone is going to come along and give them seconds. You don't get seconds in restaurants without paying a price. How long you gonna pay the price chasing after Sean, Viv?"

"Well, Jerome," I said, dragging out the last syllable of his name for emphasis, "if you must know, I'm not sitting at any restaurant table and I'm sure as hell not waiting for anybody to put food on my plate. I'm not studying Sean or any other man for that matter. I'm on a man diet."

"Huh?" he said.

"I'm not focusing any more energy on getting with Sean. I've set my sights on loftier goals," I said enthusiastically.

"Oh really," he said. "Do tell."

"Well," I sighed, "I've decided that I don't want a man—I want me. A healthy, successful, great mom who's in love with herself. All these years I was focused on having Sean because he's the father of my child, he was my first love, and I was raised to believe that people who make babies together should stay together. But I've realized that he doesn't love me back the way I deserve to be loved. Hell, I didn't love myself the way I deserve to be loved. So now I'm being selfish—for myself and for my child. A boy needs his daddy, but he also needs a mom who can show him she enjoys what she does for a living, who's healthy enough to stay alive to see him graduate and make something of himself, and who's just . . . happy. When I focus on me, and not you men, my life with my son becomes exponentially better. I mess with you boys, and my life is a shambles. I don't like messes, so I've cleaned me up."

Daddy was silent, but only for a moment. Then he made a half-hearted last-ditch effort. "That sounds all good and well, Viv, but what about the Vow? You know, a brother would be willing to help you meet your deadline if you gave him half a chance."

"Man, fuck the Vow," I said, laughing. "Can you call somebody and get this gossip crap straightened out, please, so that people don't think

I'm sleeping around to get my stories? I have an interview with *Newsweek* tomorrow, and the last thing I need is for them to think I'm not a serious journalist."

"*Newsweek*, huh?"

"Yes, *Newsweek*. They're looking for a new L.A. bureau chief who'd be responsible for covering entertainment in a much more meaningful way than planting paparazzi pictures in the gossip columns and making up stories to sell magazines."

"Shee-it, all of them are the same—rags that don't ever tell the truth," Daddy said. "But I'll do you that solid, Ms. Evans, 'cause you're my girl. No problem."

I breathed a sigh of relief. "Thanks, Jerome. I really mean it."

"Yup," he said and hung up.

I spent the rest of the afternoon at home, preparing for my interview and running through worst-case scenarios of what I would do if I didn't get it. Joel was going to fire my ass for sure, so I'd probably be stuck freelancing until something else more stable came along. Sean could put Corey on his insurance plan, and I could stretch the child support out with my savings to make ends meet. When I wasn't thinking about fresh ways to make new money, I was praying that none of Corey's little friends had said anything to my son about the *Herald* item. I wasn't quite ready to explain to him what any of it meant, and I was sure he wouldn't understand, anyway, but I'd crafted a little something in my mind that I thought would adequately explain to a seven-year-old that gossip isn't necessarily true, and that he shouldn't believe everything he reads or hears—not until he checks it out for himself. And who better to tell him the truth than his mama? By the time five P.M. rolled around and his dad brought him home from soccer practice, I was ready.

What I didn't prepare myself for, though, was Sean's reaction. Not that I really cared what he thought; we hadn't really spoken to each other, save for the necessary parenting conversations, in weeks. But it's amazing what a little gossip item can do to an already frosty relationship. "Nice picture, Jane," Sean said before he even got through the door.

"You know what, Sean? You can go screw yourself," I said simply, taking Corey's sports bag from his hand.

"Why don't you watch your mouth?" he said, as Corey walked into the kitchen, completely oblivious to the brushfire spreading in the foyer.

"Why don't you leave my house?" I shot back.

"My pleasure," he said, turning to leave. But before he could get all the way through the screen door, he reached into the breast pocket of his windbreaker and stepped back into the house. "By the way, nice spread," he said, tossing the September issue of *Playgirl* at my feet.

My eyes widened; I picked up the magazine in one quick swoop, afraid that Corey might catch a glimpse before I could get it out of view.

"Nice," I said, sarcastically. "You're such a class act."

"So is your man," Sean said. And with that, he walked out the door in a huff.

"I didn't know you cared," I said.

"I don't," he said.

"Then at least we're on the same page," I said, smiling sweetly as I watched him walk down the driveway. He tossed me a nasty look as he backed out and pulled away in a swirl of burning rubber.

"My man?" I mouthed to myself. Lord, that boy thinks Daddy and I are an item. And if I was reading him correctly, he was actually jealous. "Ha!" I laughed out loud, shaking my head. "Isn't that rich?" Usually it was me who was slamming doors and pointing fingers. How the tables have turned. I shrugged. Who gives a damn what Sean thinks?

"So, big boy, how was soccer?" I called out to Corey as I closed the front door and headed into the kitchen in search of my son.

"Congratulations, superstar!" Trista yelled as she stood on my front porch, a bottle of champagne in one hand, a box from Magnolia in the other. I'd called her just a few hours earlier, screaming into the phone in excitement about the job offer I'd received from *Newsweek*. To celebrate, Trista invited herself over for a home-cooked meal. For such a skinny girl, she sure can put it away. I happily accepted her invitation for me to cook; it'd been so long since we actually sat down and talked to one another in person, one would have wondered if our friendship had also suffered a mortal blow from the Las Vegas blow-up. I was happy to see that it hadn't.

"That's Bureau Chief to you, Miss Missy," I said, opening the door and accepting my friend's warm embrace. "Come on in."

"You better go ahead and get yourself a title," Trista said as she stepped into my foyer and handed me the box. "I can't believe they offered you the job on the spot. I figured they'd at least make you sweat a couple days before they hit you with the package."

"So did I. And you know I was sweating about that gossip item," I said. "But they almost seemed impressed that I got caught in a precarious position with a star—to them it looked like I was doing a helluva job getting a good story. In the end, that's what saved my behind at the *News*. I hope that's not a sign that they're just as ridiculous as those bubbleheads at the *News*."

"Speaking of bubbleheads, when are you going to tell them?"

"I was thinking I might walk in there tomorrow, climb up on my desk, lift my dress up around my waist, and tell them all to kiss my big brown ass, then stroll the hell out to a theme song—maybe something from early NWA, or maybe that Ice Cube song where he says 'today was a good day, I didn't have to use my AK,'" I said, putting a serious look on my face for emphasis, then falling out in hysterics. "But then I thought better of it and decided I should just tell Joel 'Fuck you' and be done with it."

"You might want to spare him the expletives and stick to a terse resignation letter," Trista laughed. "Ride out on top. I'm so proud of you, Viv. But enough about *Newsweek*—what's for dinner?" she asked, looking over my shoulder toward the kitchen. "I don't smell my prized fried chicken."

"Fried chicken?" I said, reeling back. "Girl, I haven't made fried chicken in damn near two months. Jules won't stand for it."

"Who in the world is Jules, and why is he messing up my dinner plans?" Trista asked, hands on her hips.

"Jules is my personal trainer, and he's saving your girl's life," I said.

Actually, I like to think of Jules as my knight in shining armor—a personal trainer/nutritionist who's gay and blessed with the uncanny ability to read men better than most women and dispense advice more sound than any of L.A.'s $400-per-hour psychologists. His sofa? The treadmill at Red's Total Fitness, a sweaty, hole-in-the-wall gym I joined over two months ago, shortly after Corey got out of the hospital. I didn't tell anybody I was joining—didn't ask for any referrals. I needed to lose weight without any pressure from Amaya, without overspending on some celebrity trainer Trista would surely have recommended, and without doing it to please some man—specifically, Sean. I found Jules in the Yellow Pages. He had found a way to help me lose just over eight pounds and two pants sizes in a mere seven weeks. "Jules wouldn't stand for me ruining all his work for a piece of greasy fried chicken," I said heartily to Trista as she followed me into the kitchen to check on the salmon and slice a little red onion for our salad.

"Oh really—Jules wouldn't want you to ruin all his work, huh?" she said, looking me up and down. "You look good, girl! So, um, how much work is Jules putting in?" she said coyly as she sat at the kitchen table.

"Um, get your mind out the gutter, Ms. Trista. Jules is sweeter than syrup—he ain't putting that kind of work in, trust. Damn shame, too, because he's fine as hell. But the gay ones always are. But I'll tell you, when that boy's bending over on top of me, stretching my legs? Lord, that's when I really miss getting some."

"What, no ex-sex?"

"Trista, what have you been living on—the planet Mars? I told you, Sean and I are over. I miss the sex, but I tell you, my world is so much easier to navigate now that I keep our relationship simple."

"Simple, huh?"

"Yup, simple," I said. "He picks up Corey—I say 'Hi,' hand him my child's suitcase, tell him when I'll be by to pick him up, and say good-night. He drops off his child support, I say 'Thank you,' and keep it moving. The other week at Corey's soccer game, I sat on the opposite side of the bleachers and didn't pay him any mind. And I'm proud to say that when he reneged on his weekend with Corey last Saturday, I just told him, 'No problem,' then made reservations at a vegetarian restau-rant and took my son on a date."

"Damn—'No problem'?" Trista said, cocking her eyebrows. Then she playfully looked around the room, cupped my face, and looked deeply into my eyes. "Who *are* you, and what did you do with my friend Viv?" she joked.

"I know! Right? The Viv who gave a damn would have hired a private investigator to find out where the bitch he ditched his kid for lived, so I could drive on over to her house and egg both their cars. The Viv who just a few weeks ago screamed on him for mentioning another man's *Playgirl* spread. But like Oran Juice Jones, I chilled. Just call me Mary J. Blige—no more drama for me."

"I must say, I don't quite know what to say," Trista stammered. "Viv without Sean is like, like, peanut butter without jelly, ice without water, Gladys without the Pips."

"I know, right?" I said, shaking my head.

Trista kept going. "I sure am glad you finally came to your senses," she continued. "I never could figure out what it was you saw in him."

I wrinkled my brow. "What do you mean?" I said.

"I mean, come on, Viv. Sean isn't exactly the prize you've made him out to be. He's selfish, afraid of commitment, he never gave you the respect you deserve . . . And, quite honestly, I never thought he handled his business in the father department as well as he could have, either. Thank God Corey's got you . . ."

"Hold up," I said, cutting her off. "You're my girl, so I'll take you crit-icizing my choice in men with a grain of salt. We certainly don't have the same taste in men. But I think you're out of line questioning what kind of father Sean's been to his child. He may not be perfect, but he's better than some of these other knuckleheads out here spreading their sperm from woman to woman and not taking care of their responsibilities."

"Oh, so now just because Sean cuts a check he's a good dad?"

"Sean's a good dad because he's responsible, he loves his son, and he doesn't let a day go by without letting him know it," I insisted. "Don't confuse Sean's treatment of me with the way he treats his child. Better yet, don't confuse Sean with Damon or Garrett or any of the other men in your life who've hurt you."

"Damon and Garrett have nothing to do with how I feel about Sean, Vivian," Trista seethed. "And if you're not interested in Sean anymore, why are you defending him?"

"I'm not defending Sean—I'm just asking my best friend to think about what kind of harm she's done to my relationship every time she's told me that I'm a fool for wanting to love the father of my child. You're my girl; I come to you for a shoulder to lean on, Trista. I don't need your criticism. And my son sure doesn't need you comparing his father to these trifling-ass niggas who walk away from their children as if they never existed."

"Damn—you sure told me," Trista said, rolling her eyes.

"Yes, I did, didn't I," I said, rolling my eyes right back at her. "Shit is complicated enough, my friend. Don't add to my drama. In fact, why don't you focus on your own? When's the last time you talked to Amaya?"

"Oh, see, there you go," she said, laughing nervously.

"Yeah, there I go," I said, tossing my chin up at her. "You know, life is much too short, baby. Whatever it is you and Amaya are going through, it needs to be over. She's a different animal from you, for sure, but there's something to that yin and yang thing. You guys were put on this earth together for a reason. Lord knows, I haven't figured out why, but I do know this: I can't stand it that my two best friends aren't talking, and that it's all over some dumb shit. Can y'all please just stop it already?"

"How about we make a deal right here, right now, over your bland-ass broiled fish and rabbit salad?" Trista said. "I won't get in the middle of your business with Sean, and you won't get in the middle of me and Amaya's mess. I'm finished talking about it. This is supposed to be a celebration, dammit. I don't want to fight—I want to eat. Tell me you have some mac and cheese hidden somewhere up in here."

16

TRISTA

Today is the day. I barely slept last night because I was so excited. It felt like the night before Christmas. I flipped channels most of the night and didn't drop off until around three. I even caught one of Amaya's old movies *Baby Mamma Drama 3* on BET. Lord, that girl has been in some bad movies! I thought about calling her after the movie went off but then changed my mind. I'm still pissed, and we haven't spoken since Vegas. Glancing at the clock on the nightstand, I see it's six forty-five. Garrett's side of the bed is empty.

"Garrett?" I call out as I sit up in the bed. My bedroom door opens and he walks in, dressed in dark-blue pants, a crisp white shirt, and yellow silk tie.

"Whatcha got there, hot stuff?" I ask, smiling as he places a tray of food on my lap. "I can't believe you found something in my refrigerator to cook."

"Yes, I did. And this breakfast is for the newest, sexiest partner at The Agency," he says as he sits next to me. He takes his watch off the nightstand and puts it on.

"I haven't gotten it yet," I say as I take a bite of the omelette. "What are you doing up and dressed so early?"

"Unfortunately," he says as he nuzzles my neck with his lips, "I've got a breakfast meeting, so instead of making love you'll have to enjoy this good-luck breakfast."

"That's so sweet. Thank you, baby."

"Anything for you, baby," he says as he slips on his suit jacket. "Now, call me as soon as you get the word that you are officially the most powerful black woman in Hollywood, and then we're celebrating all night. I've planned our entire evening."

"Oh, I can't wait. But are you sure you don't want to stick around for a few more minutes?" I ask suggestively as I let the sheet drop down to my waist.

"You're not playing fair," he groans as he slips back into the bed. I wrap my arms and legs around his body. "You know I'd rather stay here, but I've got to go."

"Okay, buddy, but you don't know what you're missing," I joke.

"Oh, I know all right," he says as he kisses me and then cups my face in his hands. "I love you, Trista." Before I can help myself the words slip out: "I love you, too, Garrett." I could barely hide my smile. Oh, my God. Did we say we love each other? I kiss him back as he says it again and then I say it again. He finally pulls away, smiling tenderly. "I'll see you later, baby."

I watch him walk out of my bedroom. Squealing, I lean back against the pillows. He loves me!

I wolf down the rest of my breakfast and then jump into the shower. I put on a white Jil Sander suit with a strapless red silk top that I'm sure will be perfect for wherever Garrett is taking me later to celebrate. Once dressed, I slip my feet into strappy black stilettos and pin a polka-dot silk flower to my lapel to complete my look. Time to go to work.

In addition to partner announcements being made today, it's also bonus time. From a thousand dollars for the guys in building services to seven-figure checks for some of the partners, an obscene amount of money will be handed out as each employee is called into Mr. Banks' office. People have been buzzing all week about the new toys they were going to buy. I have my eye on a cute little silver Mercedes SLK 350 Roadster that I plan to have dropped off at the end of the week.

Jake, the valet in the parking garage who only parks for the partners and visiting VIPs, misses my wave as I walk by his small office. We'll have plenty to talk about later when we're scouting out my new parking space. Stepping into the lobby, I glance at the limestone plaque on the wall with all the partners' names engraved on it. By the end of the week, there will be a new plaque up there with my name on it.

When I get to Adriene's desk I see she's sporting a conservative brown bob. I guess she decided to tone it down since she will be seeing Mr. Banks today, too. A bouquet of pink roses rests on the corner of her desk.

"Someone has a secret admirer," I say, bending over to smell the fragrant flowers. "Which one of your many men are these from?"

"Those aren't for me," she says mischievously. I carry the flowers into my office before opening the card taped to the vase.

> Good luck today, superstar! I'm proud of you.
> I hope you get everything you always wanted. You deserve it.
> —Damon

Did he remember that I always like these flowers? I ask Adriene to look up the number to Global Investments and get Damon on the phone.

"Damon Reynolds," he says when Adriene puts the call through.

"Hi, Damon, it's Trista," I say into the speakerphone. "I was just calling to say thank you for the flowers. They're beautiful."

"I'm glad you like them. Did they make the announcement yet?"

"No, and how did you know it was today?"

"I told you, my boss is on the board of directors, so he was talking about a meeting they just had and said it was coming up."

"It's today. A company press release will go out later today."

"So, are you celebrating tonight with Amaya and Viv?" he asks.

"Actually, I have plans with Garrett," I answer. I feel self-conscious for some reason.

"Oh, okay . . ."

I interrupt him when Adriene runs into my office, gesturing for me to hang up. "Oh, Damon, I'm sorry. I've got to go. Thanks again for the flowers. I really appreciate it."

"Of course. Talk to you later. Good luck."

"It's time," Adriene says in a singsong voice after I hang up the phone. "Mr. Banks' office just called for you to come over." I whip out my compact from my desk drawer and touch up my makeup quickly.

"How do I look?" I ask Adriene.

"Like a partner," she says as she slaps me five. "Now get going so I can start packing up all our stuff to move down to the big-dog office suites, Wheezie!" As I walk out of my office, she's humming the old theme from *The Jeffersons*, "We're Movin' on Up," and the tune follows me down the hall to executive row.

I CAN'T BREATHE. All the air has been sucked out of the room. I see Mr. Banks' mouth moving but I can't hear a word he's saying. Instead of looking at his pale-green eyes, my gaze is fixated on the large pinkish mole in the left corner of his thin upper lip. As I watch the mole move up and down with the motion of his lips, I find myself hoping it's skin cancer. A single bead of sweat rolls down my back into the waistband of my pants. This can't be happening. I stopped listening after he said I didn't make partner. My hands are clammy and shaking. I wipe them on my pants.

"Look, Trista, the other partners and I just don't feel that you're quite ready. You've done some fairly respectable work this year, as is reflected in your bonus," Mr. Banks says as he slides a piece of paper across his desk with my bonus figure written on it. I take the paper automatically, without looking at the number. My eyes are burning with tears. "We think you could use some new challenges, so we've decided to restructure your area to allow you to focus on some new areas of development. We'll consider you again for partner in another couple of years."

Those bastards! I can't believe they are doing this to me. I busted my ass for this firm and this is what I get? Not only was I not making partner, but they're reshuffling my client roster and giving Jared and Cassidy to Steven—the new partner. I have to get out of here before I do something crazy. I stand up while Mr. Banks continues to speak and walk out. I hear him calling my name but I don't turn around. They fucked me!

As I make my way down the hall, I can tell that word has started to circulate. Conversations cease as I make my way past clusters of coworkers. When I get to my office I don't say anything to Adriene. I just grab my purse and go down to the garage. I see Jake stenciling Steven's name on the wall. That's why he wouldn't look at me this morning because he'd already gotten the names of the new partners so he could start working on their parking spaces in partner row.

I am soaked with perspiration. I get into my car and turn on the air conditioning full blast and throw my blazer into the backseat. The stale air blows out of the vents as I rest my head on the steering wheel. I'm not sure I can make it home. Salty tears fall into my mouth. I'm devastated.

I glance at the digital clock on the dashboard and see that it is just after eleven. Suddenly all I can think about is getting to someone who will understand what's just happened to me. I call Garrett's office but his assistant tells me he called in sick today. That's strange, he said he had a breakfast meeting this morning. Maybe he's finished the meeting and is working on our celebration. I call his house, but when the machine picks up I don't leave a message and instead head over there.

When I pull into the circular driveway I see Garrett's Range Rover parked in front of the house. Good, he's here. As I begin to walk up to the door to ring the bell I hear the sound of splashing water and loud rap music coming from the backyard. I follow the grassy path along the side of the house, and as I step under the portico the sun momentarily blinds me as I scan the pool area.

Garrett, who has his back to me is seated on the top step leading down into the shallow end of the infinity pool. Stepping around the large radio on the cement that's blasting Ja Rule, I notice a pair of bright red swim trunks floating in the water beside him. Just as I am about to bust him for playing hooky from work I see something that makes me stop dead in my tracks. There is someone else in the pool. Between his legs a long dark body bobs in the water. Garrett, who has his eyes closed throws his head back in ecstasy as he aggressively pushes a man's large bald head up and down in the water.

"Oh my God!" I try to scream, but I'm almost breathless and hardly make a sound. I step back and trip over the radio and fall down onto the hard cement.

"Trista!" Garrett says as he pushes the naked man away from him and scrambles out of the pool. As I start to get up I hear a familiar voice behind me.

"Hey, save some of that for me, man," says Mike as he opens the sliding glass door and comes out in a neon-orange spandex thong, holding a bottle of beer. Now I know whose underwear I found under Garrett's bed. Mike drops the bottle when he sees me on the ground. The sound of the shattering glass causes all of us to jump.

The naked man in the pool floats off toward the other end of the pool, on his back, his two gold nipple rings glinting in the bright sunlight. Garrett, his erection gone flaccid, grabs for a towel and wraps it tightly around his hips. He gestures for Mike to go back into the house. Out of the corner of my eye I see the muscular stranger slowly raise himself out of the water.

"I'll be inside if you need me, G," he says as he walks past us without bothering to dry off. He switches his narrow hips as he walks by and strokes a long finger along the droplets of water on Garrett's shoulder. I don't recognize his face but he's sending me a message that they are lovers.

When Garrett reaches down to help me up I slap his hand away and get up on my own and sit on the lounge chair.

"You're fucking gay?" I say, shaking my head back and forth. How can he be gay? We've been seeing each other for nearly a year. How could I not know? For the second time today I'm speechless.

"I'm not gay, Trista," he says as he rakes his hand through his wet hair.

"Oh, if you're not gay, then why was your dick in that man's mouth? And what is Mike doing here? He's married, for God's sake!" I scream at him as I point at the house.

"Trista, I'm not gay," he says again. He sits down on the lawn chair next to me and begins to talk. "Look, Trista, I'm sorry you had to see this. But I'm not gay." I barely hear what he's saying as the scene from the pool keeps replaying. Hadn't he said he loved me this morning? Something penetrates my cloudy head.

"What did you say?" I ask, sure I didn't hear him correctly.

"I said I love you, Trista. We can still build a life together. We don't have to let this come between us."

"Are you fucking crazy?" I look at him, sure I couldn't have heard him correctly.

"Trista, lots of people have problems when they are first starting out, but I promise you this will never happen again."

"How long has this been going on?" I start to cry hot angry tears for the second time today. I couldn't look him in the face. I think back to all the times he's mentioned hanging out with Mike and other guys, how after the gallery auction he'd gone off with him. They had spent the entire weekend together, doing God knows what. Well, actually I guess I do know what they were doing. Some freaky group shit.

"Trista, I'm not gay. This was just a thing. It doesn't mean anything. I was just having a little fun. It will never happen again," he mumbles feebly. "We can still have a life together, I swear. This will never happen again. I love you." Hearing this, I snap.

"You lying bastard!" I scream at him, standing up and grabbing for the first thing I can to hit him across the face. "We made love last night! You told me you loved me. You were fucking men while your were sleeping with me!" I'm in a blind rage now. I pick up the radio and hit him across the shoulder and then toss the offending object into the pool. He turns away to deflect the blow. Grabbing the small plastic side table, I lift it up and try to swing it at his head. But Garrett easily takes it out of my hands and throws it out into the yard. He tries to grab my arms as I swing at him but I keep swinging wildly, scratching at his face with my nails. As we struggle, the towel loosens from around his hips. The nakedness I had enjoyed this morning offends me now. I knee him sharply in the groin. He releases me and drops to his knees, clutching his balls. As I look around madly for something else to hit him with, the two guys come running to help their friend.

"Don't you fucking touch me," I scream hysterically at Mike as he steps between me and Garrett's moaning figure, now curled in the fetal position on the ground. My hands are balled into fists, my nails digging into my palms. My heart is beating a mile a minute, like it might jump right out of my chest.

The stranger, who has now put on an LA Sports T-shirt and long nylon basketball shorts, helps Garrett onto the lounge chair and then sits beside him. He touches him with gentle concern and familiarity.

"Who are you?" I demand from the stranger seated cozily next to my boyfriend.

"I'm DJ," he answers frostily, draping a towel across his lover's lap. Garrett tries to push him away but he won't leave his side.

"And you and Garrett are lovers?" I question, incredulous, my voice catching in my throat. "And Mike, too?" Before DJ can answer, Garrett jumps in.

"Trista, I'm not gay," he exclaims earnestly. It's sick; it's like he believes it.

"Could have fooled me," DJ and I both say at the same time. DJ is clearly offended that his lover won't acknowledge him. Mike, apparently wanting no part of the discussion, slinks back into the house.

"Tell me this, are you using condoms? Do you have any diseases?" I whisper. The thought that he might have something suddenly makes me very scared. What if he or one of his partners is HIV-positive? I wait for his answer.

"I'm totally clean, Trista. I swear."

"Well, you'll excuse me if I don't actually believe anything you say," I shoot back. I realize there's nothing more for us to say. Garrett can deny he's gay until the cows come home, but I have no patience for his lies. As I get up and begin to walk away, both Garrett and his friend flinch, as if I might strike him again. I'm tempted but keep walking. But I have one last thought as I step through the gate.

"No wonder your bitch-ass couldn't eat pussy very well," I toss nastily over my shoulder. My legs are shaking as I slip into the car and try to start it. It almost starts, so I try again. It catches the second time I turn the key, and I peel out of the driveway. I can't get home fast enough.

MY HOUSE STINKS. The pile of dirty dishes in the sink, open containers of Chinese food, foils of Mexican, pizza boxes, and overflowing ashtrays in the living room have my normally immaculate condo smelling like a frat house. When the doorbell rings I step around the maze of newspapers, unopened mail, and magazines to make my way to the front door. I stuff a bunch of crumpled bills into the delivery boy's outstretched hand and snatch the white paper bag. I know he thinks I'm rude but after six days of deliveries to the same address he ought to be used to the crazy black woman in the stained sweats and T-shirt. On second thought, who cares what he thinks.

Carrying the bag of food back into the living room, I clear off a space on the coffee table by pushing the pile of mail and empty cigarette cartons onto the floor. Dinner is served. I flip the channel back to the *Good Times* marathon I've been watching on TV One. Perfect, this is the one where JJ accidentally trips Thelma's fiancé, Keith, as he's walking down the aisle of the church, ending his football career and once again dashing the Evans family's hopes of moving out of the ghetto. As I stuff a forkful of steaming shrimp fried rice into my mouth, I think to myself: So this is what a nervous breakdown feels like.

I haven't left my condo in a week. As soon as I got home from Garrett's I shut all the blinds, changed my clothes, and laid my black ass on the couch. I'd had the television on all day and night because I couldn't stand the silence. It was like voices were jumping out of my head. *I'm not gay. We're not making you a partner.* The nights were the worst. I couldn't sleep, so I'd take a sleeping pill, and then I'd wake up in a fog—until everything would come rushing back to me. The betrayals.

When I first got home, the phone was ringing off the hook. I let the calls go to the answering machine because I couldn't deal with talking to anyone. Garrett left long messages. He said he was sending over a copy of his medical records to prove that he was clean. Whatever. Even Damon called twice a day. It was hard to ignore his persistent voice. I cut off my cell and BlackBerry and only picked up my house phone when I heard Viv's insistent voice saying she was coming over there with the fire department to break down my door if I didn't answer the phone. I assured her I was still alive, gave her an abbreviated version of what went down, and told her I needed to be alone.

In the space of twenty-four hours—hell, a mere three hours, actually—my whole world fell apart. I'd lost my job and my man. While TA hadn't fired me, they had all but said I had no future at the firm. Steven, with the help of Sloane, had gotten the fruits of all my hard labor in the end. And as for Garrett, I couldn't believe what I had seen. His little freak fest had left me shaken to my core. I scheduled an emergency appointment with my gynecologist, Dr. Woodard, for an AIDS test. It had been hard to request but I knew it was something I had to do. And while Garrett and I had always used condoms during sex, if he was sleeping with men, I couldn't take any chances. Dr. Woodard told me I was doing the right thing and said the test results would be available in a week.

I thought I'd had it all. After Amaya, Viv, and I first made the Vow at Elise's wedding, I focused on finding a husband. I thought I had everything in perspective with my checklist of attributes: loving, supportive, smart, well-respected, solid career.

I look around the living room. Is this, at thirty-two, all I have in the end? This place, this perfect place that I created. I filled my life with all the things a woman could want: a nice home, beautiful car, a closet full of more clothes, shoes, and handbags than I could ever hope to have the time to wear. On paper I have everything.

I grab the remote and turn up the TV volume. When I hear the phone ring I wait impatiently for the answering machine to pick up. And then I hear my sister's voice.

"Trista, it's Tanisha," she says. "You have to come home. Daddy's in the hospital." I grab for the receiver off the floor.

"Hello," I say breathlessly into the phone.

"Trista, Daddy collapsed," she says, her voice catches on the words. "I'm calling you from the hospital. Please come."

"I'm on my way," I say, immediately standing up straight. I rush up to my bedroom, taking the stairs two at a time. I stuff my feet into my sneakers and throw on an old sweatshirt. I grab my purse off the night-stand and race to my car.

My DAD IS LYING in a hospital bed in the Intensive Care Unit. As I stand there, looking through the window into the small room, there are countless tubes coming out of his nose and arms, and an oxygen mask covers most of his face. Daddy has been lapsing in and out of consciousness for the last two days. The cancer has spread. Dr. Irby told us it wouldn't be long now. My sister and I keep a rotating vigil outside his room, drinking endless cups of bad coffee from the vending machine.

As Najee, the kind Haitian nurse who is caring for Daddy today, updates me on his condition, I see my sister walking down the hallway. She looks as tired as I feel. Her brow is furrowed and her normally neat Halle Berry crop cut is brushed back. I fill Te in on what Najee said, that there is no change. All they are hoping for at this point is to keep him comfortable. She asks me if I want to grab a bite from the McDonald's downstairs. We are both silent in the elevator ride down to the first floor. Once we receive our trays of food, we walk over to a booth in an empty corner of the restaurant.

"How's Ty?" I ask as I open a ketchup packet and squeeze the contents onto my french fries. I am wondering how my nephew is handling this crisis.

"He's okay. Trying to be strong for his mother," she says, smiling at the thought of her son and picking absently at her own french fries. "But I don't know how he'll handle Daddy's passing. Daddy's been around all his life, and without his own father there . . ."

"I know, Te," I say. "This must be so hard for him to understand."

"Yeah, but he's strong, he'll get through it. We all will, right?" As she asks this last question, it's as if she is asking me to confirm that we'll survive. It is the first time I've ever seen my older sister look or sound so vulnerable.

"We will, Te," I say as I reach across the table and put my hand on top of hers.

"So, what's going on at work?" she asks, trying to change the subject. Her voice is noticeably devoid of her normal biting sarcasm; she sounds genuinely interested. The stress of the last few days has, strangely, not had us at each other's throats as usual.

"Daddy mentioned you were up for some big promotion. How did it go?"

"I didn't get it," I say. This is the first time I have said the words out loud in over a week. The events of the last two days have taken some of the sting out of the words.

"What happened?" she asks. I tell my sister the whole story about how I'd been working so hard for the last year, about Sloane's plan for my new client, and, finally, about how the firm planned to strip me of all my important clients. And once I start talking there's no stopping me, so I tell her also about the Vow, about Garrett, and even about Damon. By the time I finish, I can barely look at her, so I take a couple of bites of my now cold Big Mac.

"Trista, I'm so sorry," she says. It's her turn now to reach over and take my hand. "That story sounds like something straight out of one of your movies."

"Yeah, but I doubt anyone would believe it all happened to one person," I snort in disgust. "My career is over and my boyfriend is fucking men."

"What do your girlfriends say you should do?" she asks.

"Well, that's the other problem."

"Is something wrong with you and your girlfriends?" she asks. I tell her about the trip to Las Vegas and the fight between me and Amaya. Recounting the story I feel ashamed.

"I can't believe I said those things to her," I say.

"I can," says Tanisha softly. "I mean, Trista, you've always been very judgmental, especially about people that don't fit into your way of thinking or acting."

"What do you mean?"

"C'mon, Tris, you've always been that way. Even with me," she says softly.

"I never judged you," I say, shaking my head emphatically.

"You may have never thought you were judging me, but I felt it in the way you looked at me and the way I was living my life when we were growing up. I never felt that I was as smart as you and I knew that I couldn't measure up in Mommy's eyes."

"Why would you even care what Mommy thought?" I snap.

"Because, Trista, even though she wasn't perfect, she was our mother. And even if you didn't see it, she was really proud of you. She was always talking about how smart you were. And she never talked that way about me, so I got attention from other places."

"Mommy talked about me?" I ask, very surprised at this bit of information. I don't remember my mother saying a sober word to me, let alone bragging about me. Most of the time I just tried to stay out of her way.

"All the time. And she would ask me why couldn't I be more like you," she snorts bitterly. "That was why I was always running the streets. Who wants to come home to a house where your mother is constantly riding you about not being as good as your little sister." I am surprised. Was that why she seemed to hate me—because Mommy was comparing us to each other and making both of us feel like we were falling short?

"But now even I know that Mommy probably had her own demons

to deal with and there was nothing that you or I could do to help her," she says. "She was sick and she couldn't stop drinking."

"I never knew any of that," I admit. "And here, all this time, I was jealous of you because you were the popular and outgoing one in the family who everyone always wanted to be around."

"You? Jealous of me?" Tanisha laughs.

"Yeah, why do you find that so hard to believe?" I ask. "You were the fly girl that everybody wanted to hang out with. People couldn't believe we were sisters."

"Yeah, well not so fly anymore," she says, laughing.

"What are you talking about? You're the woman. After Darnell died, you went on to raise an amazing boy on your own. You've put your whole life on hold to be around to take care of Daddy. You're amazing, Tanisha."

"But that's just it, Trista. I didn't put my life on hold. You think because I don't have some high-powered job like you that I can't possibly be happy. Just like you think that the way Amaya chooses to live her life isn't right. But that's just it, Trista—after the terrible relationship I had with Mommy, all I ever wanted to do with my life was have a family." As I look at her, tears begin to flood her eyes.

"I know you never thought much of Darnell, thought he was just some gang banger. But I loved him, Trista, and he loved me. We had a plan. We were talking about him leaving the gang life, and once I got pregnant he promised me he would. We just didn't get out in time. After Darnell died I was determined to go on with our plan and give our little boy a loving home life. I never wanted him to feel like he didn't measure up in my eyes. I wanted Ty to know that his mother loved him unconditionally. I know my little job down at the phone company isn't much, but it allows me to put food on the table and clothes on my child's back, and we've got health insurance. And it allows me to give my son a positive example, and that's what matters most to me."

Listening to her talk, I realize for the first time who my sister is, and I even feel like I am beginning to have a better understanding of who our mother was. She's right—I judge people. I judged our mother, who I thought had turned her back on us because she didn't care. I judged Tanisha and the important life she had created for her and her son. And I judged my friend Amaya.

"I'm so sorry, Tanisha," I say, looking at my sister. "You're right. I'm very sorry."

"I'm sorry, too," she says.

"For what?" I ask.

"For never telling you how proud I am of you. By not doing that, I'm doing exactly what Mommy did. I *am* proud of you and what you've accomplished. And most importantly I'm sorry for not accepting your help all these years more graciously. You didn't have to write all those checks. Mommy was right—you were the smart one and you used your brains to get out of the neighborhood and follow your dream. I admire that in you. And it's because you did those things that I'm able to live with my son in a nice home in a safe neighborhood and don't have to worry about him ending up on the same dead-end street as his father."

"But you know what? Now I don't think I was totally doing all those things selflessly. I think there was a part of me that was trying to buy your respect with every check I wrote. With the house, the expensive gifts, the monthly checks. And if I couldn't be there with you, Daddy, and Ty, it was because I was working so hard, I wanted you guys to have everything you needed and to make sure that I made enough money so none of us ever had to go back to the ghetto. I was making sure you guys were secure. And to prove to everyone that I was good enough to belong. All I wanted was for you and everyone else to respect me."

"I've always respected you," she says earnestly. We both were quiet for a few minutes. Each lost in our own thoughts. I took a sip of my melting chocolate shake.

"So what are you going to do now?" Tanisha asks.

"I have no idea," I said, throwing my hands up and letting my own tears fall onto the paper place mat on my tray. "For the first time in my life I don't know what I'm going to do. Looking at my so-called master plan now, I don't know what I'm going to do next. And for the first time in over ten years, I don't even care. I'm just tired, you know?"

"Yeah, I know," she said coming over to my side of the booth. Sitting down next to me she put her arms around me for the first time I can remember. I let it all go and cried softly in my sister's arms. I cried for my daddy who was dying upstairs. I cried for my wrecked career. I cried for ever giving Garrett even a piece of my heart. And I cried for Amaya and the horrible things I said to her. And I cried for the missed relationship with my sister, and I cried for my mother.

"Oh, goodness," I say when I pull away from her. "I've made such a mess." I looked down at her blue blouse, which was soaked with my tears. I dabbed at the top with one of the paper napkins and then wiped my own face and nose.

"That's okay," she says sincerely. "Now, if you can stand some more sisterly advice, I think you might need to give that guy Damon another chance."

"We've been through so much stuff this year that I don't think we could ever have what we used to have," I say, shaking my head. Although I haven't been able to stop thinking about him. I know he will be the one person who could really understand what this all means to me, who knows how hard I worked, how complicated my family relationships are, and won't judge me, but I can't bring myself to pick up the phone and return his calls. Not yet. Everything is too raw.

"I don't know, Trista," Tanisha says and sips the last of her soda. "It sounds like that man still has serious feelings for you. Besides, your first love never dies." I know she's talking about Darnell as well as Damon. We both laugh softly and begin to pack up our trays when we hear an announcement.

"Code blue, Dr. Irby, room 306," calls Najee's urgent voice over the hospital's PA system. My sister and I both freeze as we realize that Daddy's doctor is being paged to his room. Grabbing our purses, we hurry out to the elevator.

WE ARE SHADED from the blazing afternoon sun by the white canvas tent. After Tanisha, Tyquan, and I take our seats on the brown plastic folding chairs in front of the polished oak casket I look around at all the people who have come out today. I am surprised to see that nearly a hundred people have come to his funeral. There are old men from the GE plant where he worked for 35 years, friends from the neighborhood, and my sister's coworkers, and other family members I haven't seen in years. Aunt Brenda, flanked by her sons, Jason and Jamel, faces us on the other side. Our family minister, Reverend Brooks, reads through the final rites and then calls Aunt Brenda up to sing "Amazing Grace."

After Daddy passed away, I stayed at the house with Tanisha to help make the final arrangements. When we called Crenshaw Gardens, where Mommy was buried, we found out that Daddy had planned his homecoming down to the last detail so that there was really very little for us to do. A steady stream of visitors came by the house to pay their respects and to drop off meals. The dining room table was barely visible under the weight of aluminum-foil-covered containers of casseroles, stews, chicken, and cobblers.

I reach across Tyquan to take Tanisha's gloved hand so we could walk up and place flowers on the casket. We both close our eyes and say silent prayers for his easy passage. After I lay one of the roses onto the casket, I return to my seat.

When Reverend Brooks asks for Tyquan to come up to read a poem he and I had worked on to conclude the service, I'm not sure he'll be able to do it. He turns to his mother and she kisses him, and when he takes the microphone from Reverend Brooks, he stands up straight and reads the three stanzas he had written for his grandfather. I look over at Tanisha, who is beaming at her son through her tears. When Ty reaches the closing words there isn't a dry eye under the tent.

"I love you, Grandpa. I'll always love you," Tyquan says as he wipes his eyes and places the single rose on top of the casket. Aunt Brenda starts humming "Amazing Grace" again as the line of mourners pay their final respects.

After the service I tell Tanisha I will meet her and the rest of the family back at the house. I need to do something. I walk over to my mother's plot, the heels of my shoes sinking into the grass. I haven't been back to see her since the day she was buried. I kneel down on the ground and place my hand on her headstone. Bowing my head, I think about my conversations with Tanisha over the last few days. I am starting to get a better understanding of my mother. Tanisha showed me an old yellow hat box she had found in the top of Mommy's closet after she passed that held all of my report cards and citations. She said the morning after I left for college she had walked in on Mommy looking through this box. I couldn't believe she had kept all those things. A few of my tears fall on the sun-warmed marble, and then I place a rose at the base of the headstone.

"I love you, Mommy," I say. Then I say a short prayer for my parents, who are now reunited. When I start to get up I feel a hand on my shoulder. Turning around, I put my hand up to shield my eyes from the glare of the sun and I see Amaya's face. I start crying again and hug her.

"Amaya, I'm so sorry for those horrible things I said." The words come rushing out as I cringe inwardly for all the hateful things I said to her in Las Vegas. Tanisha was right, I had tried to judge her life and her choices and hold her accountable to my own ridiculous standards. How can I ever hope she'll forgive me?

"I know, girl," Amaya says, wiping away her own tears with a handkerchief. "It's okay. I'm sorry, too." We hug each other tightly, and then, looking over her shoulder, I see Viv standing behind her.

"How did you guys even know to come today?" I ask as I wiped my eyes and walked over to give Viv a hug.

"I got the message you left when your father passed and then Tanisha called me at the magazine yesterday and gave me the details," says Viv, holding my hand. "We just wanted to be here for you. Elise gets in tonight. I hope you're not upset with Tanisha for calling me."

"How could I be upset with my sister for calling my best friends in the world?" I say, laughing for the first time in a few days. "I'm so glad to see you guys," I say as I pull Viv and Amaya close and hug them both.

"Ahem," says another voice, coughing. "Are you glad to see *all* of us?" It's Damon making his way from around the side of the tent. His suit jacket is draped over one arm and his shirt is wrinkled and his tie loosened. I look at Viv and Amaya quizzically.

"Girl, after I called his office yesterday and told him about your dad, he flew back from New York this morning to be here," whispers Amaya in my ear. Both of them smile at me.

I walk over to Damon and hug him. "What are you doing here?" I ask, hoping for one simple answer.

"I thought you might need me," he says hopefully as he takes me in his arms and hugs me close. I wrap my arms around him and close my eyes. He's right.

17

AMAYA

"Hey, it's Clarence," my lazy agent greets me as soon as I answer my cell. "I just wanted to double-check that you were all set for your meeting tonight."

"For the fifth time, I'm all set," I answer totally exasperated. "Now quit calling, Clarence, you're making me nervous."

"I'm so sorry, kitten," he continues, "this dinner was just so hard to arrange."

"Clarence, please. I understand how hard it was for you to get this together. But you've only told me a thousand times," I retort. "I do not want to talk about it anymore." Lord have mercy, he can be so annoying. If Clarence were actually halfway competent, I guarantee it wouldn't have been such a problem.

"Okay, okay, angel, I hear you. Not another word. The last thing I want is for you to be upset at the dinner."

"I thought you said you weren't going to say another word?" I question sharply.

"You're so right. Real quick before you go, I just confirmed next week's Dead Straight in-store appearance at the Target in South Central. It shouldn't be too long, maybe two hours."

"Jesus, I totally forgot about that," I sigh. "How much am I getting for that?"

"Um, lemme check. Okay, here it is. This one is a five-hundred-dollar appearance."

"I swear this movie can't drop soon enough. I promise I'll never do another one of these godforsaken Dead Straight appearances again," I complain bitterly. "All those hateful women coming out just to see if my hair is a weave. That and psycho stalker-men, talking about they just want to get a box signed for their wives—whatever!"

"Don't worry, it's almost over."

"Yeah, yeah. I'll call you when I finish if it's not too late." And with that, I decisively shut my phone.

I'M ABOUT TO meet Carter James! I feel giddy just thinking about it. I've been a fan for so long, I can barely believe that we're actually going to be working together. Carter is one of the few African-American A-listers in Hollywood. He's costarred alongside everyone from Julia Roberts to Harrison Ford, and easily earns eight million a movie. Nowadays, Carter has the ability to green-light any project he wishes. His word is gold. And if I have anything to do with it, after working on this project with him I won't be trekking across Los Angeles for another open casting call as long as I live.

I asked Clarence to set up this dinner so that our first meeting will be in a more comfortable environment than the first principal-cast read-thru session next month. After several weeks of going back and forth between Clarence and Carter's management team, they were finally able to pin down a window of time in the veteran actor's schedule when he and I could get together for a little meet-and-greet.

I'd done my research on Carter and discovered that he is an avid fan of seafood, so I requested that Clarence make reservations for us at Crustaceans in Beverly Hills. Luckily, the restaurant is only a hop, skip, and a jump from my apartment, so for a change, I'm able to be on time for a dinner. As I walk across the aquarium in the entrance floor, I spot Carter in a corner of the balcony. God, he looks good! In black slacks and a fitted black knit top, it's easy to see why he's consistently voted one of *People* magazine's top ten eligible bachelors. Following the maître d' over to a hostess waiting to escort me up to our table, I say a quick prayer for the strength not to giggle like a little child in front of this man. As I near the table, Carter stands to greet me. For the first time in my life, I have the distinct feeling more eyes in the room are directed at the man I'm dining with than on me.

"Amaya, what a pleasure it is to finally meet you," he says as he takes my hand and kisses it. Every hair on my arm stands at attention as his voice rumbles in his chest.

"The pleasure is truly all mine, Mr. James," I respond with a shy smile. Wow, I can't believe that this man is making me nervous.

"Please, call me Carter. So I understand that you picked this restaurant," he continues once I'm comfortably seated in my chair. "Great choice, I love seafood."

"Really," I answer, feigning ignorance. "I'm so glad."

"You're all right with me if you know your fish," he says, flashing a perfect smile.

"Well, I definitely want to be all right with you," I answer coyly, feeling my confidence returning as I catch him peeping down the V-neck of my silk, lilac and cream spaghetti-strap Betsey Johnson cocktail dress.

"Mmm, I hear you," he answers just as the waiter approaches the table to fill my glass with the white wine that Carter has already requested for the table and ask if we're ready to order. "May I have the pleasure of ordering for you, Amaya?"

"Please be my guest," I respond graciously as I sit back and cross my legs.

"Great. We'll start with an order of steamed oysters for the table, then I'd like the one-pound lobster and garlic scallop over pumpkin pilaf with asparagus for the lady, and I'll take the one-and-a-half-pound lobster with the sautéed spinach and the scalloped potatoes, thank you," he states authoritatively.

"Mmm, it all sounds so delicious," I say as the waiter walks away.

"I'm glad that you're pleased," he responds with a devilish grin.

"I am. And let me just say what an honor it is to be chosen to work with you on this film," I start as I sip from my glass of wine. "As I'm sure you know, *The Black Crusader* will be my very first major release."

"Well, have no fear, Amaya, this will be my second Soular Son production. Adolphus is an amazing director and producer. Not to mention, I think you're a perfect fit for the part of Tatiana. You should have absolutely nothing to worry about when it comes to the actual filming," he says and leans into the table.

"Just when it comes to the filming, huh?" I joke.

"Well, how you get along with the cast, or should I say your costar, is completely up to you," he says as he reaches across to stroke my hand and stares with a raised eyebrow.

Despite my initial attraction, there is something in his tone that sets off a huge alarm in my brain. This feels wrong. Still smiling, I slowly pull my hand away from him and say, "Aww, you're so sweet, Carter. I'm sure the two of us are going to get along magnificently. But unfortunately I'm in a very committed relationship right now," I exaggerate ever so slightly. "Perhaps you know my boyfriend, Troy . . ." His laughter interrupts me before I finish my sentence. "I'm sorry, did I say something funny?"

"Not at all. And, yes, you could say I know your boyfriend Troy. As a matter of fact, I play golf with him at least once a month."

"Really? I had no idea," I answer, instantly annoyed at Troy for failing to mention this to me, and at myself for not following up on his whereabouts while I was running around with Keith.

"Yes, really. Honestly, why do you think I made time to meet with you? I've heard all about you from your boyfriend Troy," he continues with a slight sneer.

"I'm not sure I understand exactly what that's supposed to mean," I ask, measuring my words as I remind myself that I'm seated across from my future costar and not some random man that I can curse out from top to bottom and never see again.

"What it means, my dear," he says in the same tone of voice as he puts his hand firmly on my knee and rubs under the edge of my dress, "is that you've been the talk of the golf course for months. You're his girlfriend, all right—maybe his Los Angeles girlfriend. But trust, he's got one in every city that he travels."

I am stunned. I can't believe this is happening to me. I'd worked so hard on my career and this is what it was all going to come down to? Ruined by straight-up locker-room gossip? This whole time I thought I was using Troy and that low-life bastard was putting my business out in the street. Luckily, the waiter arrives at that exact moment with our order of oysters. Carter casually pulls back his hand off my knee and sits back in his chair.

"Don't look so surprised, my dear. From what I've heard you're one of the best he's ever had," Carter states smugly as soon as the waiter walks away. "He's been talking about you ever since that first night after the Rap Renegade party. Whipped cream and honey on the first date? My, aren't you a naughty girl, huh?"

More than anything, I want to dump the entire bowl of steaming oysters on his head. But instead of reacting, I calmly reply, "I don't know what it is you think you've heard. But I assure you that you've somehow gotten me confused. And if you don't want me to press charges for sexual harassment and begin the biggest smear campaign you've ever seen in your life as soon as I leave this restaurant, you will pretend this conversation never happened. I assure you I'm not playing with you, Carter." I stand up and gather my belongings, as I watch the color drain from his face.

I walk away from Carter almost completely numb with anger. I can barely see straight for the tears clouding my vision. I'd been played by my own pawn. As soon as the valet pulls the car up, I jump in without even bothering to tip and peel off. I'm about to K-I-L-L Troy Bennett.

As I SCREECH to a halt in front of Troy's mansion, I'm completely emotionally exhausted. I'd called Elise to brief her on what happened and see what she thought I should do. While she was shocked and agreed that Troy was a complete waste of space, she begged me not to do anything too crazy. But, I mean, what's really too crazy, considering that this man practically ruined my entire career trying to show out for his boys?

Now that I was actually here, I didn't know what to do next. I briefly toy with the idea of burning down his home like Left Eye had done to Andre Rison's Atlanta mansion but I realize that I don't care enough. I don't love Troy, never did. I'm certainly not about to go to jail over him. I'm just pissed because he embarrassed me. What the fuck did he think, that I was never going to get to the point where I was working with someone as large as Carter? Acting like he was so happy for me when I got the part . . . Whatever. I just need to get my shit and get as far away from him as possible . . . oh, and maybe key his new tricked-out Cadillac truck as a parting gift.

As soon as I open the front door, I hear Jay-Z's *The Black Album* blasting from the playroom. Huge surprise—his little sidekicks are over again. I head directly up to the master bedroom, hoping that the music is loud enough to muffle the security system's entry-notification beeps. Thankfully, Troy had only given me the keys to his place a couple of months ago, so I don't have that much stuff at his place yet. I quickly jam all my clothes, shoes, and lingerie back into the same Louis Vuitton travel duffel that I'd brought them over in. As I walk out of the bathroom with the last of my beauty products, Troy appears in the doorway.

"Hey, sexy, I didn't even hear you come in," he says, his lips curved in his characteristic lopsided grin. As he surveys the pulled-out drawers and empty hangers on the floor, he quickly changes his tune. "Whoa, what the fuck is going on here?"

Without even bothering to respond, I put the last of the beauty products in my bag and proceed to zip it up. I survey the room one last time to make sure I haven't forgotten anything and start to walk out the bedroom door.

"Hello . . . earth to Amaya. What in the hell is going on?" he says, grabbing my arm to stop me from passing by him.

"Get your fucking hands off me," I hiss from between clenched teeth.

"No. Not until you tell me what's up. 'Cause this ain't cute. You got my house looking like a tornado ran through it and you walking out with all your stuff, looking like I shot your mom dukes or something. I want to know what's going on," he answers refusing to release my arm from his tight grip.

"I said, get the fuck off me," I scream as I pull from his grasp and push him away from me. "You want to know what's going on? Why don't you ask your golf buddy, Carter, what the fuck is going on! Wait, why bother, since you've already taken the liberty of telling everyone what's going on, you pathetic little piece of shit."

"Yo, for real, you're gonna lower your voice . . ." he responds as he nervously pulls at the collar of his white T-shirt and quickly shuts the bedroom door.

"No, Troy, I'm not gonna do a damn thing that you tell me. Why don't you go tell your New York trick or your Detroit whore to lower their voices. The only thing I'm gonna do is walk up out of this bullshit house and never look back at your sorry ass," I respond, heading past him out the door.

"Please, just let me explain, Amaya . . ." Troy calls from behind me.

As soon as I hear my name, I stop, turn back around, stare him dead in the eyes, and warn him, "For real, keep my goddamn name out your mouth. I have worked too long and too hard to build up a reputation, and the last thing I'm about to do is let your trifling, young behind come along and ruin it. So trust me when I say, whenever you see me out, act like you know, and keep it moving. Don't get embarrassed. 'Cause I will embarrass you."

I rush down the stairway only to discover Troy's tired-ass boys all gathered at the bottom, eavesdropping like a bunch of bitches.

"Oh, hey, Amaya. What's happening, girl?" they greet me uncomfortably.

"Puh-lease, fuck all y'all." I shoot back as I walk out the front door.

6

As I JUMP BACK on the highway, I feel only a brief sense of relief before I start to work myself up again. I wonder how many others are privy to the details of our sex life. Lord knows that it only takes a minute for hot gossip to get around Black Hollywood. Negroes kill me, I tell you. I knew I shouldn't have bothered giving his young behind a real taste of the goodies. Shit is so good, he didn't even know how to act. But the worst part is, none of this would have ever happened if I hadn't been trying to impress Keith. And for what? I still haven't seen any divorce papers. In fact, the only difference between now and ten months ago is that now he'll return all my pages, come to see me three times a week, occasionally spend an entire night, and, oh yeah, toss around the word "love" a whole lot. However, we're still running around after hours, denying our relationship, and acting like it's something to be ashamed of in front of folks. Bottom line, absolutely nothing that's getting me any closer to an engagement ring. Fuck that. It's time for me to play all the cards left in my hand. I pick up my cell and call Keith.

"Hello?" he answers in a slightly hushed voice.

"I need to see you right now," I say urgently as I turn down my Eminem CD.

"Huh? Amaya? It's late. I'm already in the house."

"I don't care what time it is," I whine, my voice getting slightly louder. "Baby, please, I need to see you right now. Meet me at my house in forty minutes."

"What's wrong?" Keith asks, his voice starting to sound strained. "Why are you tripping? Can't you just tell me? Or can we do this in the morning?"

"I'm not tripping, Keith. It's important. And I promise you, it'll be worth the little drive," I say confidently and hang up the phone before he has a chance to further protest.

I cannot believe he just said, "It's late." So goddamn what? As many nights as he allegedly spends in the studio working till the wee hours of the morning? Let me find out that he is laid up with Trixie and that's why he doesn't want to come back out. Whatever the case may be, all I know is Keith had better bring his black behind out of that house tonight. He doesn't want me to come ring his front doorbell.

FORTY-THREE MINUTES later, my front doorbell sounds. Ha, I knew it— that Negro knows he can't tell me no. Changed out of my dinner dress, I open the door in a hot-pink satin robe and a pair of clear Lucite hooker heels that I've been saving for a very special occasion, to find a very annoyed Keith huffing on my doormat.

"Yo, this better be some shit," he says, pushing past into the candle-lit apartment.

"So much for the sweet talk, huh?" I reply sarcastically, still bitter from earlier.

"Listen, you know I'm not for all this drama. I said I was already at home, and you dragging me back into the streets all crazy is just gonna make things hot for me."

"Keith," I answer, trying to soften my tone as I close the door and follow behind him. "I don't want to make things hot for you. It's just that I had a very disturbing evening and it's forced me to rethink a lot of what's going on in my life."

"I don't know what the hell happened to you, but this shit is not cool," he replies dispassionately, sitting down on the edge of my beige suede couch.

"Fine, Keith. It doesn't even matter what happened, the bottom line is that you're here with me now." I stand in front of him with my hands on his shoulders and slowly push him back into the deep couch. I start to massage his shoulders as he parts his legs further to allow me to stand closer.

"Mmmm, Amaya, you can't be acting like shit is an emergency for nothing," he grumbles into my stomach as he massages my naked butt under the flimsy robe.

I slowly end my massage and climb onto his lap facing him. Slowly kissing on his neck, I untie the robe so that my body is fully exposed. It's obvious from the change in his breathing pattern that I'm going to have to say what I have to say before we get caught up. I gently grab a hold of his chin and raise his face until our eyes meet. "This *is* an emergency," I state firmly. "You know how much I love you, right?"

"Of course," he replies trying to tug his face from my hand so that he can focus on the breasts in front of him.

"Wait, Keith," I gently reprimand with a quick kiss and devilish grin. "Let me say what I have to say and then we can do whatever you want."

"Fine," he pouts like a bad five-year-old. Looking at him makes my nipples hard.

"So, like I was saying, you know I love you. You turn me on physically and mentally. It's obvious that we're made for each other—both of us are happiest when we're together. Or at least that's what you always tell me."

"Yeah, okay so what's your point, Amaya?"

"My point . . ." I pause for emphasis, "is that I'd like nothing more than to spend the rest of my life as your woman—your real woman. Not your piece on the side." I can feel his body tense beneath me but I know that it's now or never, so I continue. "And if you haven't already, I want you to start the divorce proceedings tomorrow morning."

"Amaya! I know that this is not what you dragged me out of my house at the middle of the night for!" he explodes, then pushes me off of him and immediately stands up. I scramble to my feet, struggling to retie my robe.

"Yo, I'm out," he says as he strides toward the front door.

"You're out? That's all you have to say?" I ask as the situation spirals out of control. I can't believe that I just poured my heart out to him and this is all he has to say. I have hit a wall with Keith Cooper. This selfish bastard will never change.

"Hell yeah, I'm out. This shit is crazy. Enough with the mad pressure. You're acting stupid, and I really don't need this. I told you that those things take time and I'll do it when the time is right. You act like a nigga don't have kids and responsibilities. I can't just drop everything because you think you need something. Grow up. I want a mature woman, not a spoiled child who's throwing temper tantrums in the middle of the night!"

"No, Keith, what you want is a fool! Someone willing to wait the rest of her life until the time is convenient for you just because you manage to squeeze out an 'I love you' every once in a while. Well, I'm not her!" I yell back.

"Amaya, you're bugging. Why don't you go bother your little ball-bouncing boyfriend until you get it together," he angrily replies.

"Yeah, well, why don't you go lay up with your dyke wife until you get it together," I fire back.

"What the hell did you just say to me?" Keith stops dead in his tracks.

I grab the envelope with the photos of Trixie and her lover from off of my coffee table and throw it at the back of his head. "You heard me," I respond as he turns around and picks them up off the floor. "This whole time you keep pushing me off because Trixie and the kids can't handle you leaving . . . Well, take a good look, Keith. Um, it seems to me like Trixie can handle herself just fine!"

I smirk with satisfaction as Keith opens the envelope. His jaw drops as he slowly examines each photo. That's right, you punk, go on home to that, I think to myself.

"Where did you get these?" he growls at me.

"Does it even matter?" I ask.

"I know you didn't have my wife followed by some damn photographer," he asks menacingly as he starts walking toward me.

"Actually, I didn't even need the pictures. I overheard her having phone sex in the Armani showroom during my fitting right before Awards Week. But I knew you'd never believe me if I just told you. So I decided to get proof," I answer, standing my ground as he continues to advance toward me. "For the love of God, don't ask me why. Guess I'm just the fool trying to do everything I can to make you love me back."

"Bitch, I cannot believe that you had my wife followed. Are you out of your mind?" he roars in my face.

"Who are you calling a bitch?" I instinctively yell back.

Just as I get the last word out of my mouth, Keith grabs me by the collar of my robe, lifts me slightly off the ground, and starts shaking me violently. "Are you fucking crazy? Who do you think you are?" he continues. As the satin starts to choke me, I swing my arms, trying to punch him in his face to make him release me. When he finally drops me to the ground, my robe is torn but I barely notice. I jump right up and start scratching his face and beating on his chest.

"I hate you! I thought you loved me! Fuck you, Keith, fuck you!"

"No, Amaya, fuck you," he answers, shoving me to the ground with a hard push. "I should have left your crazy behind years ago."

This time the wind is completely knocked out of me. I lay in a crumpled heap on the floor, my body racked by sobs. Shortly after the door slams, I hear the sound of Keith's car screeching away from the curb. I start screaming like a wounded animal.

WHEN I AWAKE the next morning, the sun is shining brightly through my living room window. I'm still curled up in a ball on the floor. As I slowly pull myself off the ground, every bone in my body aches. I wince in pain with each breath. I hobble upstairs to the bathroom to get a full-length view of the previous night's damage.

The image in the mirror horrifies me. My face is puffy from crying and my hair is a matted mess. There's bruising around my neck and along my left upper arm, where I landed when he shoved me. Three of my fingernails are torn. I look a wreck.

I turn and head back into my bedroom. My chest tightens and the tears slowly start to fall. I can't believe what happened last night. After all this time waiting and praying, how could he just walk out on me like that? Didn't anything that we shared matter to him? I gave that bastard two years—how dare he choose Trixie over me. She obviously doesn't give a fuck about him. I love him. But maybe that's the problem. Maybe I need to not give a damn for Keith to feel me. Well, I've got something from him all right. Ain't no man ever going to put his hands on me and get away with it. I'm going to show Keith what it feels like when I don't give a damn about you. I grab my phone off the nightstand and dial number seven on my speed dial.

"This is Vivian Evans," she answers before the fourth ring.

"Hey, girl," I croak into the phone.

"Amaya? Girl, why do you sound like that?" she asks.

"Chile, you wouldn't believe me if I told you," I respond, my throat burning from the effort of trying to speak. "But lemme ask you this question right quick. My girl has some dirt on a high-profile person that she wants to get out quickly but it can't come back to her. Who should she call?"

"Oh, a friend, huh? I know all your damn friends. What's going on," she demands.

"Nothing, Viv, I promise. Trust me, I just can't talk about it right now. Okay?"

"Fine," she sighs. "Your 'friend' should call Nikki Brown at *Tattleteller* magazine. Have her tell Nikki that I sent her. She's practically the sole source for Industrywhispers.com. So this better be some shit that your 'friend' is taking to her."

"Oh, this is some shit, all right."

"Amaya, at least tell me if you're okay or not."

"I'm *going* to be, girl. I may be heading out of town for a few days, but no worries, it's all good. Let's just say I need to get some beauty rest before I have to report to the set in Toronto. I'll bring you up to speed when I return. Thanks for your help."

"All right, well, hit me as soon as you return," Viv insists as we hang up.

I immediately dial information and get the main number at *Tattleteller* magazine. Keith may have stormed out of here last night with the proofs and the negatives, but I've got a high-resolution pdf file on my hard drive with Nikki Brown's name all over it.

"LADIES AND GENTLEMEN, we will now begin boarding Flight 883 direct to Catalina, Arizona. All first-class passengers please report to Gate 45," announces the friendly voice over the intercom.

It's forty-eight hours later and my body still feels like crap from all the bruises, though my spirits are slowly recovering. A couple of weeks at the Mirival Spa and Resort is just what I need to get me back on track. I slowly stand and grab my carry-on. As I pass the trash can, I pause to take one last look at the cover of the special-edition *Tattleteller* that was released earlier this morning before casually dropping it in. There's a split cover with a photo of Trixie and her blond lover alongside a photo of Trixie and Keith at the Corcoran Gallery. The bold yellow headline reads: TRIXIE COOPER TAKES A LOVER! KEITH NOT MAN ENOUGH?

Checkmate, Negro!

18

VIVIAN

Mommy? Why you always mad at Daddy?"

That's a question I was neither expecting nor prepared to answer. At least not in terms that a seven-year-old, with whom I'd just been discussing card tricks and which color shorts he liked most, would understand. We were in his room, packing his suitcase for his bimonthly weekend stay-over at his dad's when Corey dropped the bomb. I was quiet, but I knew better than to leave him hanging; seven-year-olds, my son included, are notorious for holding on to a question until they get an answer. I decided quickly that my response should be slow and deliberate; I chose to deny, which isn't exactly a lie. I'm not mad at Sean. I just choose not to have any words with him. It keeps things civil.

"I'm not mad at your daddy," I said, folding his swimming trunks into quarters and stuffing them into the bag.

"If you're not mad at Daddy, why ain't you speaking to him when he comes over?"

"It's not 'why ain't you,'" I said, part stalling, part correcting his grammar—can't have my child walking around speaking Ebonics, like his mama doesn't have control over the King's English. "It's 'why *aren't* you.'"

"Why aren't you speaking to Daddy?" he said, quickly correcting himself.

I took my time answering—pulled his underwear out of his dresser drawer and packed them neatly on top of his jeans and T-shirts. "Sometimes," I spoke slowly, "grown-ups have differences of opinion, and rather than fight about it, they just go on about their business without really talking, so that they don't get into arguments."

"Well, if you're not mad at him, then why are you worried about getting into an argument with him?"

"Sweetie, what's happening between your dad and me isn't really something you should be worrying yourself over," I said, sitting on the bed and pulling him over to me. I hug him; he eagerly accepts my embrace.

"I wish that you and Daddy and me could live together," he said.

"I wish you, Daddy, and I could live together," I counter. "You don't say 'me' in that sentence."

"You, Daddy, and I," he says, exasperated.

"Well, sweetie, take it from Mommy: You can't always get what you want," I said and leaned in to kiss his cheek. I got up off the bed and grabbed his knapsack out of the corner of his closet. "How about you pack up whatever toys you want to take over to your father's house in your bag? He'll be here to get you soon enough."

I wasn't studying anybody's Sean. It was his sister Jalene that I was focused on. She'd called me all out of the blue to ask me if I'd go with her to Paint Shop, a hip nail salon in Beverly Hills. She said she wanted to catch up with her nephew's mom and ask me something, though she wouldn't tell me what it was. I was a little apprehensive about her cryptic call for a meeting, but not too much; Jalene was a constant presence in Corey's life—whether it was baby-sitting for Sean when Corey was over for the weekend, or coming by my house to pick him up herself— and we got along easily. Besides, I was looking forward to the fresh pedi and a few good laughs before I settled in for the weekend to finish up a story for *Newsweek* (a piece about the impact of criminal laws and police surveillance on hip hop that I pitched several times to my editors at the *Daily News* but was summarily dismissed as irrelevant by all of them).

"*Newsweek*—that's great for a journalist, huh?" Jalene said, flipping through a magazine as we sat out in the waiting area of Paint Shop.

"Sure is," I said, nodding my head. "Sure is."

"I knew you'd be great at writing for those magazines," she said. "What's up with your girls? How are Amaya and Trista?"

"Girl, they just started speaking after months—can you believe it?"

"Damn, what happened?" she said, resting the magazine on her lap. I gave her some sketchy details about the Las Vegas blow-up, and how just a few days ago, I tried to coax Trista into speaking to Amaya so they could work out their differences, how Trista's dad had passed, and the crazy reunion.

"Trista was icier than the top of Mount Everest," I said, shaking my head. "I just couldn't get through to her. I swear, she's about the most judgmental person I know, and when she gets it in her mind that she's figured you out, she runs with it. I'm glad she's working on that flaw—there's no way in the world she'd have been able to be Amaya's friend again if she wasn't. It's pretty easy to come to some hard-and-fast conclusions about Amaya, but that's not what friends are for. I'm glad Trista's finally realizing that."

"Sounds like Trista and Amaya both needed to get over themselves," Jalene said just as we were signaled to take a seat in the pedicure chairs. "Actually, though, Viv, I didn't come here to talk about Amaya and Trista. I came here to talk to you about Sean."

I snapped my neck around so quickly to look Jalene in the eye that I damn near gave myself whiplash. "Sean?" I asked. "What's to talk about?"

"Well, after your baby daddy came over to my house last night, spilling his guts and asking me for advice, I think there's plenty," she said.

"I'm lost," I said flatly, dipping my toes into the warm milk-and-honey bath. "What do you mean?"

I listened intently as Jalene explained how Sean dropped by her house with a pint of Häagen-Dazs and a dilemma he begged her to help him work through. He told her that Corey had been pressuring him to explain why his mother and father weren't together, and that the questioning had become so persistent that he figured he'd better come up with a good reason to tell his son. But the more he thought about it, the more he realized that there was no good reason—he and I had grown apart over something that, with just a little bit more discussion and understanding, could have easily brought us closer together had we not been so incredibly pig-headed.

"And that's exactly what you two have been over the past few years," Jalene announced. "Pig-headed."

"Hold on there, honey—I don't think you have any place passing judgment on the decisions I've made as a mother or as the ex-fiancée of Sean Jordan . . ." I began.

Jalene held up a manicured finger. "Let me finish," she said. "Just hear me out."

I sat back in my chair, but I refused to look in her direction. I stared at my big toe as the pedicurist dragged a wet cotton ball across my nail.

"I'm not saying you need to forget everything that went wrong between you and Sean. I'm just saying that when he came by last night, he seemed contrite and willing to at least be civil, if not more than friends, with the mother of his child—not only for the sake of Corey, but because he still loves you."

"He what?" I said.

"You heard me. He didn't exactly come out and say it in those words, but the sentiment was there. And I know my brother. I think that at the end of the day, if he could turn back time and start all over again with you and Corey, he would."

"Well, it's a shame that you really can't erase over seven years from your memory, because then maybe something like that would be possible, but I don't see that happening," I said softly. "And maybe the next time my child's father calls you for a little chat and chew, you should tell him that you're not interested in getting in the middle of our private affairs."

Jalene sucked her teeth then sighed. "Look, Viv, I have no interest in getting in the middle of anything. I just want my brother and my girl to be happy. You've gotten yourself together over these past few months, and we're all proud of you for that—even Sean. So you probably don't need any help in the man department. But if I can help you have a happy life with the man you've spent a lifetime loving, then I'm going to do that. Love doesn't come often, Viv—don't throw it away because you're too busy holding up the stubborn flag."

"I'm not being stubborn," I said simply. "I just don't feel like it's necessary to rehash all of this. I've moved on, and I came here today to relax and enjoy my pedi." And with that I sat back in my chair, turned on the chair massage, and buried myself in the latest issue of *People*. I wasn't reading shit, though. My mind was too busy trying to process what Jalene had just said.

WHEN I'M UPSET, or stressed out, I scrub. Everything. I can't help myself. I start at the top of the stairs, work my way through the bathrooms, the bedrooms, the linen closet, and the office, then back downstairs and through the kitchen, into the dining room and living room, the music room, the foyer, and downstairs into the basement. When I came back home from my pedi date with Jalene, I headed straight for the kitchen, where I proceeded to mop, scrub, and buff the appliances until they practically screamed for mercy. Sean loves me? Loves me? He lusted for me, that much I was sure of—but only when he was looking for a quick piece of booty. Nothing like ex-sex to cure that one. But love? Me? Sean? What was I supposed to do with this information? I'd finally gotten my son's father out of my system, purged him from my mind—carefully filed him under the category I'd neglected to put him in all these years: baby daddy, nothing more. And now that I'd finally gotten over him, I was supposed to fall for him all over again?

The crack of thunder shook me out of my haze. I hadn't noticed how cold I was until I heard the rain driving against the kitchen window. I shoved the Mr. Clean, Pine Sol, and Murphy's Oil Soap back into the cleaning bucket under the kitchen sink, washed my hands with scented hand wash, and went upstairs to my bedroom. In no mood to even read the contents page of a magazine, much less write a story for one, I buried myself under my comforter and waited for sleep to come. The ringing phone jarred me from my sleep.

"Hello?" I said groggily into the receiver. I was surprised that darkness had fallen outside, lifted only by the full moon peeking through the clouds. I looked at the clock. It was 8:42 P.M. I'd been asleep for almost three hours.

"Viv. We need to talk," Sean said.

I shifted against my pillows, and instinctively pulled the covers up to my neck. Was I ready for this?

"Jalene told me that you and she talked today," he continued. "I was going to wait until I brought Corey back home to speak to you, but I can't hold on any longer. The truth is, Viv, you and I have too much to lose to keep going at it like we do."

"Sean, I don't know that . . ." I started, but Sean didn't let me finish.

"Just wait a minute, Viv—let me talk," he interrupted. "You never let a brother finish what he's got to say. It's one of the things I've always loved and despised about you: You say what's on your mind, but it always comes at the expense of not listening to anyone else. I need you to hear me out tonight, okay?"

I waited for him to continue.

"Wow—I thought for sure I'd be hearing a dial tone by now," he laughed, but my silence made it clear I wasn't amused. He cleared his throat. "Anyway, over the years, we've made some tough decisions, you and I, and a lot of them, I think, were smart moves that helped us get to be the people we are today. There were times when we didn't always agree with each other's decisions, but they were ultimately very necessary choices. I've never questioned the decisions you've made, but I've always felt unjustly maligned by you for making the choices that I've made. My choices, however, were always made with you and my son in mind."

"Where in your mind? Couldn't have been the front, because it's always seemed like we've played second chair to your interests. So explain to me exactly when you made a decision on all of our behalf. Please. Do that," I said, fast becoming annoyed.

"See? That's what I'm talking about, Vivian," Sean said, his voice rising. "You've always jumped to conclusions about me—assumed the worst first. I can't stand that about you."

"You can't stand what?" I said, incredulous.

"Your assumptions, Vivian," he said, annunciating each of the syllables in the words for emphasis. "You assume that every woman I'm either out with or near is someone I'm boning. You assumed that I was the reason why Corey had an asthma attack, even though the doctor said that anything could have set it off. Hell, you even assumed that I didn't care about my son enough to come see him at the hospital when asthma almost suffocated him to death, even though I had a perfectly logical explanation for why I wasn't there."

"Sean, forgive me if I don't take you at your word, but I have good reason to assume that caring for my child and me aren't at the top of your things-to-do list," I said quietly. "My child has lived a lifetime in a single-parent home because you abandoned him and his mother to pursue your own dreams, without once taking into consideration how we'd fit into them. Don't blame me if I see only the worst in your actions."

"First of all, Corey is *our* son," he said. "Let's get that straight. Second, you never let me explain why I wanted to put the wedding off. You just tossed my ring in my face and walked out."

I ignored the "our son" comment. "Okay, Sean, tell me this brilliant reason for why you wanted me to raise my son on my own and pursue my dreams of being a journalist without the help that comes when you've got a partner to help you keep your life in order. Come on, I want to hear it."

Sean was quiet for a moment. He spoke slowly and clearly. "There was no way that I could care for you and a baby and do well in med school. I figured that if I focused, I could get out and then scoop you and Corey up and make you a doctor's wife. I would have felt like a failure if I had you both living in poverty and I flunked out of school because I couldn't concentrate.

"See, Viv, I thought I was making the right decision for us. What I didn't realize was that a decision about us should have included just that—us. I was wrong for putting you in the position of having to fend for yourself. I hadn't thought that part through. And you were so angry when I told you that you wouldn't give me a chance to explain, and it all fell apart because we were both too caught up in our own points to hear each other's reasoning. And for that, Vivian Evans, I'm so sorry."

He had me at "I thought I was making the right decision for us." Tears ran hot down my face, dripping off my chin and onto my chest, soaking my bra. What was there to say? I could barely speak. He was saying what I'd always wanted to hear, and he was sincere about it, and I believed him. It was true.

"Viv? Are you still there?" Sean said.

"Where's our son?" I said, gathering my composure.

"He fell asleep about an hour ago," Sean said quietly. "I took him to a ball game, and he was exhausted from all that cheering."

"He sure does love a good game, huh?"

"Yes, he does."

We listened to each other breathe for what seemed like an eternity. Sean broke the silence. "Viv, why don't you come over," he said easily.

"But it's raining outside."

"I'd come over there, but Corey's in the bed. Come on, put on your galoshes, grab your umbrella, and come over. We can talk some more."

It wasn't talking that I wanted to do. I pushed back the comforter, hopped out of bed, and made a beeline for my lingerie drawer. I tossed everything out, and considered kicking myself for constantly passing up the bra-and-panty sets for the more reasonably priced big-girl drawers. I thanked the heavens that my nicest black lace bra was clean, and that I'd splurged a couple weeks ago for a pair of those lace short-shaped underwear—Victoria's Secret was practically giving them away, so I bought one. I stood in the mirror, admiring my purchase: I never realized how cute sets actually looked, especially on my new-and-improved body. The shorts sat low on my ass, providing the perfect showcase for my firm stomach and curvy hips. I slipped into a simple sky-blue cotton wrap shirt, and a gray flared skirt, both of which skimmed me in places I'd long been too afraid to accentuate, and popped on a pair of black stilettos before thinking better of it. Sean wouldn't appreciate me trying too hard. I threw the pumps back into the closet, grabbed my black thong sandals out the foyer closet, the biggest black umbrella I could find, and my keys off the kitchen counter, and hightailed it over to my son's father's house.

Sean met me at the door wearing a robe and nothing else. His locks hung around his shoulders; the porch light made the green in his eyes sparkle. He pulled me into his arms and I fell happily into his embrace. "I love you, Vivian Olivia Evans."

"I love you, Dr. Sean Jordan."

We hugged and danced our way into his living room. Anita Baker's "Angel" was playing softly on the stereo. Sean hummed the melody, and when Anita made it to the chorus, he sang along with her—all off-key, but he sang it from the heart nonetheless.

I felt the extra hands on my hips, but I didn't immediately process that Corey had snuck into the room to dance with his parents until he spoke. "I love this song. Daddy says it reminds him of you," Corey said. I looked at Sean, smiled, then shook my head and turned around to greet my child.

"I thought you were sleeping," I said.

"I'm not sleepy," Corey whined. His smile stretched from one ear to the other. "Can I stay up for a little while, please?"

I smiled, too, then looked back at Sean. "You'll have to ask your dad," I giggled.

"Dang, man," Sean laughed. "Okay, you got fifteen minutes, then it's time for bed. Fifteen, man," he stressed.

"Okay, Daddy!" Corey said before snuggling back into my butt. His arms were just long enough to stretch around my hips and halfway around his father's.

YOU ARE CORDIALLY INVITED TO JOIN

COREY AJANI JORDAN'S PARENTS

VIVIAN OLIVIA EVANS

AND

DR. SEAN ALLEN JORDAN

AS THEY JUMP THE BROOM INTO

HOLY MATRIMONY

SUNDAY DECEMBER 31, 2006

8:00 P.M.

THE GRAND PALAZZO RESORT AND SPA

ST. THOMAS, VIRGIN ISLANDS

ATTIRE: BEACH CHIC

19

TRISTA

I have a slight hangover. As the warm sunlight streams into my bungalow, the sea breeze cools the small room. I inhale the salty air and my eyes open slowly and begin to focus on the copper silk dress hanging on the closet door. Sitting up, I push back the sheets. Thankfully I didn't get so twisted on that wicked Sangria last night that I didn't remember to take some aspirin and raid the mini-bar for water before I went to sleep. I push back the mosquito netting attached to the canopy and stretch. Glancing at the digital clock on the nightstand I see it's only 10:30. Good, I've got plenty of time to chill before I have to meet Amaya and Elise in the hotel's garden to take pictures.

The terra-cotta floor feels cool against my feet as I walk into the tiny bathroom. Looking in the mirror, I'm happy to see that the two-strand twists I got on the beach yesterday withstood the night. The humidity is murder on a sister's style, so this was my last hope to look cute. Letting the water heat up, I tuck the twists of hair under my shower cap and then call the hotel restaurant to order some breakfast.

After ordering, I step into the shower and chuckle at the memory of Viv, Amaya, and Sean's daiquiri-induced limbo contest on the beach last night. Hopefully they can both stand up straight this morning. They had tried to pull me into their wild antics but I was content to watch a very pregnant Elise and Will stroll along the surf.

It's going to be a small wedding. It's a special day that's been over ten years in the making. My girl Viv got her man.

We all flew to St. Thomas yesterday morning to celebrate with Sean and Viv. And in just twenty-four hours I've fallen in love with this tiny island paradise. I planned to stay for a few more days after the wedding because there would be plenty of work waiting for me when I got back to L.A. And who knows when the next time will be that I have a chance to take a vacation.

After my father passed away I stayed with Tanisha and Tyquan to help get things organized. And in addition to Daddy's affairs there was one other important thing I needed to take care of. Tanisha went with me to the doctor's office to get the results for my AIDS test. She held my hand as Dr. Woodard read the results: negative. My sister and I hugged each other and cried, repeating "Thank you, Jesus" over and over again. Dr. Woodard recommended I schedule a follow-up test in six months, as it can take six months for HIV antibodies to show up in the blood, then she lectured me for at least twenty minutes about safe sex and the alarming numbers of black women contracting HIV.

The next day I had called my HR contact at The Agency, Nichelle Edwards, a sister who knows where all the bodies are buried. She told me she would personally put through the necessary paperwork for an extended leave for me. Nichelle said this should buy me some time so that I could get my head together and think about what I wanted to do.

I talked over the work situation with Damon. He'd gone back to New York for a funeral but called every day. I told him that there was really no way I could stay at the firm. He agreed that by turning me down for partner and stripping me of my clients they were saying I had no future at TA. The question for me, he said, was what was I willing to do about that. I'd worked really hard to get where I was, and I didn't want to just take their shit. I sat down in the living room with a calculator and a pad of paper and started running numbers. My bonus had been just over $300,000 this year. I then called my private banker to discuss selling my beloved home. Since the condo had been bought in foreclosure and renovated he thought I'd realize a sizable profit. I told him I needed to move quickly and that I would be staying in Compton until we settled.

Next I went over to Office Max and bought a laptop computer, had one of Tanisha's friends down at the phone company install a new line in the dining room, and set up shop. My first call was to Adriene to ask her to email me all my contacts. I needed to do that quickly because as soon as TA realized what I was up to, they'd freeze all my files. I told her I didn't expect her to come work with me and that I was sure that Nichelle would take care of her if she wanted to stay with TA. Within two hours she was at the house with copies of all my files.

"So what's the name of this bootleg start-up?" she asked as she popped her gum. Her fiery red curls bounced up and down.

"I don't know. I haven't even thought about it," I said.

"You need a name," she said. "How do you expect me to start calling folks if we don't have a name?"

"We?" I asked. I didn't have the nerve to ask her to sign on to my half-baked plan and was shocked that she'd even think of coming on board.

"What?" she asked with a grin. "You think you're going to just ride off into the sunset with the business I helped create and leave me at TA?"

"I think Trista T. Gordon and Associates has a nice ring to it," said Tanisha, walking into the room.

"It's kind of catchy," said Adriene.

"But I don't have any associates," I said, looking at the two of them.

"What the hell am I?" said Adriene. "Chopped liver?"

"And me," said Tanisha.

"And me, too," chimed in Tyquan, who was sitting on the floor, labeling folders with a list of names I had given him earlier.

"Are you guys serious?" I asked. Apparently they were. Adriene said she'd defer part of her salary to be rolled into an equity partnership because she hoped to work her way up to full partner and wanted to own a piece of the business. Sounded like a great idea to me. Tanisha couldn't afford to quit her job but said she and Ty would help out in any way they could.

Next we began working the phones. By the time I'd finished notifying my clients of my impending departure from TA, only three were willing to leave with me. Unfortunately I wasn't able to reach Jared directly, so I left a message on his cell phone. I also left a message for Cassidy but didn't expect to hear back from her.

Amaya surprised me by stopping by the house the next day. She said she just *happened* to have a copy of her agreement with Clarence in her bag. I skimmed the document and highlighted several clauses to show her how Clarence was ripping her off. I also took a look at her contract for the Soular Son picture and rattled off a few ways in which she could optimize this new agreement.

"So it looks like I need a new agent, huh?" she said, smiling at me across the cluttered dining room table.

"Really, you want me to manage you?" I said, surprised.

"I like what you're doing here. Plus, you're going to get a lot of buzz when you launch, so I figure an opportunistic sister such as myself ought to ride that wave."

Finally I got a call from Jared's mother, Lynda, requesting a meeting. Conscious of the mounting expenses, I asked Adriene to set the meeting up for someplace not too pricey.

"Are you crazy?" she said. "If you're going to make money you've got to look like money. Especially to these guys. Especially in this town. Jared's getting wined and dined all over the place. You can't go out looking like you can't run with the big dogs."

"You're absolutely right," I said, coming to my senses. "Book The Ivy."

I had expected Jared's mom to urge her son to stay with TA but was surprised that she wanted to hear my pitch. When they arrived, Heather was with them. I had assumed they'd broken up after all the stuff in the paper linking him with Kimberly and after her suicide attempt (Sloane earned every penny of her exorbitant retainer by keeping *that* out of the papers). I walked them through my plan for his career and talked about how I saw him growing into a star. Sure, I said, Steven can make the fast money pushing all the predictable projects, but if you want to build a serious career as a respected actor then I was the only one who can help him do that.

"Look, Trista," said Lynda as she pushed her Dior sunglasses up into her hair, "we know you can guide Jared's career. You believed in him from the beginning, and we're confident in that, but I gotta tell you, the only reason we're taking this meeting is because of what happened to little Heather here."

"My mom's right," Jared said as he wrapped an arm around his fiancée's slender shoulders. "I need the kind of people around me who can help me steer my professional life while respecting and protecting the boundaries of my personal life."

"No problem," I said confidently.

"Good. Send your agency agreement over to the house by the end of the day. Also, we haven't signed the Paramount Pictures deal yet, although Steven's been hounding us every day. Can you take care of that? And of course, we'll need a new publicist."

"That's for sure," I said. If Jared hasn't signed the Paramount papers yet, I'll be kicking off our new business with a four-million-dollar deal!

By the time I got back to the house in Compton, Amaya had forwarded an email with an excerpt from Industrywhispers.com.

> TO: Tgordon@yahoo.com
> FROM: Astarisbrn@yahoo.com
> Subject: FW: The Dish
>
> Is the new action hero Jared Greenway a two-timer?
> Sources spotted the Hollywood hottie chowing at The Ivy with
> AWOL TA agent Trista Gordon this afternoon. Hmmm . . .
> Somebody better tell TA wonderboy Steven Banks before
> Gordon the Great steals the $4 million man right from under
> his nose . . .

As expected, TA went crazy when they heard I was opening my own shop. They immediately filed an injunction against me to keep me from taking any of their clients. But by the end of the second week, we were up and running with Jared's new $4 million Paramount deal as our first signing. Our plan had been to start off small and grow slowly, but Adriene pushed me to sublease a small space in Beverly Hills so we could post a proper address on our letterhead.

AFTER I WASH up in the shower, I slather Bobbi Brown Body Polish on my body. The blazing Caribbean sun has given my skin a sexy glow, and the lotion's hint of sparkle shows it off to perfection. A knock at the door interrupts my thoughts about my new business. I grab the yellow hotel robe from the back of the bathroom door and belt the soft material tightly around my waist.

"Who is it?" I ask before opening the door.

"Room service." The muffled voice has a slight island accent.

"Wow, that was fast," I say as I open the door and step back to let the attendant wheel in the cart. But instead of a uniformed waiter standing in my doorway, I see Damon, dressed in dark-blue jeans and an orange T-shirt, standing behind the dining cart. A small brown leather overnight bag is slung across his chest.

"What the . . ." I say, suddenly very conscious of being naked under the thin material of the robe. "What are you doing here?" He smiles and wheels the cart past me into my room.

"Just thought I'd deliver your breakfast," he says with a twinkle in his eye. "Nice shower cap." Shit. I rip the plastic cap off my head and try to fluff out my hair. He removes the leather bag and drops it in a corner by the door, then wheels the squeaky cart out onto the small balcony. I follow him out on the small terrace.

"Hmmm, looks good," he says, smiling as he sits down and removes the tops from the dishes.

"Uh, Damon, what are you doing here?" I ask as I try to squeeze behind him and slip into the other seat. Once seated, I adjust the robe to make sure I am fully covered. I'm suddenly mindful of what happened the last time we were in a hotel room together.

"I'm here for the wedding," he says as he butters a slice of toast and looks out into the ocean. The stubble on his cheeks is so sexy. Why haven't I ever noticed that before? "Man, it's beautiful here."

"You were invited?" I ask as I pick up the carafe and pour myself a cup of tea and then add a couple of cubes of brown sugar. "Viv didn't tell me that."

"So how's business? Did that lawyer I recommended work out?" he asks, ignoring my comment.

"Oh, yeah, Chris is brilliant. We're working together very well."

"Good. I told him to take extra-special care of you."

"Thank you," I say, suddenly feeling a little shy.

"I like your hair," he says, reaching across the table to brush back one of the curly tendrils. I try not to stare at the muscles flexing in his strong arms and the T-shirt fitted across his broad chest.

"Oh, thanks," I say. "Just something I thought I'd try on vacation."

"It's cute," he says.

"Thanks," I say again, still confused about why he's here.

"I read in the paper that you signed that kid Jared. That's big, right?"

"Yeah. Huge, actually." When he brought up my most famous client I started talking excitedly about the new business, my plans for expansion, and the great meetings I had lined up once I returned to L.A. He smiles at me as if he knew I could do it all along, and then gives me the name of a good accountant to help with my billing. When I ask him about things at Global, he tells me things are going well and that he'll probably be heading soon to Singapore for a few weeks on a new deal.

"Oh, really," I say, trying hard not to sound disappointed. After my dad's funeral Damon and I spoke a lot on the phone. We hadn't seen each other because he seemed to always be flying back and forth to the home office in New York and I was working around the clock on the new business plan. He had given me a lot of valuable advice and hooked me up with some key contacts. He never asked me what happened with Garrett, so I never mentioned it. I wanted to know if he was seeing anyone but didn't think I had any right to ask. After all, we were just friends, right?

"How's Amaya doing?" he asks when I tell him that I'm representing her now.

"She's good. I've lined up some good meetings for her when we get back to L.A. I really think with the right representation that girl is going to go places," I say and laugh to myself.

"Yeah, she always was a star, even if it was only in her own mind back in the day," he says and chuckles. He leans back in his chair and folds his hands behind his head. His T-shirt creeps up to expose his hard stomach and the dark trail of hair leading down into his boxers. Damn, it's hot out here. I feel my nipples harden and I know he can see through the thin material of the robe. I need to put some damn clothes on. I excuse myself from the table and then try to make my way around his chair. As I try to pass he reaches out and grabs my arm and pulls me onto his lap. The bottom half of the robe falls open. I try to close it as much as I can to cover up the tops of my thighs. Something hard pokes into one of my thighs.

"Damon, what are you doing?" I ask.

"What does it feel like I'm doing?" he asks as he nuzzles my neck and his hands slip under the robe. "Mmm, you smell good." I am finding it hard to think clearly but know I need to get up before we start something that neither one of us can finish. I try to get up but he holds me in place.

"Why are you always running away from me," he says softly in my ear. "Just stay still for a minute. Just stay still for a minute." I can feel his heart beating rapidly through his T-shirt. I am sure mine is beating just as fast. Suddenly, I feel one of his hands opening the robe and pushing it off my shoulders. Damon continues to caress my breasts and tenderly kiss my shoulders and then moves up to my waiting mouth. I savor his lips by tracing the fullness with my tongue. I think we are going to get something started when I feel him fiddling with something in his pants.

"What are you doing, Damon?" I say, trying to twist around to see. When I look down, he's pulled a small, weathered leather box from his pocket along with a folded-up piece of newspaper.

"What's that?" I ask, my voice catching in my throat.

"I told you that I had some unfinished business to take care of," he says as he places the box in my hand and begins to unfold the paper. What is he talking about?

"I don't understand," I say and push back behind my ear the hair that had fallen in my eyes. "What is this?"

"Something that belongs to you," he says, tipping up my chin with his finger to make me look into his eyes. "Open it."

I take a deep breath and open the small box that looks a little beat up. Inside, tucked into a black velvet lining, is a small diamond ring.

"I don't understand," I say, looking up at him and back at the ring.

"Look at the lid on the box," he says. I don't have my contacts in, so I squint to read the gold foil lettering on the inside of the box.

"Mitchell's Jewelry?" I read. "Why does that name sound familiar?" He doesn't answer me as I repeat the name softly. Then I remember. Mitchell's was the name of the little jewelry store that Damon worked at our senior year in college. But why would he have a ring from there?

"Mitchell's is still open?" I ask, still confused.

"No, they closed a couple of years after we graduated," he says and he smiles, enjoying my confusion.

"Well, I don't understand, then. How did you get this ring?"

"You know, for a big-time businesswoman you aren't very bright sometimes," he says jokingly as he kisses my neck and takes the ring from the box. Then he holds up the piece of newspaper so that I can read it. It's a yellowing front page of the newspaper he started in college with the large headline TRISTA, WILL YOU MARRY ME? Holding up the ring for me to see, he then says, "I bought this ring eleven years ago, made up this copy of my newspaper, and planned to propose to you on our last night together."

"What?" I can't believe what he is saying. "Oh my God, Damon. I can't . . ." I choke back tears.

"Now, I've held on to this ring for eleven years, and I flew out here to give it to you. Like I said, it belongs to you," Damon says as he takes the ring out of the box and slips it on my finger. "Trista, when I saw you last year I realized I never stopped loving you. I thought I was over you, but I never stopped loving you. But I also realized there were some things that you needed to do for yourself before you could fully make room for me in your life. And I didn't want to crowd you. I know what happened last year with that girl was crazy. But please believe me when I tell you that we had broken up before the wedding and I swear I had no idea she was going to fly out there. And I certainly didn't plan for us to sleep together. But when I saw you again I just couldn't stay away. And later, I hated seeing you with Garrett, especially since I knew he'd never appreciate you. Not the real you, like I do. I know we're meant to be together."

"That's over, Damon," I say. "That's all over." I leave out most of the details but confess to him that Garrett and I have broken up because I found out he was gay. Even if Garrett didn't believe he was gay, I did.

"Wow," he says, shaking his head at this new information about Garrett.

I can barely see him through the tears welling in my eyes. I put my hands on the sides of his face and bring his lips down to mine and kiss him. I love this man, I think to myself. I've always loved this man.

"Trista Tanya Gordon, will you marry me?" Damon asks as he brings my fingers up to his lips and kisses them one by one, and I let my tears fall onto his shoulder. I can't believe this is happening. It all feels like a dream that is too good to be true.

He picks me up and carries me into the bedroom and kicks the patio door closed behind him. Placing me gently on the bed, he stands over me and looks into my eyes and then unties my robe and opens it. Looking down at me he quickly takes off his clothes and then lies on top of me. I am ready for him. I had never wanted him so badly. I open my legs to welcome him but he won't kiss me.

"You didn't answer my question," he says, looking deeply into my eyes, searching for an answer. He raises himself up on his outstretched arms. "Will you marry me, Trista?"

"Yes, Damon. Yes, I'll marry you," I say, still crying softly as I arch my body up to meet him. He slips a condom on quickly and then slides into me as my nails tease his back and shoulders. I wrap my legs tightly around his waist.

"Trista, I love you," he moans in my ear.

"I love you, too, baby," I say as I grab his face. "Look at me, Damon. I love you, Damon. I've always loved you."

"Oh, Trista," he says as he grips the bed's headboard to brace himself as he thrusts deeply inside me and we make love.

After our breathing returns to normal, he pulls one of the sheets up over our bodies and then rests his head on my breast. I stroke his hair with one hand and stare at the ring on my left hand with what I am sure is a stupid grin on my face.

"What are you looking at?" he asks playfully as he kisses my breast.

"I'm looking at the most beautiful ring in the world," I say as I turn my hand to admire it from different angles.

"Well, actually I thought that when we got back to L.A. we could go and pick out something more appropriate. That ring was just the only thing I could afford back in the day. Besides, I wouldn't want your girls to clown you over this diamond dust."

"Are you crazy?" I say, pushing his head off of my breast so I can sit up in the bed. "This is the most beautiful ring I've ever seen in my life and I'll never take it off."

"Are you sure?" he asks, raising an eyebrow as he looks up at me. "I mean, I'm not tripping if you want something else. You know, a brother's got a little change now, so we can go to one of those fancy jewelers when we get back to L.A. if you want."

I throw my leg over his body and straddle him, moving my hips around suggestively.

"Damon Jackson Reynolds, this is the ring that you bought me eleven years ago when you first wanted to marry me, and this is the ring I'm going to wear forever," I say, looking into his eyes. "This little ring means more to me than anything else we could pick out today." I lean in to nibble on his lower lip, biting gently.

"I guess my wife has spoken," he says and then falls back against a pillow and closes his eyes.

"You're damn right," I say. "You're damn right."

20

AMAYA

"Goddamn technology," I mumble under my breath as I swipe my electronic room key through the slot for the third time. At the sound of the lock finally clicking open, I push down the handle, shove open the door, and release a loud sigh of relief. The last thing I am in the mood to do right now is walk all the way down to the front desk to haggle with the night manager for a replacement key card.

As soon as I enter the room I place my half-empty glass of bubbly on the nightstand and kick off my copper-colored, strappy Anne Klein Collection sandals. The cool clay tiles provide an unspeakable relief to the burning balls of my feet. Whoever coined the phrase "cuteness kills" ain't never lied. But although I'd like to blame the slow, throbbing sensation on poorly fitting shoes, I know it's really just the price I have to pay for dancing the night away at yesterday's preceremony celebration. I was getting my grind on to Beenie Man with Sean's handsome baby cousin Frank from Maryland. I swear that little twenty-one-year-old wore my old behind out on the dance floor!

A soft breeze wafts the strong scent of the Caribbean through the bungalow's open window, and I follow the stream of moonlight over to the window. There's nothing quite so beautiful as the sight of a full moon in the islands; it makes the soft hair on my arms stand at attention. I slowly rub my arms to try and settle them down. Vivian and Sean are truly blessed with a perfect night.

Once my feet cool off somewhat, I turn and drift into the bathroom—

time to touch up the face. After spending the previous afternoon loung-
ing on the beach, debating baby names with Elise, I really don't need
more than eyeliner, mascara, and a fresh coat of gloss to accentuate my
sun-kissed look. This is definitely going to be a quick touch-and-go.
As I sit down at the vanity I'm relieved to see that the humidity hasn't
completely ruined the sweeping wave effect that frames my face. I can
hear the sounds of the band jamming and people celebrating in the distance. For such an intimate little party, we sure are a loud group of folks.
But, then again, considering the sort of year it's been for everyone—
especially Vivian, Trista, and me—there's certainly a lot to celebrate and
be loud about. The events of the past two months replay themselves like
a runaway train in my mind . . .

It wasn't until almost the end of the second week at the Better Day Spa
that the bruises on my neck and arm finally faded. By then I had decided
it was time to call Benita and share the details of my confrontation with
Keith. For the first time in two years I was absolutely sure of the status of
my relationship with Keith: it was over. It might break her heart to hear
the news, but as for me, personally, I was more than okay with it.

"Hey, Benita," I greeted her when she finally answered the phone.

"Amaya, darling! I wasn't expecting to hear from you!" she
responded, the sound of undeniable happiness still apparent in her
voice.

"Can't your only child give you a call?" I snipped before I could
catch myself.

"No need to be smart. Of course you can call me. I'm just surprised
is all."

"I'm sorry. I was actually calling to share some news with you," I
softly apologized.

"Let me guess, Keith popped the question, didn't he? I knew he'd
come around!"

"Actually . . . no. More like Keith shook the hell out of me and threw
me around my very own apartment. Not quite a proposal, huh?"

"What?" she gasped. "Has he lost his mind?"

"Long story short, I hired a private investigator to follow his wife to dig up some dirt on her. And, basically, I discovered that she was having an affair . . . with a woman. When I confronted Keith with the information, he flipped out on me," I rushed through the story.

"Goodness, I thought that story in *Tattleteller* was completely fabricated," she gasped. "But I simply cannot believe he had the nerve to put his hands on you over a woman that's cheating on him with another woman. He's trash. I'm so sorry that this happened to you. It's no secret that in the past I've been a fan of Keith's, but this is unacceptable."

"It's fine. I just thought you should know what's going on."

"Well, certainly you're going to be fine. After all, you're my daughter. And there are plenty of other men out there besides Keith. In fact, our new neighbors have a son who works in finance . . ."

"Um, thanks but no thanks, Benita," I quickly cut her off. "I think it's time for me to put more energy into loving Amaya and a lot less into looking for Mr. Right."

"Well, of course, dear, of course. I was only just trying to be helpful . . ."

"You know what, Benita? For once I actually believe that you genuinely were trying to help, and I appreciate that. I'm going to be okay," I say with the most conviction I've ever felt in my life. "I'll call you soon. Take care . . . Mom."

"Yes, well, you take care, sweetheart," Benita answered softly.

As soon as I returned to Los Angeles I did something I'd been promising myself for years—I fired Clarence's trifling behind. If I was making a fresh start, this was the right place to start. Honestly, it felt like a rebirth. The sight of Clarence choking in disbelief as I walked out of his office is a memory I'll always treasure.

"What, what, what do you mean I'm fired?" he stammered, jumping to his feet and clutching his chest like my decision was going to give him another heart attack.

"J-J-Just what I said, Clarence," I spitefully mimicked as I stood holding the copy of my contract that he'd so kindly provided moments before. "Your ass is fired." As I walked out past his assistant, I flipped her the middle finger for good measure.

Then I called an emergency girls night at my apartment where I confessed everything that had happened with Troy, Trixie, and Keith. They were incredulous. "I cannot believe that fool put his hands on you," screeched Trista, leaping up from my chaise.

"Girl, please. You know he was the devil," I calmly responded as I sipped on my glass of merlot. "Don't even bother getting yourself worked up—or, worse, spill that red wine—over it."

"I knew Keith wasn't about shit, but damn—Troy?! What a bunch of little punks," fumed Vivian, picking at her salad. Since her engagement to Sean, Viv had gone hardcore healthy to tone up for her big day.

"Hey, y'all, it's fine," I insisted. Matter of fact, I might need to send both of those fools a thank-you card."

"I hear that," said Viv between bites.

"It's just so crazy. This whole time you were away I thought you were probably worried sick about Keith, and now I come to find out this mess," mumbled Trista, still pacing.

"I'm just mad that I wasted my Vow on two Negroes who ain't worth the spit coming out of their mouths," I said. "And y'all know how I feel about losing."

"Girl, please, you ain't the only one," started Trista, finally snapping out of her mental tirade. "But at the end of the day, you've gotta focus on everything you do have. Your career is about to blow up, you've got your health, and we're all behind you. Surely Keith and Troy are not going to be the last men in your life."

"I know that's right," cosigned Vivian.

"As long as you know," I said with a smile and a snap of my fingers.

I almost fell over laughing as they described the havoc that ensued from the special edition of *Tattleteller* with the exclusive photos of Trixie and Sam versus Trixie and Keith on every front of the entertainment industry while I was away. Apparently within hours of the magazine hitting newsstands the story was picked up and reported on by MTV, BET, and every online and print gossip column, not to mention the celebrity news TV shows like *Extra* and *Inside Edition*. In fact, Viv is pretty sure that she even read something about it on the Associated Press wire service that same day. When the news first hit, Keith and Trixie tried to present a united front and refused to comment. But I guess Trixie's agent broke down for her how hot homosexuality is in Hollywood right now, because not even four days later, homegirl sits down with Diane Sawyer and comes clean. Not only did Trixie admit that the photos were real, but turns out it wasn't just a random lesbian affair. She's in love. During her hour-long interview, Trixie told Diane about how she'd been unsatisfied for years with Keith and how relieved she was to finally live her life openly.

"You should've seen the crocodile tears sliding down her face," insisted Viv. "That woman is coldhearted. She filed for divorce the same day she signed her new movie deal with Miramax Films. The rumors say, it's a drama about a woman seduced by her sister-in-law. Now you know!"

"Last I heard she was suing for full custody and asking for damn near twelve thousand dollars a month in child support," added Trista.

Needless to say, after Trixie's little primetime confession, Keith Cooper's name wasn't worth a damn in the streets. Nobody wanted to deal with or be too closely associated with him. Beat Down Records has become a joke—I mean, how do you expect people to believe that you're running shit when your own wife prefers the pleasure of a woman to you? Industrywhispers.com has it that he'll be replaced as the CEO by the end of the month.

I almost felt bad for him . . . but then again, not so much. For a while there he kept leaving me threatening messages on my cell. But after I politely left a message with his assistant, Andrew, warning that if he continued to harass me with the phone calls and pages I'd file for a restraining order, it stopped. Considering the last thing he wants or needs right about now is more messy press, I'm pretty confident I won't be hearing from him.

I never spoke to Troy again—which suited me just fine. Of course, Industrywhispers.com was the first to break the news of our breakup. I laughed out loud when I read the exclusive interview Troy had given, claiming total responsibility for the breakup, insisting he was a changed man and begging for my forgiveness. I figured he should probably save some of that energy for the paternity suit he'd just been slapped with by a woman in Nevada. She came forward, shortly after the Stingers lost the finals, claiming that her baby twins were his sons. My, oh my, karma is a bitch!

A couple weeks later, I signed on with Trista's new agency. The ink had barely dried on the contracts before she had me sequestered in my apartment reading the revised script for *The Black Crusader*. I was only allowed to leave home for my acting classes and the gym. Tris insisted that I know every single line backward and forward before I left for Toronto in January. "There is no wiggle room for you, Amaya," she explained. "You need to be so good that no one can deny you." About three days before the first principal-cast read-through, I stopped by her office on my way to the gym and confessed what happened at the dinner with Carter. She was livid. Turns out that he had harassed one of her clients a couple of years back and she was very familiar with his antics. She put an immediate call into Carter's management team on my behalf. I don't know what exactly Trista said to them, but I sure heard a whole lot of "sexual predator," "filing charges," and "next special edition of *Tattleteller* magazine" coming from her side of the conversation. Needless to say, the largest bouquet of white roses, white calla lilies, and orchids I've ever seen in my life arrived the next day for me at Trista's office. And best believe the moment he saw me at our principal-cast read-through, he was the perfect gentleman. If I hadn't been the one sitting in the restaurant, I would never have believed that incident ever happened. Can't nobody tell me my girl ain't the fire!

Of course the ceremony was an amazing Vivian Evans affair, but I gotta say that Trista almost stole the show with her surprise proposal. I should've known that she and Damon would end up together. Ever since

they started dating in college, they've been meant for each other. Seeing the way her entire body lights up when she speaks about him is
enough to make even me teary-eyed. And you know I'm not about getting worked up and ruining good makeup for any ol' body! To think, if
only she hadn't been so hard-headed back in the day, Trista would
already be married to that man! I'm just glad that they finally got it
together. But I sure hope she takes some of that glow with her to the
jewelry store and puts a little more bling in that little-ass ring Damon
gave her.

So with Viv now happily married and Trista engaged, that just leaves
me—still. I haven't come anywhere near accomplishing our Vow. If anything, I took about twenty leaps in the opposite direction. Yet I can't say
that I'm upset. In fact, this total independence feels good. I never realized just how capable I am until I cut all the safety nets. Granted, every
once in a while, it gets a little lonely in my bed, but that's the reason for
my trusty vibrator and the porn channel.

Thankfully, with Keith, Clarence, and even Troy to a certain extent
supplementing my lifestyle for so long, I had more than enough money
stashed away to hold me over until the first check from the film came
through. So I haven't been stressing about the rent and whatnot. I
mean, the usual bill collectors continue to harass me, but I just chalk it
up to fodder for the future tell-all. Not to mention, Trista is already in
the middle of negotiating a possible Gap campaign and a run on Broad-
way in a new August Wilson production. She thinks I need to branch out
with something more artistic. Can you imagine me in New York? Whew,
those Negroes aren't ready!

THE SUDDEN rustle of the curtain startles me back to reality. Time to get
back to the reception. I hurriedly finish applying my gloss. As I study
myself one last time in the mirror, I pause and smile. Flawless. I head
back into the bedroom to search for the sandals I kicked off my feet
earlier. While searching, I flip on the television to see if I can catch
the weather report. My flight to Miami is scheduled to depart from

Saint Thomas first thing in the morning—I plan to spend a few days in Miami with Benita before I head back to L.A. and start packing for Toronto. Hopefully, this visit will be the start of some type of reconciliation. I booked an open ticket so that I can always leave at the drop of a hat, just in case. As the TV comes into focus, my very first Dead Straight television commercial begins. I pause and watch my image fill the screen. Damn, it's good to be me! I grab my glass of champagne off the night table and raise it in a silent toast to me, myself, and I.

21

VIVIAN

We screamed one of those sorority-sister screams—the screeching kind that makes whoever is standing in a five-mile radius turn, take note, and shake their heads in disgust at the ruckus being made. I didn't care who was looking, though. It's my wedding day, which means that I've walked down the aisle and exchanged vows with the man I've loved a lifetime. Can't think of a better reason to act a fool with my girls.

"I'm just saying—peep the ring," Amaya said, grabbing my hand and thrusting it into Elise and Trista's faces. "Honestly, I don't even know how you made it back down the aisle without a separate attendant to hold up your left hand. That's at least four carats, right?"

"I haven't a clue—you know I don't know anything about diamonds," I said, smiling and holding my hand out to admire my ring finger. "The first time I even saw it was when Sean put it on my finger. He and Corey picked it out."

"Well, your boys sure got some serious taste," Amaya said. "Um, Trist—maybe you should get Damon a tutorial with Viv's little man so he can hook you up properly."

Trista rolled her eyes and passed her ring finger under Amaya's nose. "Don't hate," Trista said. "I got the ring I've always dreamed about—one from the man I love."

"That's right," I chimed in after taking a sip of champagne from a glass I grabbed from the waiter as he passed by. "No ring size, price tag, or stone can ever be as precious as the sentiment behind it. I love your ring, Trista. Congratulations, girl."

"Thank you, Viv," Trista said, shooting a fake dirty look at Amaya. "When you get a man, then maybe you can take some lessons from me and your girl here on how to keep him and get yourself one of these."

"And you better hope he's an ounce as romantic as Sean and Corey," Elise said, throwing a high five to Trista and me for emphasis.

Sean's proposal was, indeed, out of this world. I hadn't expected it to come so suddenly; we'd been back together for only about a month when he pulled off an enormously extravagant and elaborate proposal/engagement party. One beautiful, balmy evening in October, he dispatched a fleet of limousines across Beverly Hills, Hollywood, and Compton, to pick up thirty of our family members and closest friends and bring them to an undisclosed location. No one knew what was up— Amaya told me later that the drivers just showed up to everyone's doorstep with a single rose and a hand-stenciled invitation beckoning them to get in the limousine and head for an "unforgettable celebration of the woman who's taught my heart to sing."

While everyone was being snatched up around town, Sean showed up to my office to take me to what I thought was going to be a movie-and-dinner date. It was obvious something was up, though, when he drove back to his place—he claimed he'd bought the movie tickets and left them in a jacket at his house—and we were met at the door by a group of three women who ushered me into his rose-filled home. "Sean? What's going on," I said, a frown crossing my face as the three welcomed us and grabbed me.

"Just do as the nice ladies say," he said, smiling.

In his bedroom there were three beautiful dresses laid across the bed; at least ten pairs of shoes stood at attention by the closet. The women sat me at a vanity by the fireplace and proceeded to fuss with my hair and paint my face and body with makeup and all kinds of exotic potions, then helped me into a gorgeous, strapless rust-orange gown that boasted a tight bodice with a long, flared skirt, accented with a stunning flower at the waist. I was slipping into a pair of brown lace sling-back pumps when Sean came into the room about an hour later.

"You take my breath away," he said.

"Sean? What's going on? No one will tell me what's going on," I said, half smiling, half demanding answers.

Sean didn't say anything at first; just watched as the women cleaned up their things. Then he turned to me, took me by my hands, and said simply, "Come with me."

Rose petals painted the carpeted hallway and the spiral staircase. My eyes filled with tears as we headed downstairs—I knew what was about to happen the moment I saw my mother, Sean's family, and a roomful of my closest friends all crowded at the bottom of the staircase, grinning from ear to ear and clapping like they'd just seen an encore at a Janet Jackson concert. Mom, Amaya, and Trista each reached out and gave me hugs, and then Sean took my hand and led me over to the picture window in the living room. There, my son, in an adorable gray pinstripe suit, was sitting in a grand chair. A ring box was in his little hand.

Sean raised his hands to quiet the crowd, and then turned to me. By now, I was a blubbering idiot, completely incapable of saying so much as my name. Luckily, Sean and Corey did all the work.

"Vivian Evans—there is no other," Sean said, taking my hands in his. "You are the mother of my child, my best friend, my confidante, my lover, and I couldn't imagine my life without you in it. When I wake up in the morning, I want to see you. When I'm headed for work, I want to see you. When I'm eating lunch and dinner, I want to see you. When I go to sleep every night for the rest of my life, the last sight I want to see before my eyes is you. Because no one has ever made me feel like you do, and no one ever will. I am a lucky man because I've found the woman who has made my heart sing. I don't want that feeling to ever go away."

And then he got down on bended knee, and Corey got out of the chair, stood next to him, and opened the ring box. "Vivian Evans, will you be my wife?"

I was so overwhelmed with emotion, and trying so hard to keep my tears and nose from running over my makeup that I didn't respond immediately. Corey took my hand and gently reminded me that I should answer his dad. "Mommy," he whispered, "you have to say yes."

The room burst into hearty laughter. As did I. "Yes, Sean Jordan. I'll marry you."

We had just shy of two months to pull our wedding together. Sean liked the idea of having it in the Caribbean. That way we could keep the guest list short—just those we truly wanted to witness the ceremony. We all arrived in Saint Thomas three days before the wedding to enjoy the island and party together, and the day before the ceremony, Sean and I spent the majority of the day together with our son.

"Are you excited, Son?" Sean asked Corey, who'd been picking over his food and pretty quiet over lunch.

"Yeah, I guess," he said.

"Corey?" I said, giving him a stern look.

"I mean yes," he said quickly.

"You don't seem like it," Sean said. "Is there anything wrong? Or are you just tired?"

Corey was quiet for a moment. And then he finally spoke up. "My friend Victor is really sad because his parents are getting a divorce and now he has to live with his mom in a different house and his dad moved out and his family is broken," he said.

Sean and I looked at each other, waiting for him to say more, but our son didn't say another word. Though he didn't ask a question, it was obvious he was looking for answers—specifically, whether his parents would meet the same fate as Victor's. Sean took the lead. "Are you worried that your family will be broken, too?" he asked his son. Corey nodded but still said nothing. Sean shot a look at me, and cautiously continued. "Your mom and I have been apart for a long time, but we're together now. Today, we're going to stand up on the beach in front of our family and friends and the ocean and the sunset and tell everyone that Mommy, you, and I are a strong family and that we love each other and will stay together forever. We've waited a long time for this, right?" Corey nodded again. "So we should be excited about the new life we're going to have, because it's filled with love. Right?"

"Right," he said slowly.

"That doesn't sound like excitement," I said.

"Sure doesn't," Sean said, reaching across and giving Corey a noogie. "Come on, champ. Nobody loves your mother like I do."

"He's got the hots for your mama—he's not going anywhere," I said, winking.

"And you know that," Sean practically yelled.

"Daaad!" Corey said, finally smiling.

"That's my boy," Sean said. "That's my boy."

I think Corey was more excited than Sean and I were about the ceremony—and we were pretty geeked. He practically galloped down the aisle with my wedding band on a small lace pillow my mother made from the lace hem of her mother's wedding dress ("I never got to wear it because I never got a wedding day, but I knew I'd be able to put it to good use," she'd said when she presented the pillow and a handkerchief she made from the material just before we left for the ceremony), much to the delight of the audience. I couldn't tell who was grinning harder as I waltzed barefoot across the sand to the precious sound of a kora player strumming a beautiful African wedding song. Corey waved and reached over to grab his father's hand as I reached the altar, and then he grabbed my hand, too, making the entire audience go, "Aw!"

"I swear, I hope I have a child as smart, sweet, and well mannered as your son," Trista said. "Did you see little man holding things down during the ceremony?"

"That's my boy," I laughed.

"You gonna work on a girl now?" Trista asked, hardly missing a beat.

"Can I let my wedding cake settle in my stomach before I start making reproductive plans?" I shot back, laughing.

"Come on now, Viv, you know you can't wait to give that man a whole basketball team's worth of kids," Amaya said. "Don't wait too long—you ain't getting any younger."

"Thank you, Jagged Edge, I have one already—if anything, I think you need to be talking to your girl Trist," I said, tossing my head in her direction. "That's right, Miss Agent Extraordinaire—you might have your little business up and running, but make sure you carve out some maternity leave," I laughed.

"Easy," Trista said. "Easy. We have plenty of time for that. If anybody needs to be pushing out a little one, it's Amaya, seeing she's a celebrity and all and it's all the rage in Hollywood to carry babies down the red carpet. Jada does it. Angelina Jolie does it. Sarah Jessica Parker, Reese Witherspoon—all of them Hollywood mommies make motherhood look hot. It's the thing to do. So how about it, Amaya?"

Amaya twisted her lips up on the side of her face and sucked her teeth. "Shoot, I'm not finished working on the first Vow, much less trying to push a baby out in the next nine months," she said. Then she looked down at her watch. "Shit, I got another twenty minutes to find me a man. Don't put another one on me."

"Oh, bump men and babies," I said. "Taking a vow to find and marry a man in a year was perhaps the craziest thing I've ever done in my life—just stupid and foolish. I'm amazed that we actually emerged from the year with men, frankly. Somehow, we did, despite ourselves."

"You better preach, Rev Vivian," Trista said.

"Besides, New Year's resolutions weren't designed for the opposite sex—they're for us," I said, lifting my glass. "I propose that at the stroke of midnight, we make a really meaningful vow that we can realistically fulfill."

"Oh Lord—here she goes again," Amaya said to Trista. "Stop her. I'm not going to make any more promises I can't keep. My ass is too worn out for that."

"This will be an easy one," I said, looking at the clock. "We don't even have to do it at the stroke of midnight."

"And just what is it," Trista asked, intrigued.

I lifted my glass and smiled a toothy grin. "Bump men. I say we make a vow right now to be friends forever—no matter what."

"Hear! Hear!" Amaya said.

"Hear! Hear!" Trista said.

"I love you guys," I said. "Girls for life."